# LOST SOUL, BE AT PEACE

## Maggie Thrash

CANDLEWICK PRESS

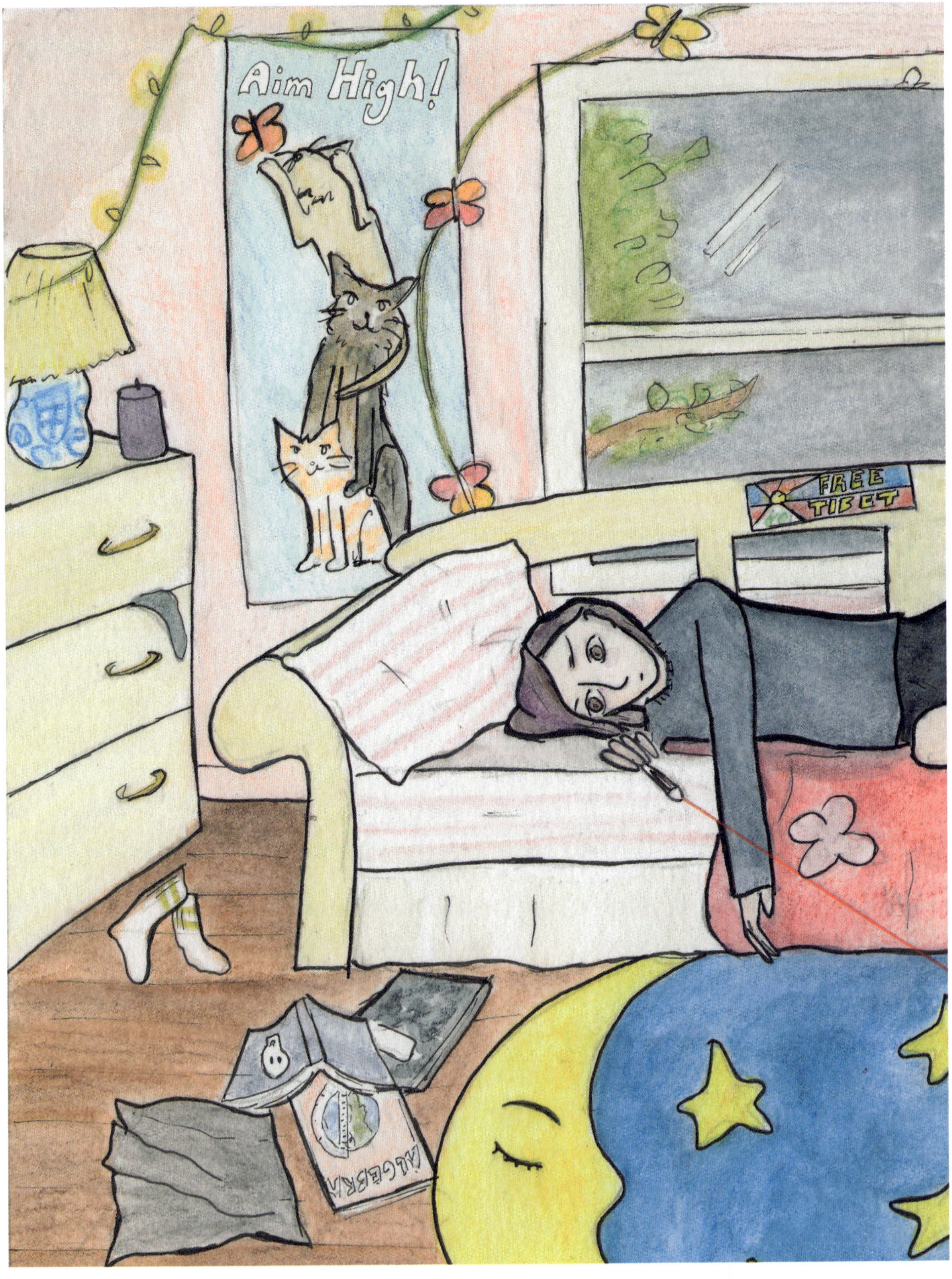
Aim High!
FREE TIBET
ALGEBRA

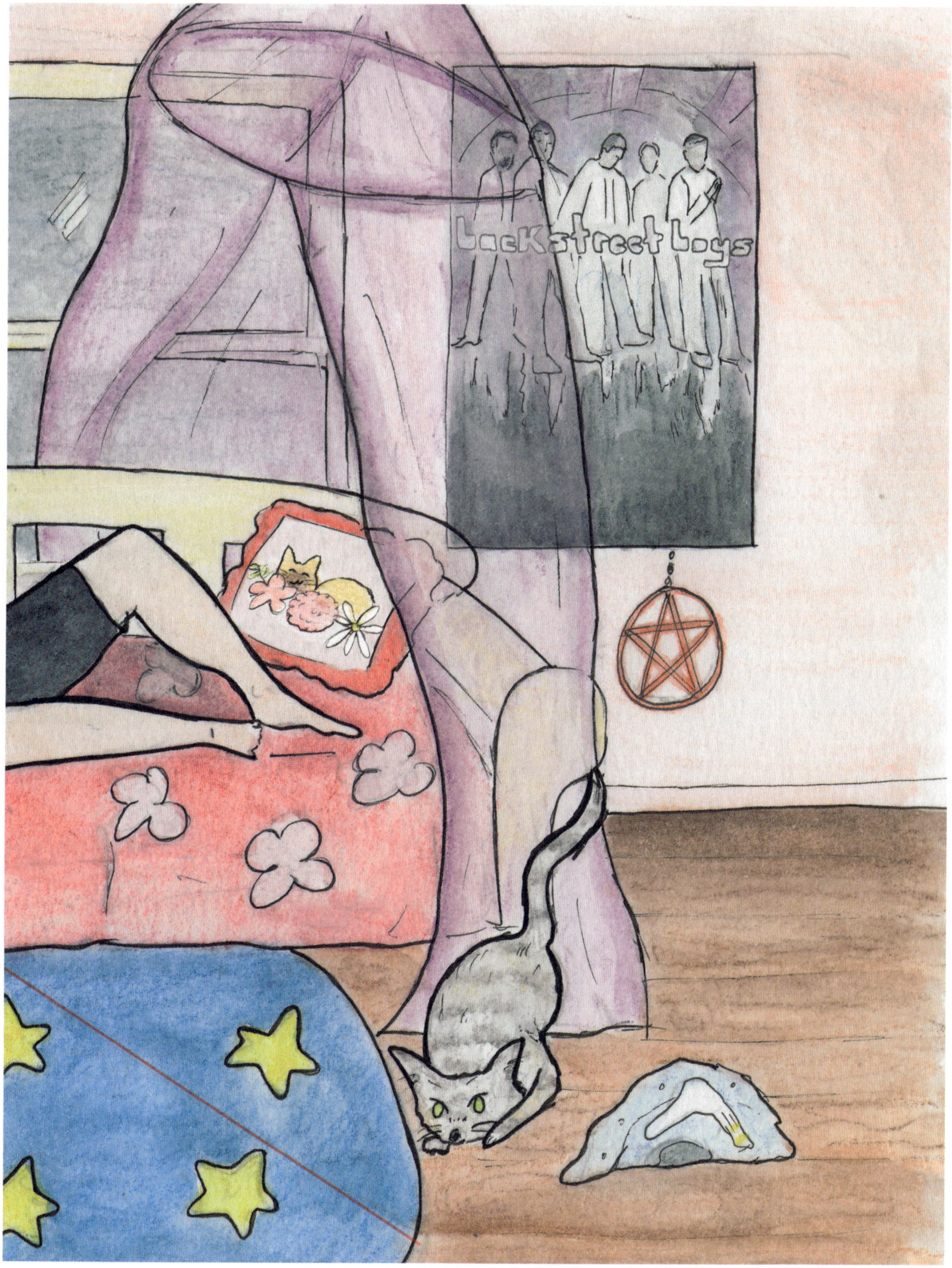
backstreet boys

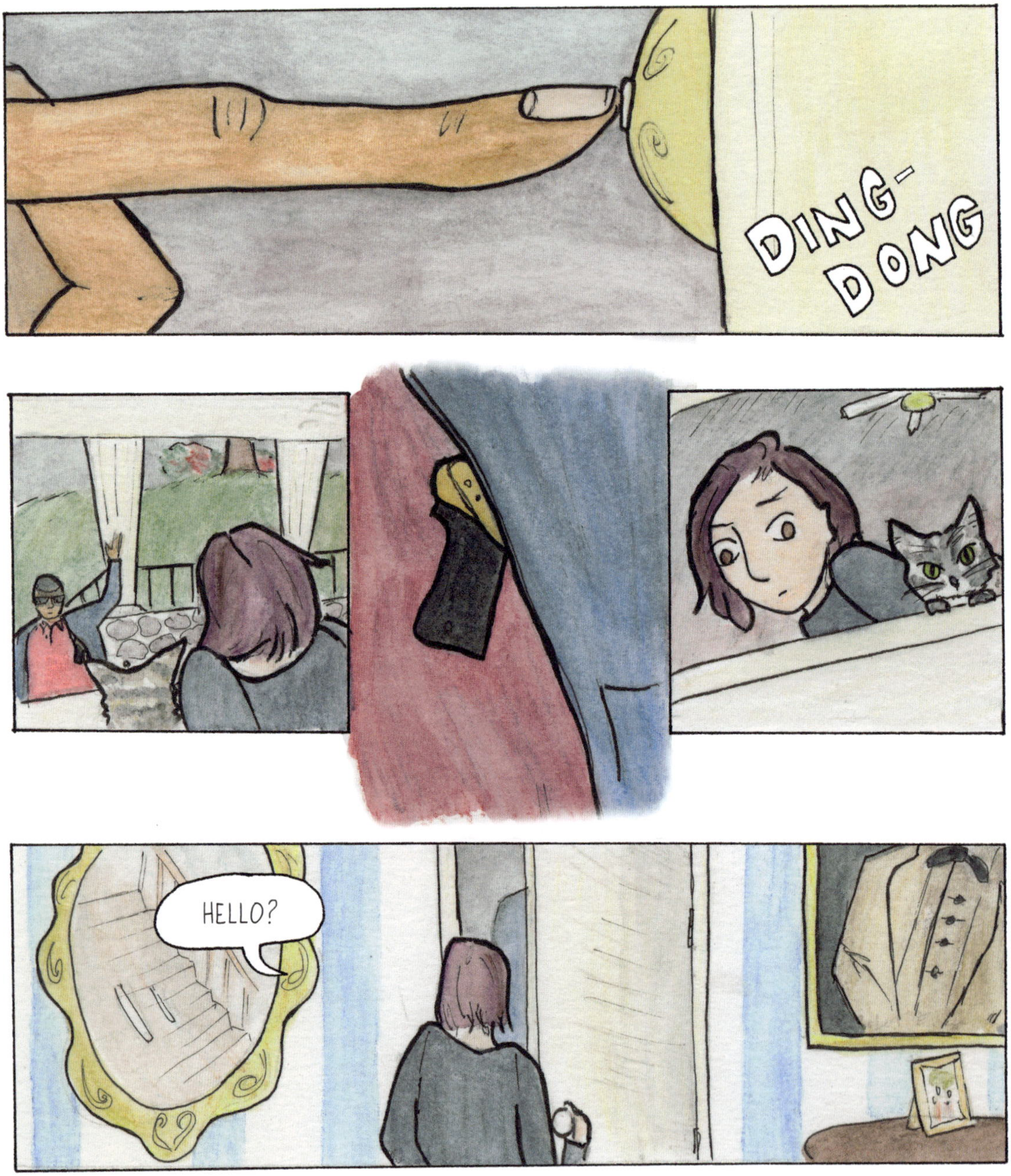
DING-DONG
HELLO?

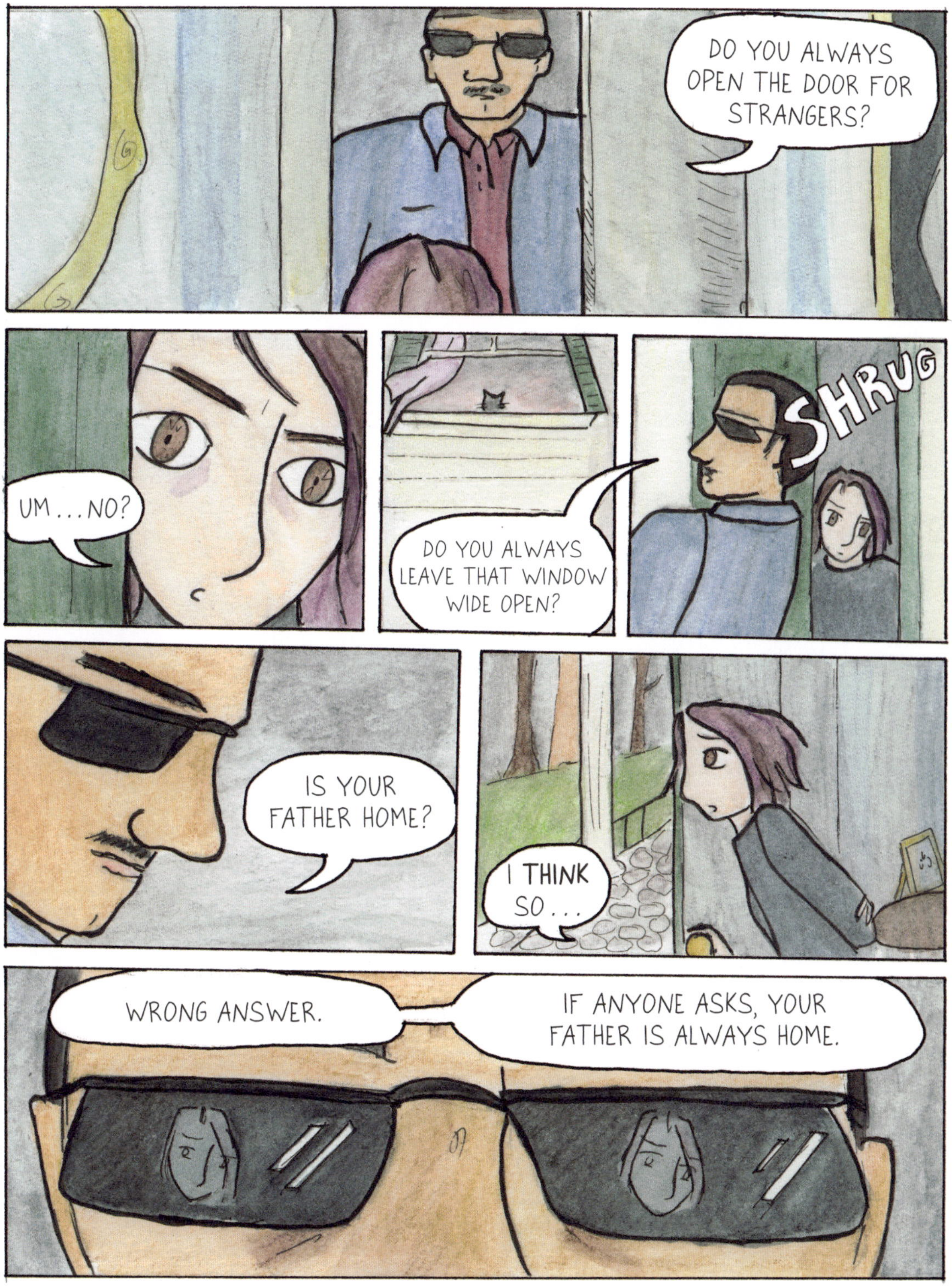
DO YOU ALWAYS OPEN THE DOOR FOR STRANGERS?
UM . . . NO?
DO YOU ALWAYS LEAVE THAT WINDOW WIDE OPEN?
SHRUG
IS YOUR FATHER HOME?
I THINK SO . . .
WRONG ANSWER.
IF ANYONE ASKS, YOUR FATHER IS ALWAYS HOME.

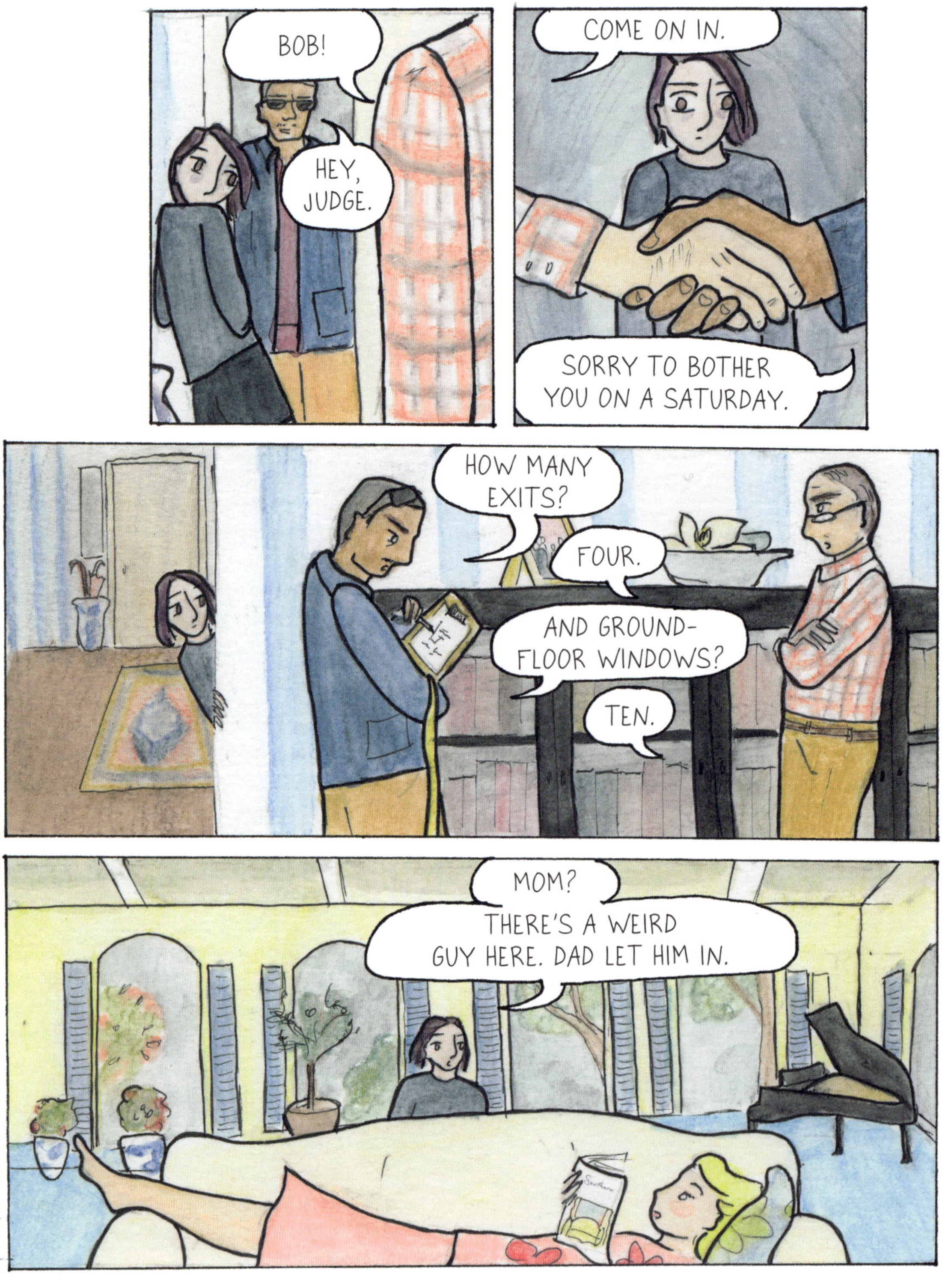
BOB!
HEY, JUDGE.
COME ON IN.
SORRY TO BOTHER YOU ON A SATURDAY.
HOW MANY EXITS?
FOUR.
AND GROUND-FLOOR WINDOWS?
TEN.
MOM?
THERE'S A WEIRD GUY HERE. DAD LET HIM IN.

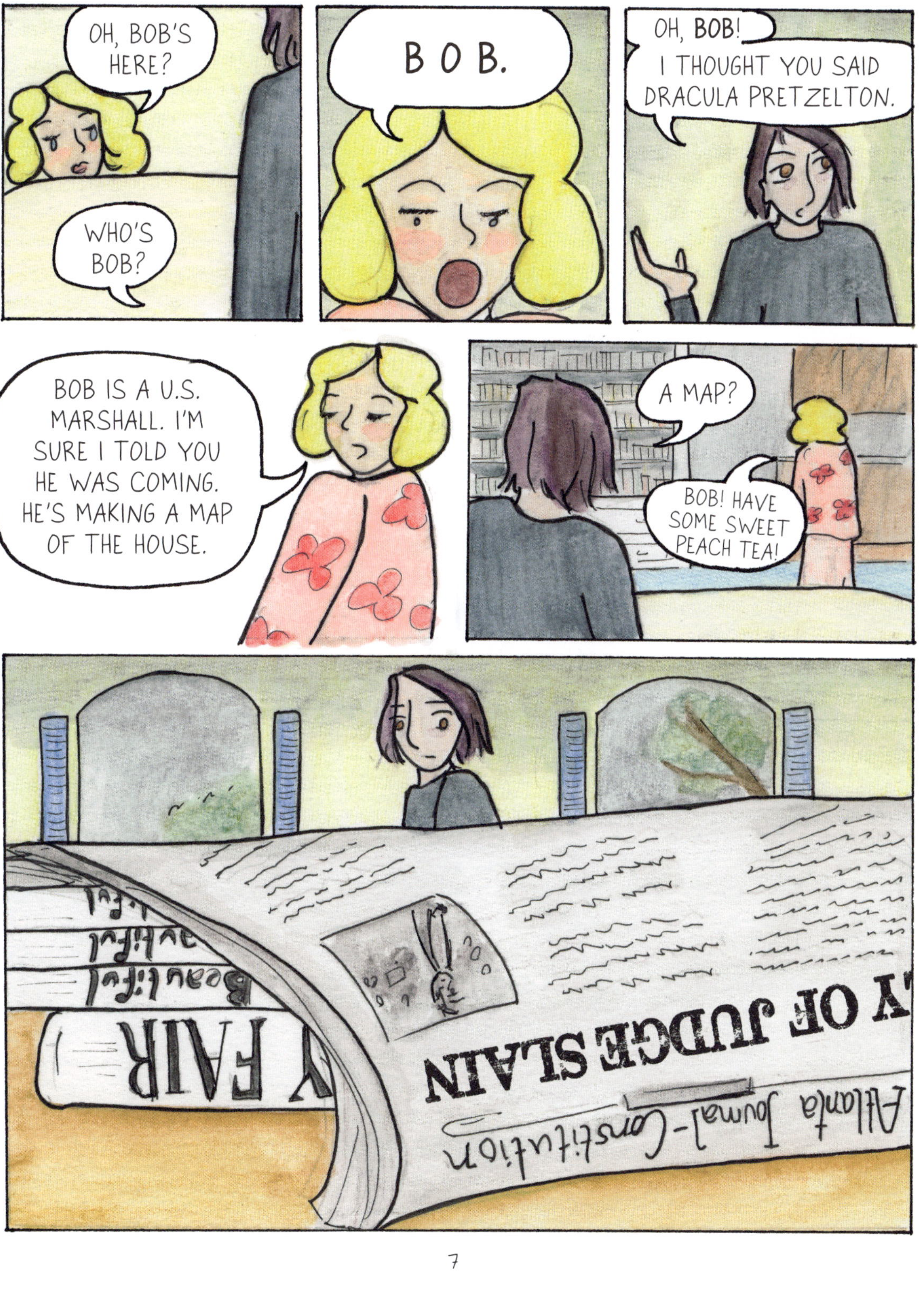
OH, BOB'S HERE?
WHO'S BOB?
B O B.
OH, **BOB**!
I THOUGHT YOU SAID DRACULA PRETZELTON.
BOB IS A U.S. MARSHALL. I'M SURE I TOLD YOU HE WAS COMING. HE'S MAKING A MAP OF THE HOUSE.
A MAP?
BOB! HAVE SOME SWEET PEACH TEA!
OF JUDGE SLAIN
Atlanta Journal-Constitution
FAIR
Beautiful

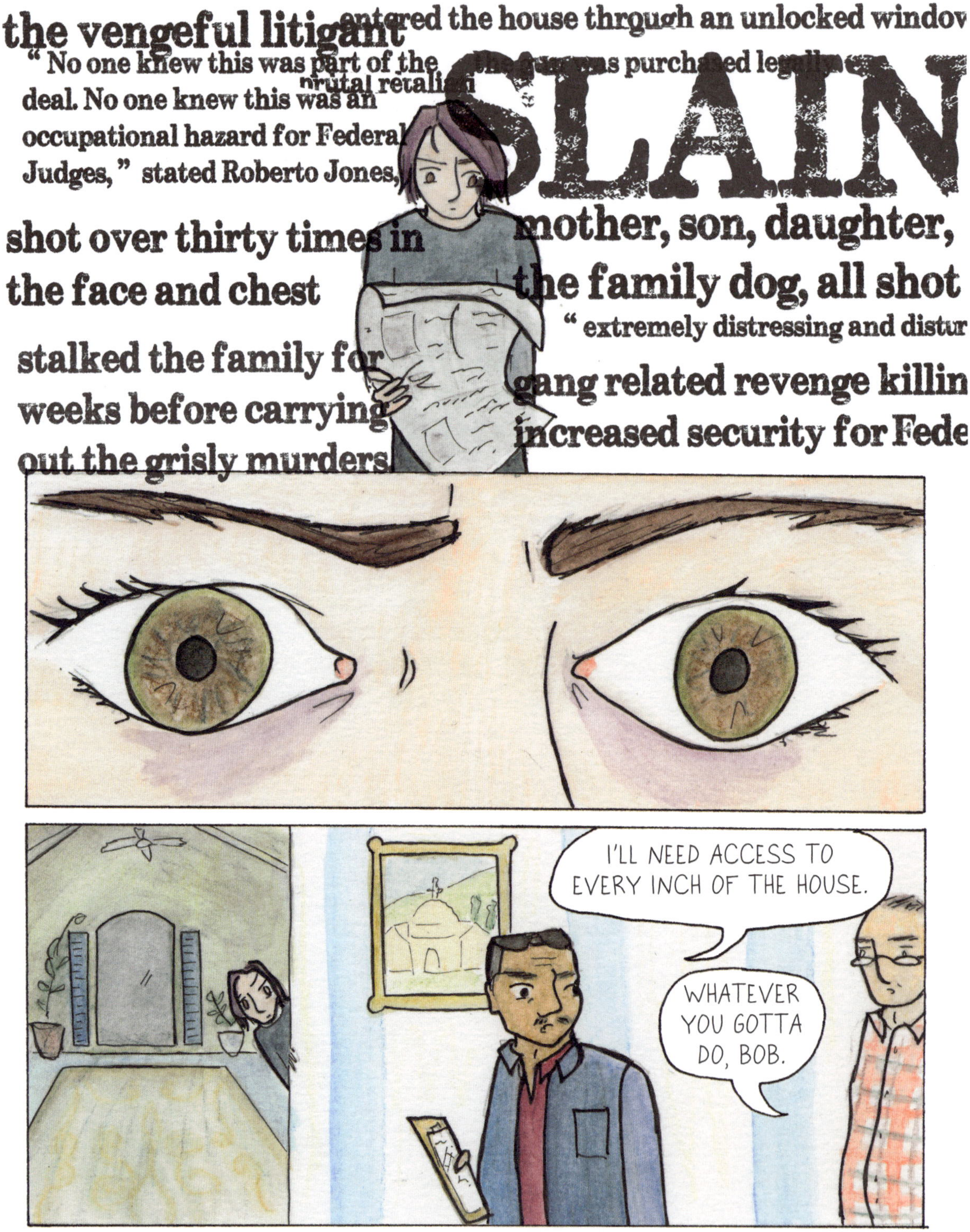
the vengeful litigant
entered the house through an unlocked windov
" No one knew this was part of the deal. No one knew this was an occupational hazard for Federal Judges," stated Roberto Jones,
SLAIN
shot over thirty times in the face and chest
mother, son, daughter,
the family dog, all shot
" extremely distressing and distur
stalked the family for weeks before carrying out the grisly murders.
gang related revenge killin
increased security for Fede
I'LL NEED ACCESS TO EVERY INCH OF THE HOUSE.
WHATEVER YOU GOTTA DO, BOB.

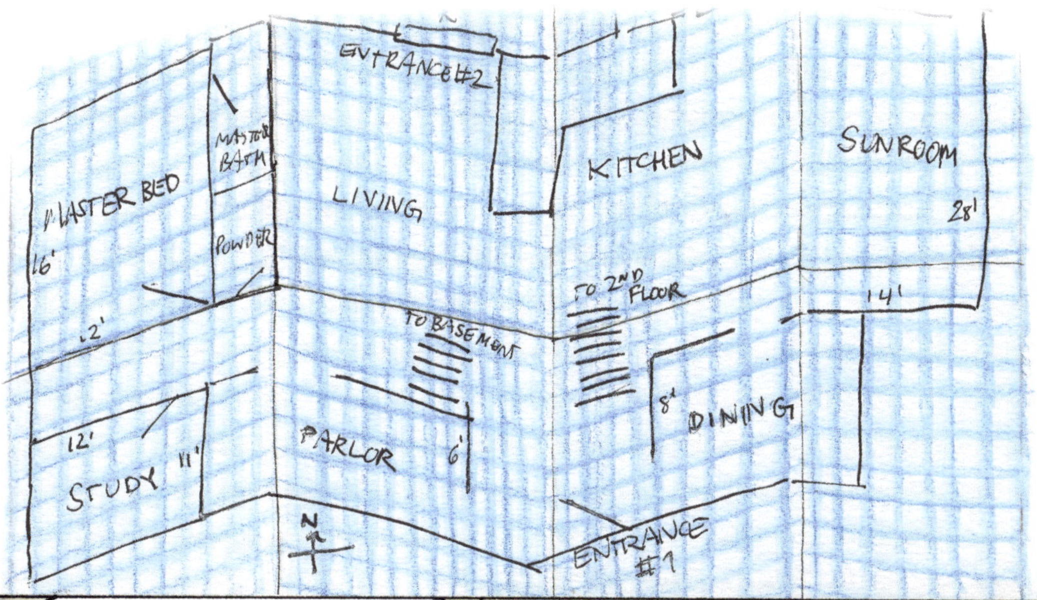
ENTRANCE #2
MASTER BATH
MASTER BED
16'
POWDER
LIVING
KITCHEN
SUNROOM
28'
TO 2ND FLOOR
14'
12'
TO BASEMENT
8'
DINING
12'
STUDY 11'
PARLOR
6'
N
ENTRANCE #1

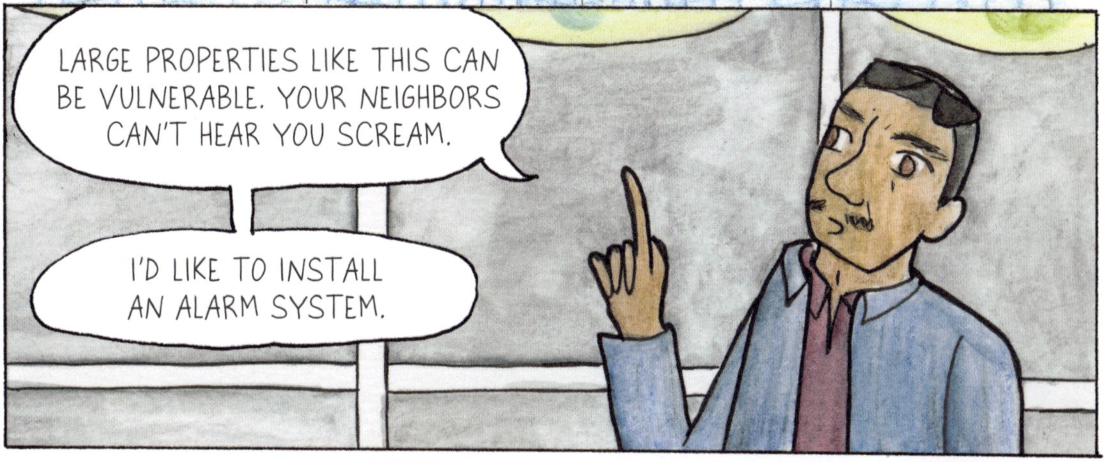
LARGE PROPERTIES LIKE THIS CAN BE VULNERABLE. YOUR NEIGHBORS CAN'T HEAR YOU SCREAM.
I'D LIKE TO INSTALL AN ALARM SYSTEM.

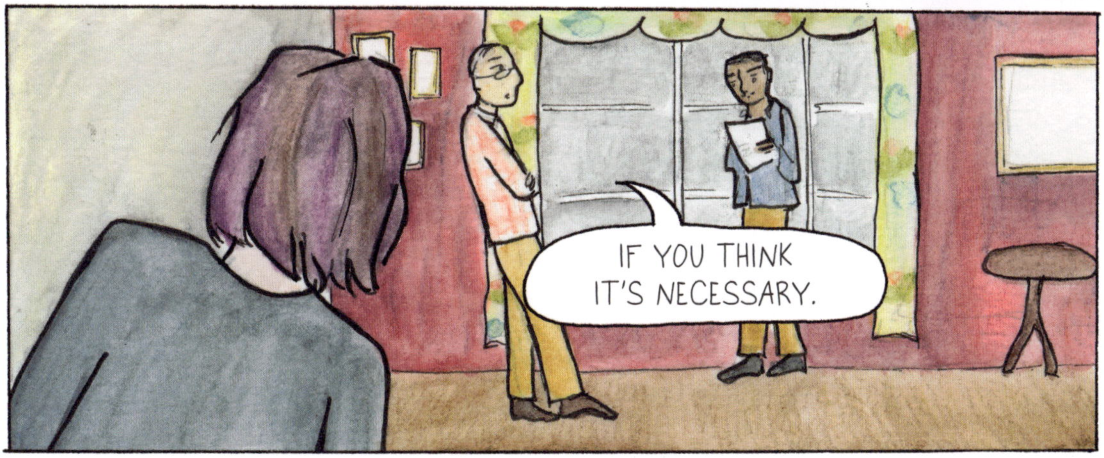
IF YOU THINK IT'S NECESSARY.

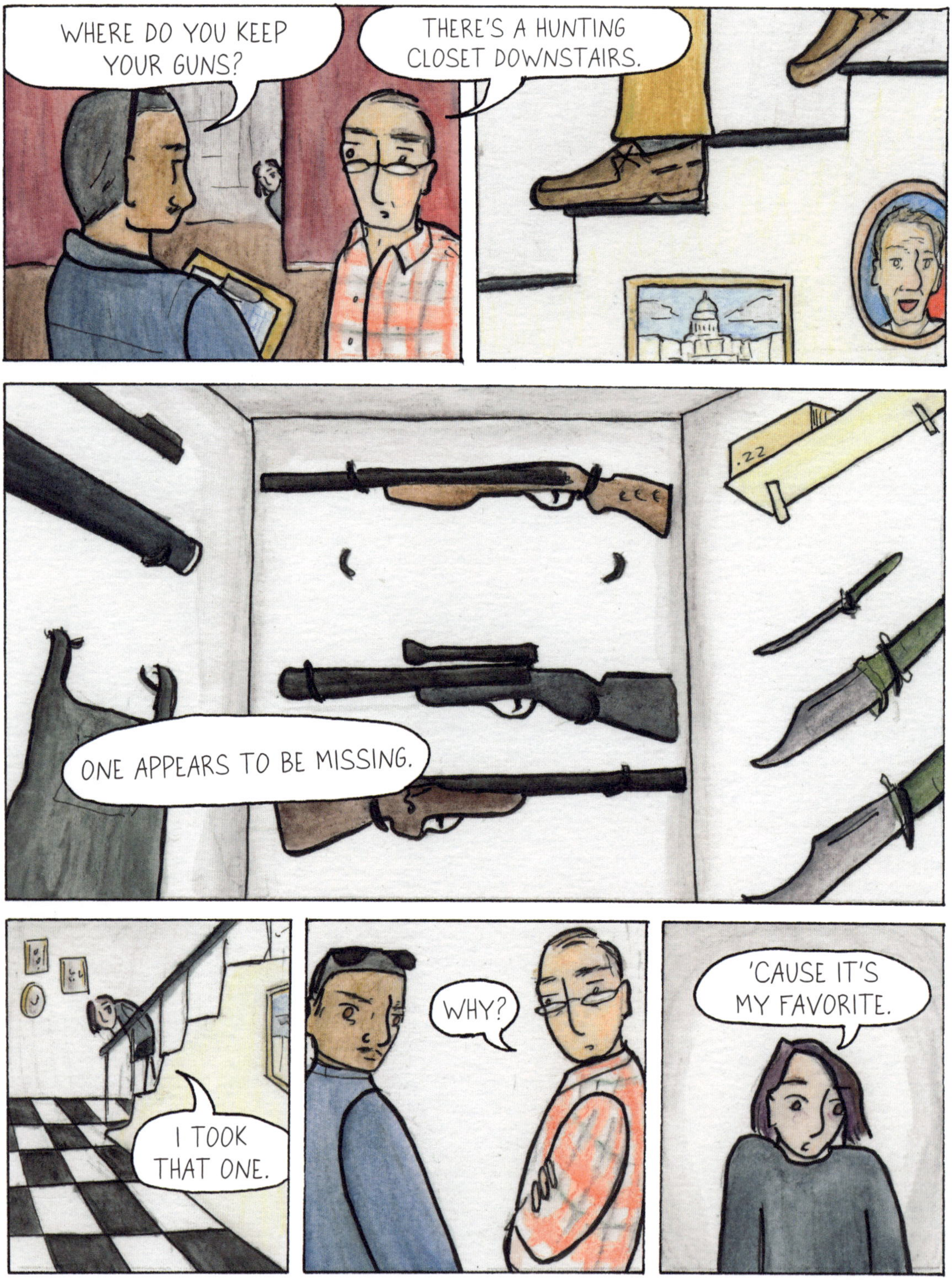
WHERE DO YOU KEEP YOUR GUNS?
THERE'S A HUNTING CLOSET DOWNSTAIRS.
.22
ONE APPEARS TO BE MISSING.
I TOOK THAT ONE.
WHY?
'CAUSE IT'S MY FAVORITE.

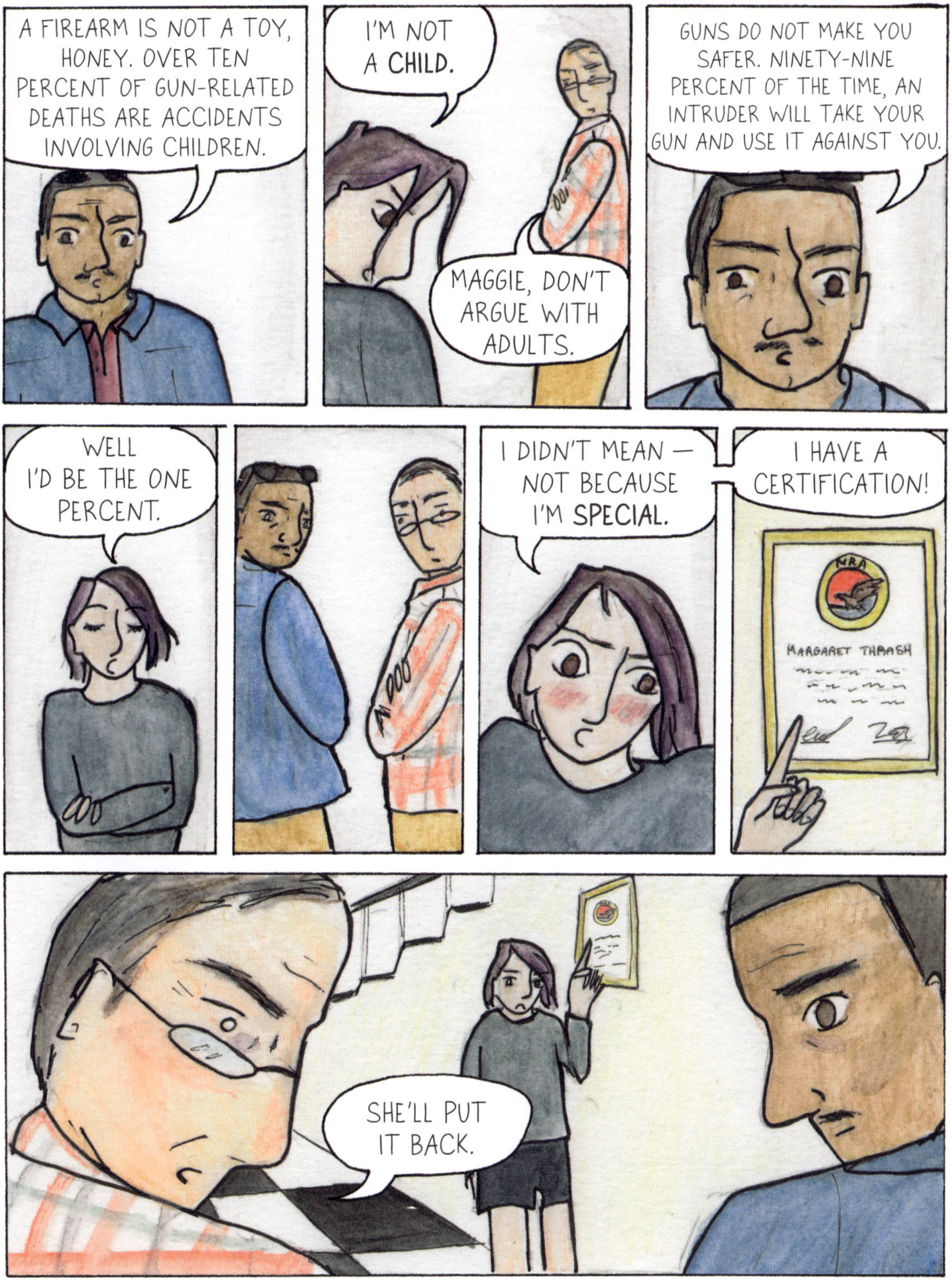
A FIREARM IS NOT A TOY, HONEY. OVER TEN PERCENT OF GUN-RELATED DEATHS ARE ACCIDENTS INVOLVING CHILDREN.
I'M NOT A **CHILD.**
MAGGIE, DON'T ARGUE WITH ADULTS.
GUNS DO NOT MAKE YOU SAFER. NINETY-NINE PERCENT OF THE TIME, AN INTRUDER WILL TAKE YOUR GUN AND USE IT AGAINST YOU.
WELL I'D BE THE ONE PERCENT.
I DIDN'T MEAN — NOT BECAUSE I'M **SPECIAL.**
I HAVE A CERTIFICATION!
NRA
MARGARET THRASH
SHE'LL PUT IT BACK.

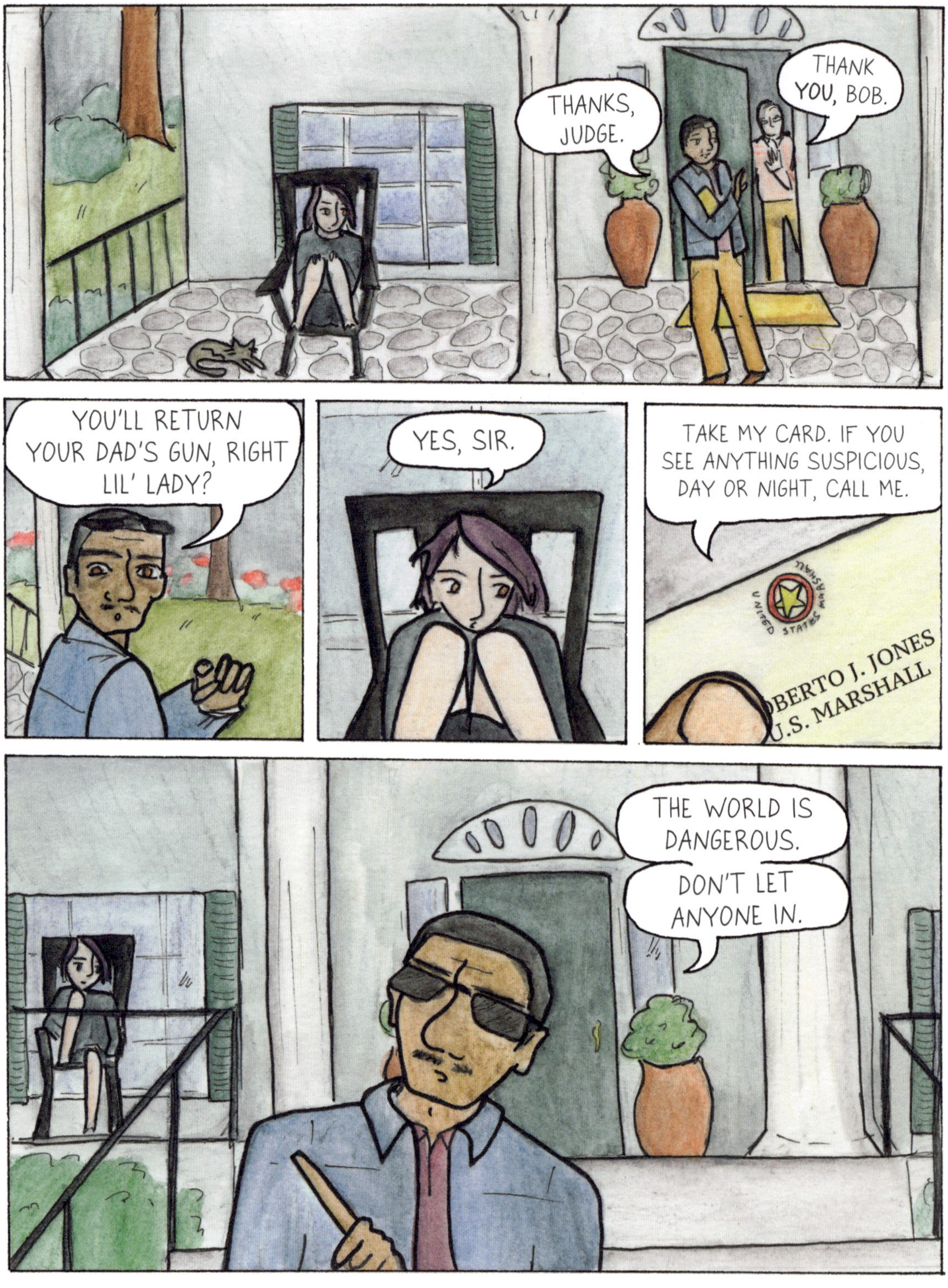
THANKS, JUDGE.
THANK YOU, BOB.
YOU'LL RETURN YOUR DAD'S GUN, RIGHT LIL' LADY?
YES, SIR.
TAKE MY CARD. IF YOU SEE ANYTHING SUSPICIOUS, DAY OR NIGHT, CALL ME.
UNITED STATES MARSHALL
OBERTO J. JONES
U.S. MARSHALL
THE WORLD IS DANGEROUS.
DON'T LET ANYONE IN.

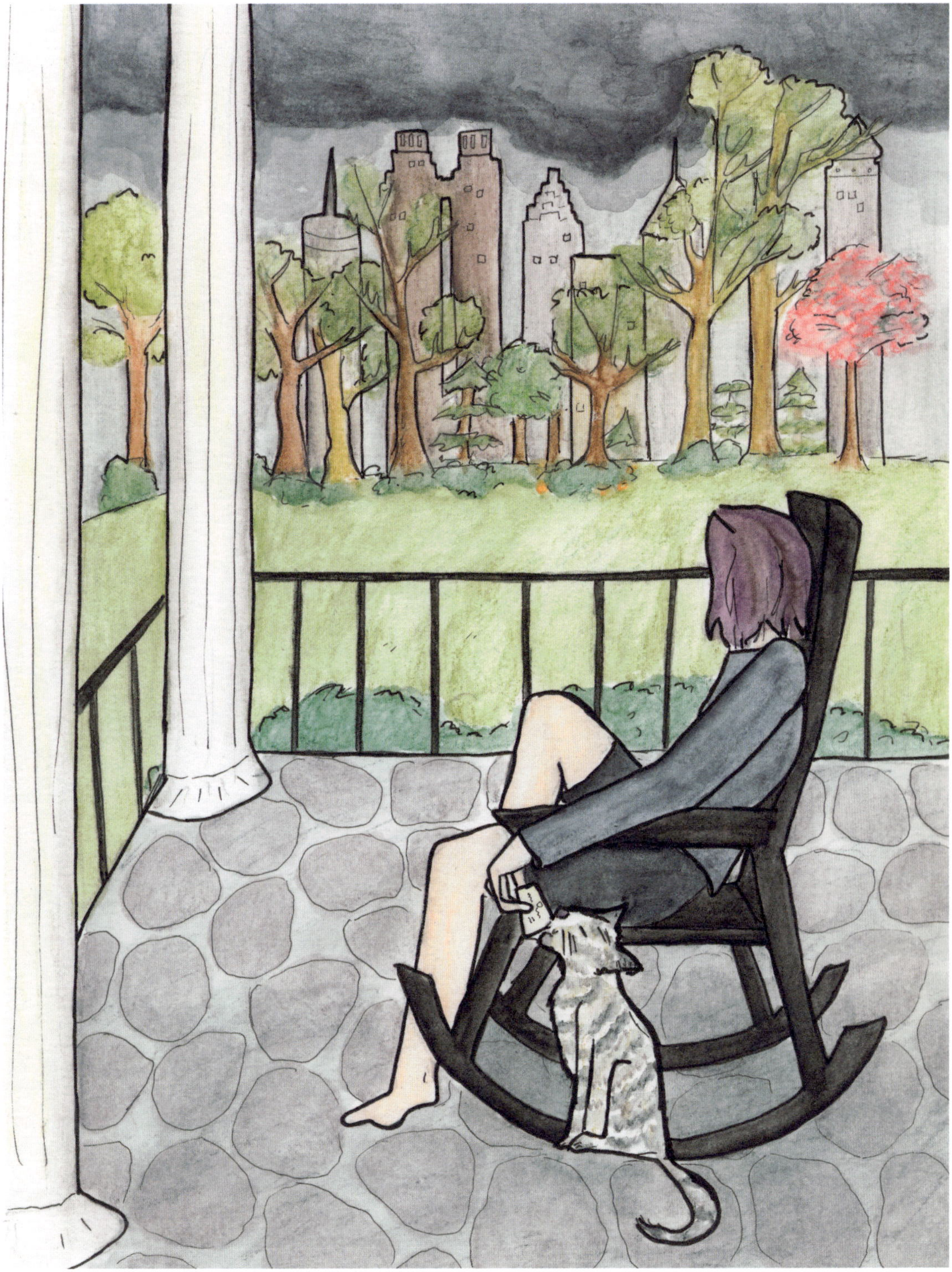

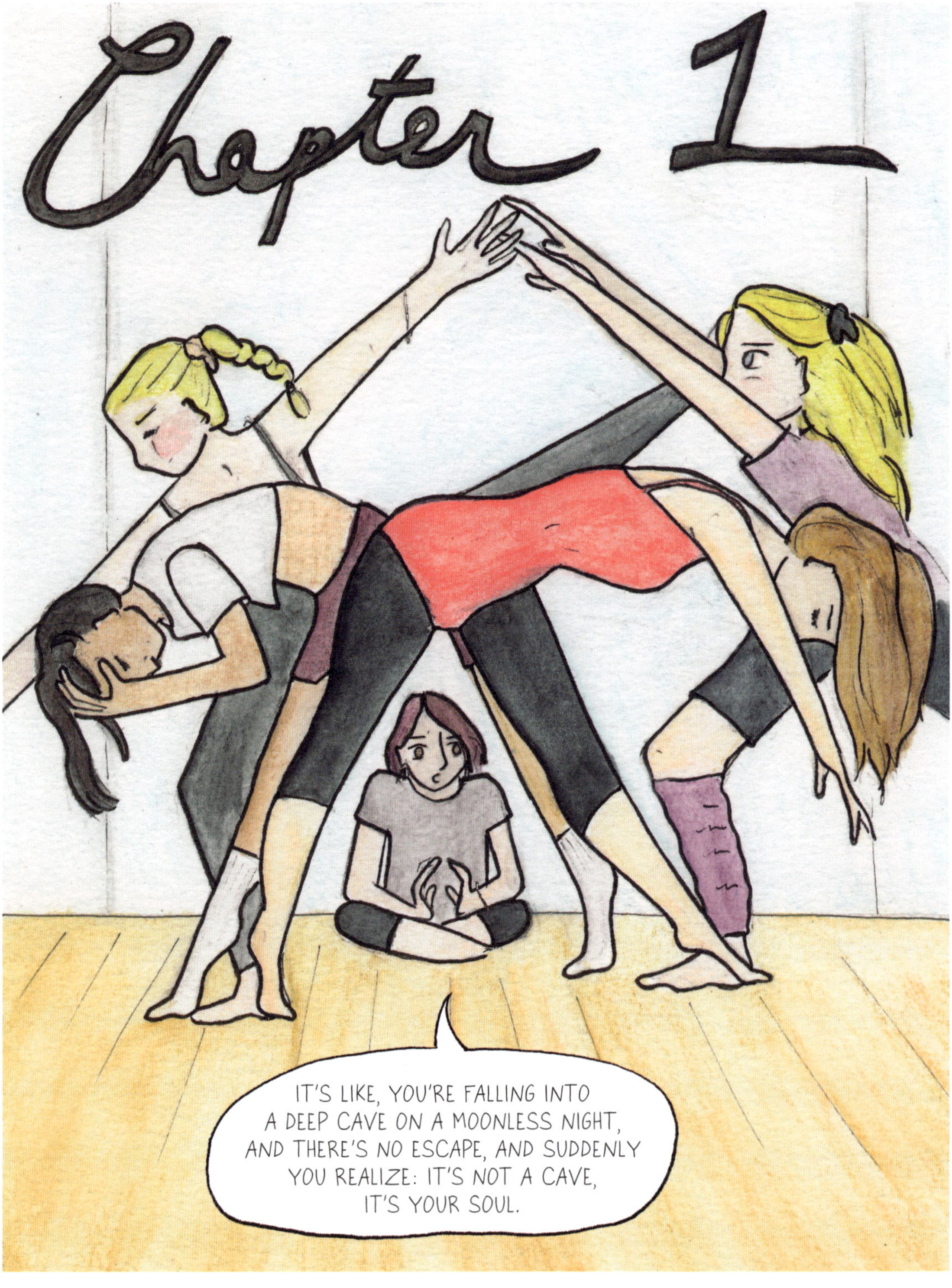
Chapter 1
IT'S LIKE, YOU'RE FALLING INTO A DEEP CAVE ON A MOONLESS NIGHT, AND THERE'S NO ESCAPE, AND SUDDENLY YOU REALIZE: IT'S NOT A CAVE, IT'S YOUR SOUL.

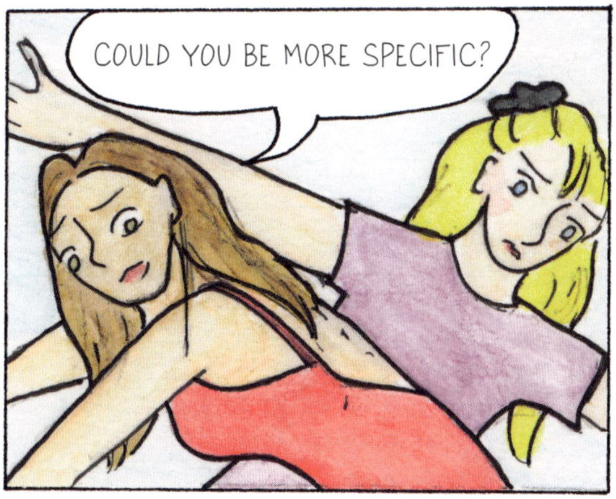
COULD YOU BE MORE SPECIFIC?

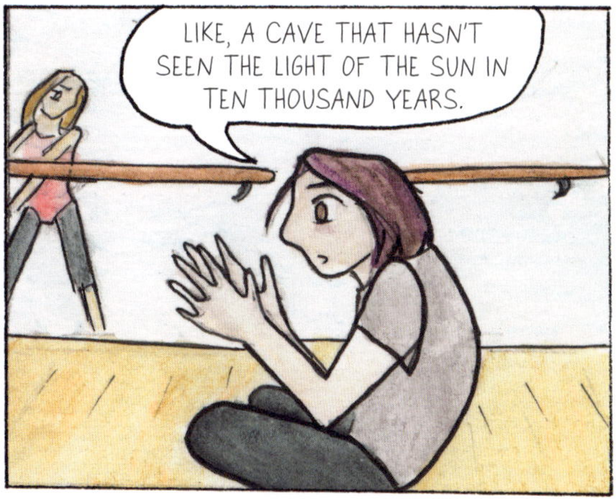
LIKE, A CAVE THAT HASN'T SEEN THE LIGHT OF THE SUN IN TEN THOUSAND YEARS.

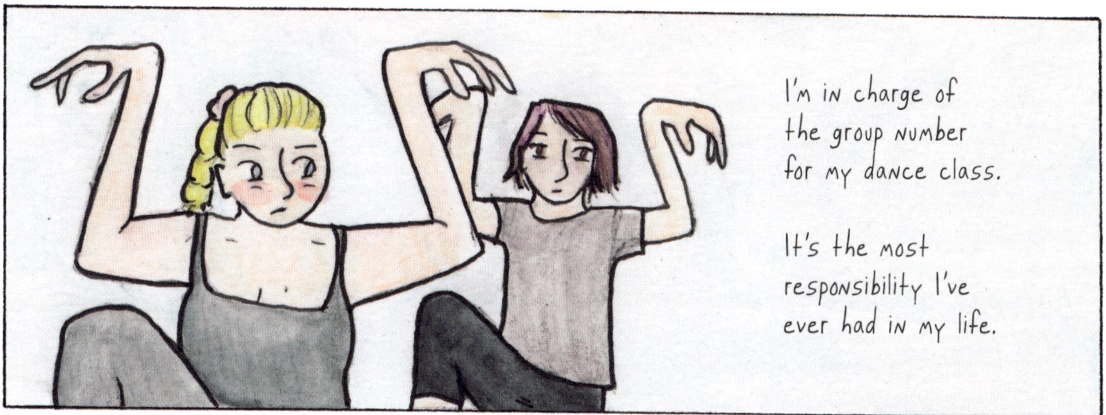
I'm in charge of the group number for my dance class.
It's the most responsibility I've ever had in my life.

I always feel really awkward touching the girls. At the beginning of the year I told a few people that I'm pretty sure I'm a lesbian. I expected the news to get around and be this big sensation. But what actually happened is that everyone just kind of ignored it. So I didn't tell my parents because I was afraid they'd ignore me, too.

Looking back, I don't know why everyone's lack of reaction surprised me: It's like shouting into the emptiness of space and being surprised there's no answer.

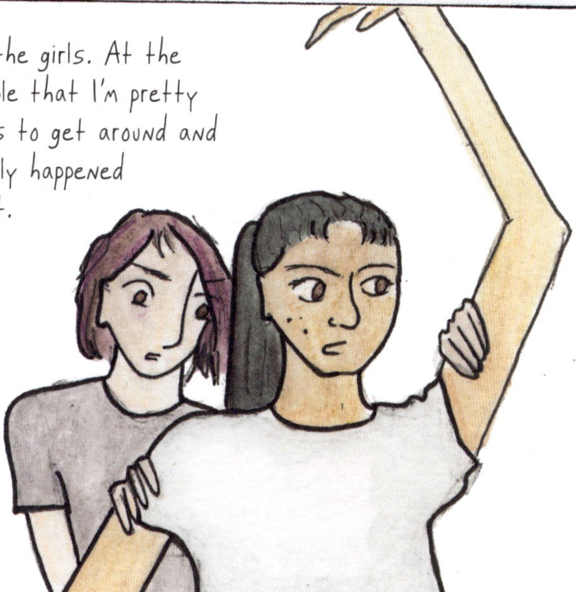

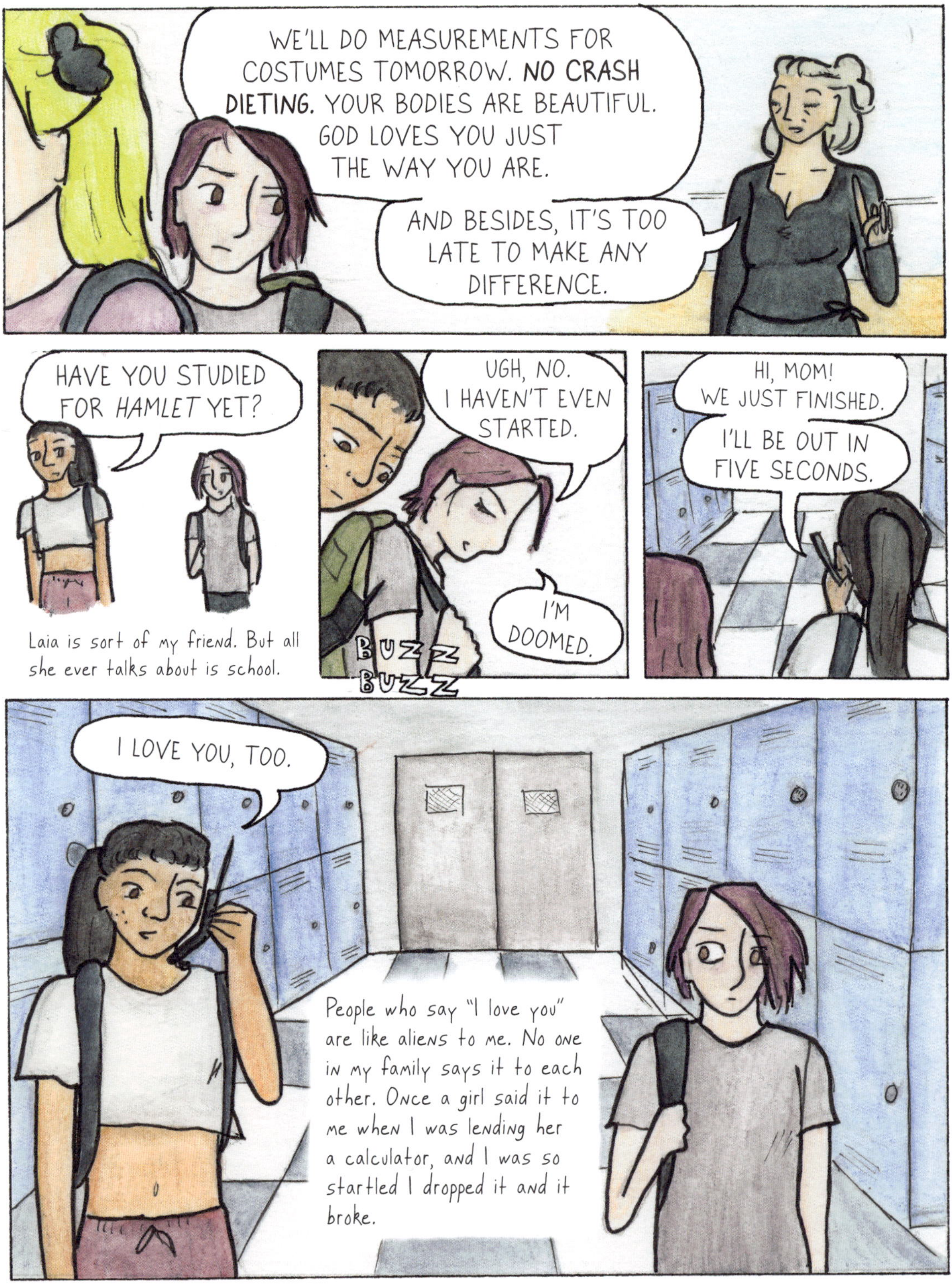
WE'LL DO MEASUREMENTS FOR COSTUMES TOMORROW. **NO CRASH DIETING.** YOUR BODIES ARE BEAUTIFUL. GOD LOVES YOU JUST THE WAY YOU ARE.
AND BESIDES, IT'S TOO LATE TO MAKE ANY DIFFERENCE.
HAVE YOU STUDIED FOR *HAMLET* YET?
Laia is sort of my friend. But all she ever talks about is school.
UGH, NO. I HAVEN'T EVEN STARTED.
I'M DOOMED.
BUZZ BUZZ
HI, MOM! WE JUST FINISHED.
I'LL BE OUT IN FIVE SECONDS.
I LOVE YOU, TOO.
People who say "I love you" are like aliens to me. No one in my family says it to each other. Once a girl said it to me when I was lending her a calculator, and I was so startled I dropped it and it broke.

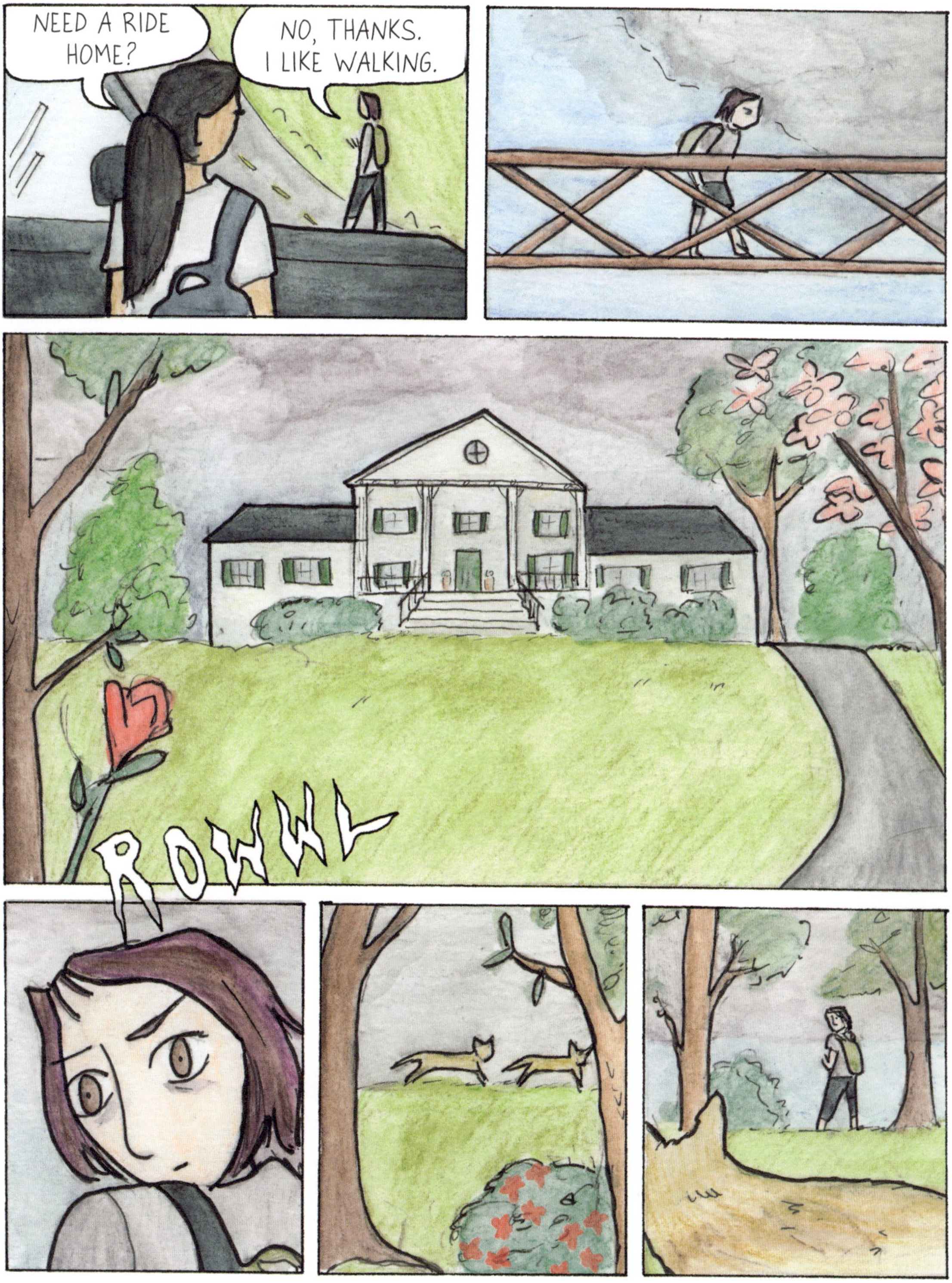
NEED A RIDE HOME?
NO, THANKS. I LIKE WALKING.
ROWWL

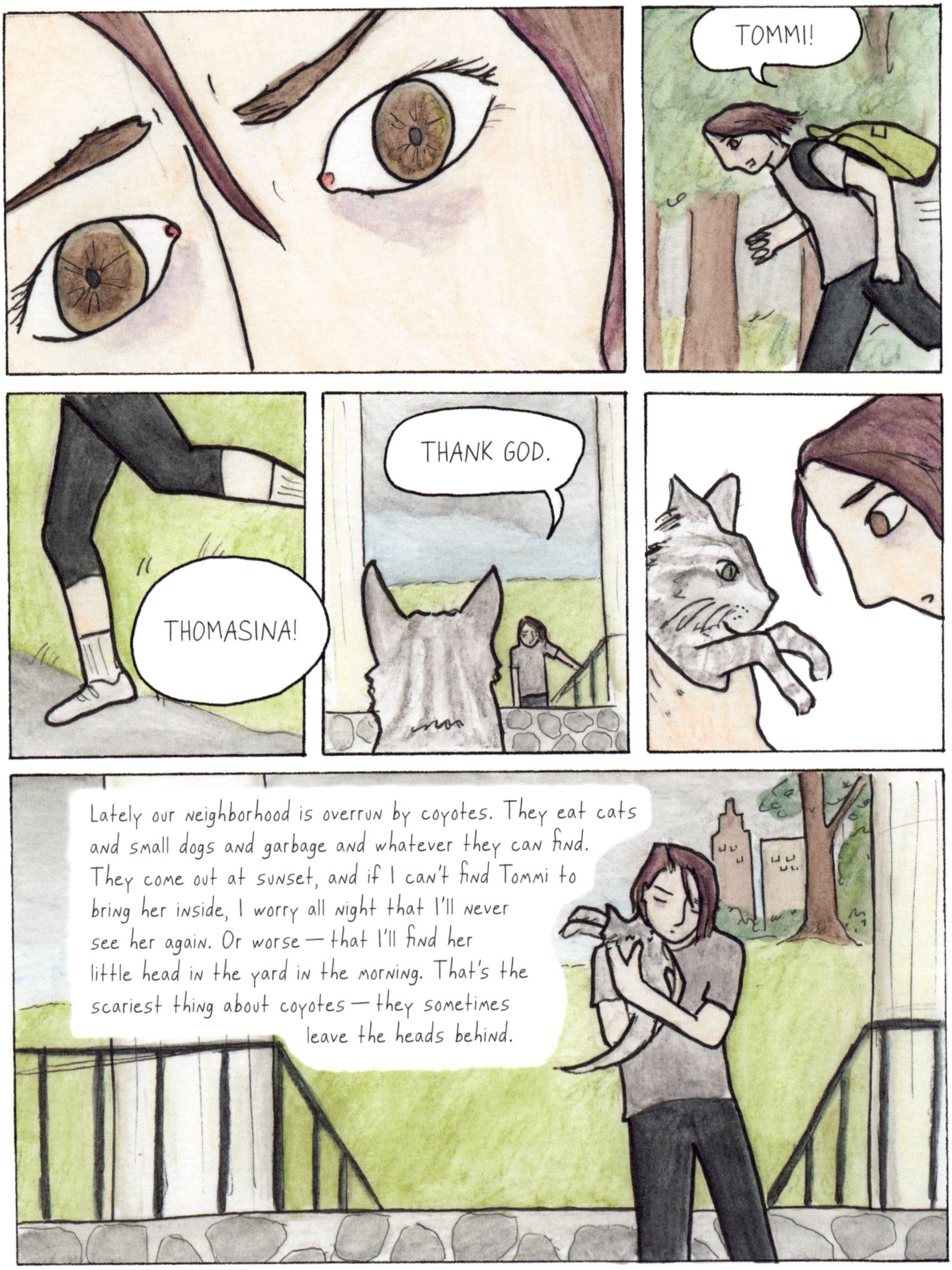
TOMMI!
THOMASINA!
THANK GOD.
Lately our neighborhood is overrun by coyotes. They eat cats and small dogs and garbage and whatever they can find. They come out at sunset, and if I can't find Tommi to bring her inside, I worry all night that I'll never see her again. Or worse — that I'll find her little head in the yard in the morning. That's the scariest thing about coyotes — they sometimes leave the heads behind.

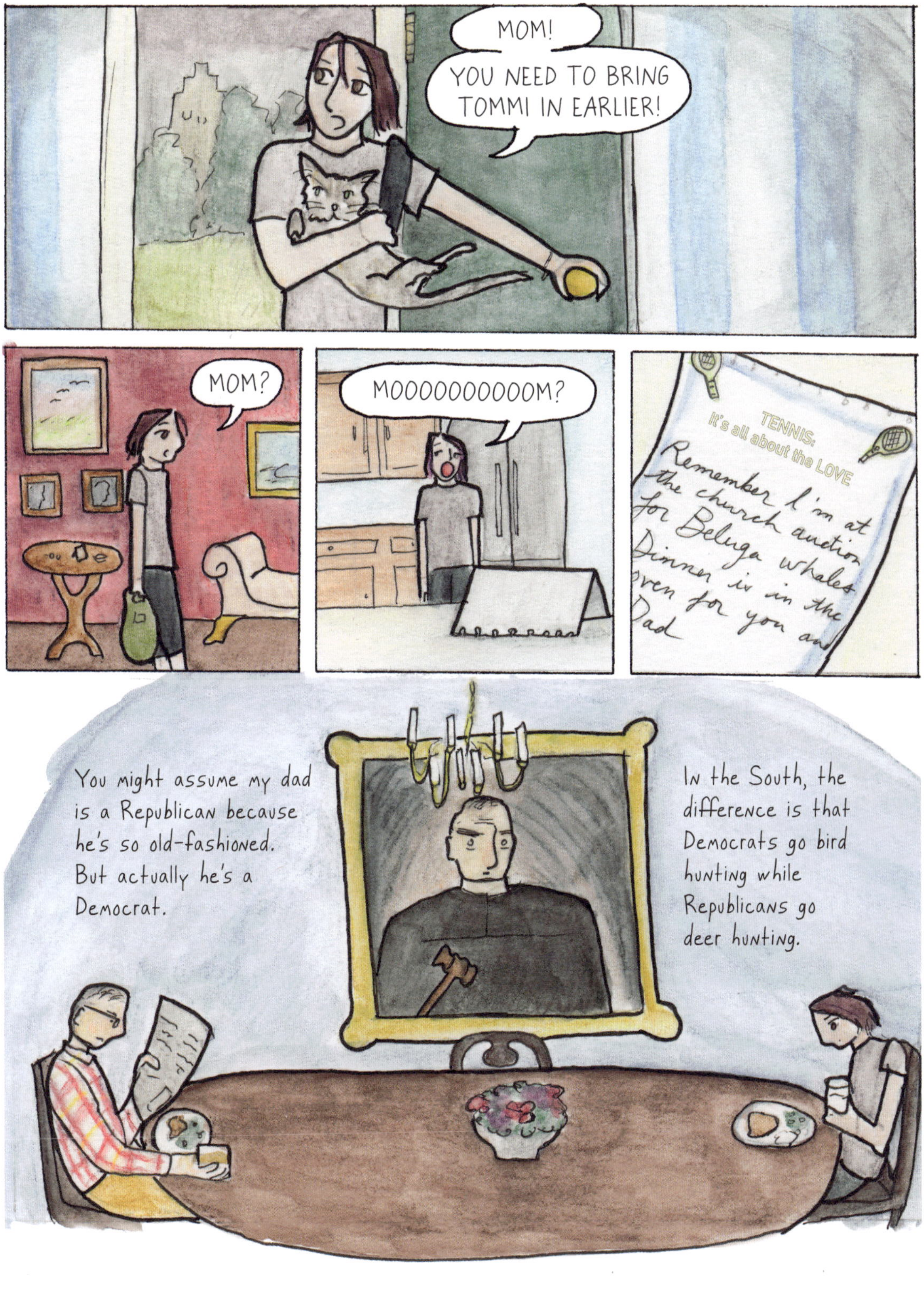

MOM!
YOU NEED TO BRING TOMMI IN EARLIER!
MOM?
MOOOOOOOOOOM?
TENNIS: It's all about the LOVE
Remember I'm at the church auction for Beluga whales
Dinner is in the
ven for you an
Dad
You might assume my dad is a Republican because he's so old-fashioned. But actually he's a Democrat.
In the South, the difference is that Democrats go bird hunting while Republicans go deer hunting.

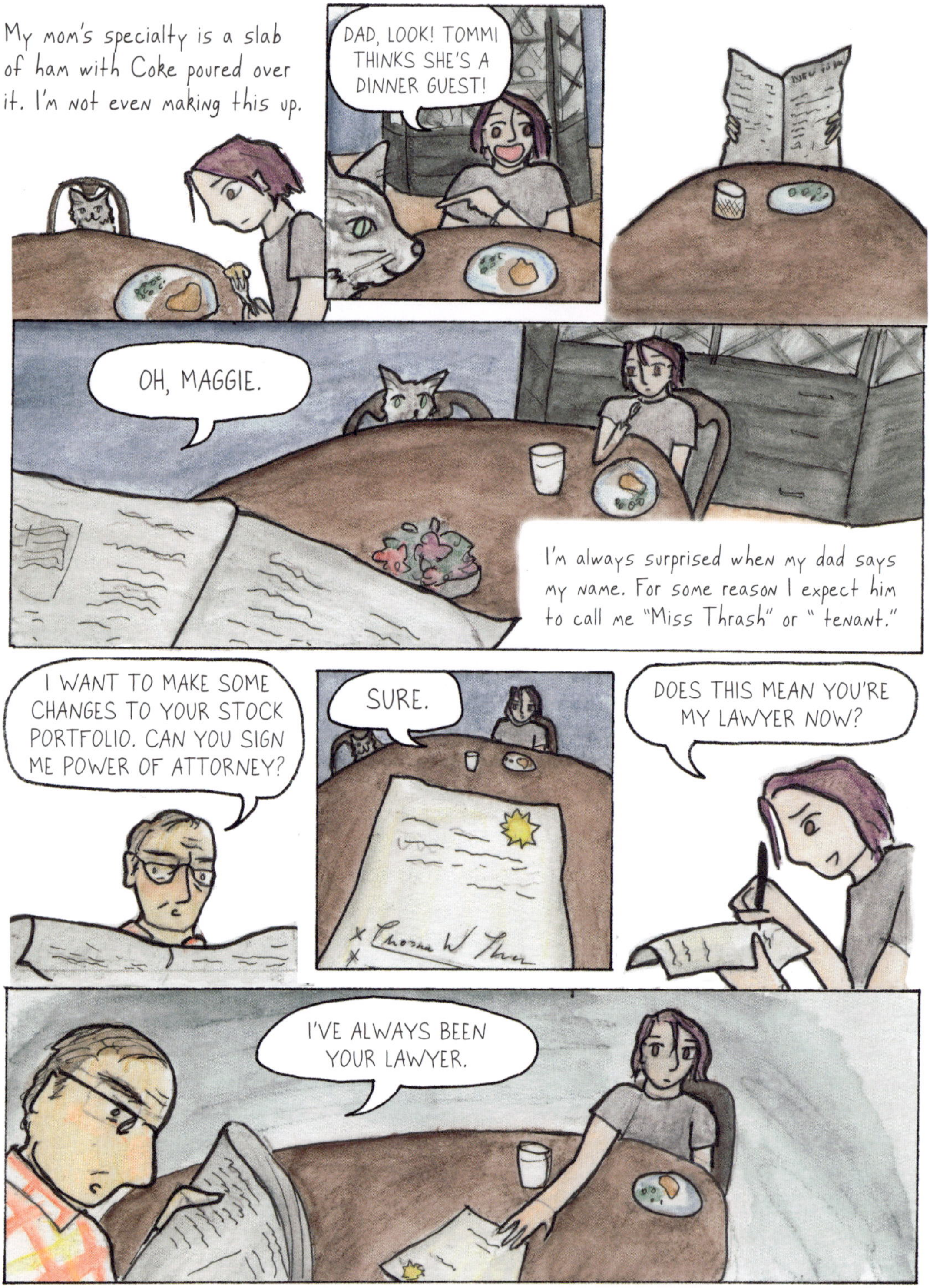
My mom's specialty is a slab of ham with Coke poured over it. I'm not even making this up.
DAD, LOOK! TOMMI THINKS SHE'S A DINNER GUEST!
OH, MAGGIE.
I'm always surprised when my dad says my name. For some reason I expect him to call me "Miss Thrash" or "tenant."
I WANT TO MAKE SOME CHANGES TO YOUR STOCK PORTFOLIO. CAN YOU SIGN ME POWER OF ATTORNEY?
SURE.
DOES THIS MEAN YOU'RE MY LAWYER NOW?
I'VE ALWAYS BEEN YOUR LAWYER.

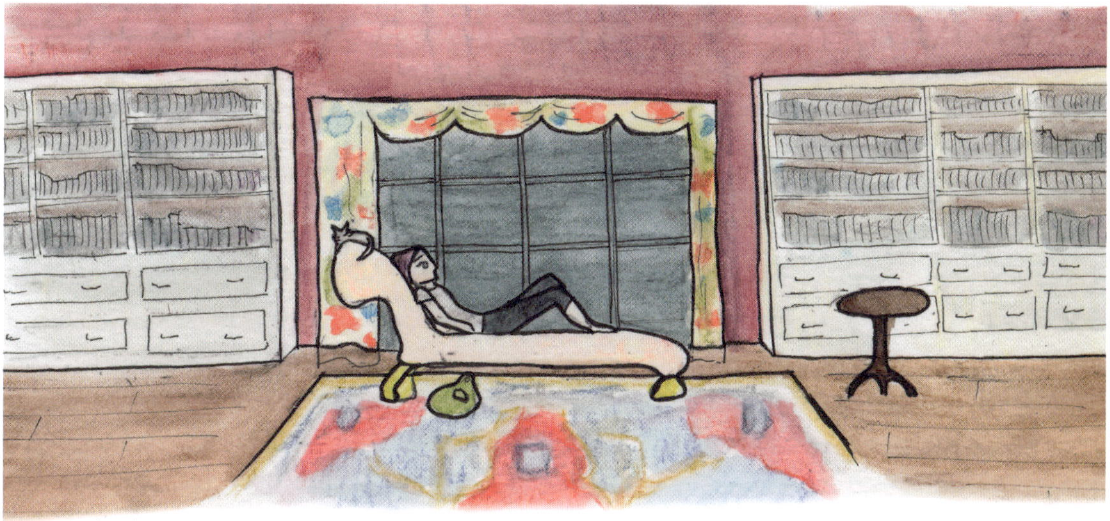

The house suddenly seemed vacuously huge when my brother left for college. It's not like he was such a sparkling, sunny presence. He's a grim introvert just like my dad. But it was nice having him around. We would watch *Babylon 5* after school and make microwave s'mores, which is fun with a friend, but by yourself is kind of depressing.

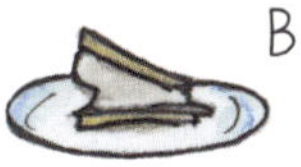

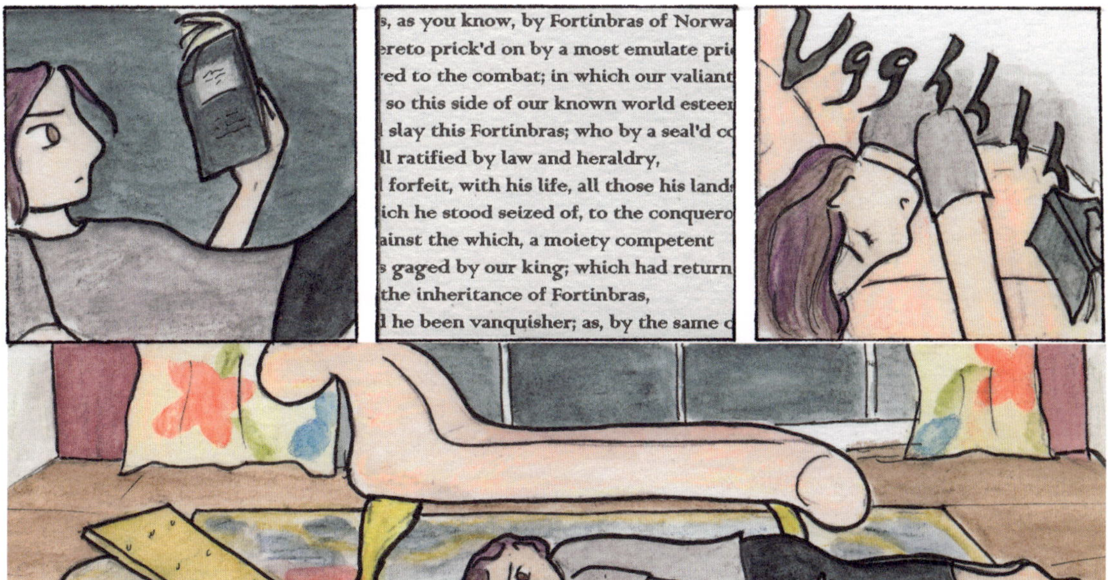
s, as you know, by Fortinbras of Norwa
ereto prick'd on by a most emulate pri
red to the combat; in which our valiant
so this side of our known world esteer
slay this Fortinbras; who by a seal'd c
ll ratified by law and heraldry,
forfeit, with his life, all those his land
ich he stood seized of, to the conquero
ainst the which, a moiety competent
s gaged by our king; which had return
the inheritance of Fortinbras,
d he been vanquisher; as, by the same c
Ugghhhh

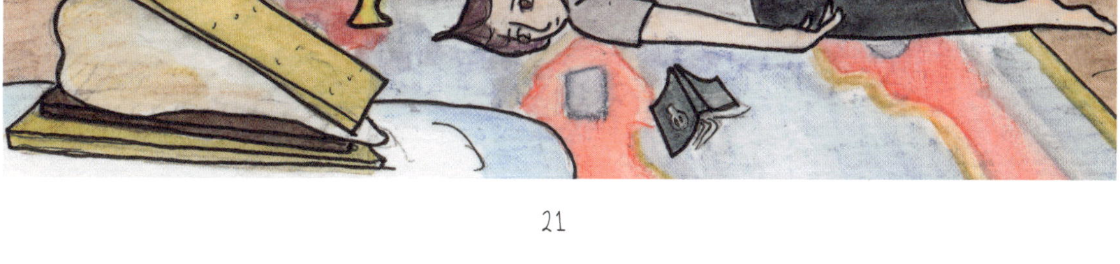

The other day I realized I'm the same age as Aurora from *Sleeping Beauty*, which makes me want to crawl in a hole and die. Not just because of the pressure that I should be taller and more charming by now, but because by the age of sixteen, Aurora had already snagged her happy ending, and her story was over.

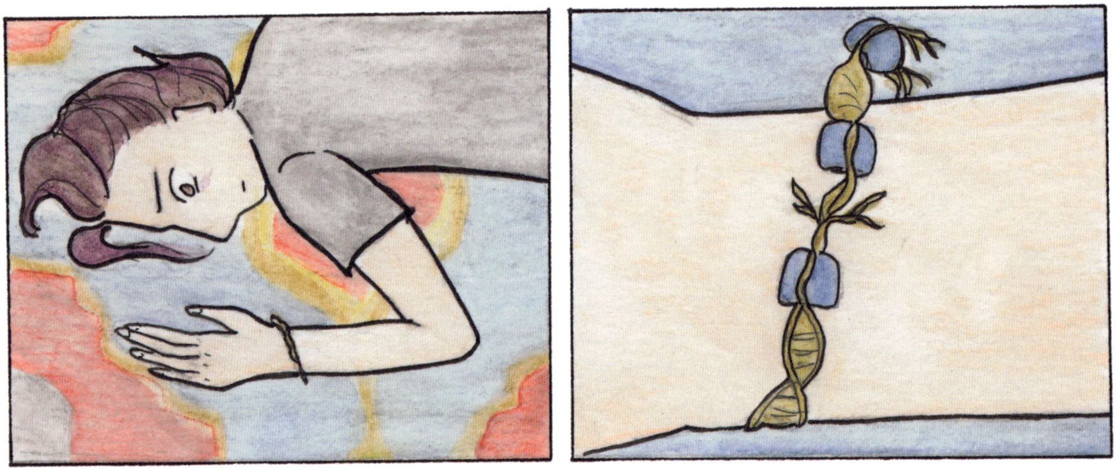

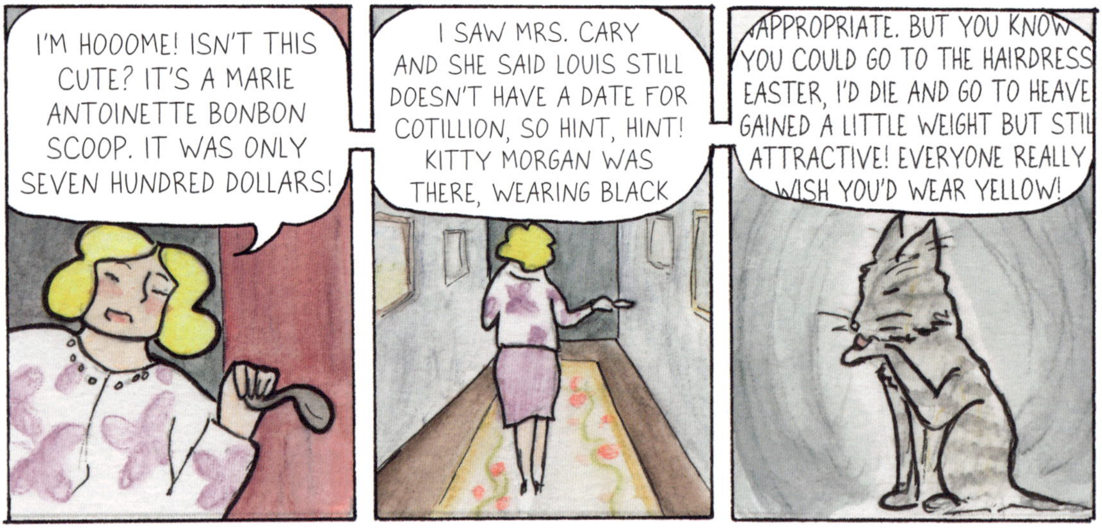

I'M HOOOME! ISN'T THIS CUTE? IT'S A MARIE ANTOINETTE BONBON SCOOP. IT WAS ONLY SEVEN HUNDRED DOLLARS!
I SAW MRS. CARY AND SHE SAID LOUIS STILL DOESN'T HAVE A DATE FOR COTILLION, SO HINT, HINT! KITTY MORGAN WAS THERE, WEARING BLACK
APPROPRIATE. BUT YOU KNOW YOU COULD GO TO THE HAIRDRESS EASTER, I'D DIE AND GO TO HEAVE GAINED A LITTLE WEIGHT BUT STIL ATTRACTIVE! EVERYONE REALLY WISH YOU'D WEAR YELLOW!

I don't know what I have to do to get my mom to notice that I'm incredibly depressed. I'm failing all my classes and I dyed my hair purple. But if I said anything about it directly, she'd just be like, "Well maybe if you studied and hadn't ruined your hair, you wouldn't be depressed!"

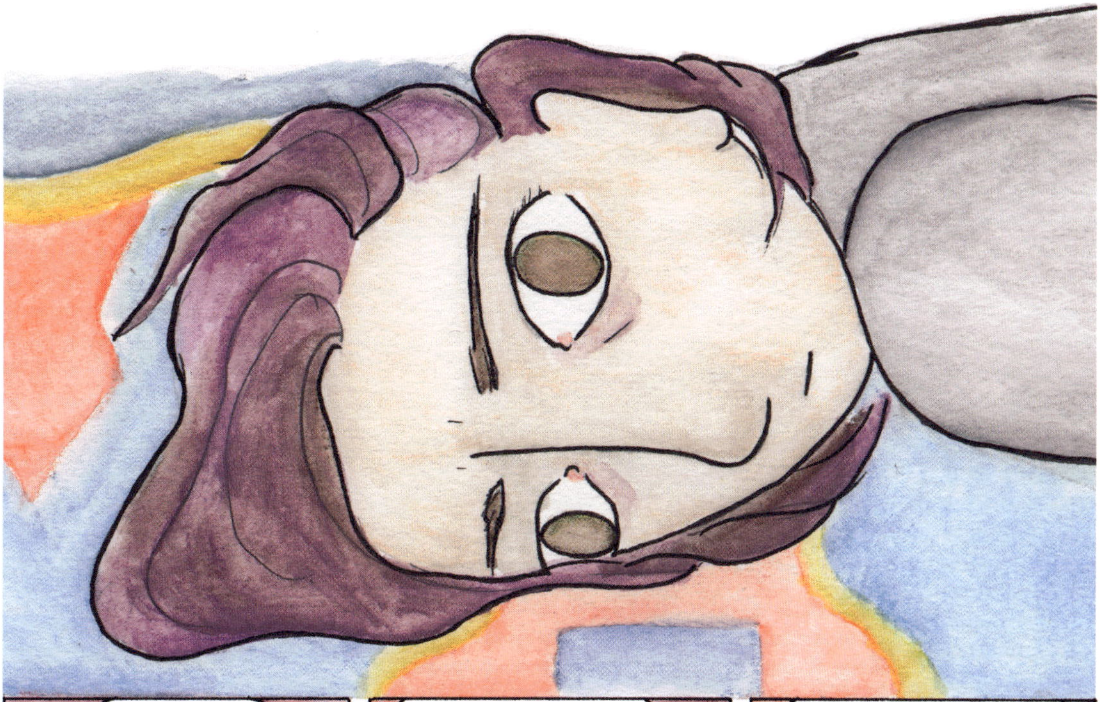

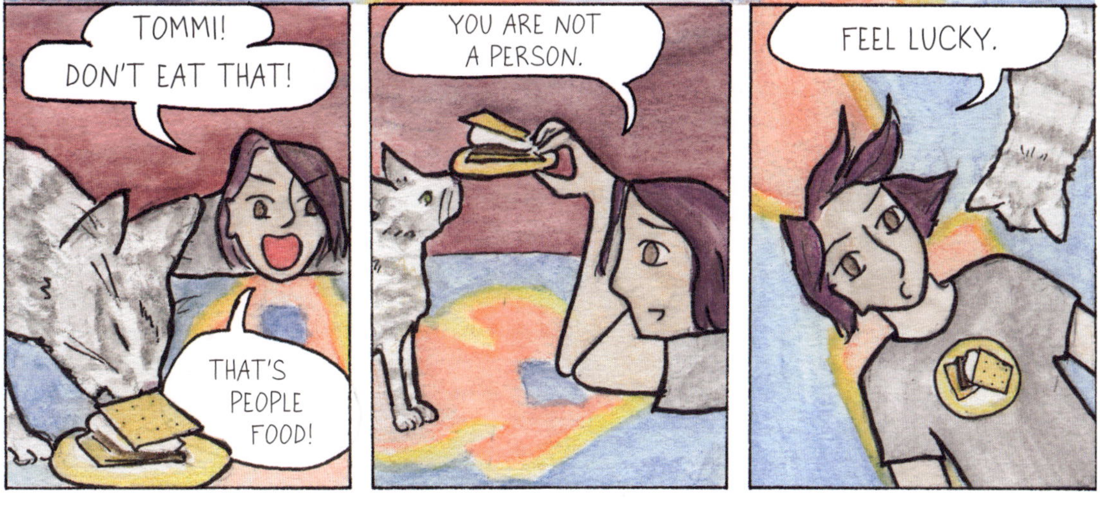
TOMMI!
DON'T EAT THAT!
THAT'S PEOPLE FOOD!
YOU ARE NOT A PERSON.
FEEL LUCKY.

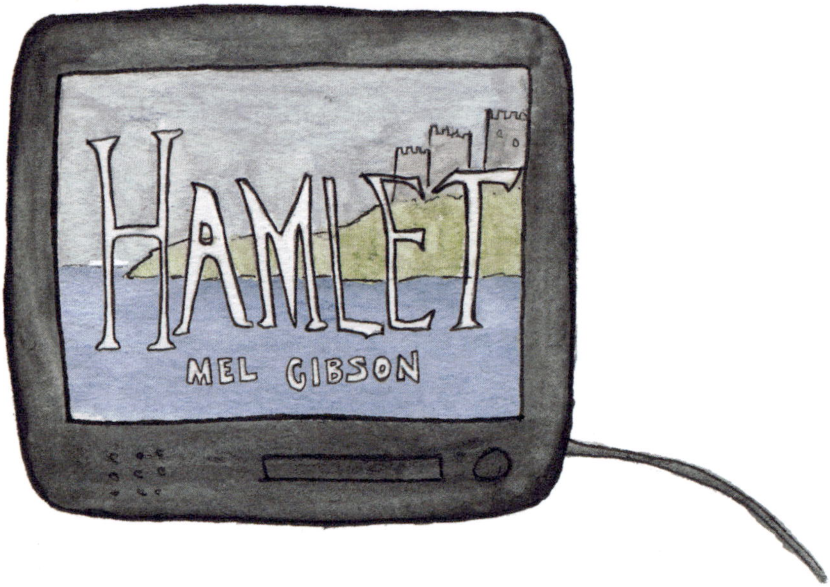
HAMLET
MEL GIBSON

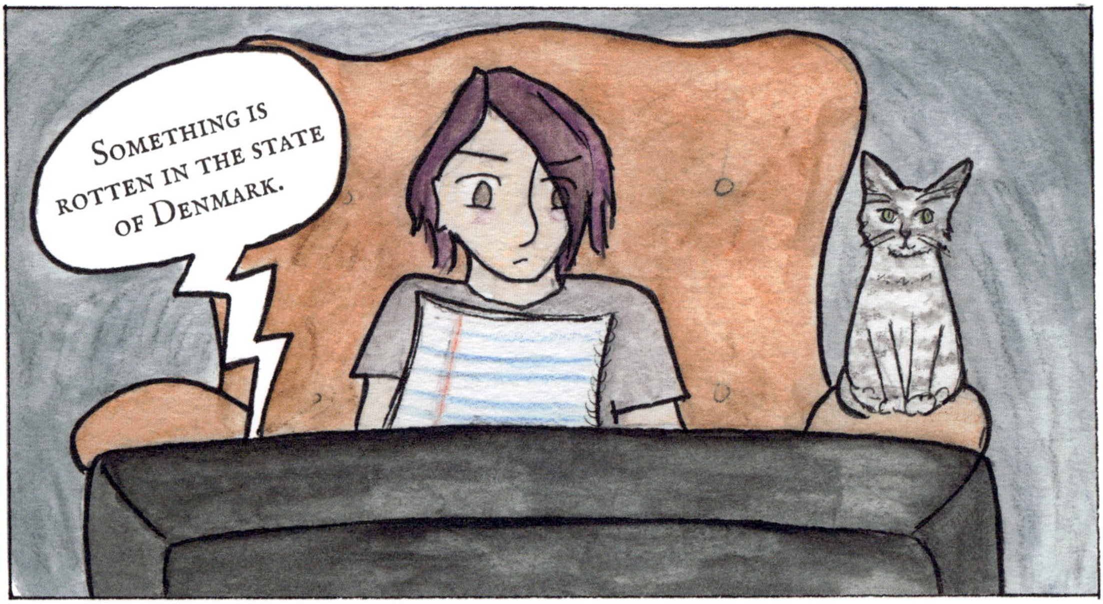
SOMETHING IS ROTTEN IN THE STATE OF DENMARK.

I **have** to pass my in-class essay on Thursday. The situation with my grades has become dire. My parents are in denial about it. My mom was Phi Beta Kappa and my dad went to Harvard, so it's a miracle of genetics that together they produced a child who is failing eleventh grade. The only reason I don't run away from home is because I couldn't leave Tommi.

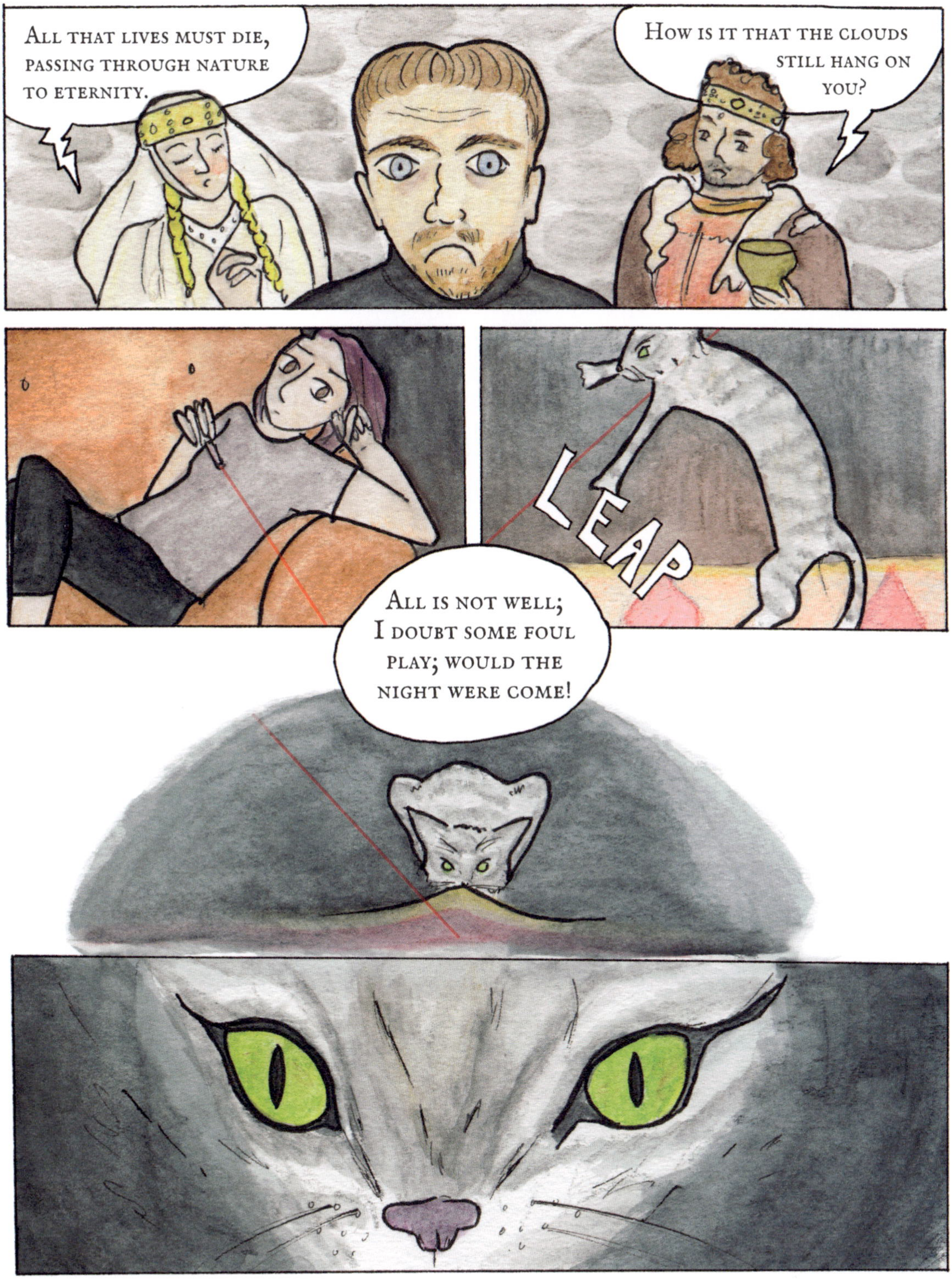
All that lives must die, passing through nature to eternity.
How is it that the clouds still hang on you?
LEAP
All is not well; I doubt some foul play; would the night were come!

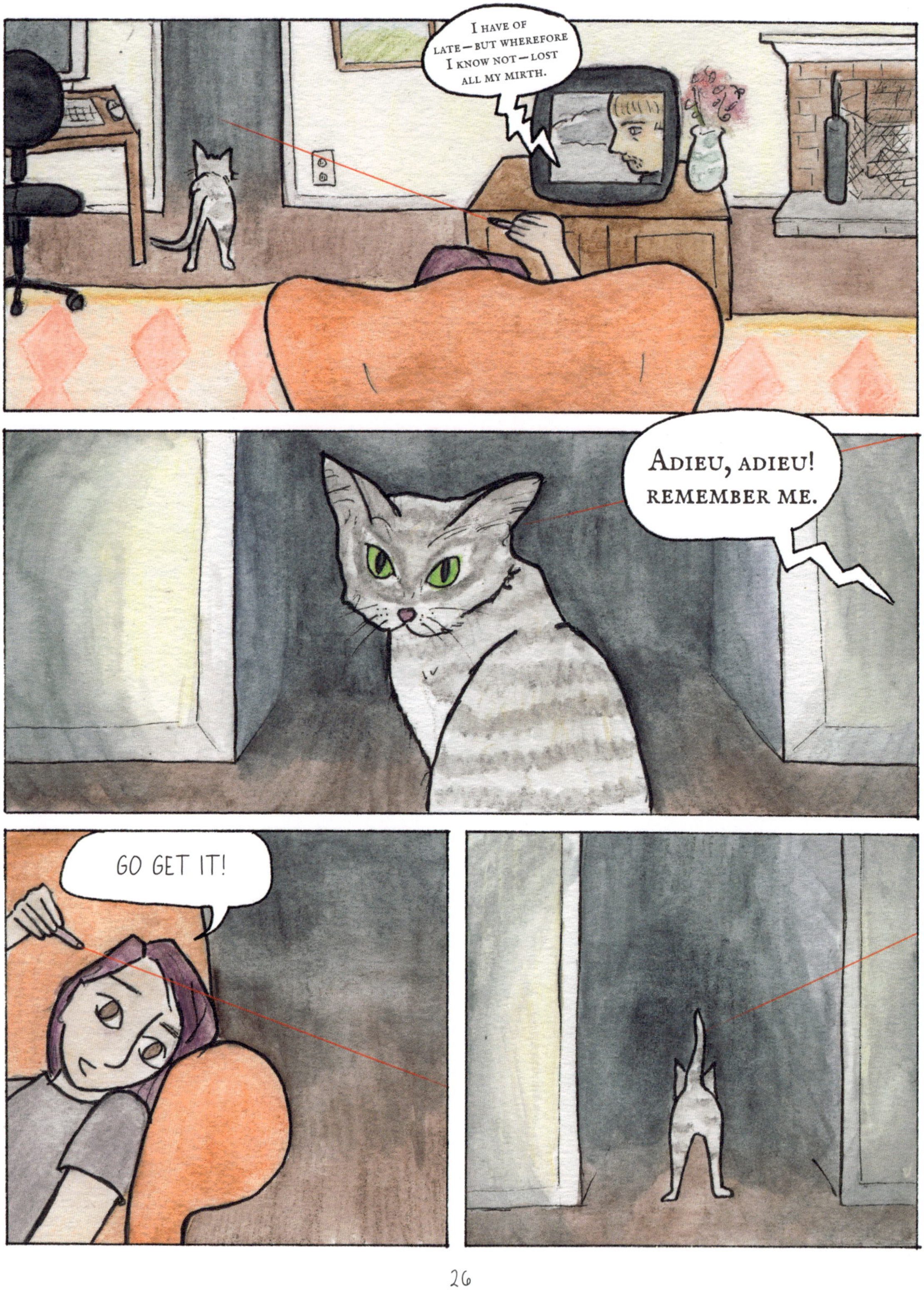
I have of late—but wherefore I know not—lost all my mirth.
Adieu, adieu! remember me.
GO GET IT!

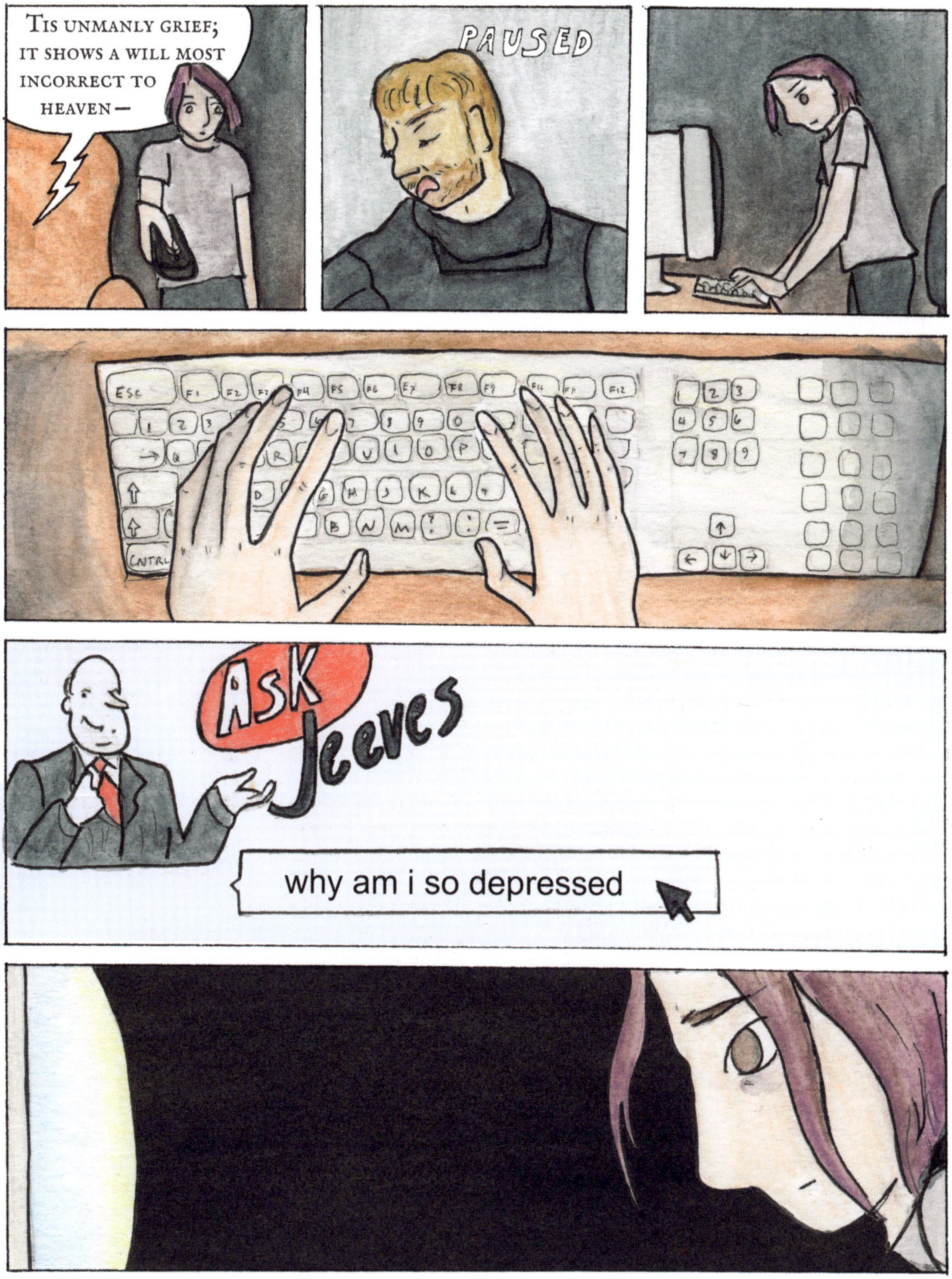
Tis unmanly grief; it shows a will most incorrect to heaven—
PAUSED
Ask Jeeves
why am i so depressed

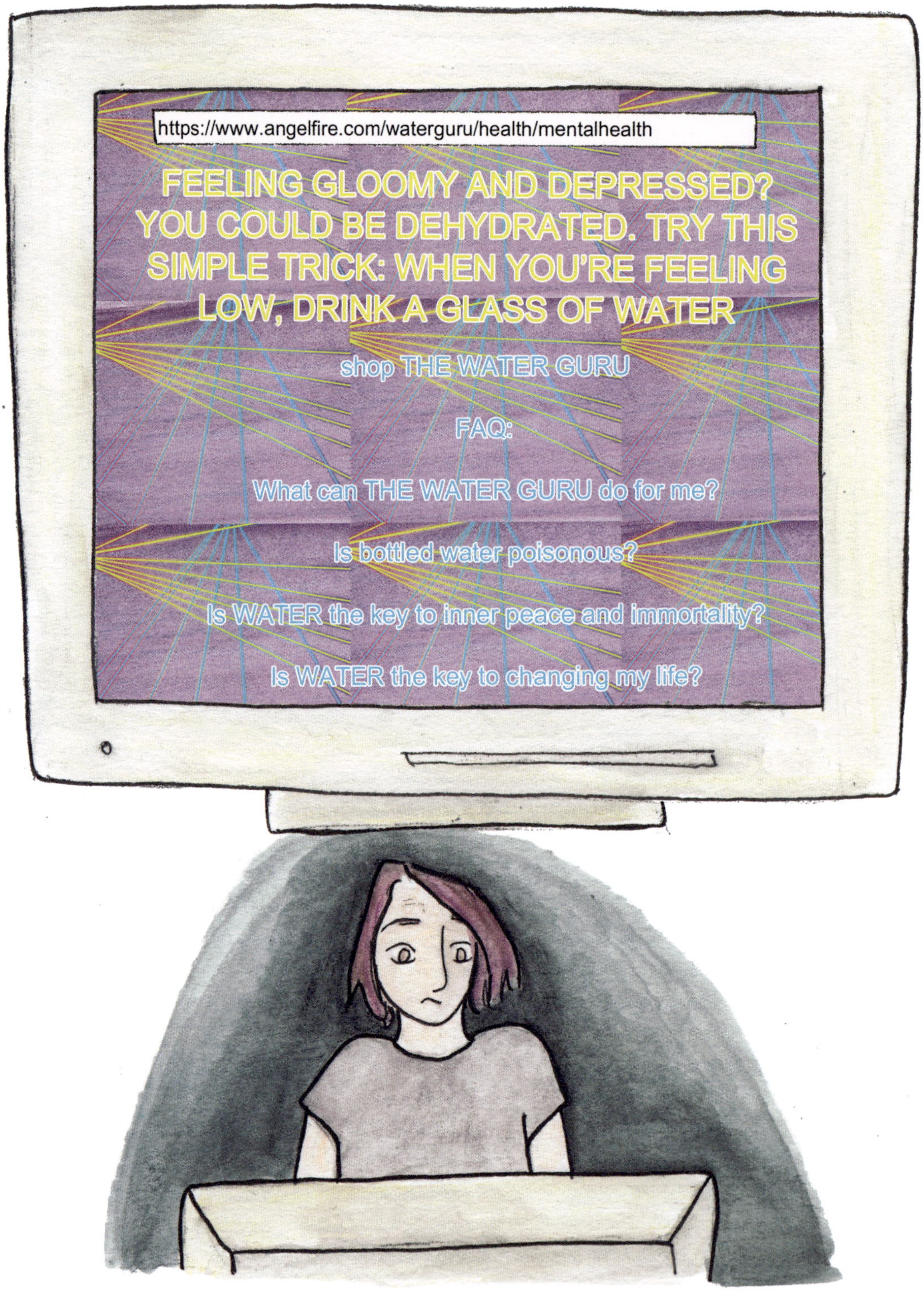
https://www.angelfire.com/waterguru/health/mentalhealth
FEELING GLOOMY AND DEPRESSED? YOU COULD BE DEHYDRATED. TRY THIS SIMPLE TRICK: WHEN YOU'RE FEELING LOW, DRINK A GLASS OF WATER
shop THE WATER GURU
FAQ:
What can THE WATER GURU do for me?
Is bottled water poisonous?
Is WATER the key to inner peace and immortality?
Is WATER the key to changing my life?

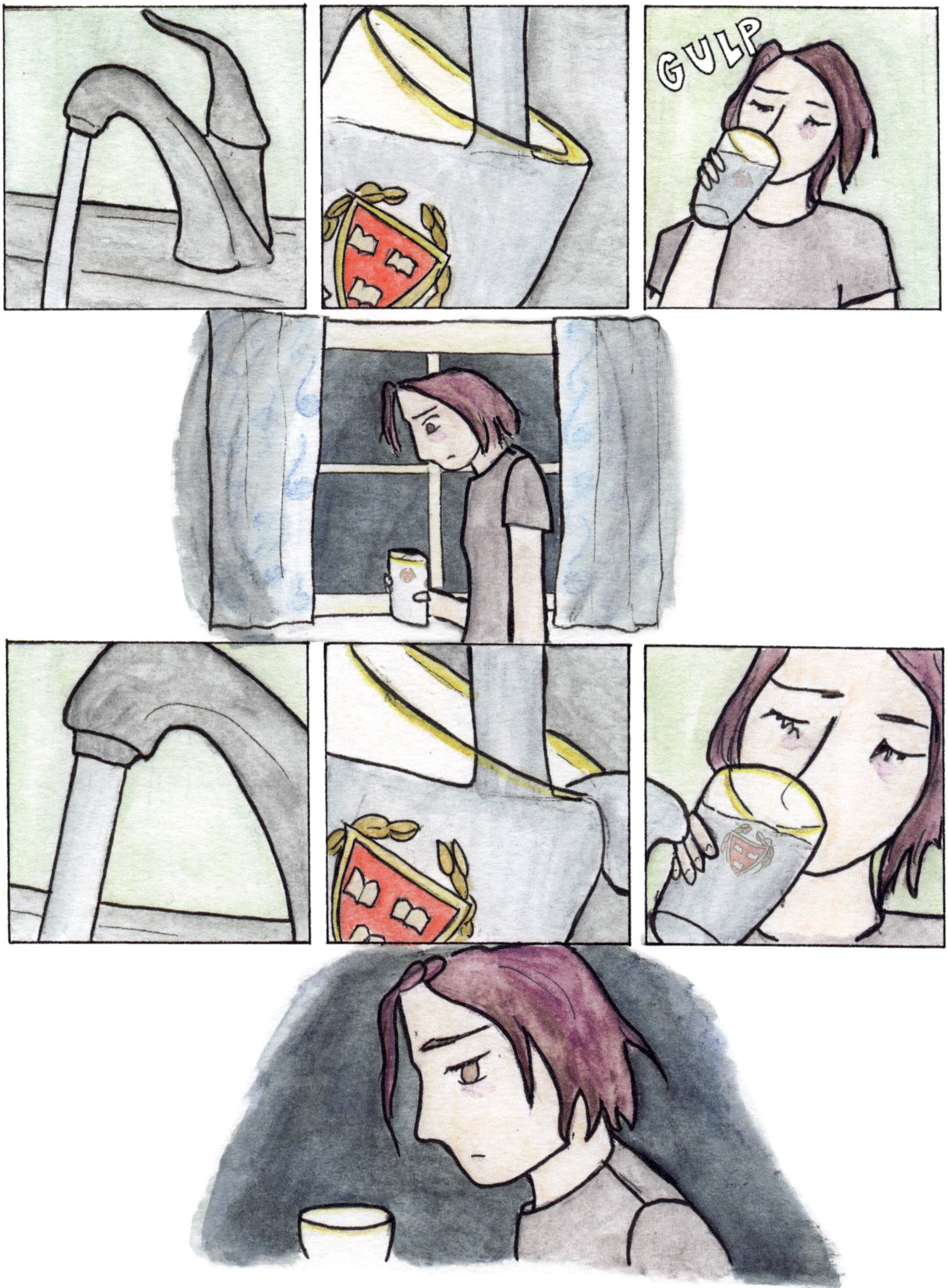
GULP

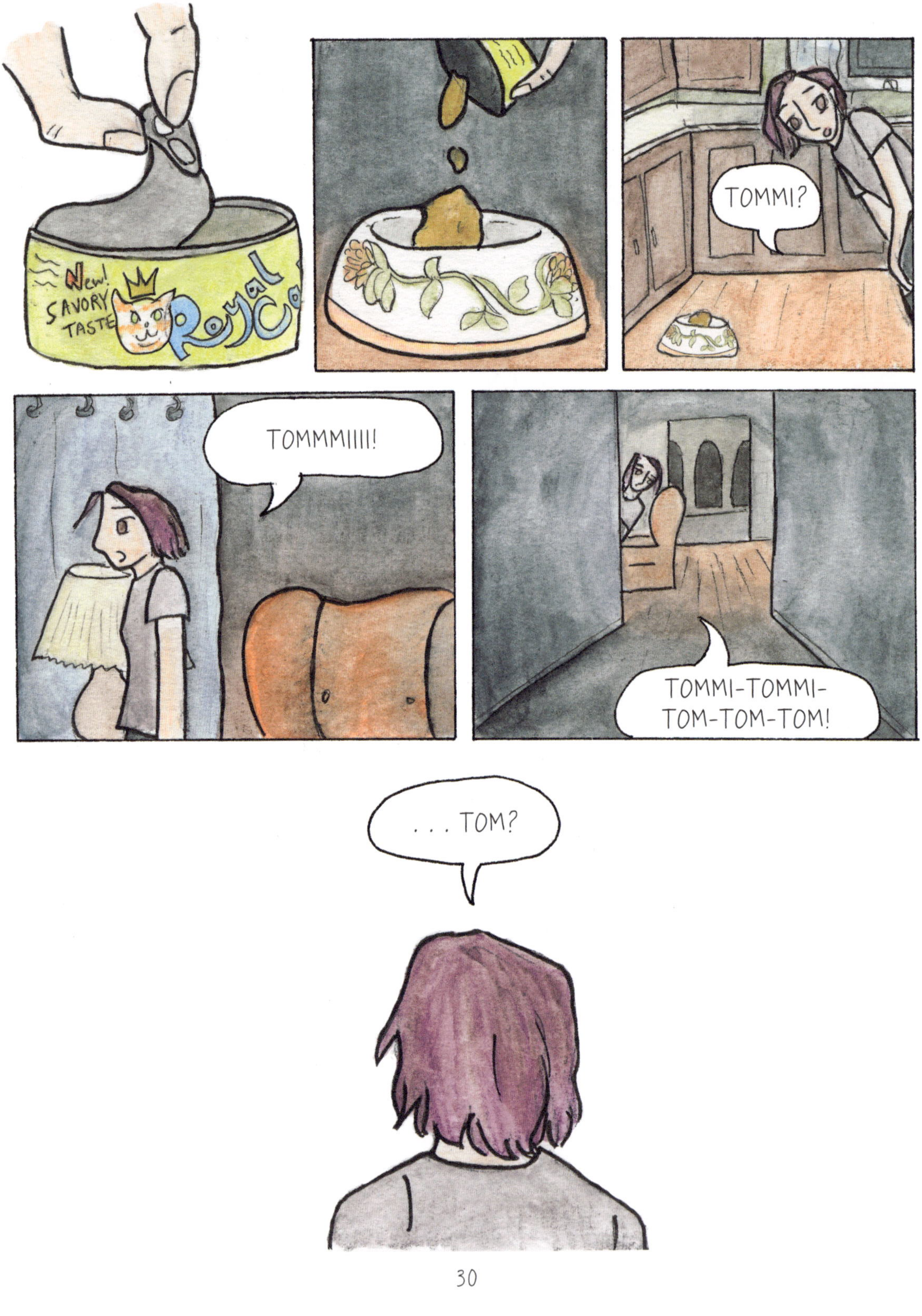
New!
SAVORY
TASTE
Royal Ca
TOMMI?
TOMMMIIIII!
TOMMI-TOMMI-
TOM-TOM-TOM!
. . . TOM?

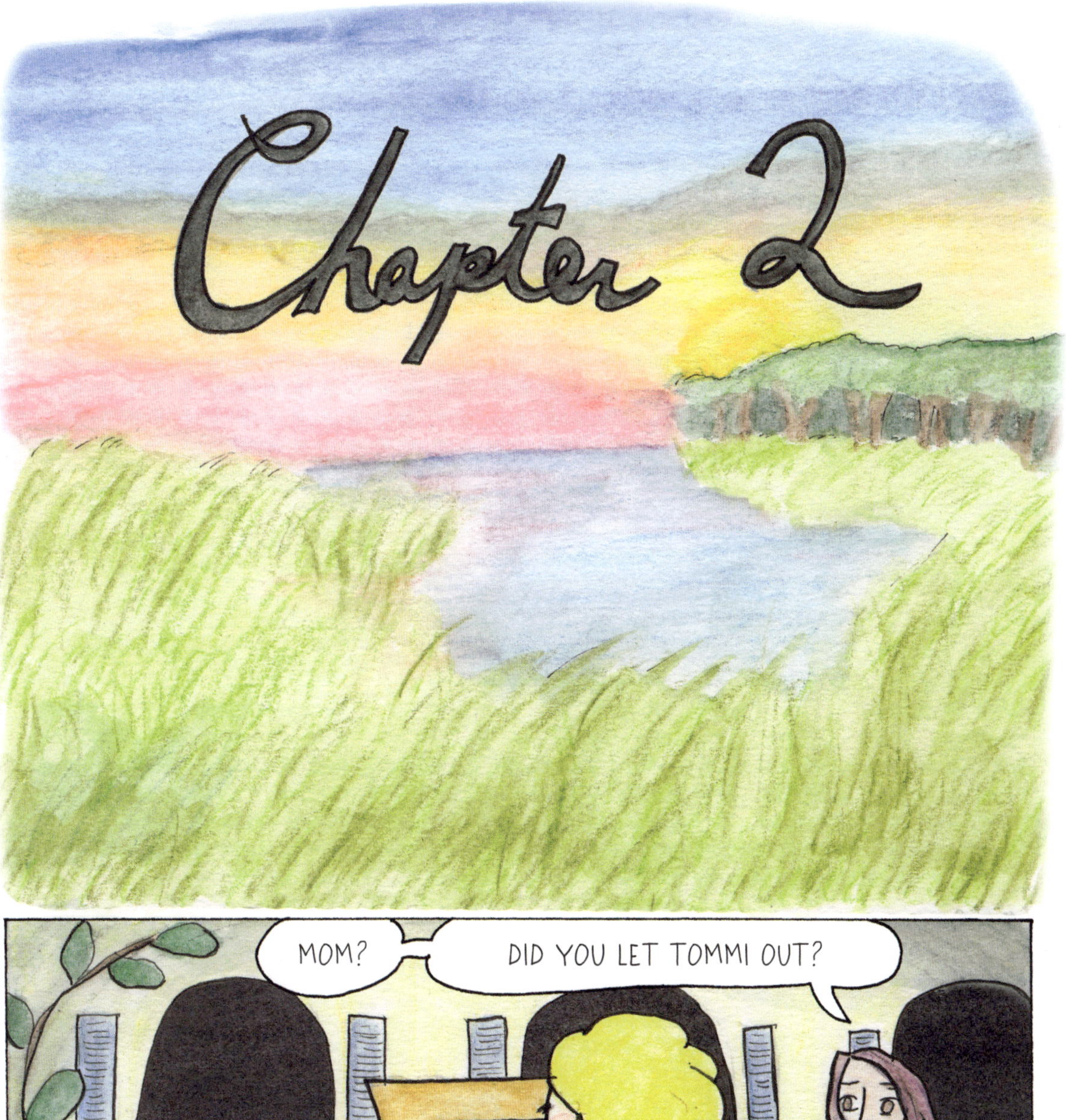
Chapter 2

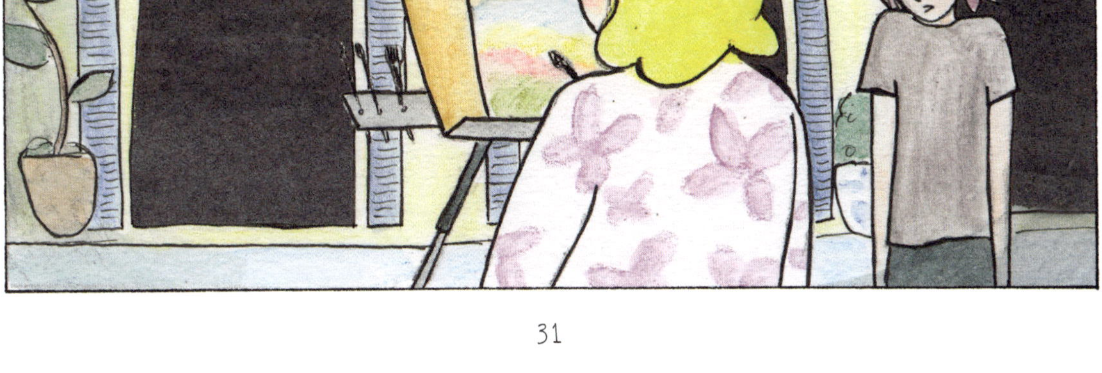
MOM?
DID YOU LET TOMMI OUT?

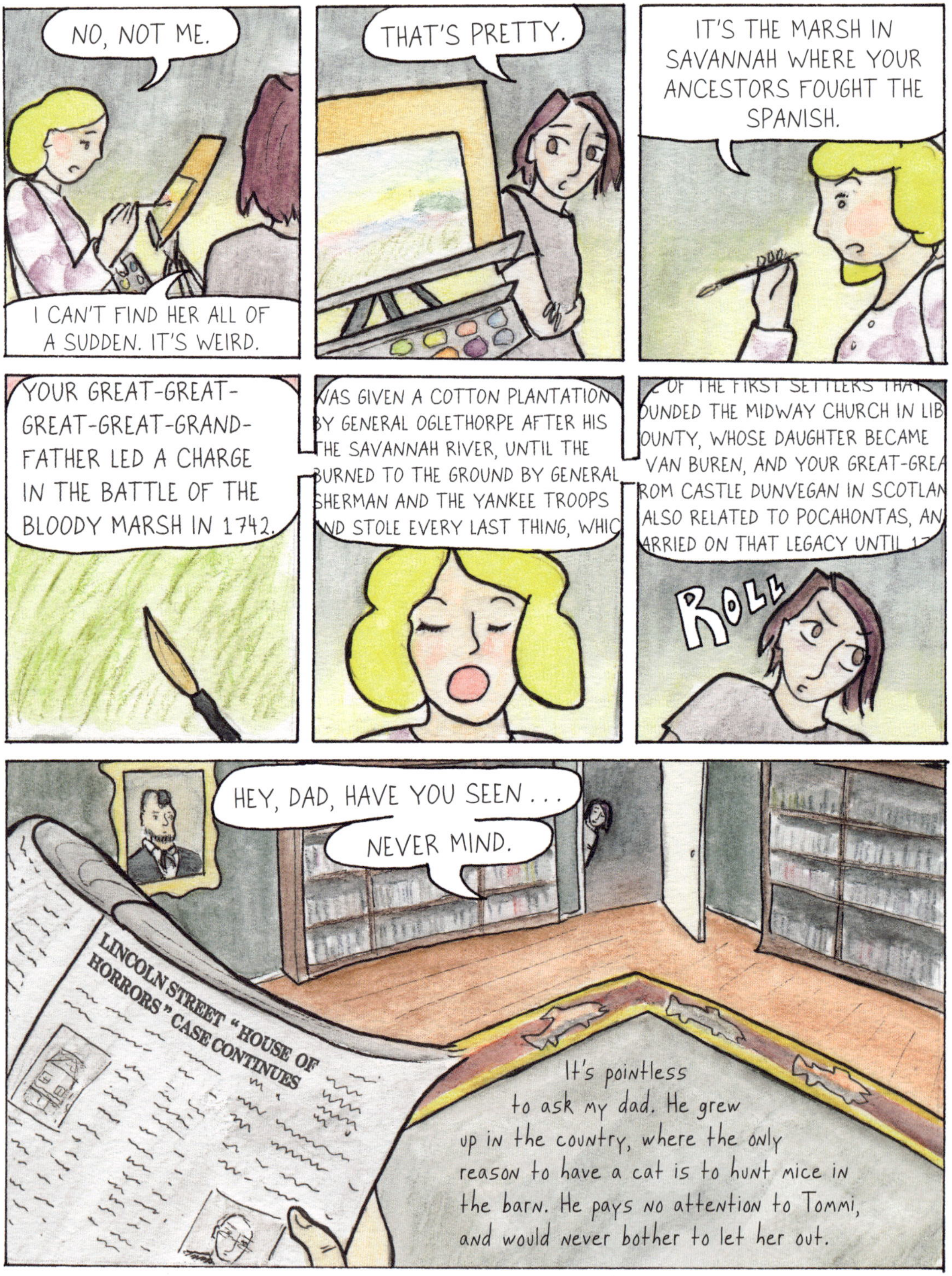
NO, NOT ME.
I CAN'T FIND HER ALL OF A SUDDEN. IT'S WEIRD.
THAT'S PRETTY.
IT'S THE MARSH IN SAVANNAH WHERE YOUR ANCESTORS FOUGHT THE SPANISH.
YOUR GREAT-GREAT-GREAT-GREAT-GRAND-FATHER LED A CHARGE IN THE BATTLE OF THE BLOODY MARSH IN 1742.
VAS GIVEN A COTTON PLANTATION BY GENERAL OGLETHORPE AFTER HIS THE SAVANNAH RIVER, UNTIL THE BURNED TO THE GROUND BY GENERAL SHERMAN AND THE YANKEE TROOPS ND STOLE EVERY LAST THING, WHIC
OUNDED THE MIDWAY CHURCH IN LIB OUNTY, WHOSE DAUGHTER BECAME VAN BUREN, AND YOUR GREAT-GREA ROM CASTLE DUNVEGAN IN SCOTLAN ALSO RELATED TO POCAHONTAS, AN ARRIED ON THAT LEGACY UNTIL
ROLL
HEY, DAD, HAVE YOU SEEN . . .
NEVER MIND.
LINCOLN STREET "HOUSE OF HORRORS" CASE CONTINUES
It's pointless to ask my dad. He grew up in the country, where the only reason to have a cat is to hunt mice in the barn. He pays no attention to Tommi, and would never bother to let her out.

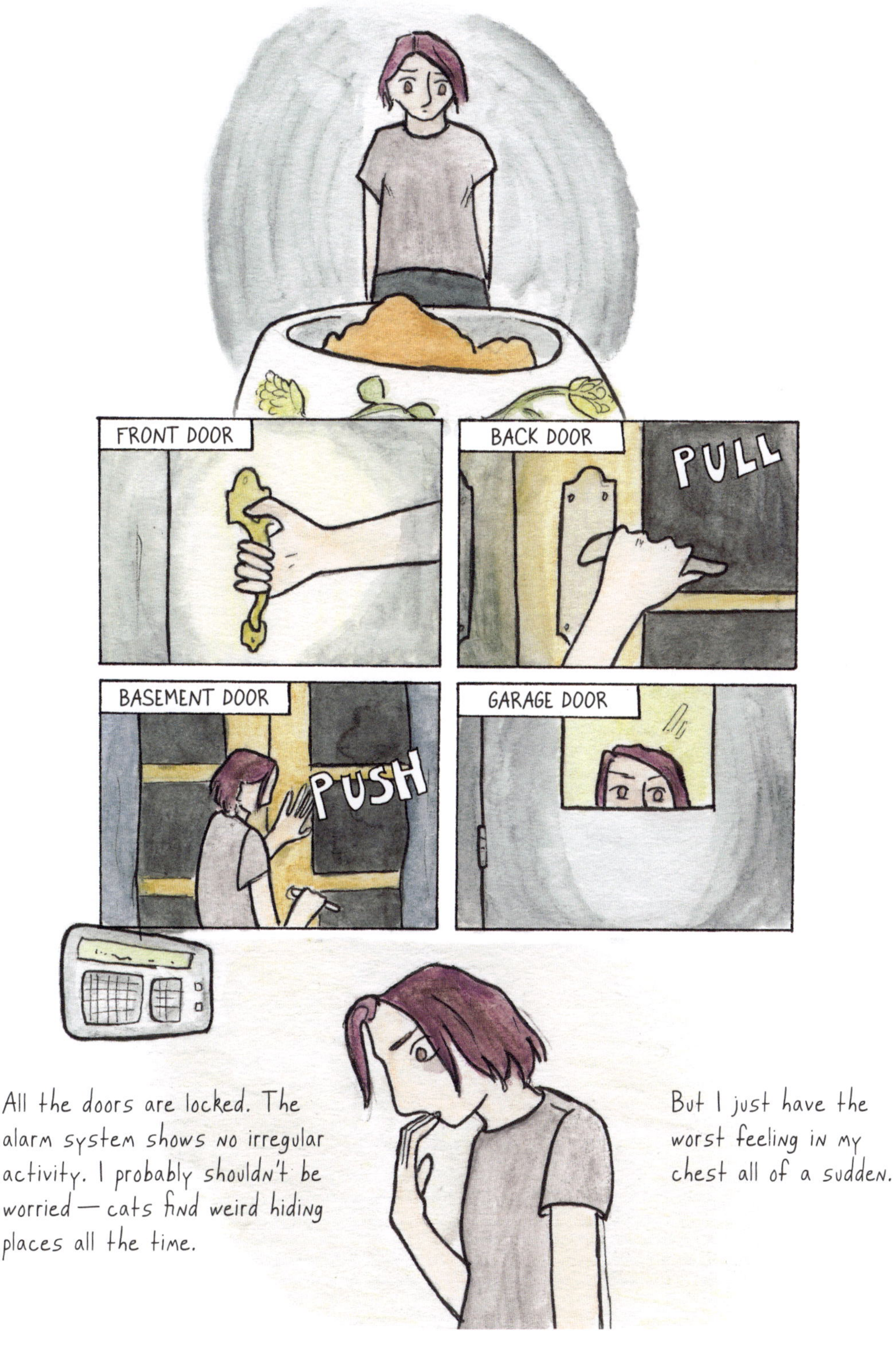
FRONT DOOR
BACK DOOR
PULL
BASEMENT DOOR
PUSH
GARAGE DOOR
All the doors are locked. The alarm system shows no irregular activity. I probably shouldn't be worried — cats find weird hiding places all the time.
But I just have the worst feeling in my chest all of a sudden.

It takes about an hour to search my whole house, which has thirteen rooms and an attic.

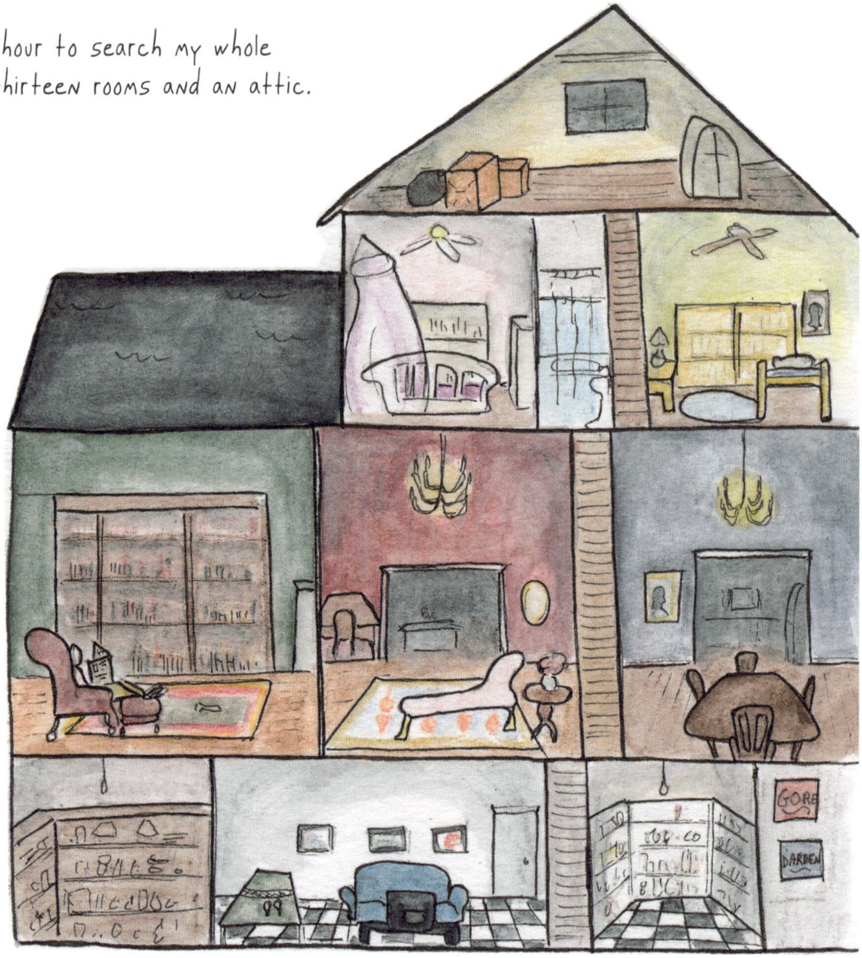
GORE

BACK OF THE HOUSE

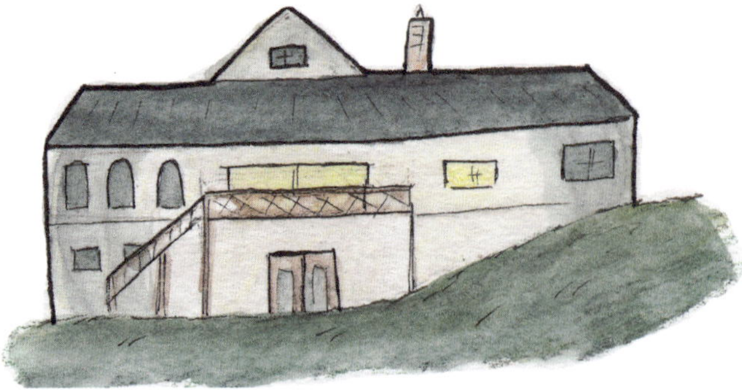

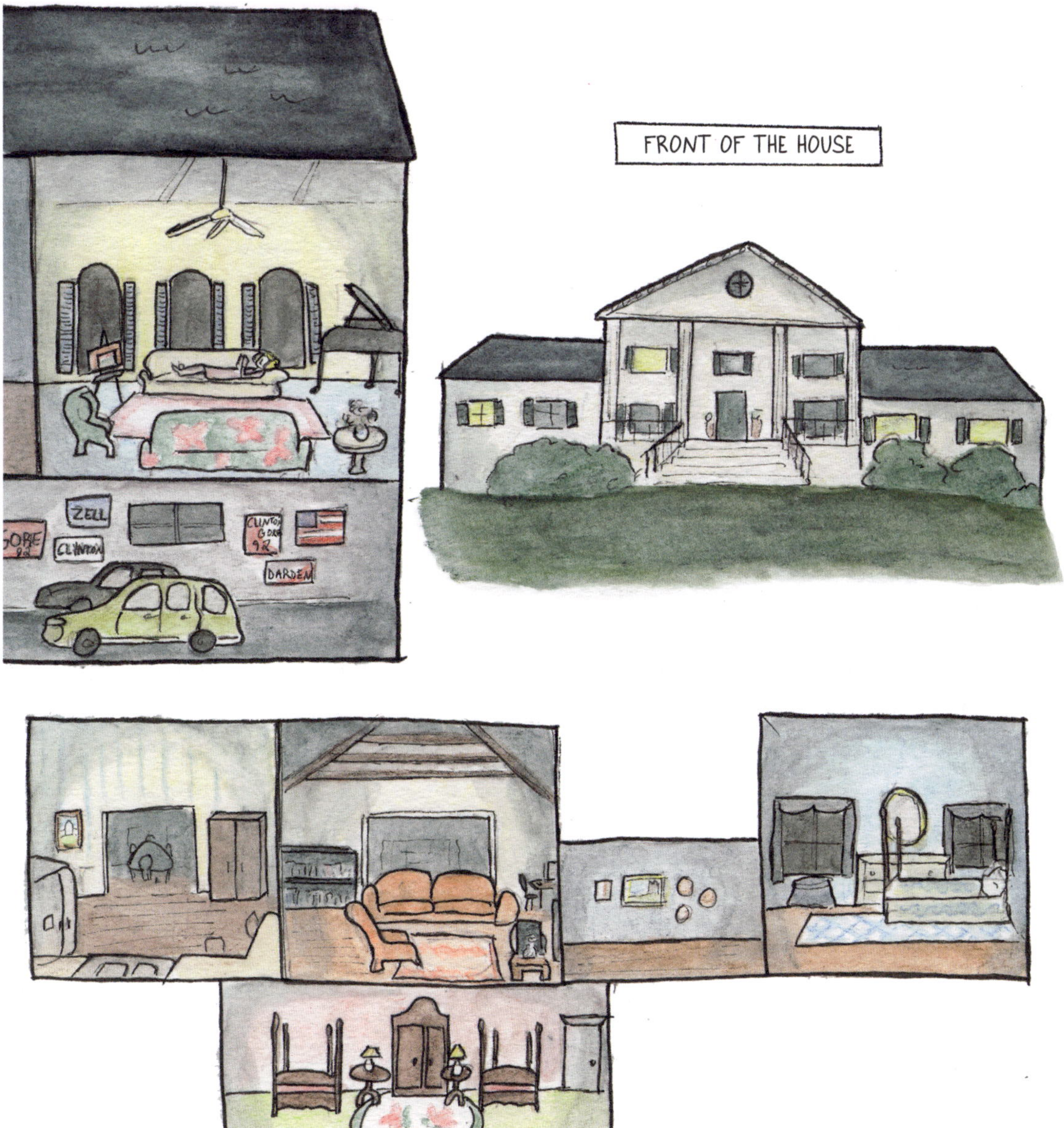
ZELL
GORE
CLINTON
DARDEN
FRONT OF THE HOUSE

I search the attic last, because it scares me.

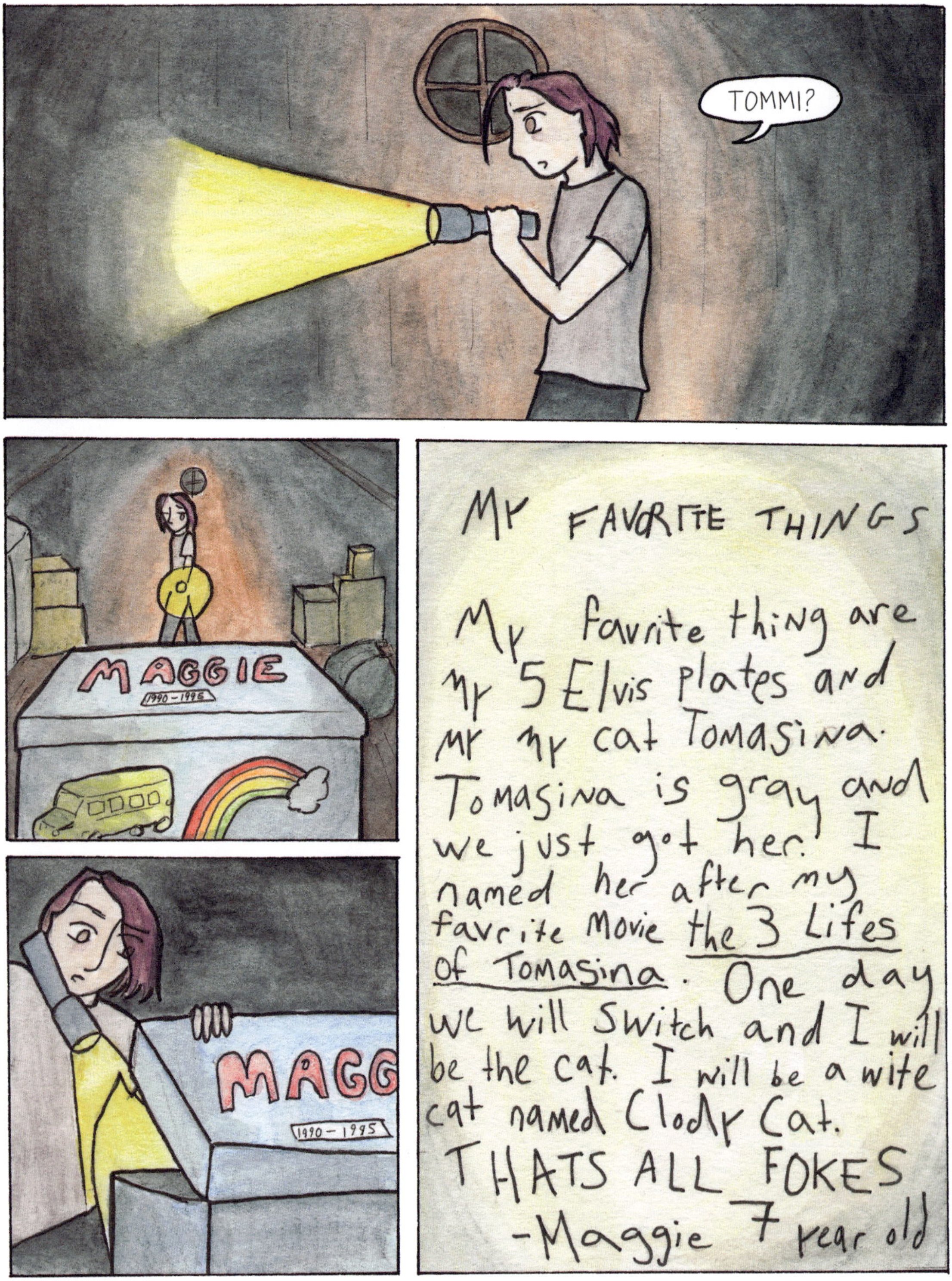
TOMMI?
MAGGIE
1990–1995
MAGG
1990–1995
MY FAVORITE THINGS
My favrite thing are
my 5 Elvis plates and
my my cat Tomasina.
Tomasina is gray and
we just got her. I
named her after my
favrite Movie the 3 Lifes
of Tomasina. One day
we will Switch and I will
be the cat. I will be a wite
cat named Clody Cat.
THATS ALL FOKES
-Maggie 7 year old

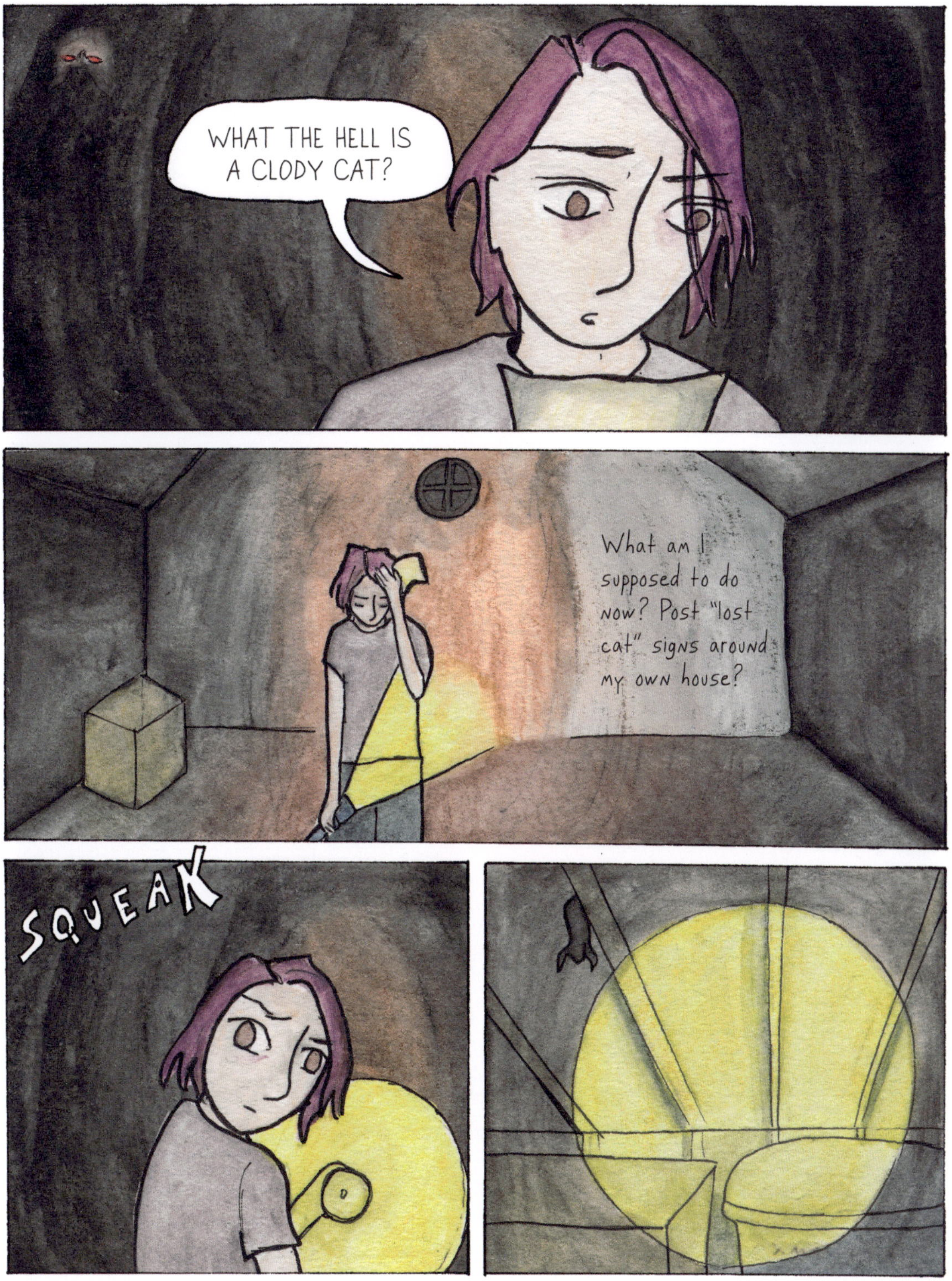
WHAT THE HELL IS A CLODY CAT?
What am I supposed to do now? Post "lost cat" signs around my own house?
SQUEAK

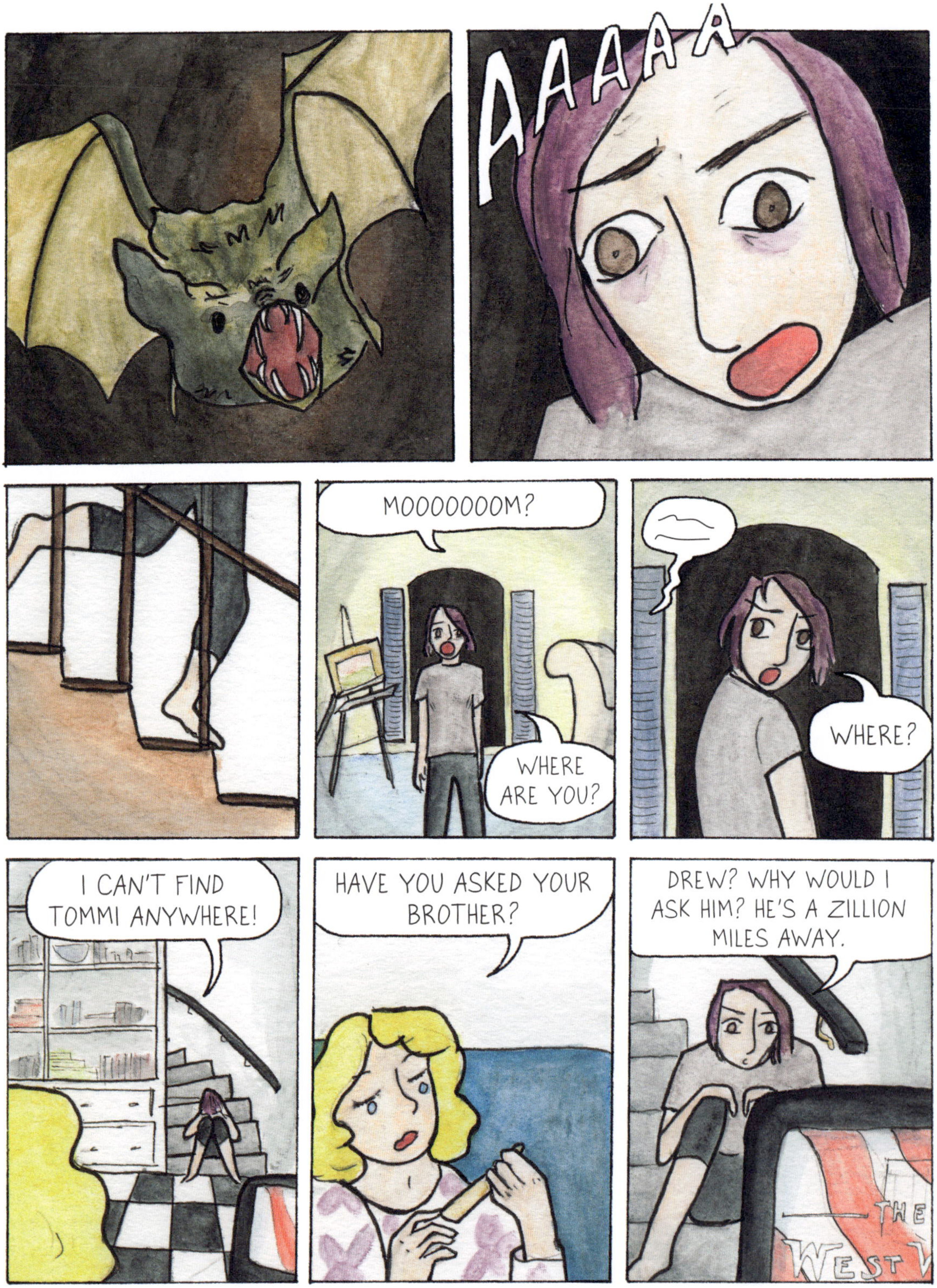
AAAAA
MOOOOOOOM?
WHERE ARE YOU?
WHERE?
I CAN'T FIND TOMMI ANYWHERE!
HAVE YOU ASKED YOUR BROTHER?
DREW? WHY WOULD I ASK HIM? HE'S A ZILLION MILES AWAY.
THE
WEST

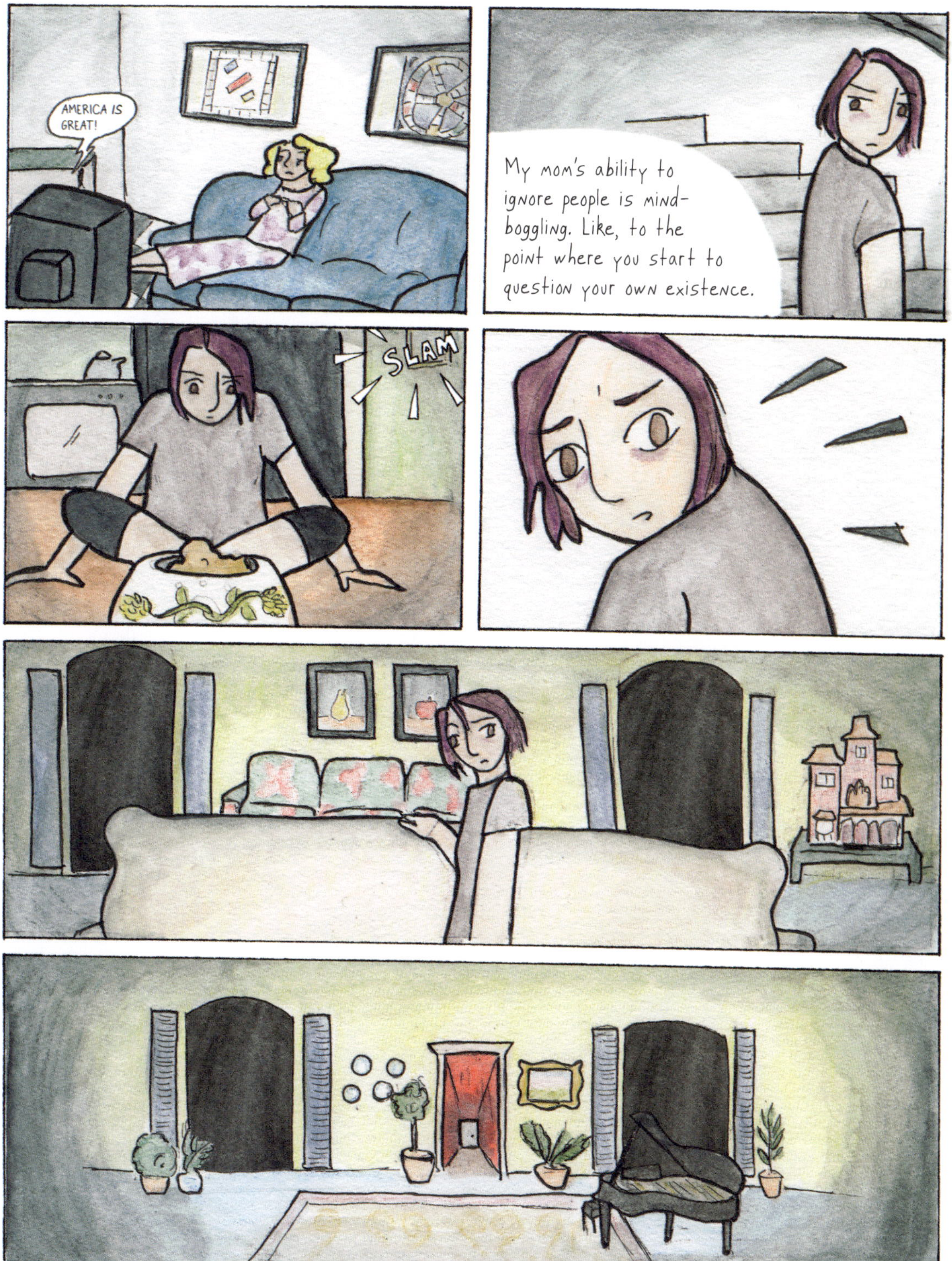
AMERICA IS GREAT!
My mom's ability to ignore people is mind-boggling. Like, to the point where you start to question your own existence.
SLAM

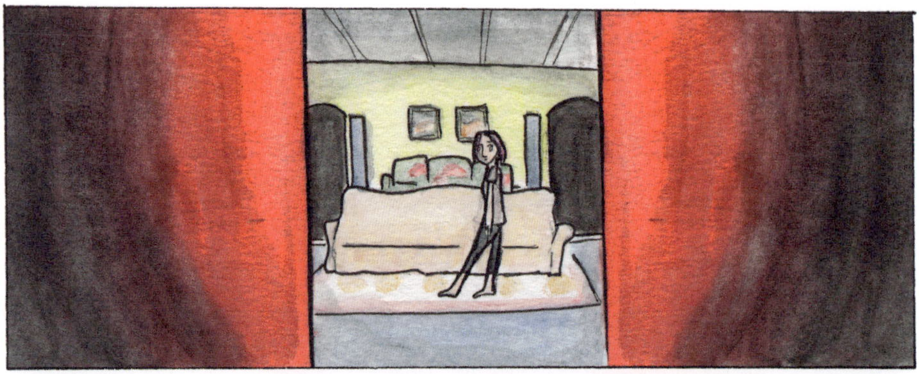

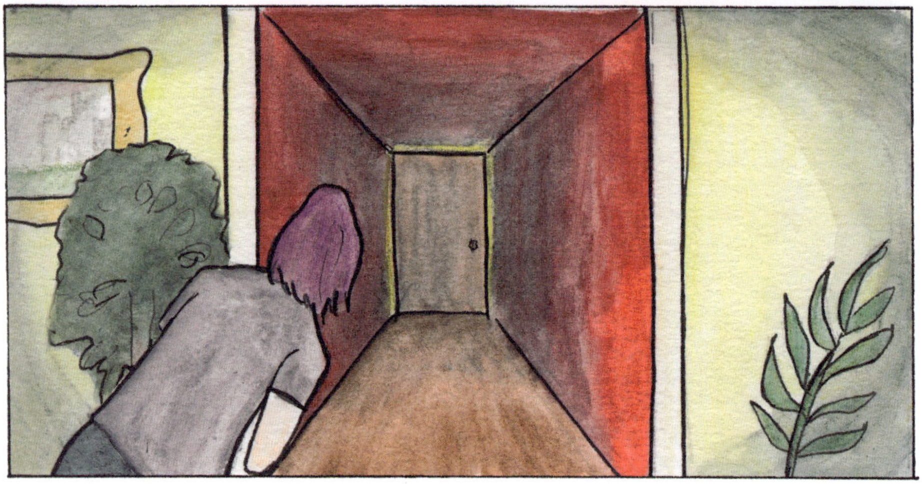

I swear to God I have never seen this hallway in my life.

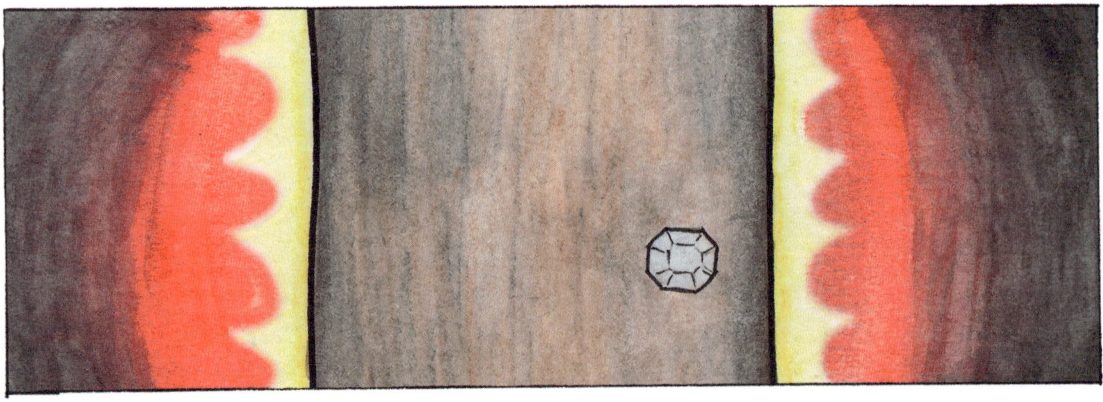

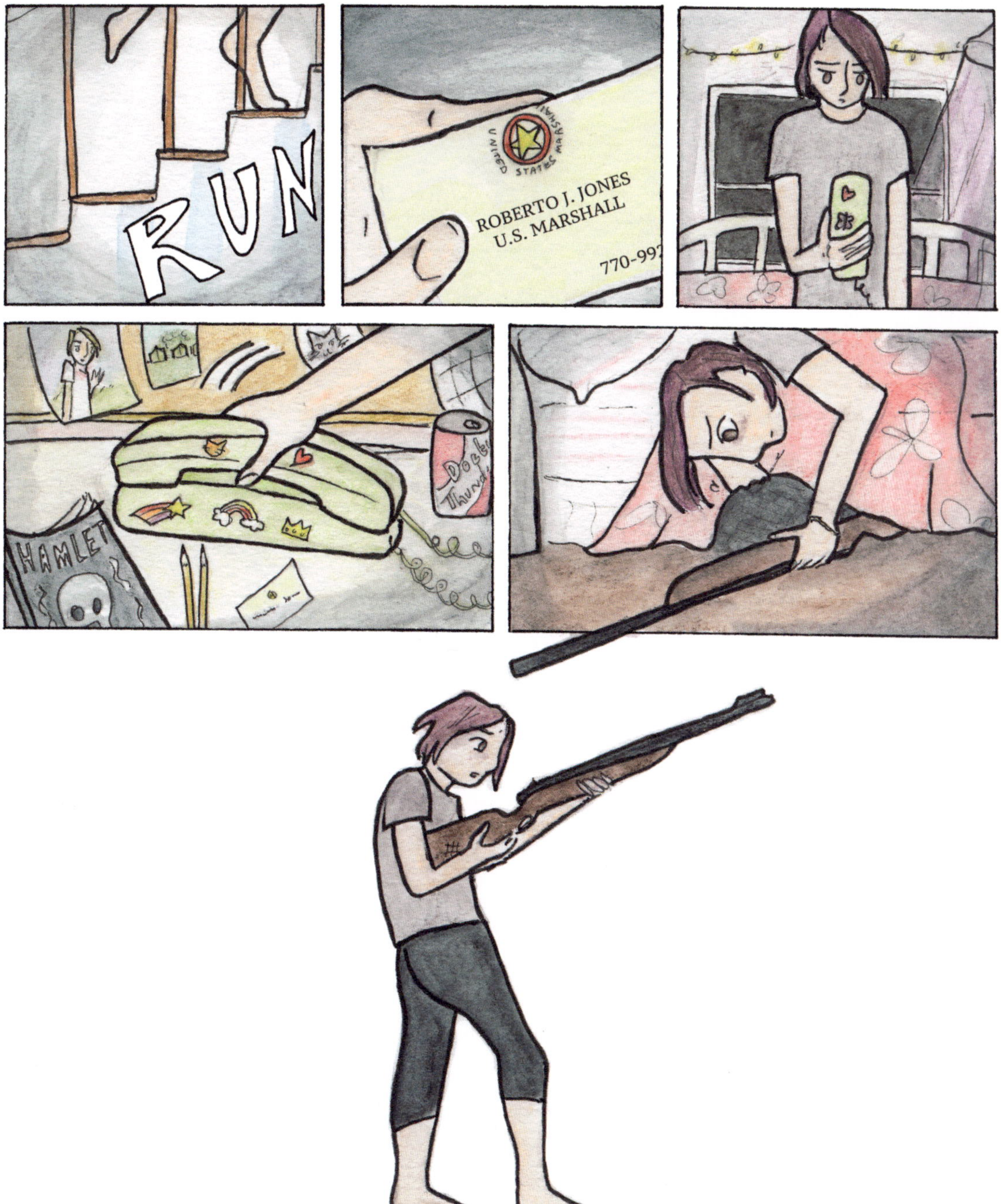
RUN
UNITED STATES MARSHALL
ROBERTO J. JONES
U.S. MARSHALL
770-99
HAMLET

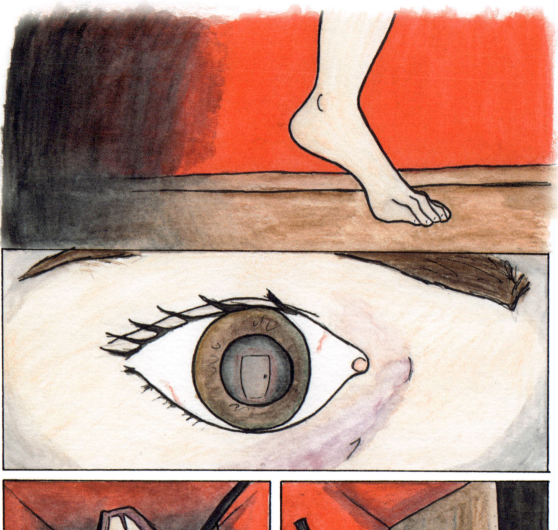

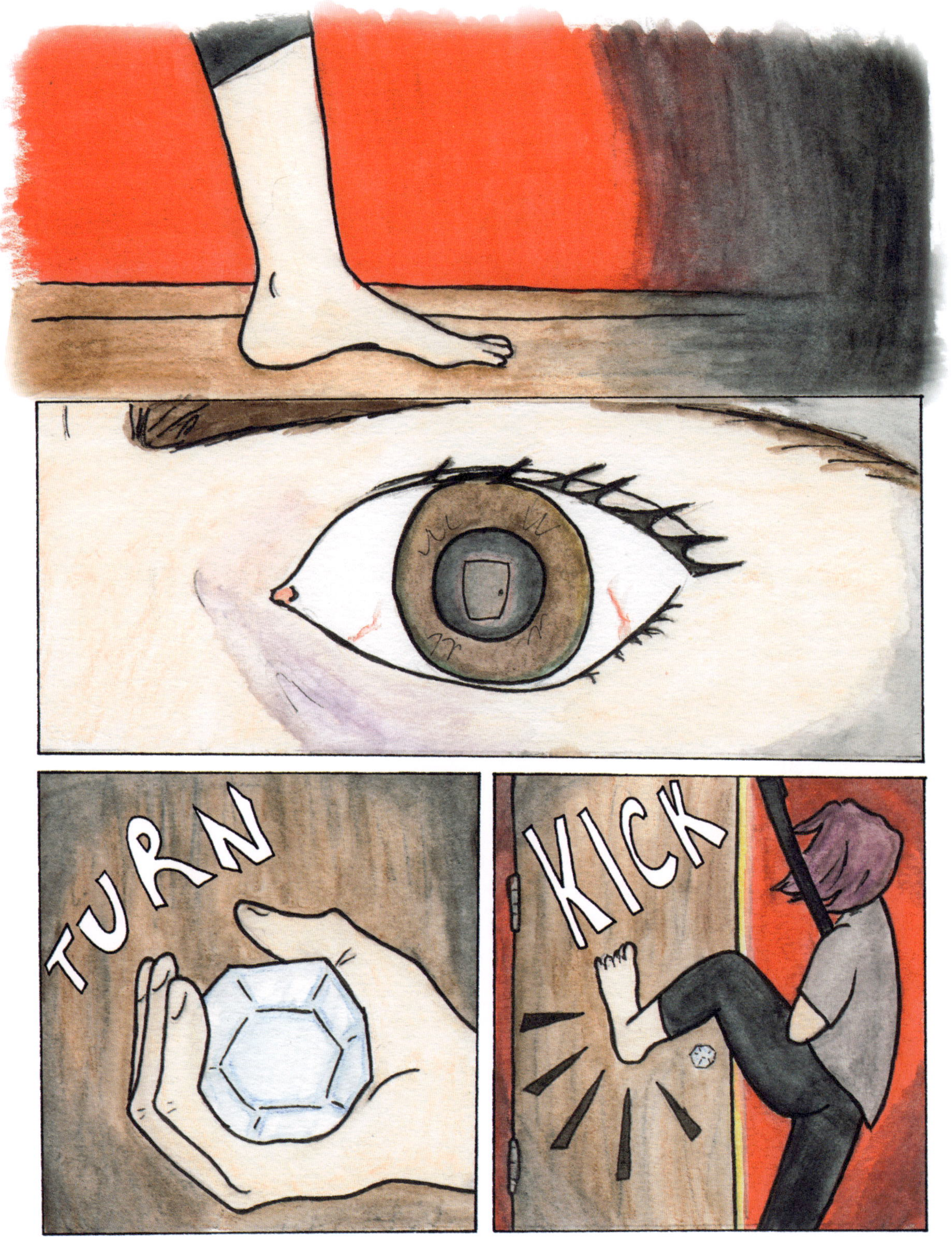
TURN
KICK

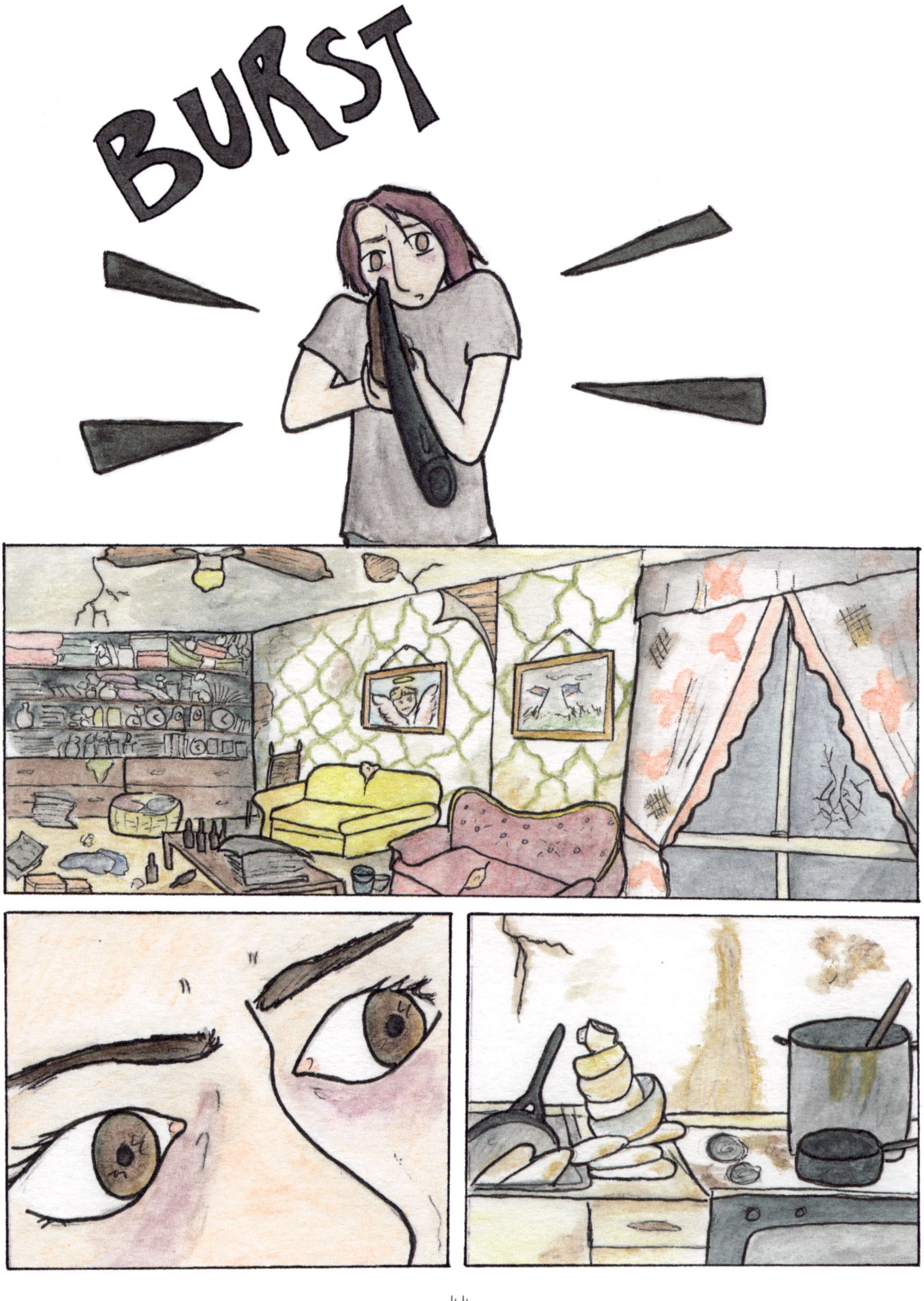
BURST

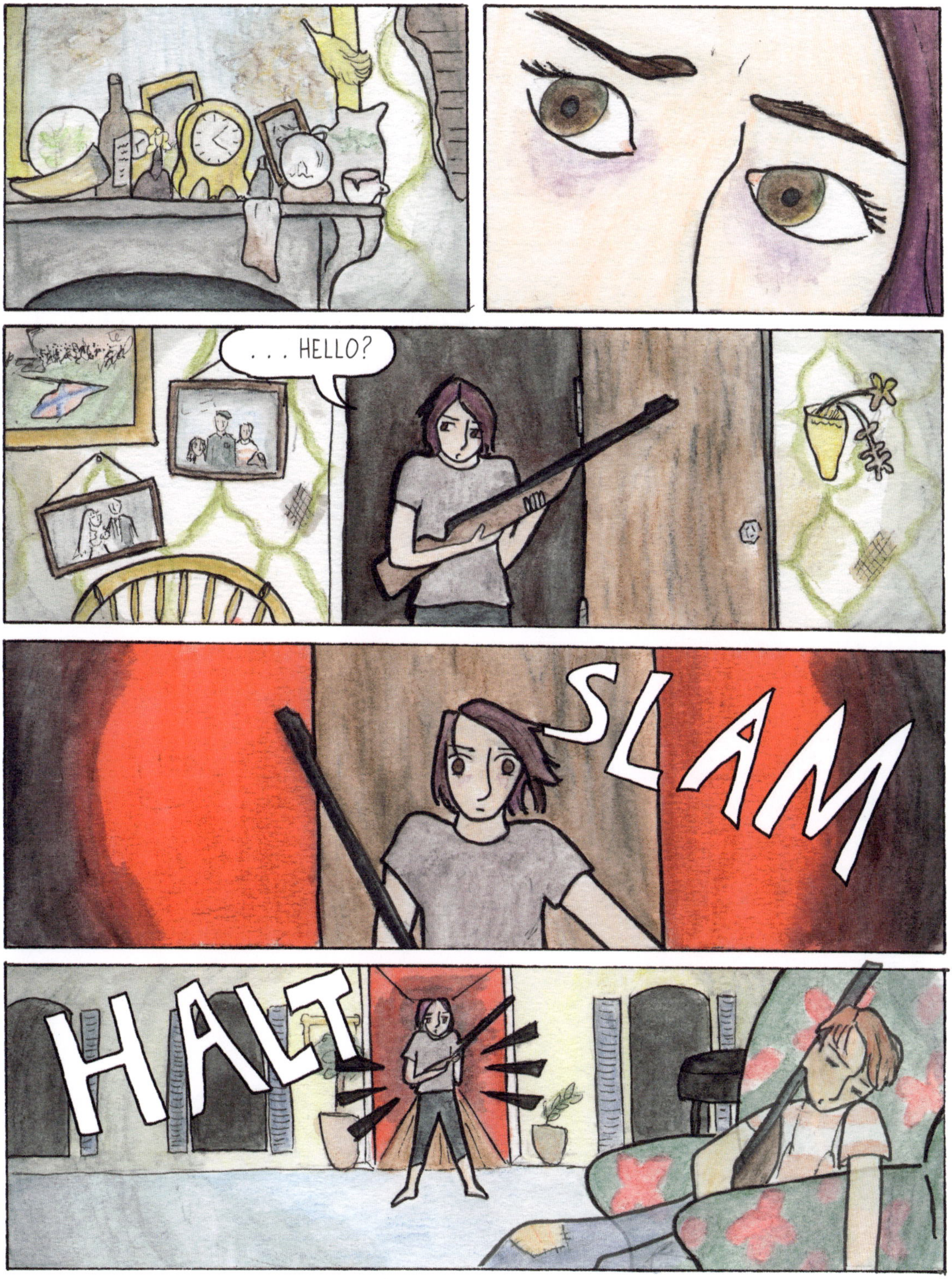
. . . HELLO?
SLAM
HALT

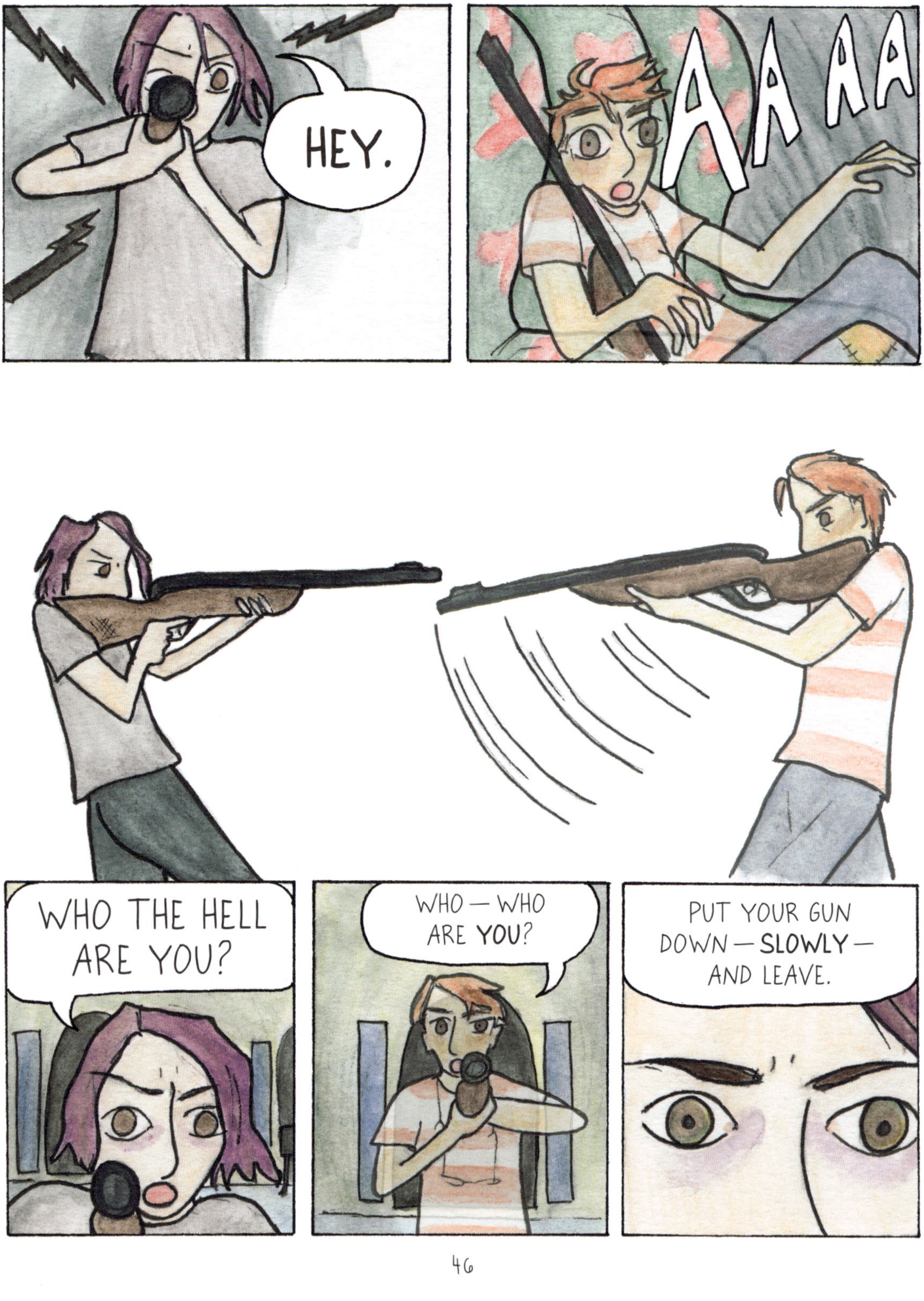
HEY.
AAAA
WHO THE HELL ARE YOU?
WHO — WHO ARE YOU?
PUT YOUR GUN DOWN — SLOWLY — AND LEAVE.

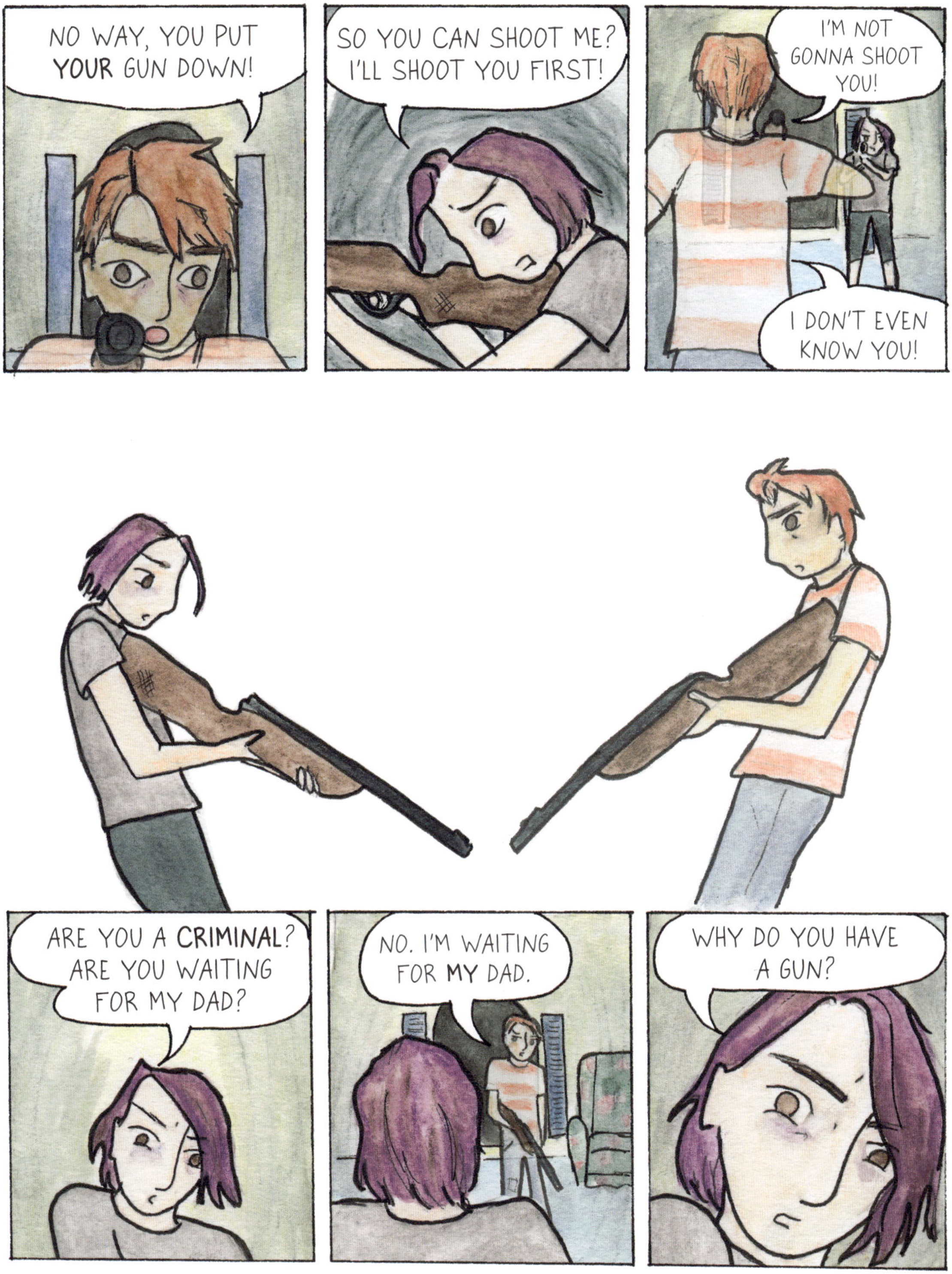
NO WAY, YOU PUT **YOUR** GUN DOWN!
SO YOU CAN SHOOT ME? I'LL SHOOT YOU FIRST!
I'M NOT GONNA SHOOT YOU!
I DON'T EVEN KNOW YOU!
ARE YOU A **CRIMINAL**? ARE YOU WAITING FOR MY DAD?
NO. I'M WAITING FOR **MY** DAD.
WHY DO YOU HAVE A GUN?

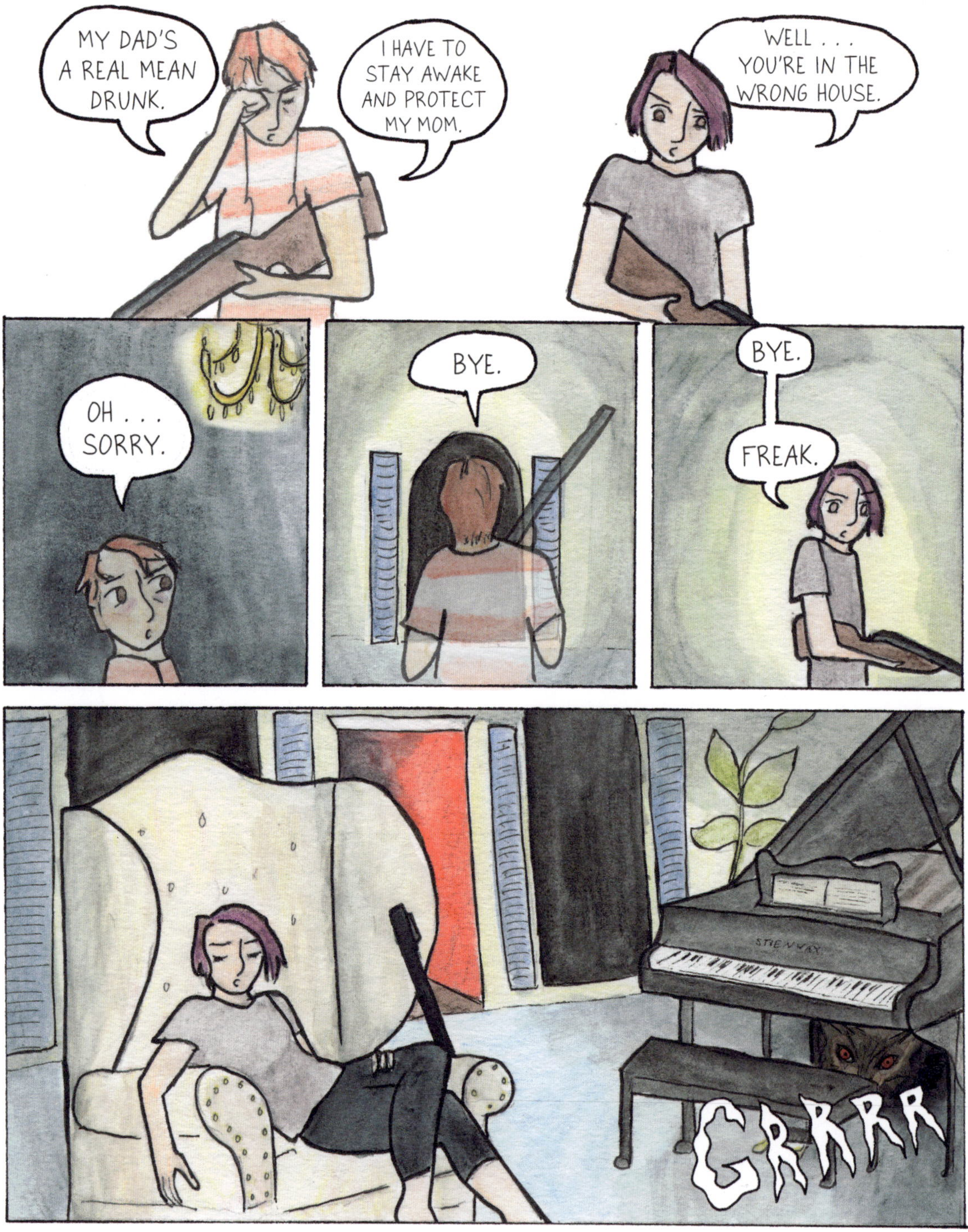
MY DAD'S A REAL MEAN DRUNK.
I HAVE TO STAY AWAKE AND PROTECT MY MOM.
WELL . . . YOU'RE IN THE WRONG HOUSE.
OH . . . SORRY.
BYE.
BYE.
FREAK.
GRRRR

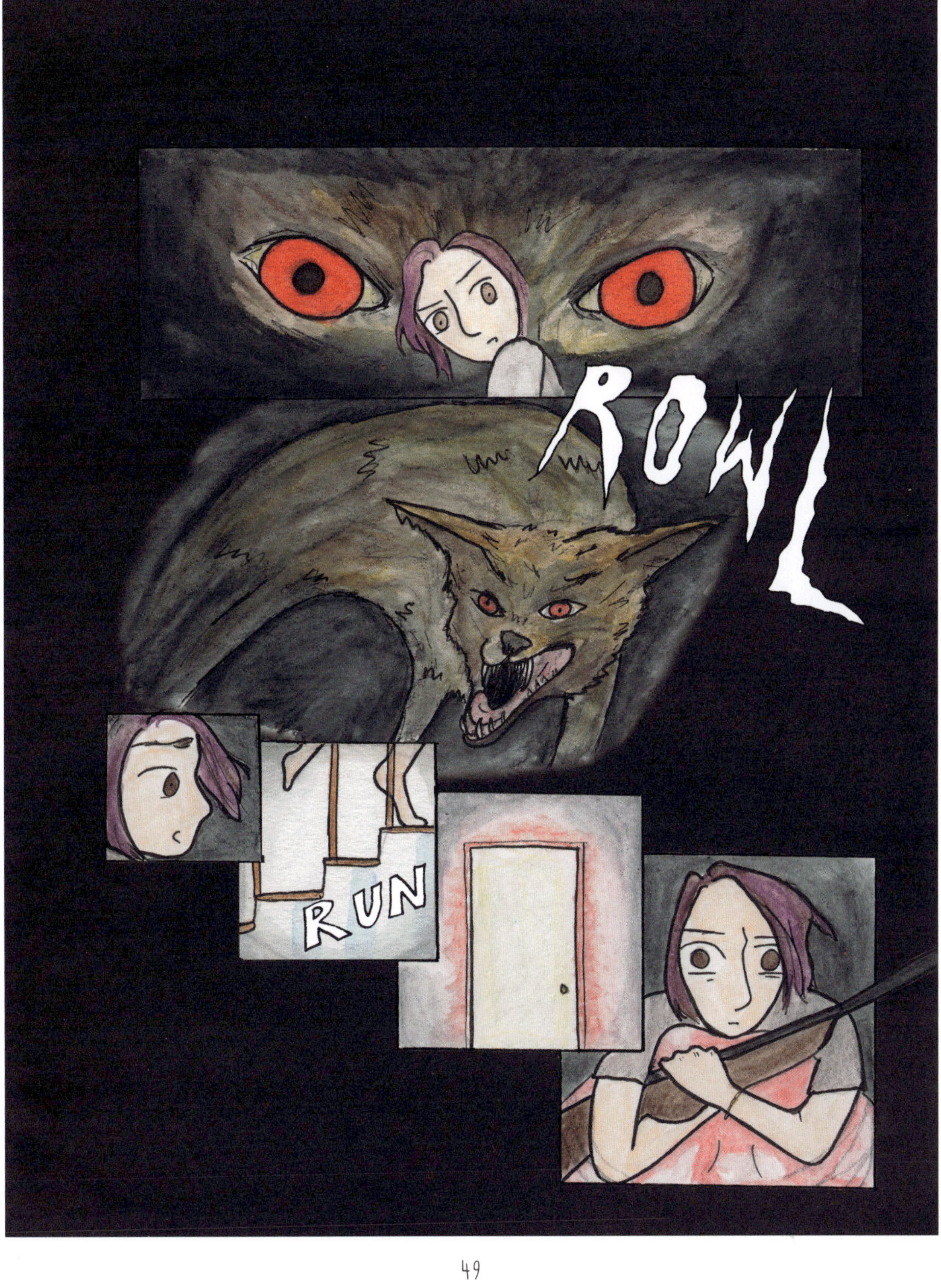
ROWL
RUN

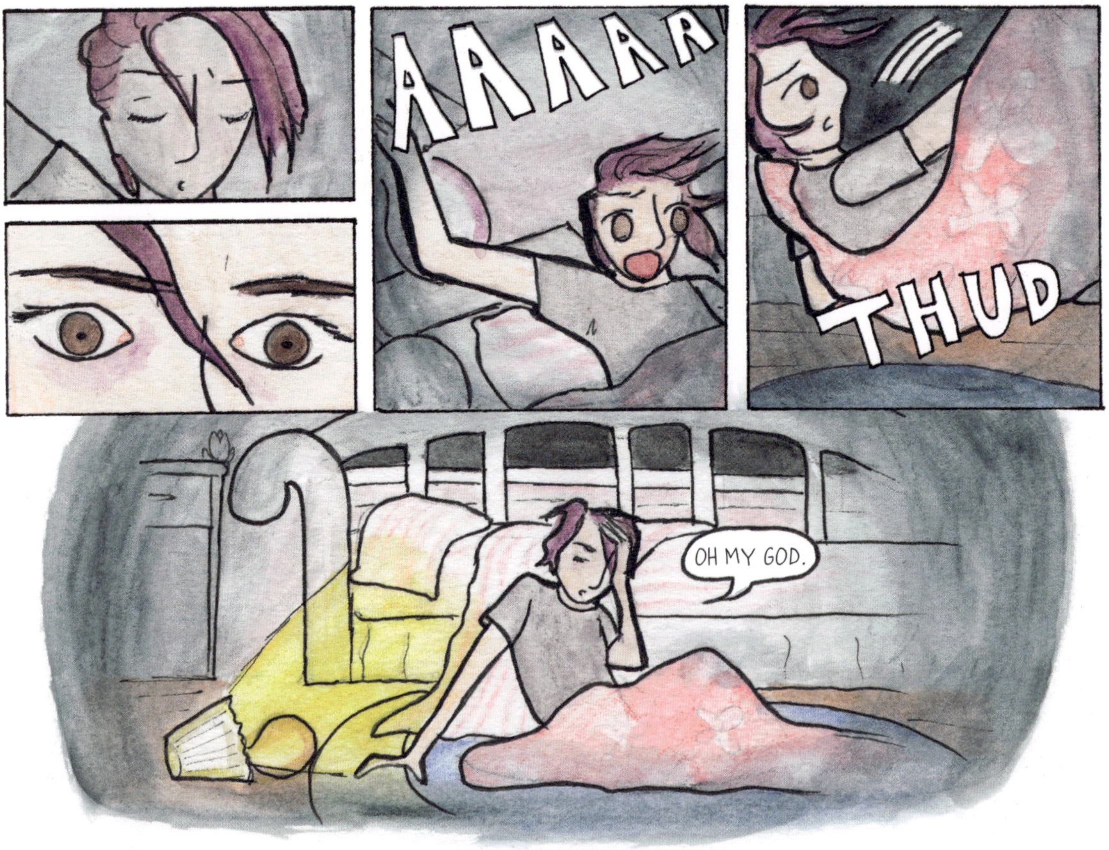
AAAAA
THUD
OH MY GOD.

I used to have a sleepwalking problem, which lately has morphed into something even more annoying. Now I wake up in the middle of the night screaming my head off. On TV, the parents always swoop in and assure the kid there's no such thing as ghosts and monsters. But my parents never wake up because their room is too far away. Since my brother left, I'm on my own up here.

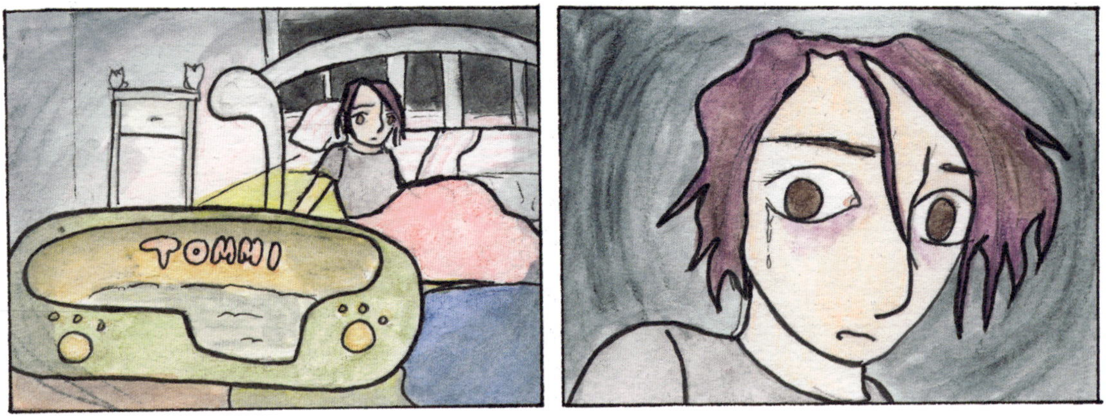
TOMMI

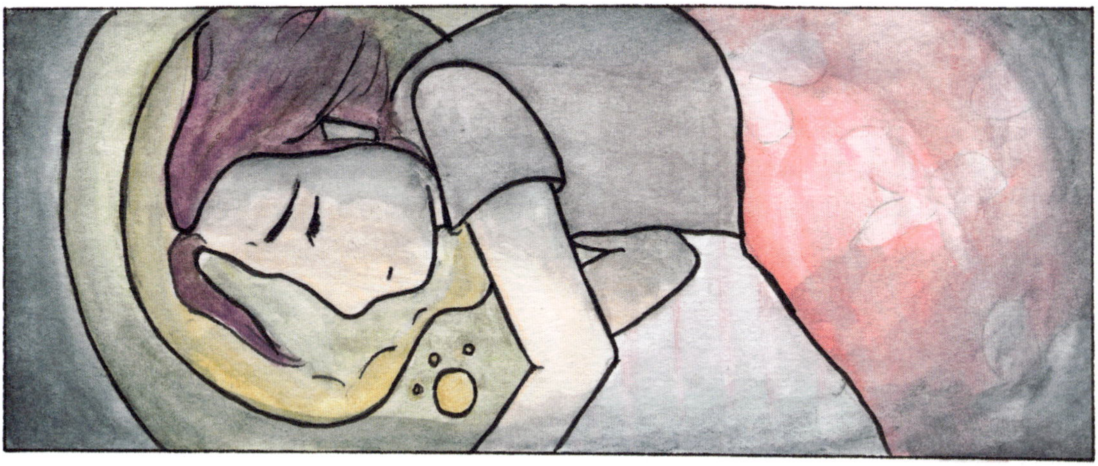

# Chapter 3

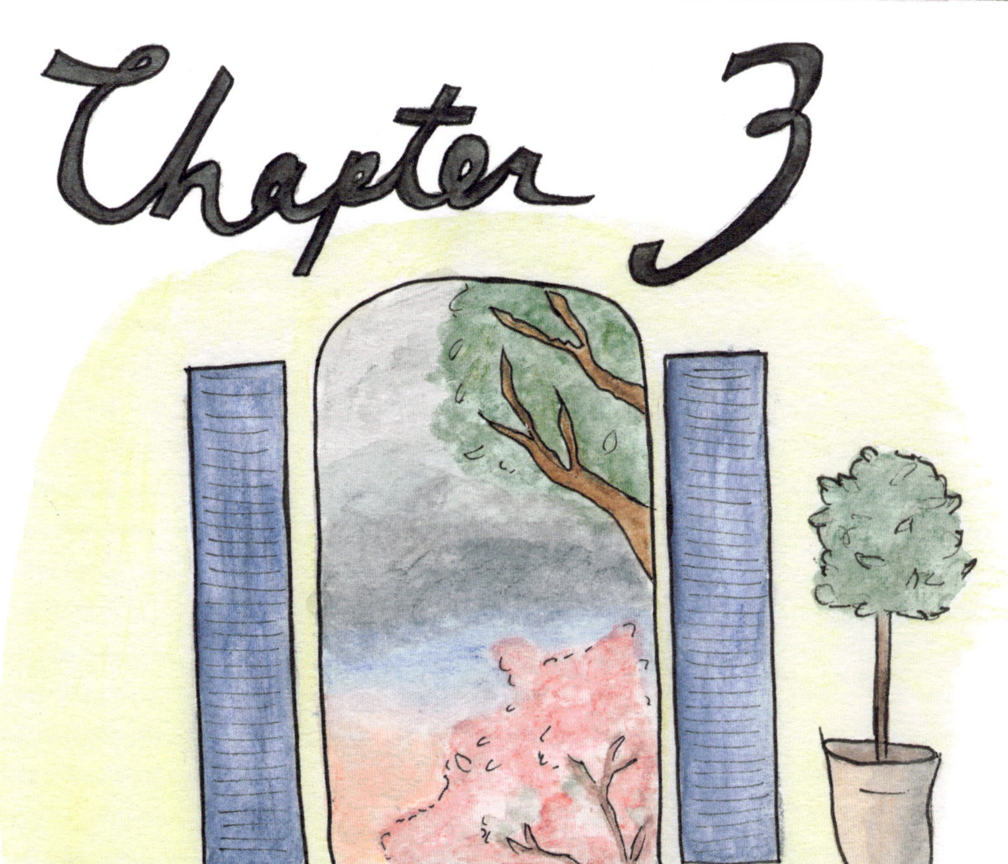

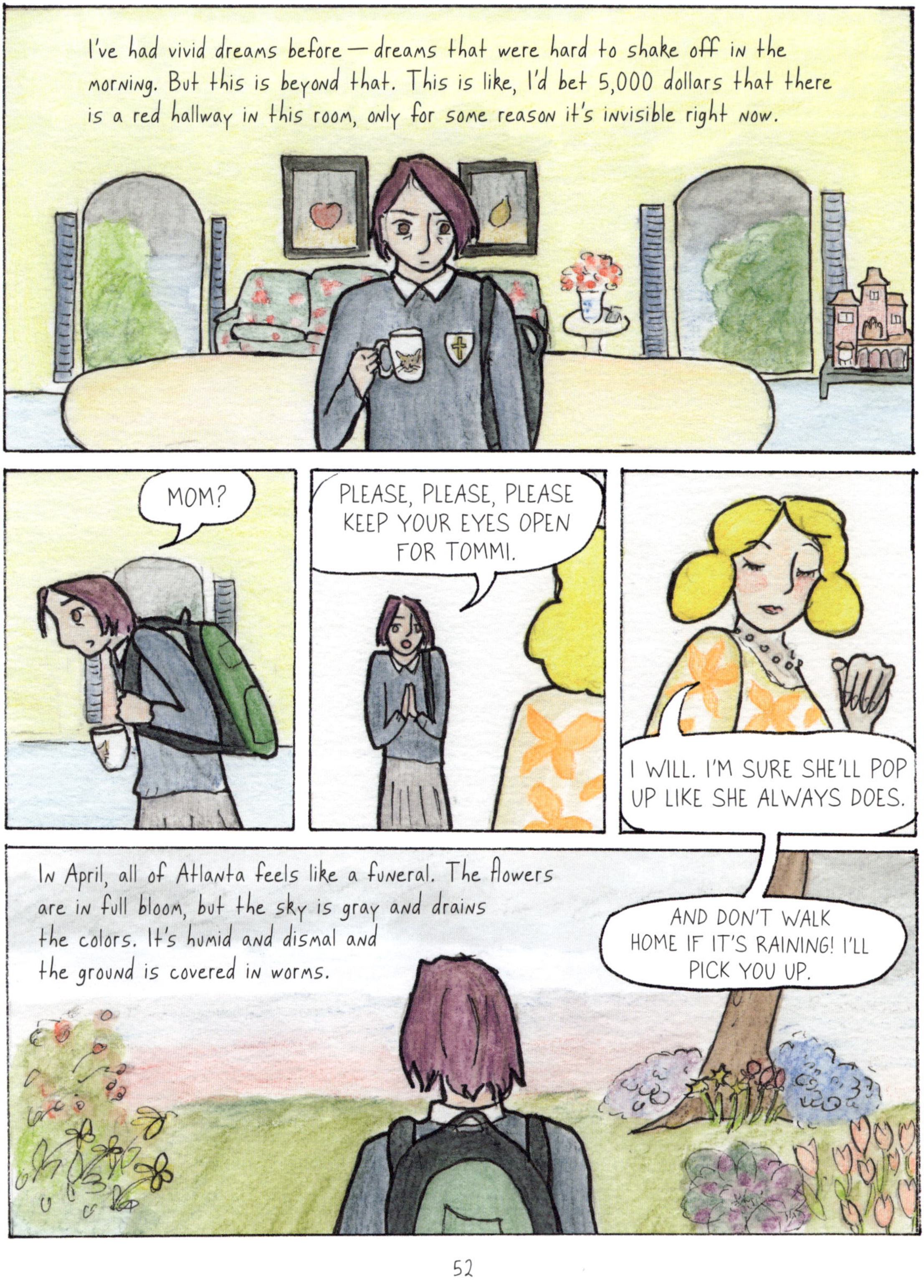
I've had vivid dreams before — dreams that were hard to shake off in the morning. But this is beyond that. This is like, I'd bet 5,000 dollars that there is a red hallway in this room, only for some reason it's invisible right now.
MOM?
PLEASE, PLEASE, PLEASE KEEP YOUR EYES OPEN FOR TOMMI.
I WILL. I'M SURE SHE'LL POP UP LIKE SHE ALWAYS DOES.
AND DON'T WALK HOME IF IT'S RAINING! I'LL PICK YOU UP.
In April, all of Atlanta feels like a funeral. The flowers are in full bloom, but the sky is gray and drains the colors. It's humid and dismal and the ground is covered in worms.

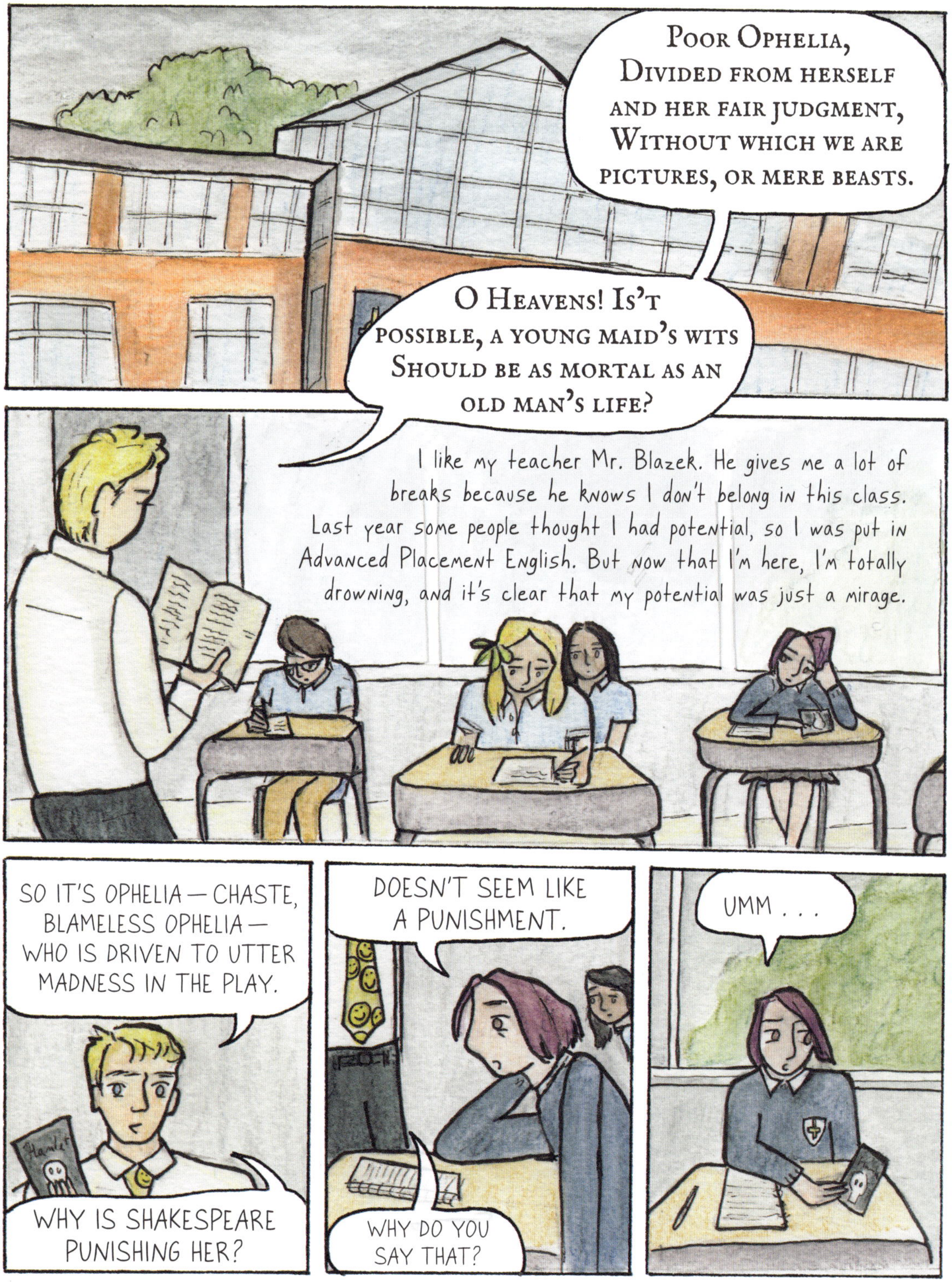
Poor Ophelia, Divided from herself and her fair judgment, Without which we are pictures, or mere beasts.
O Heavens! Is't possible, a young maid's wits Should be as mortal as an old man's life?
I like my teacher Mr. Blazek. He gives me a lot of breaks because he knows I don't belong in this class. Last year some people thought I had potential, so I was put in Advanced Placement English. But now that I'm here, I'm totally drowning, and it's clear that my potential was just a mirage.
SO IT'S OPHELIA — CHASTE, BLAMELESS OPHELIA — WHO IS DRIVEN TO UTTER MADNESS IN THE PLAY.
WHY IS SHAKESPEARE PUNISHING HER?
DOESN'T SEEM LIKE A PUNISHMENT.
WHY DO YOU SAY THAT?
UMM . . .

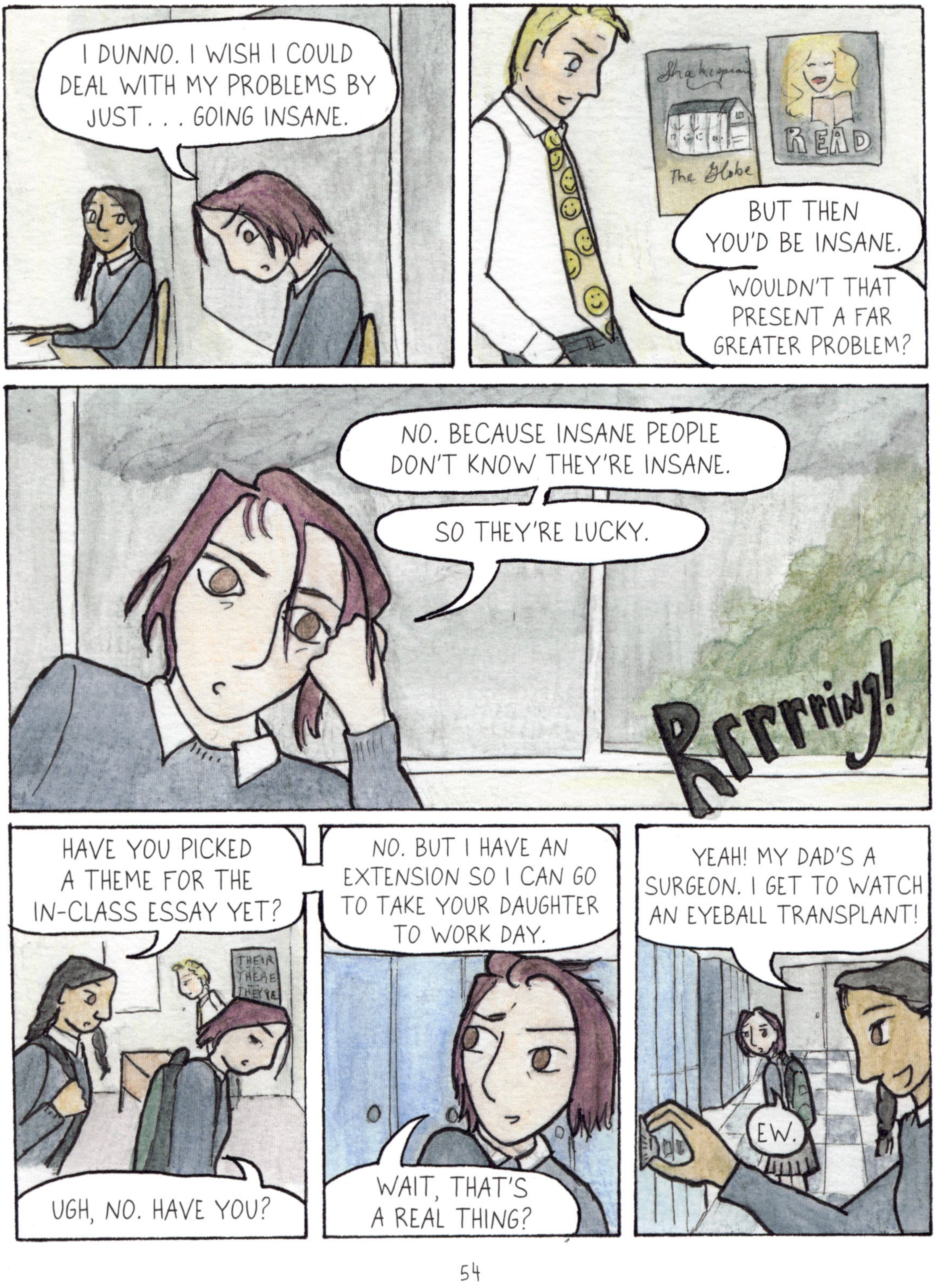
I DUNNO. I WISH I COULD DEAL WITH MY PROBLEMS BY JUST . . . GOING INSANE.
Shakespeare
The Globe
READ
BUT THEN YOU'D BE INSANE.
WOULDN'T THAT PRESENT A FAR GREATER PROBLEM?
NO. BECAUSE INSANE PEOPLE DON'T KNOW THEY'RE INSANE.
SO THEY'RE LUCKY.
Rrrrring!
HAVE YOU PICKED A THEME FOR THE IN-CLASS ESSAY YET?
THEIR THERE THEY'RE
UGH, NO. HAVE YOU?
NO. BUT I HAVE AN EXTENSION SO I CAN GO TO TAKE YOUR DAUGHTER TO WORK DAY.
WAIT, THAT'S A REAL THING?
YEAH! MY DAD'S A SURGEON. I GET TO WATCH AN EYEBALL TRANSPLANT!
EW.

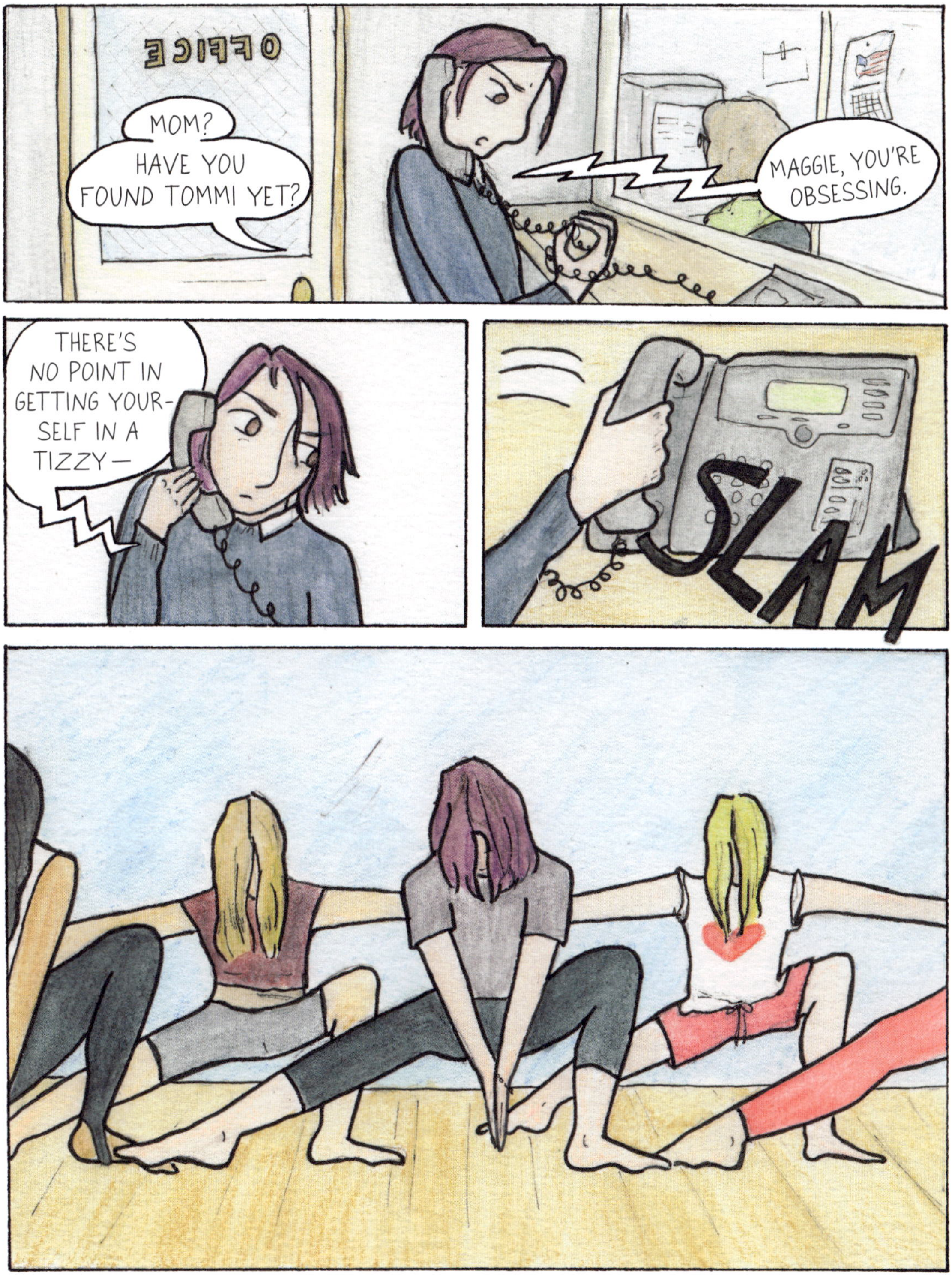
OFFICE
MOM?
HAVE YOU FOUND TOMMI YET?
MAGGIE, YOU'RE OBSESSING.
THERE'S NO POINT IN GETTING YOURSELF IN A TIZZY—
SLAM

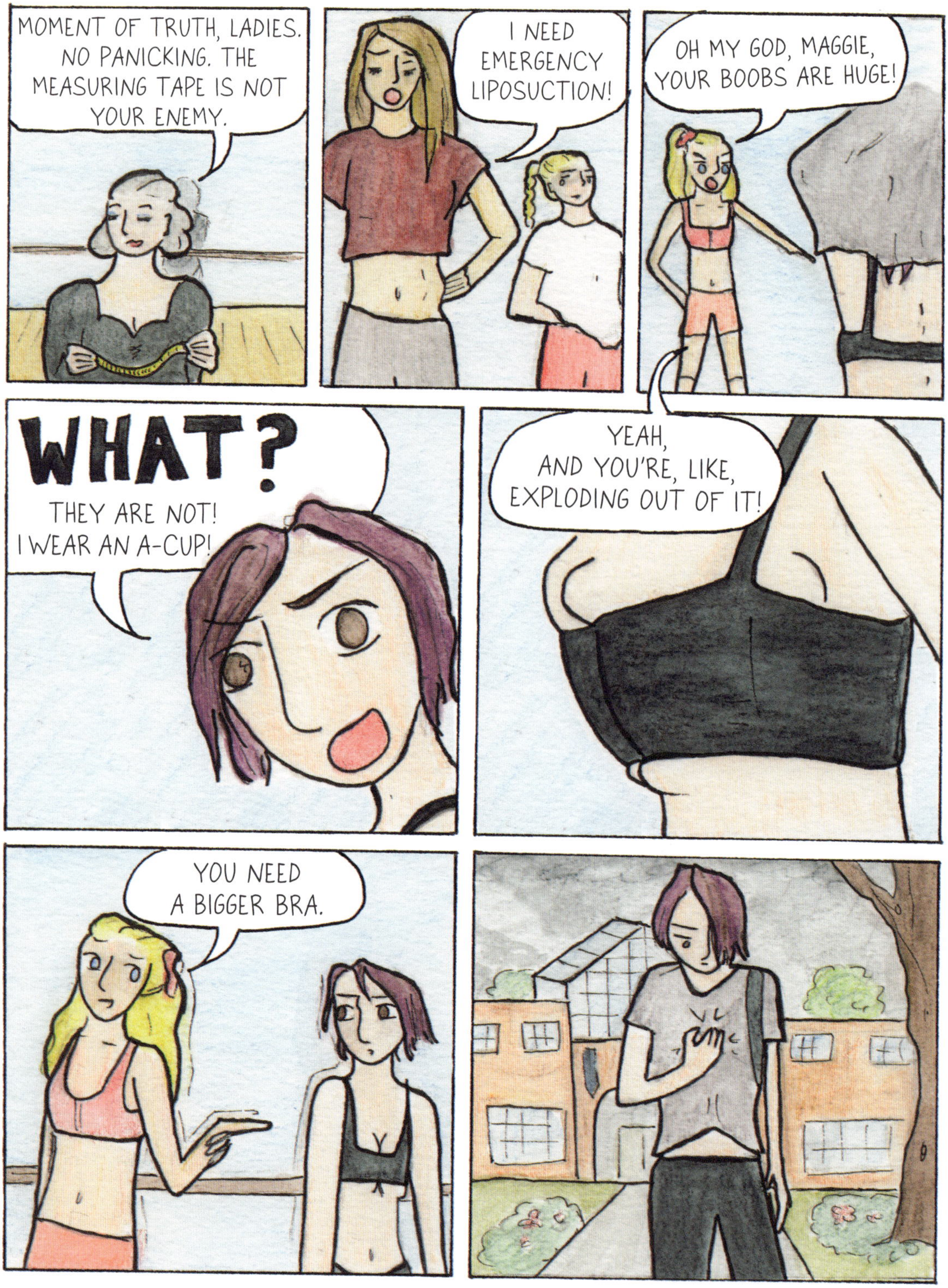
MOMENT OF TRUTH, LADIES. NO PANICKING. THE MEASURING TAPE IS NOT YOUR ENEMY.
I NEED EMERGENCY LIPOSUCTION!
OH MY GOD, MAGGIE, YOUR BOOBS ARE HUGE!
WHAT? THEY ARE NOT! I WEAR AN A-CUP!
YEAH, AND YOU'RE, LIKE, EXPLODING OUT OF IT!
YOU NEED A BIGGER BRA.

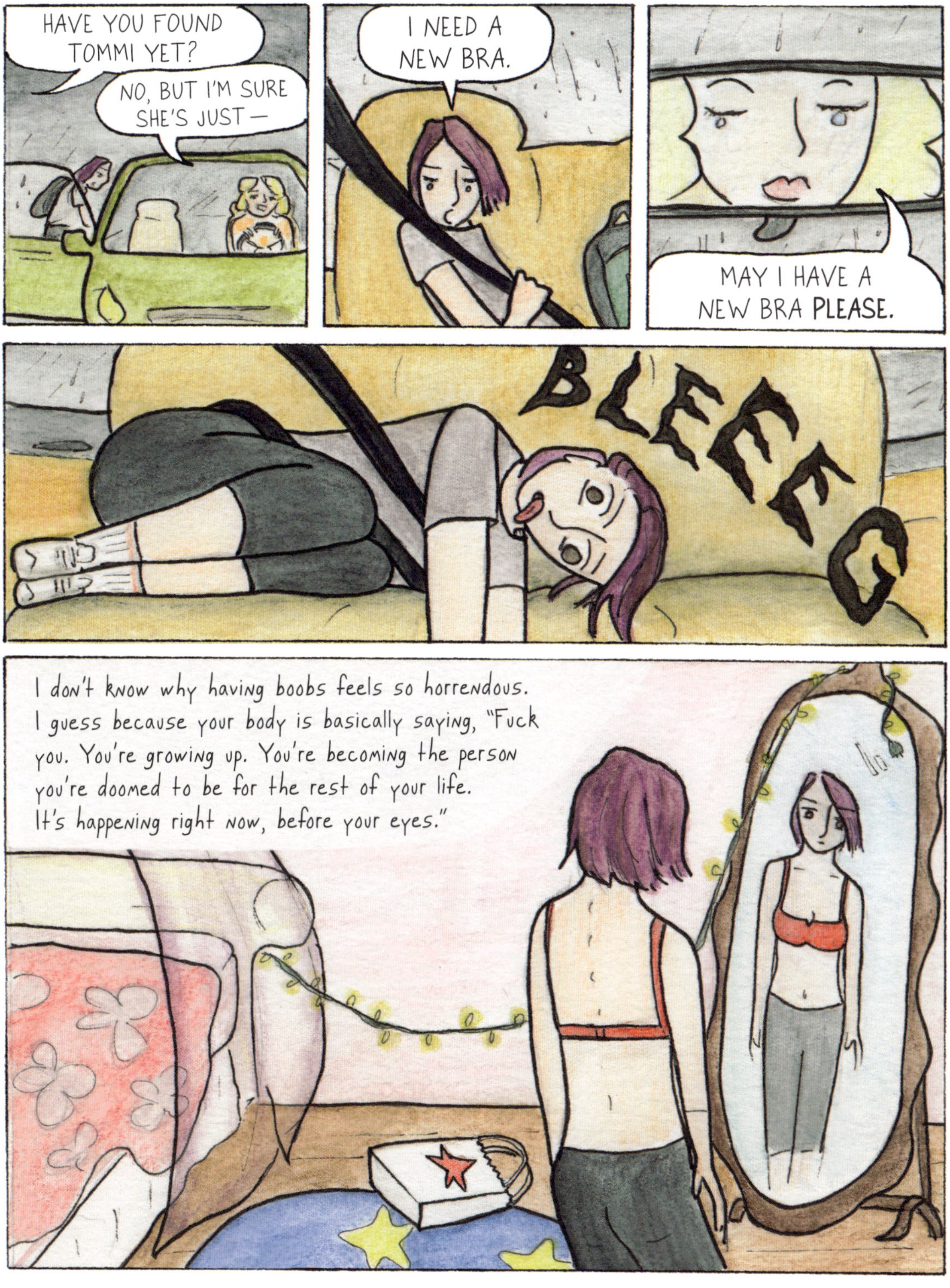
HAVE YOU FOUND TOMMI YET?
NO, BUT I'M SURE SHE'S JUST—
I NEED A NEW BRA.
MAY I HAVE A NEW BRA **PLEASE.**
BLEEEG
I don't know why having boobs feels so horrendous. I guess because your body is basically saying, "Fuck you. You're growing up. You're becoming the person you're doomed to be for the rest of your life. It's happening right now, before your eyes."

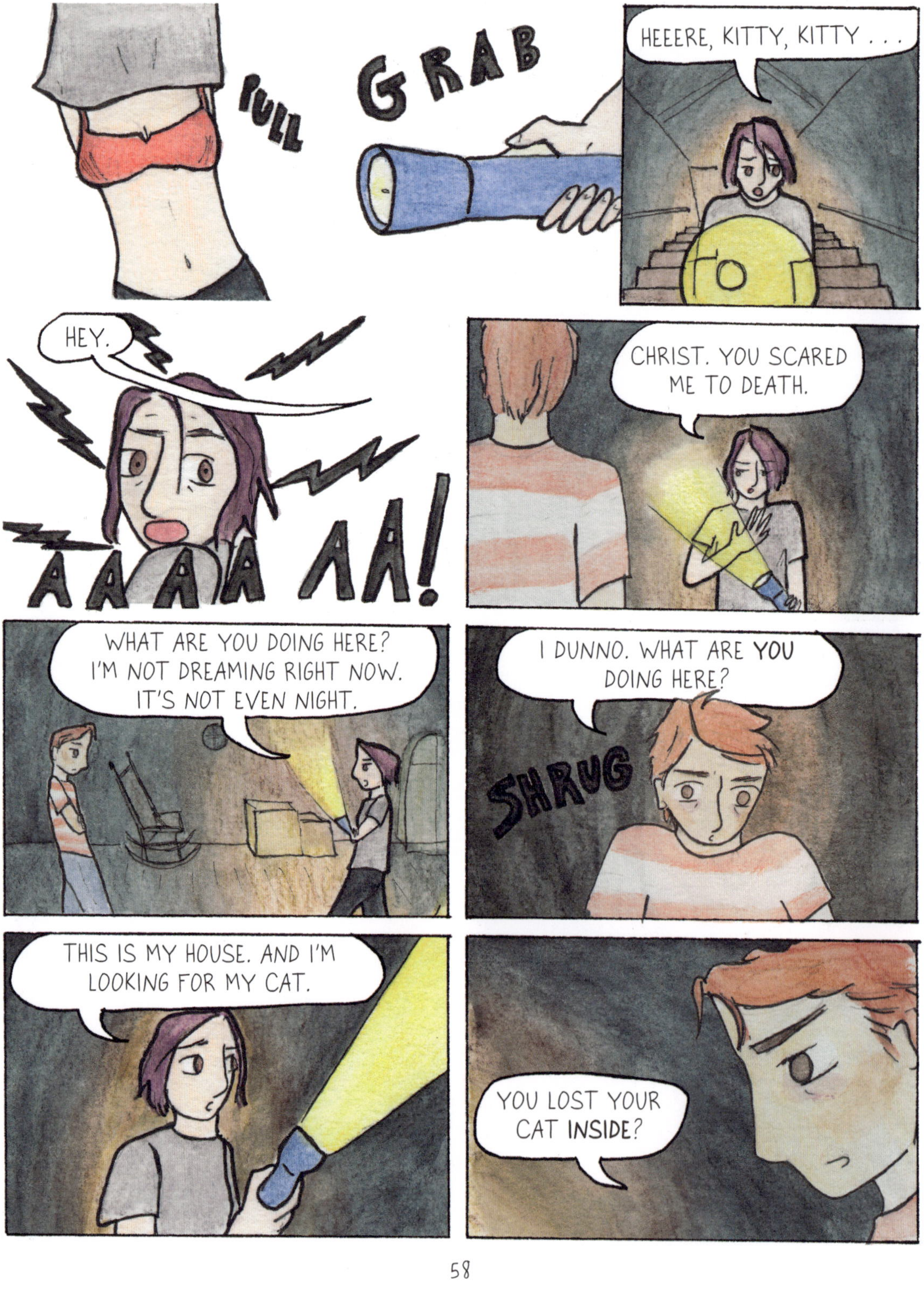
PULL
GRAB
HEEERE, KITTY, KITTY . . .
HEY.
AAAA AA!
CHRIST. YOU SCARED ME TO DEATH.
WHAT ARE YOU DOING HERE? I'M NOT DREAMING RIGHT NOW. IT'S NOT EVEN NIGHT.
I DUNNO. WHAT ARE **YOU** DOING HERE?
SHRUG
THIS IS MY HOUSE. AND I'M LOOKING FOR MY CAT.
YOU LOST YOUR CAT **INSIDE**?

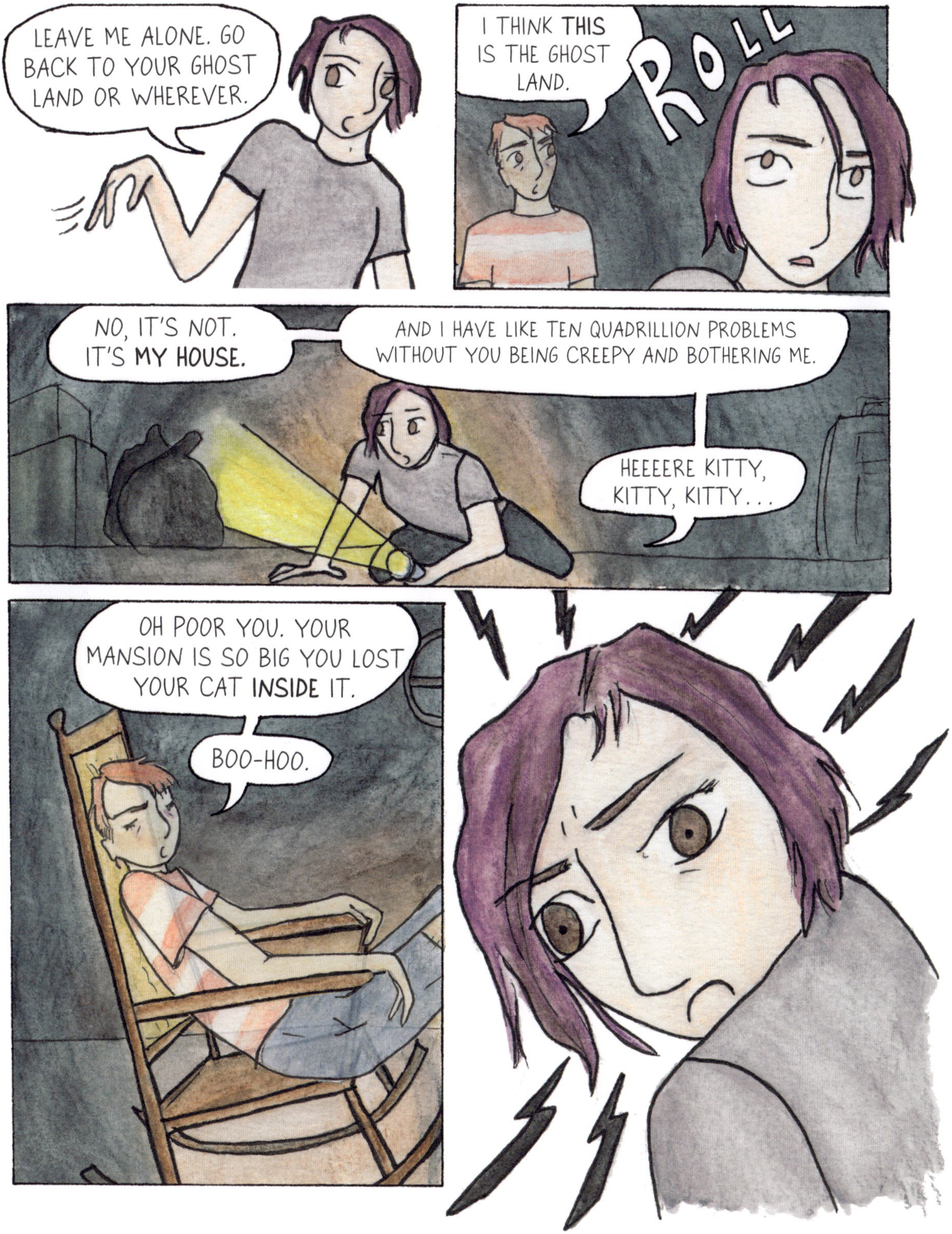
LEAVE ME ALONE. GO BACK TO YOUR GHOST LAND OR WHEREVER.
I THINK **THIS** IS THE GHOST LAND.
ROLL
NO, IT'S NOT. IT'S **MY HOUSE.**
AND I HAVE LIKE TEN QUADRILLION PROBLEMS WITHOUT YOU BEING CREEPY AND BOTHERING ME.
HEEEERE KITTY, KITTY, KITTY...
OH POOR YOU. YOUR MANSION IS SO BIG YOU LOST YOUR CAT **INSIDE** IT.
BOO-HOO.

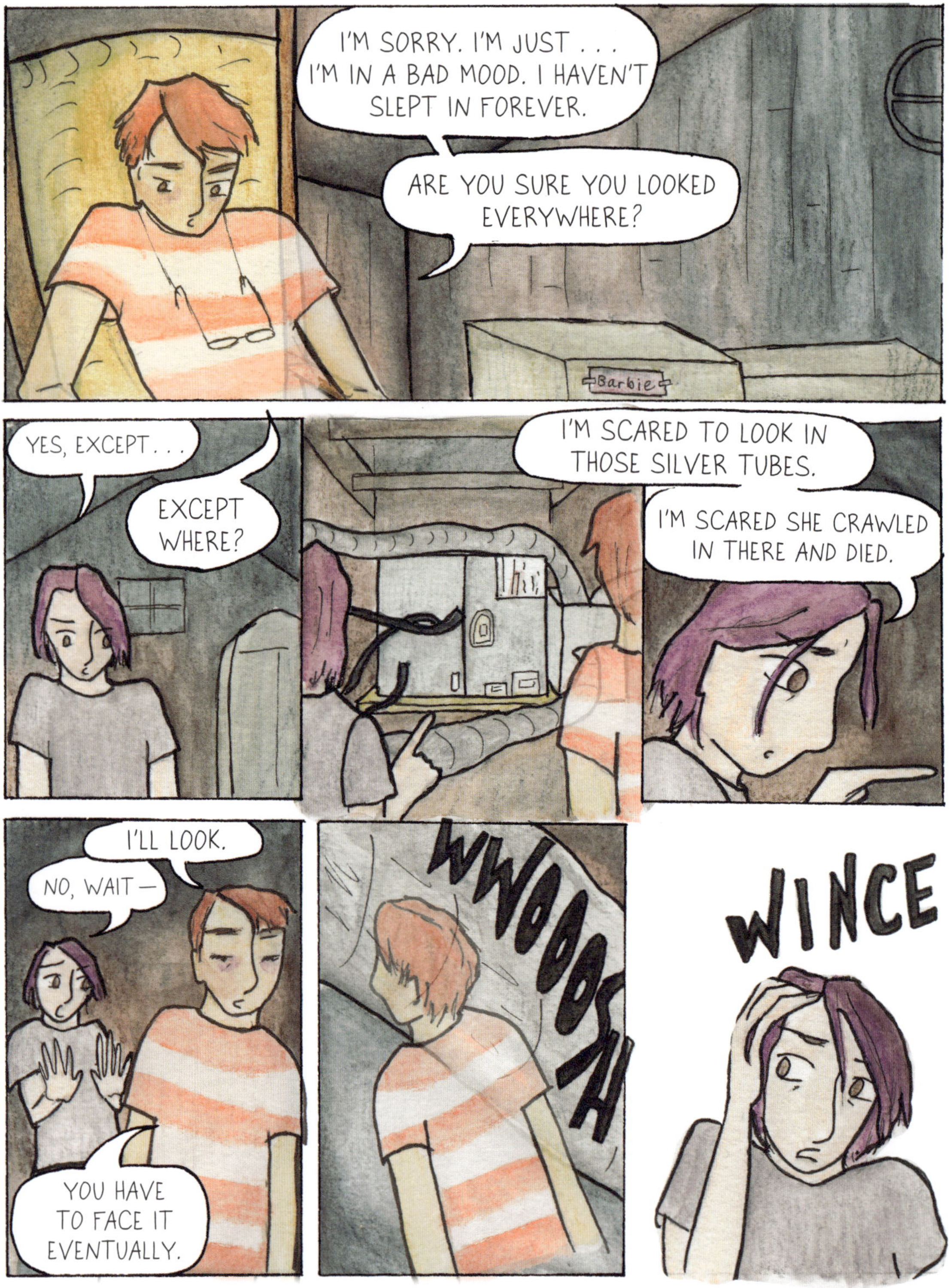

I'M SORRY. I'M JUST . . .
I'M IN A BAD MOOD. I HAVEN'T
SLEPT IN FOREVER.
ARE YOU SURE YOU LOOKED
EVERYWHERE?
Barbie
YES, EXCEPT . . .
EXCEPT
WHERE?
I'M SCARED TO LOOK IN
THOSE SILVER TUBES.
I'M SCARED SHE CRAWLED
IN THERE AND DIED.
I'LL LOOK.
NO, WAIT—
YOU HAVE
TO FACE IT
EVENTUALLY.
WWOOOSH
WINCE

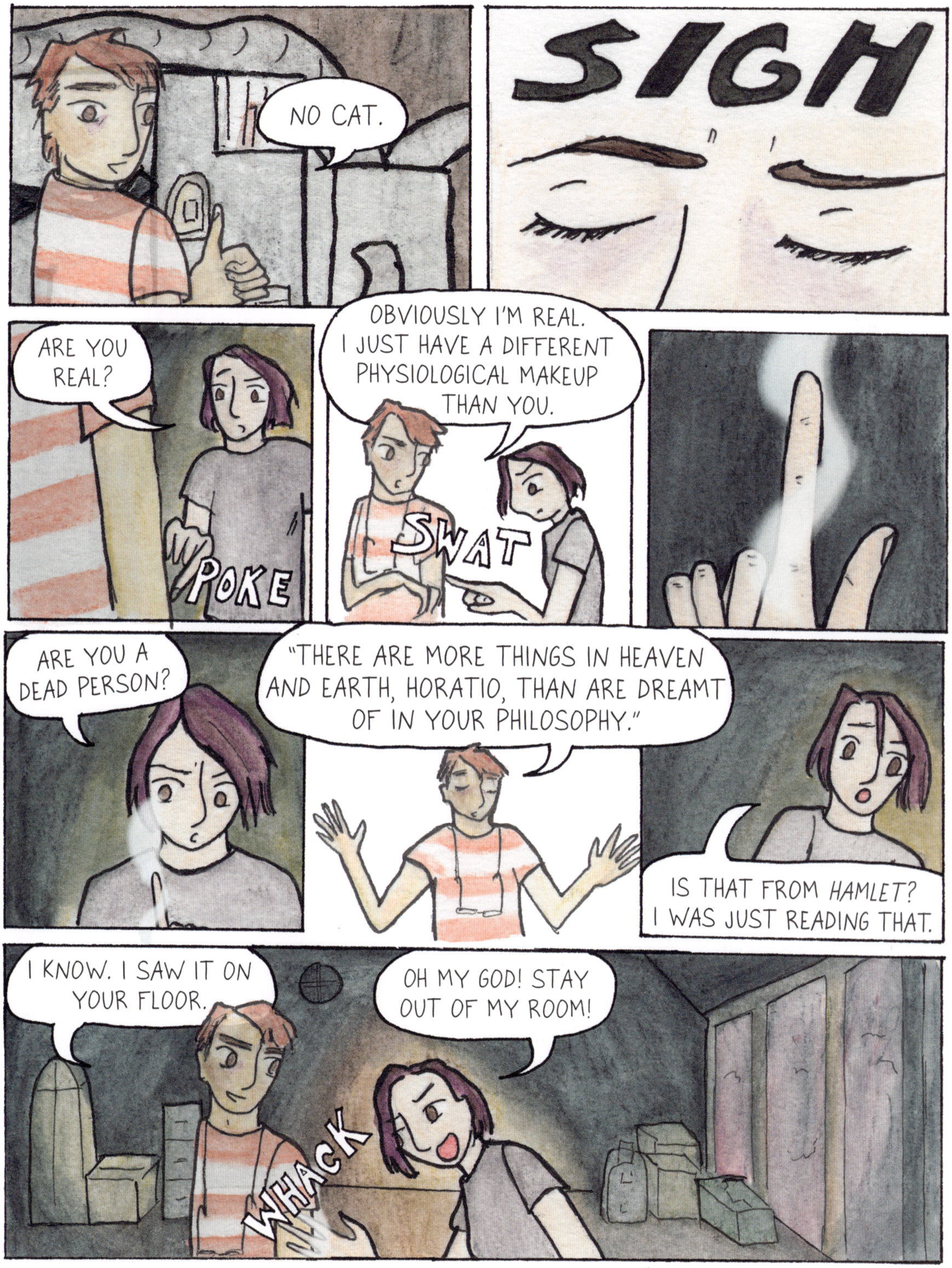
NO CAT.
SIGH
ARE YOU REAL?
POKE
OBVIOUSLY I'M REAL. I JUST HAVE A DIFFERENT PHYSIOLOGICAL MAKEUP THAN YOU.
SWAT
ARE YOU A DEAD PERSON?
"THERE ARE MORE THINGS IN HEAVEN AND EARTH, HORATIO, THAN ARE DREAMT OF IN YOUR PHILOSOPHY."
IS THAT FROM *HAMLET*? I WAS JUST READING THAT.
I KNOW. I SAW IT ON YOUR FLOOR.
OH MY GOD! STAY OUT OF MY ROOM!
WHACK

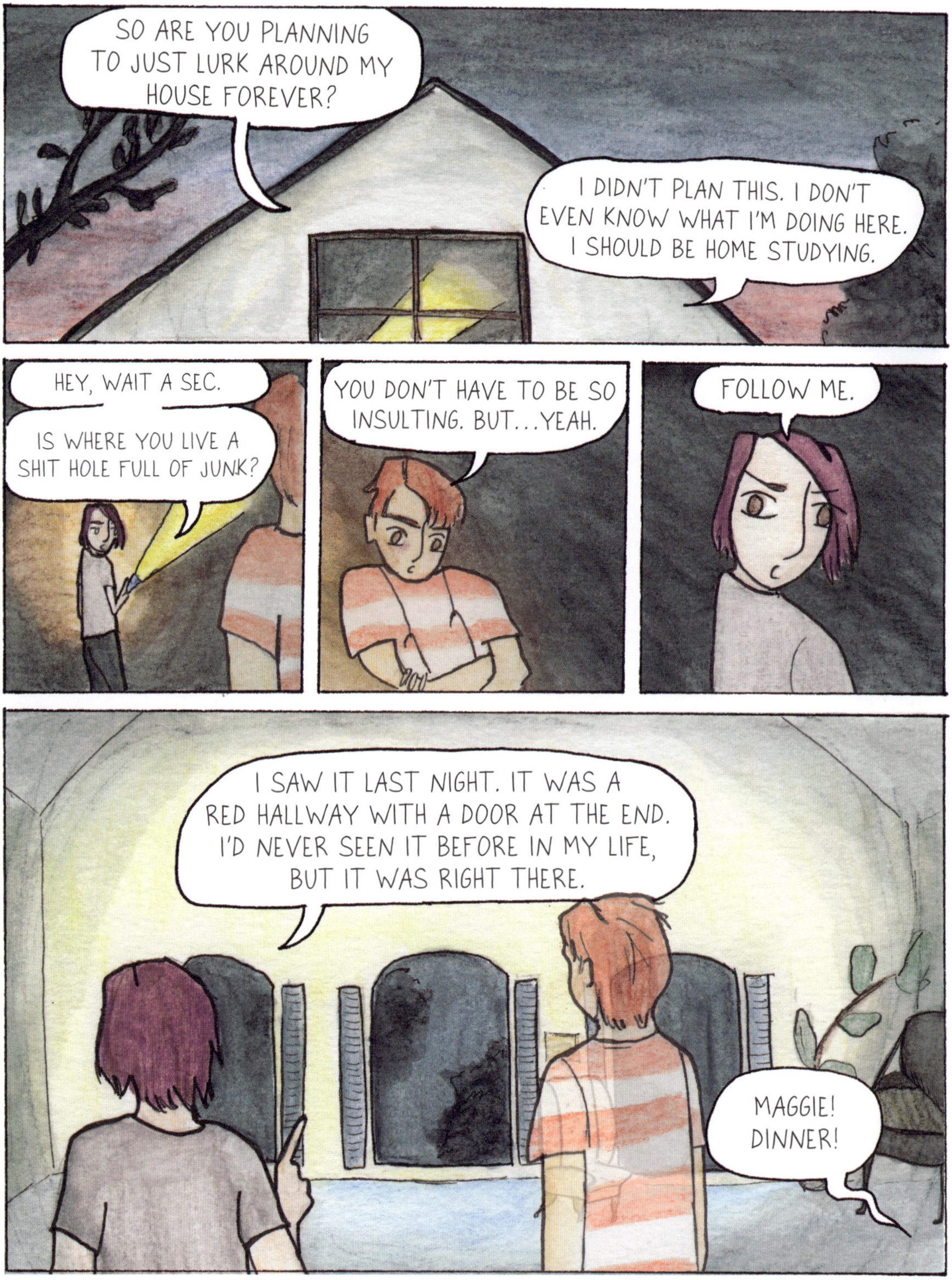
SO ARE YOU PLANNING TO JUST LURK AROUND MY HOUSE FOREVER?
I DIDN'T PLAN THIS. I DON'T EVEN KNOW WHAT I'M DOING HERE. I SHOULD BE HOME STUDYING.
HEY, WAIT A SEC.
IS WHERE YOU LIVE A SHIT HOLE FULL OF JUNK?
YOU DON'T HAVE TO BE SO INSULTING. BUT. . . YEAH.
FOLLOW ME.
I SAW IT LAST NIGHT. IT WAS A RED HALLWAY WITH A DOOR AT THE END. I'D NEVER SEEN IT BEFORE IN MY LIFE, BUT IT WAS RIGHT THERE.
MAGGIE! DINNER!

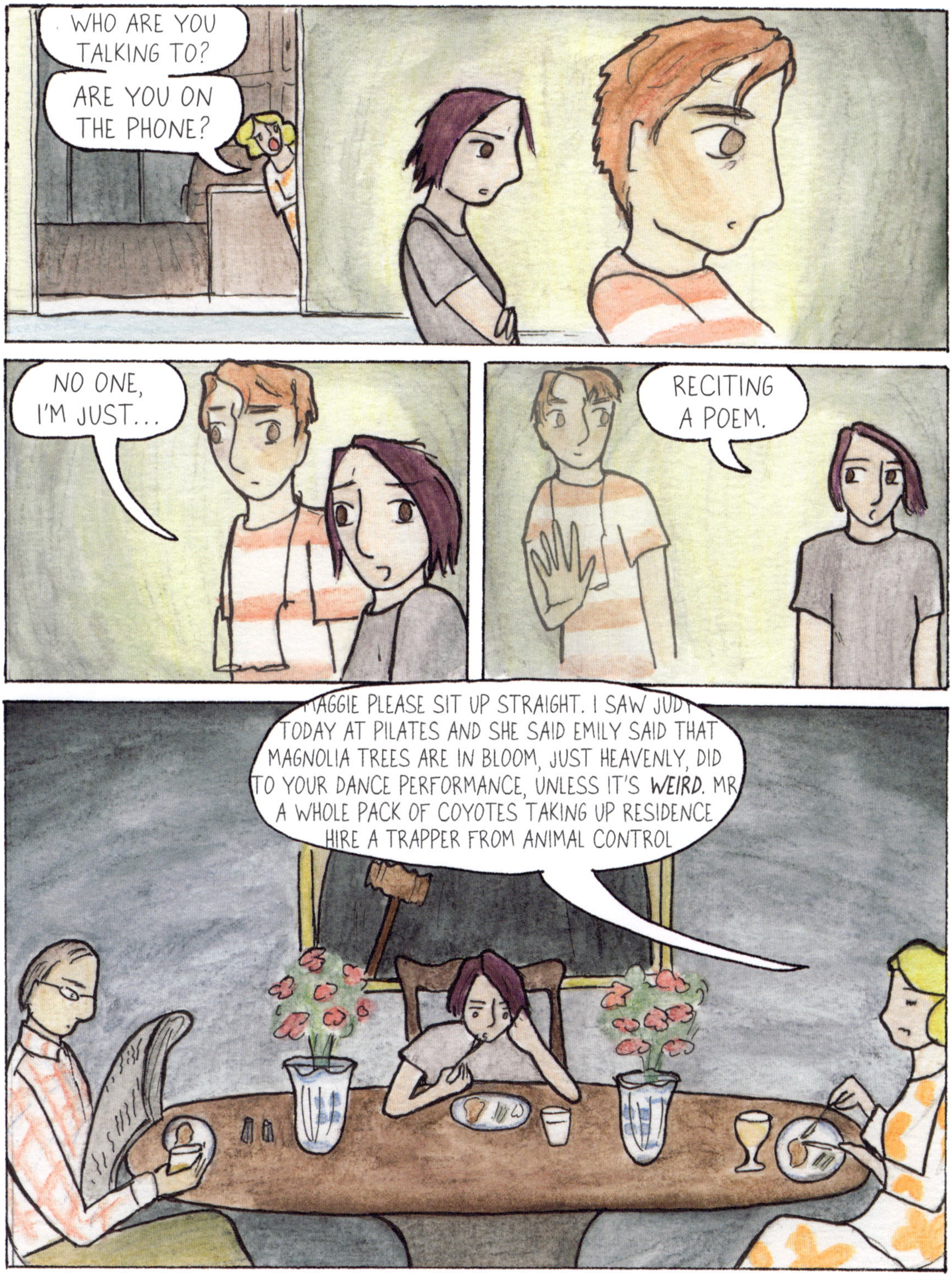
WHO ARE YOU TALKING TO?
ARE YOU ON THE PHONE?
NO ONE, I'M JUST...
RECITING A POEM.
MAGGIE PLEASE SIT UP STRAIGHT. I SAW JUDY TODAY AT PILATES AND SHE SAID EMILY SAID THAT MAGNOLIA TREES ARE IN BLOOM, JUST HEAVENLY, DID TO YOUR DANCE PERFORMANCE, UNLESS IT'S **WEIRD**. MR A WHOLE PACK OF COYOTES TAKING UP RESIDENCE HIRE A TRAPPER FROM ANIMAL CONTROL

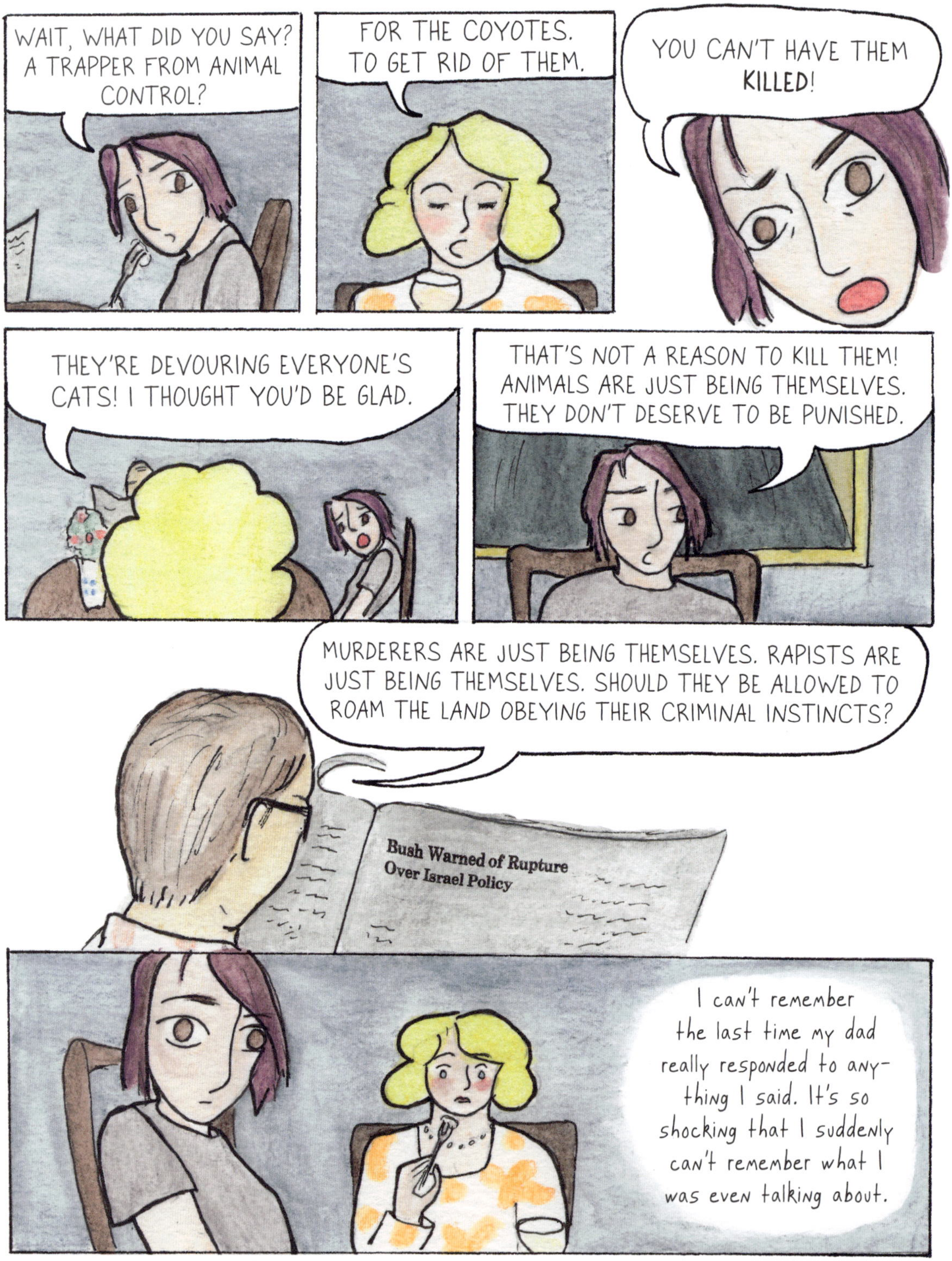
WAIT, WHAT DID YOU SAY? A TRAPPER FROM ANIMAL CONTROL?
FOR THE COYOTES. TO GET RID OF THEM.
YOU CAN'T HAVE THEM **KILLED**!
THEY'RE DEVOURING EVERYONE'S CATS! I THOUGHT YOU'D BE GLAD.
THAT'S NOT A REASON TO KILL THEM! ANIMALS ARE JUST BEING THEMSELVES. THEY DON'T DESERVE TO BE PUNISHED.
MURDERERS ARE JUST BEING THEMSELVES. RAPISTS ARE JUST BEING THEMSELVES. SHOULD THEY BE ALLOWED TO ROAM THE LAND OBEYING THEIR CRIMINAL INSTINCTS?
Bush Warned of Rupture Over Israel Policy
I can't remember the last time my dad really responded to anything I said. It's so shocking that I suddenly can't remember what I was even talking about.

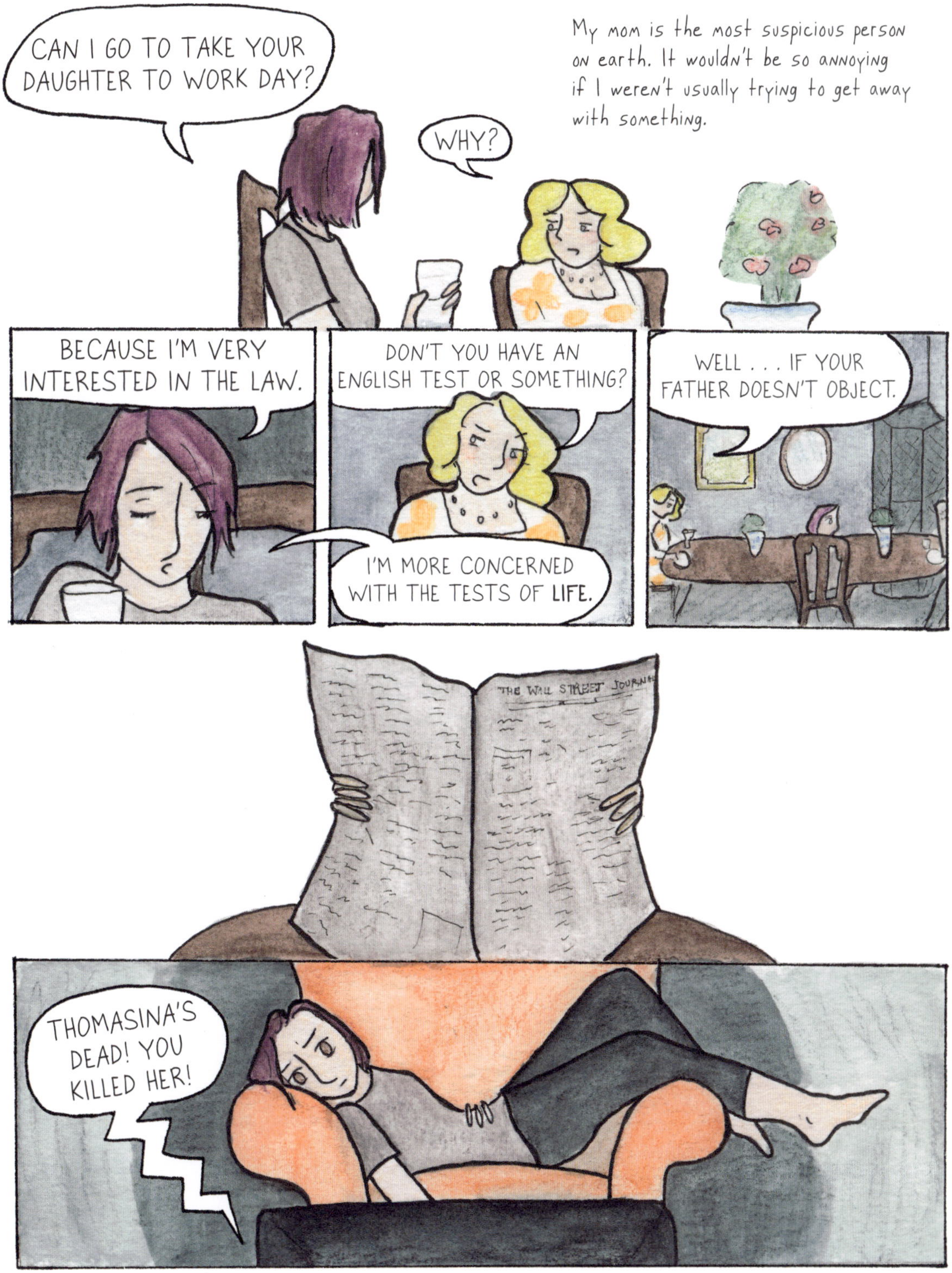
CAN I GO TO TAKE YOUR DAUGHTER TO WORK DAY?
WHY?
My mom is the most suspicious person on earth. It wouldn't be so annoying if I weren't usually trying to get away with something.
BECAUSE I'M VERY INTERESTED IN THE LAW.
DON'T YOU HAVE AN ENGLISH TEST OR SOMETHING?
I'M MORE CONCERNED WITH THE TESTS OF **LIFE**.
WELL . . . IF YOUR FATHER DOESN'T OBJECT.
THE WALL STREET JOURNAL
THOMASINA'S DEAD! YOU KILLED HER!

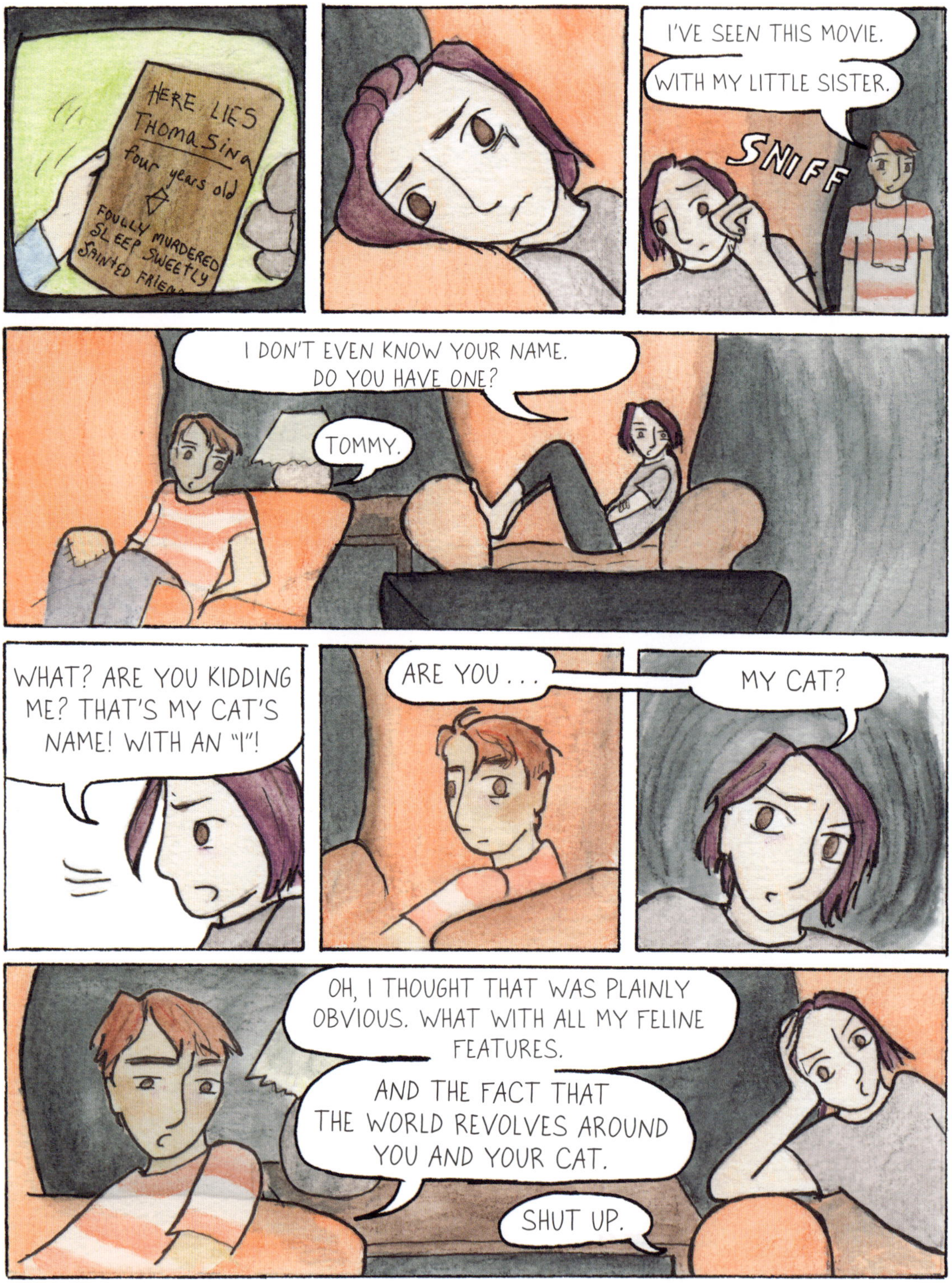
HERE LIES THOMASINA four years old FOULLY MURDERED SLEEP SWEETLY SAINTED FRIEN
I'VE SEEN THIS MOVIE.
WITH MY LITTLE SISTER.
SNIFF
I DON'T EVEN KNOW YOUR NAME. DO YOU HAVE ONE?
TOMMY.
WHAT? ARE YOU KIDDING ME? THAT'S MY CAT'S NAME! WITH AN "I"!
ARE YOU . . .
MY CAT?
OH, I THOUGHT THAT WAS PLAINLY OBVIOUS. WHAT WITH ALL MY FELINE FEATURES.
AND THE FACT THAT THE WORLD REVOLVES AROUND YOU AND YOUR CAT.
SHUT UP.

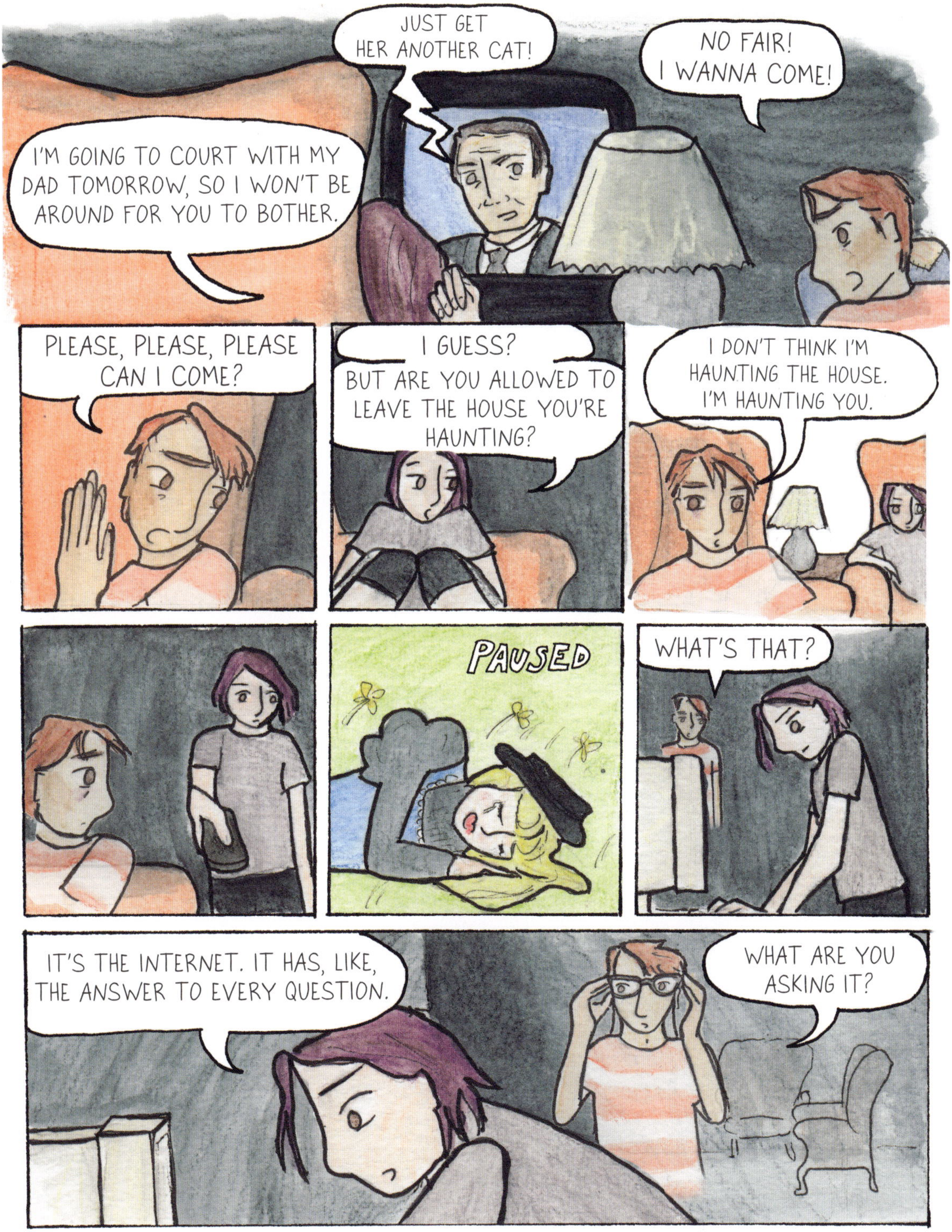
JUST GET HER ANOTHER CAT!
NO FAIR! I WANNA COME!
I'M GOING TO COURT WITH MY DAD TOMORROW, SO I WON'T BE AROUND FOR YOU TO BOTHER.
PLEASE, PLEASE, PLEASE CAN I COME?
I GUESS?
BUT ARE YOU ALLOWED TO LEAVE THE HOUSE YOU'RE HAUNTING?
I DON'T THINK I'M HAUNTING THE HOUSE. I'M HAUNTING YOU.
PAUSED
WHAT'S THAT?
IT'S THE INTERNET. IT HAS, LIKE, THE ANSWER TO EVERY QUESTION.
WHAT ARE YOU ASKING IT?

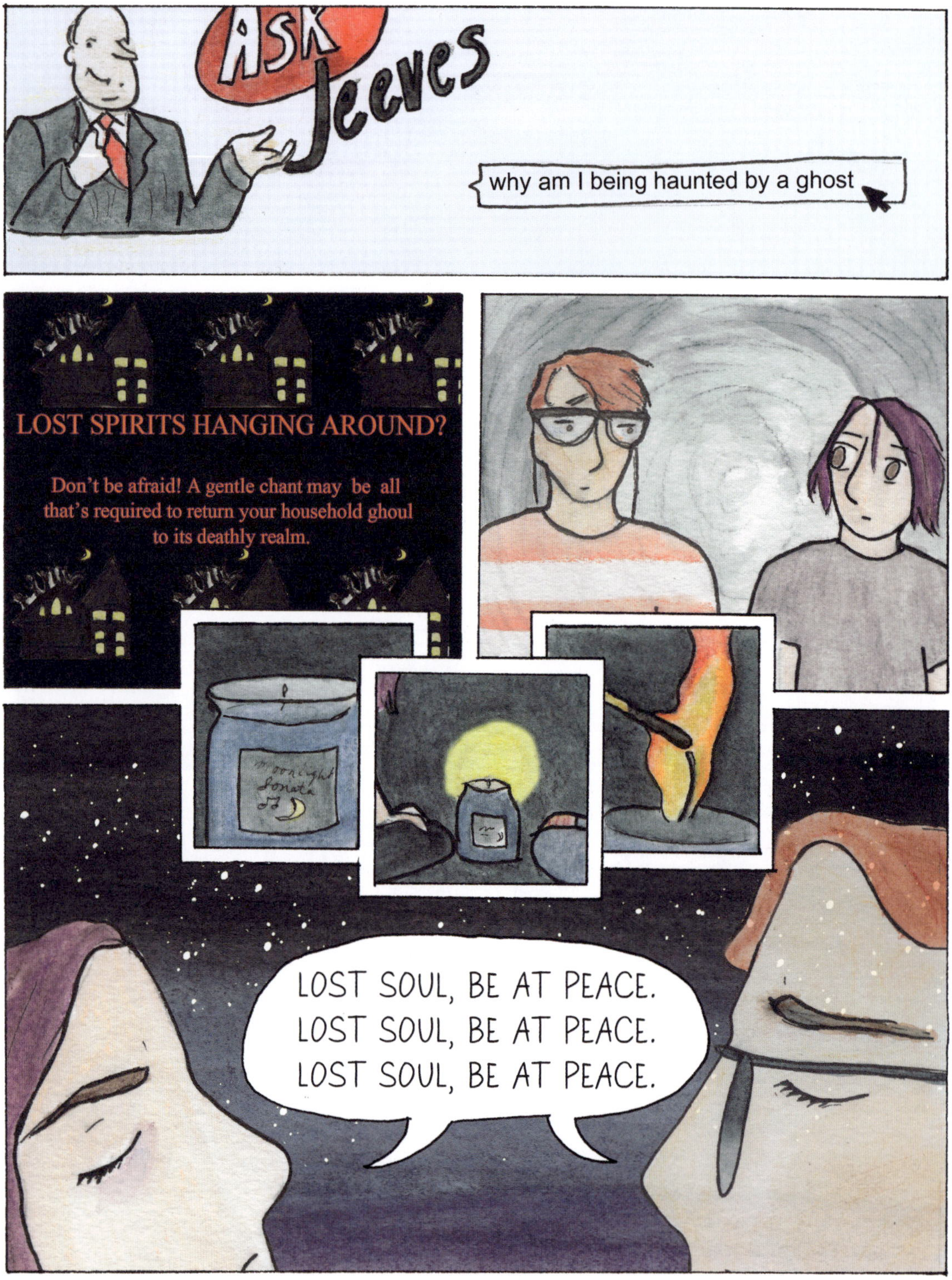
Ask Jeeves
why am I being haunted by a ghost
LOST SPIRITS HANGING AROUND?
Don't be afraid! A gentle chant may be all that's required to return your household ghoul to its deathly realm.
Moonlight Sonata
LOST SOUL, BE AT PEACE.
LOST SOUL, BE AT PEACE.
LOST SOUL, BE AT PEACE.

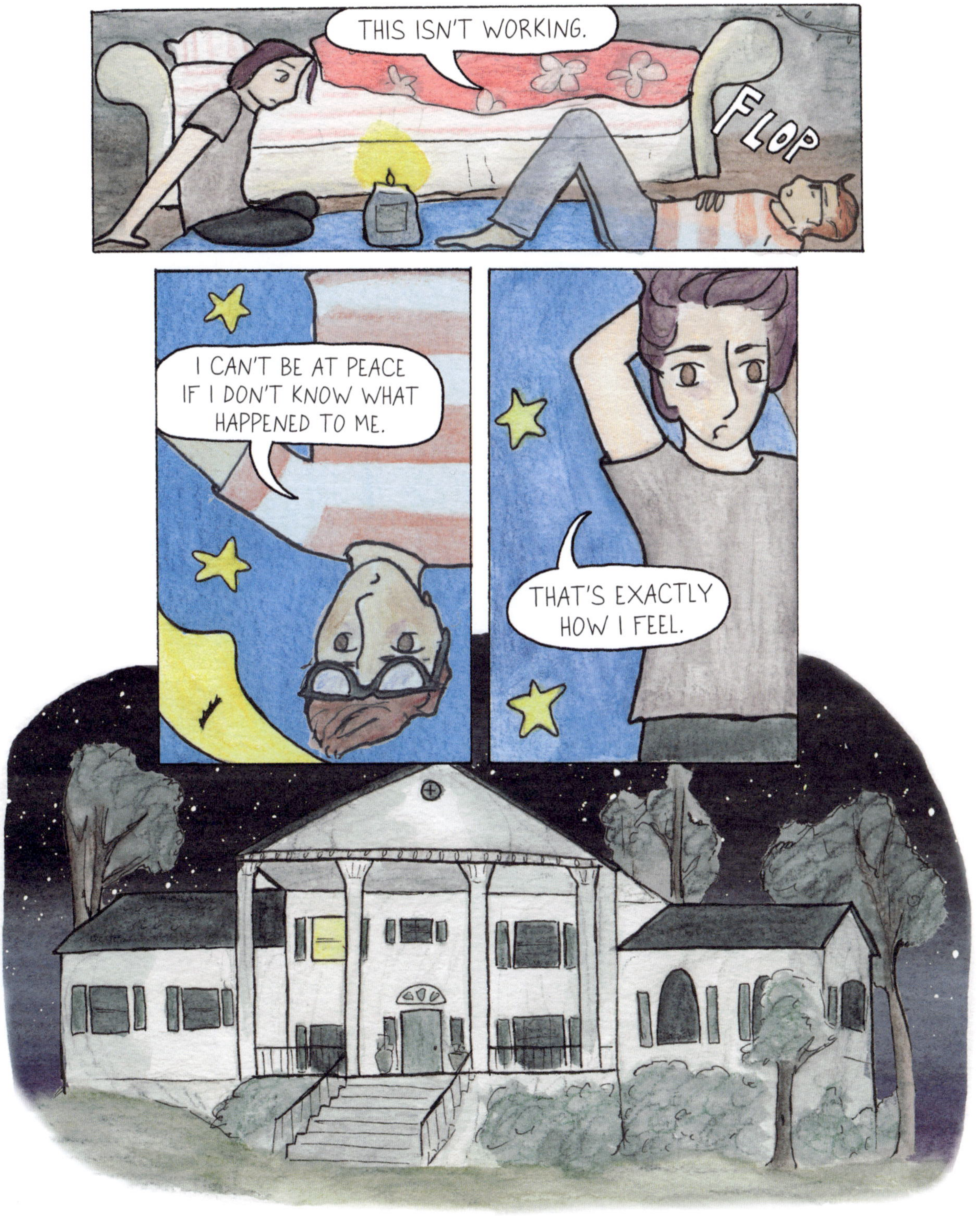
THIS ISN'T WORKING.
FLOP
I CAN'T BE AT PEACE IF I DON'T KNOW WHAT HAPPENED TO ME.
THAT'S EXACTLY HOW I FEEL.

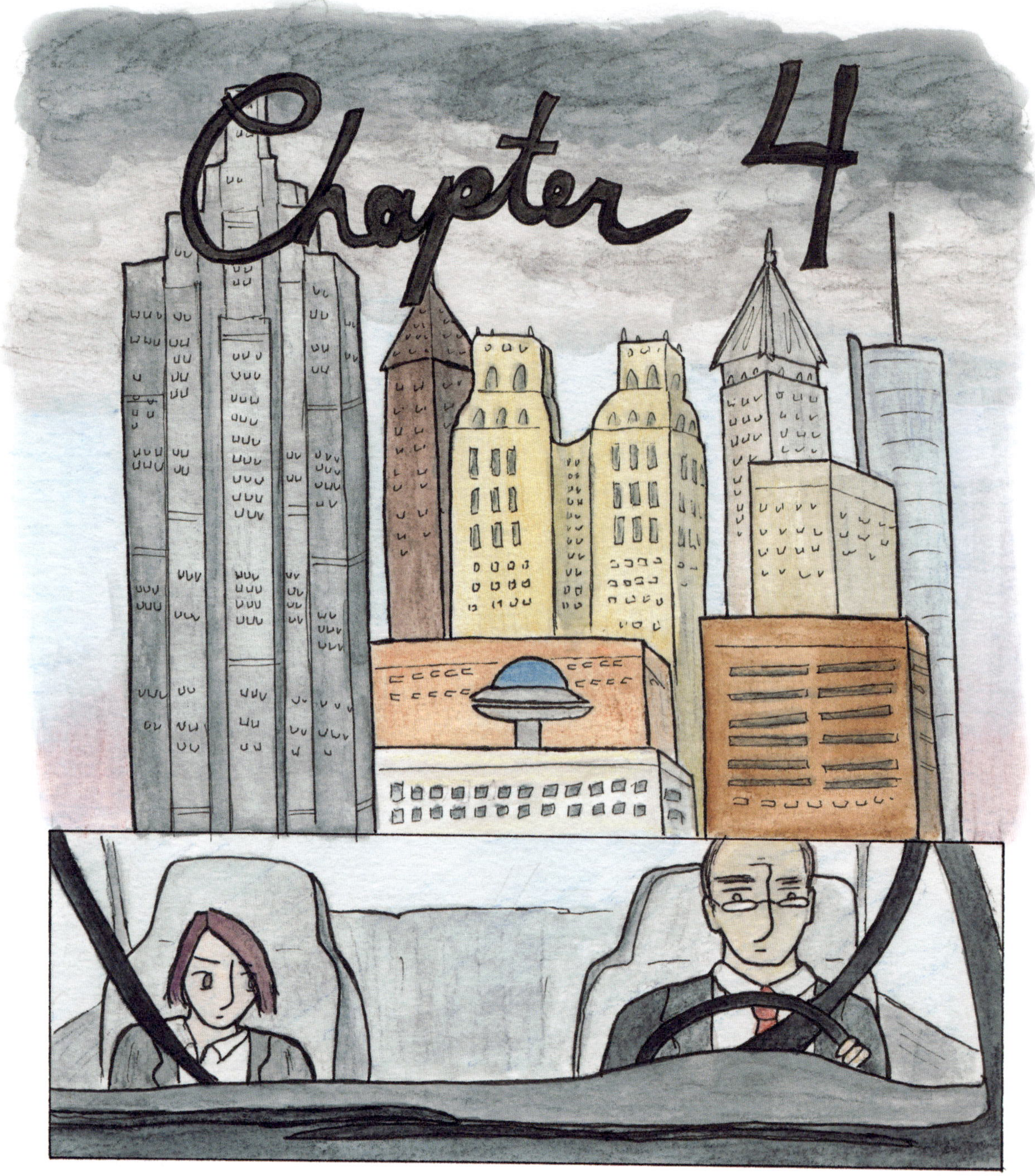
Chapter 4

Sitting in the car with my dad is always weird. In kindergarten they drill it into your head: NEVER GET IN A CAR WITH SOMEONE YOU DON'T KNOW. But what they don't say is how you can live in the same house as someone and still be total strangers.

I don't know what my dad would be surprised or unsurprised to learn about me. That I'll never go to Harvard? That I'm a lesbian? That I can see a ghost in his car at this very moment?

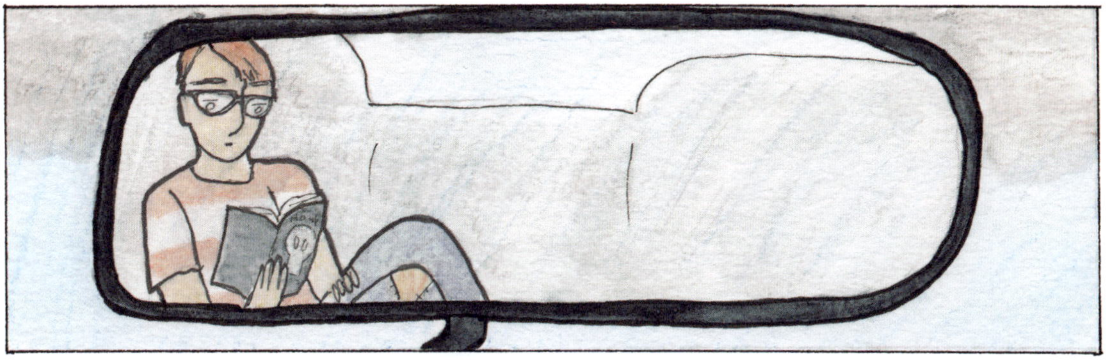

It's hard not to notice the ugly blocks of cement surrounding the courthouse. They're to prevent killers from filling their cars with explosives and crashing them into the building.

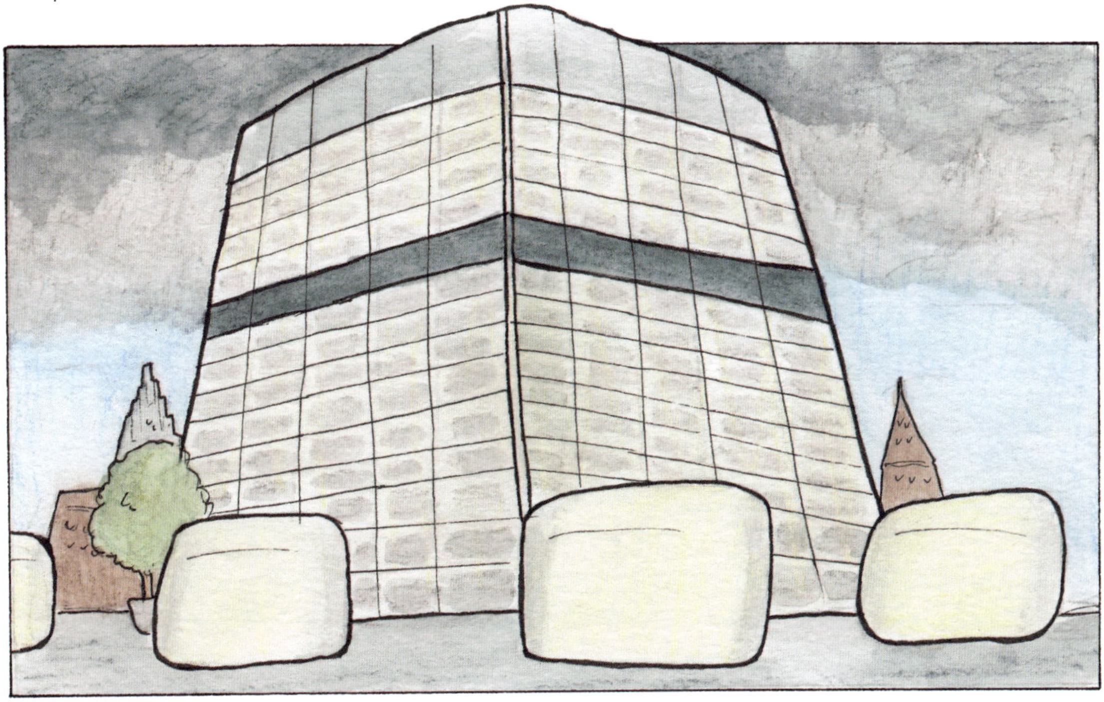

I can't believe it's some people's jobs to anticipate all the ways mass murder could occur in a situation. Like, at what point do you just give up, if the killers are so determined, and if everyone dies in the end anyway?

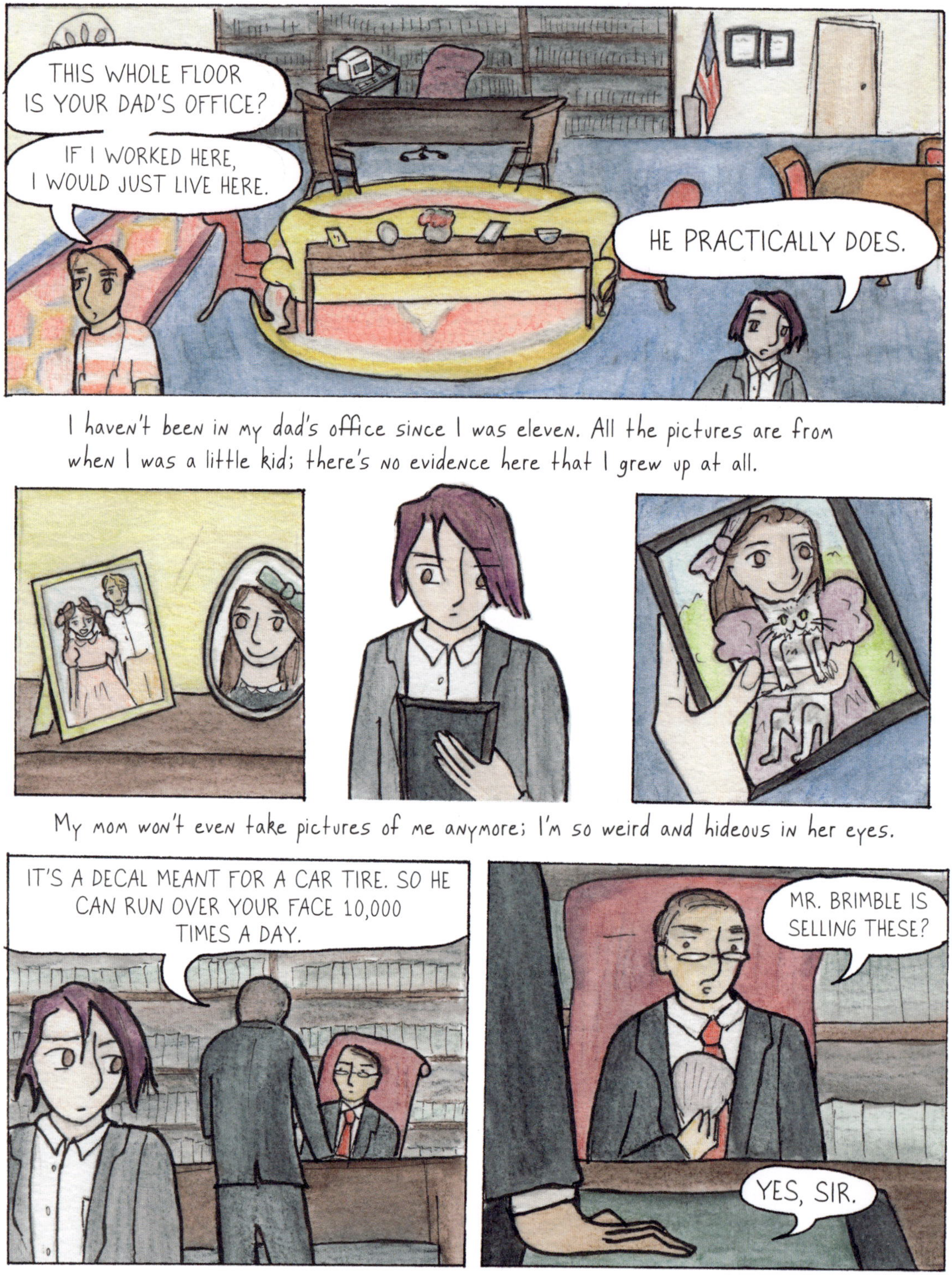
THIS WHOLE FLOOR IS YOUR DAD'S OFFICE?
IF I WORKED HERE, I WOULD JUST LIVE HERE.
HE PRACTICALLY DOES.
I haven't been in my dad's office since I was eleven. All the pictures are from when I was a little kid; there's no evidence here that I grew up at all.
My mom won't even take pictures of me anymore; I'm so weird and hideous in her eyes.
IT'S A DECAL MEANT FOR A CAR TIRE. SO HE CAN RUN OVER YOUR FACE 10,000 TIMES A DAY.
MR. BRIMBLE IS SELLING THESE?
YES, SIR.

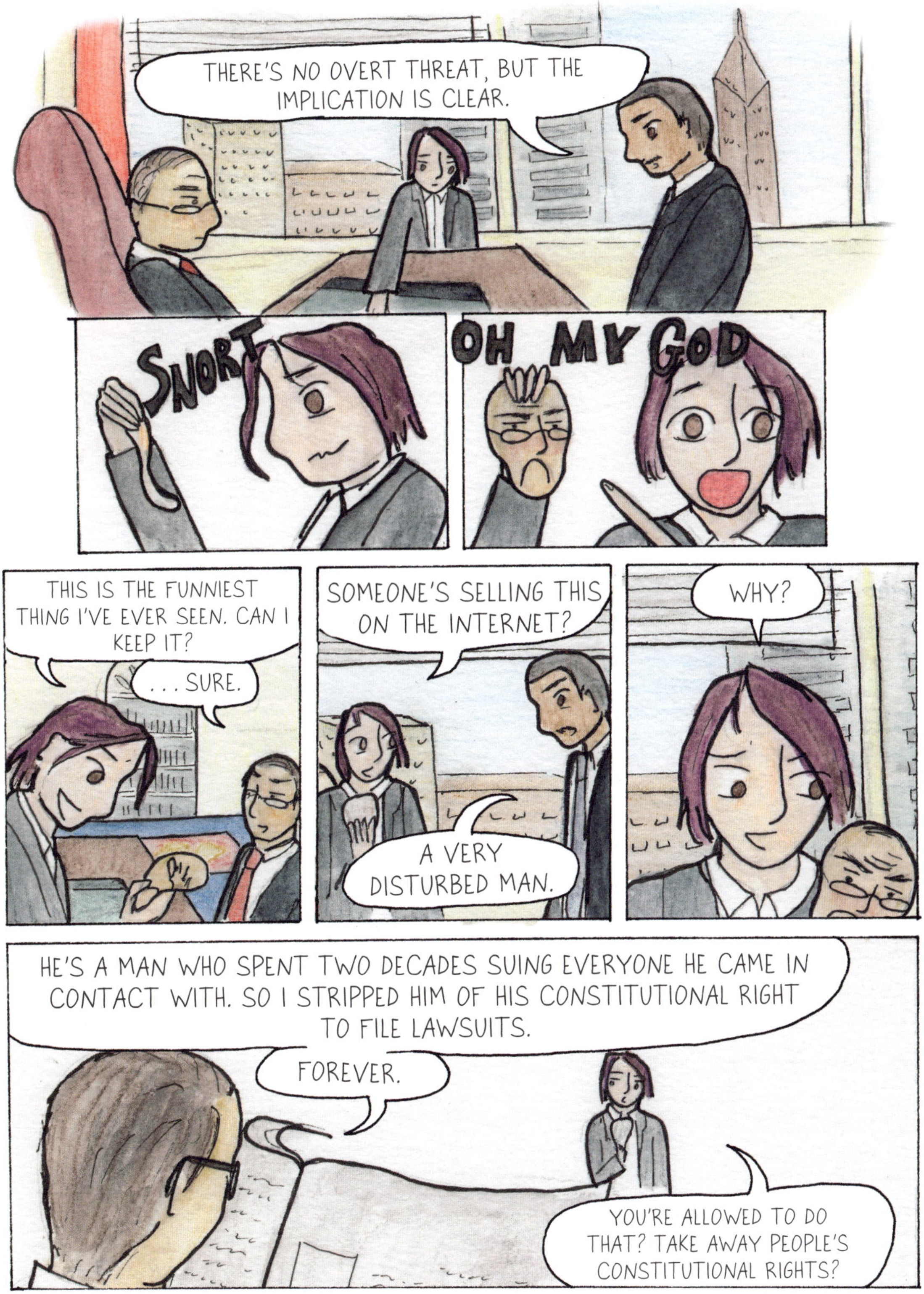
THERE'S NO OVERT THREAT, BUT THE IMPLICATION IS CLEAR.
SNORT
OH MY GOD
THIS IS THE FUNNIEST THING I'VE EVER SEEN. CAN I KEEP IT?
. . . SURE.
SOMEONE'S SELLING THIS ON THE INTERNET?
A VERY DISTURBED MAN.
WHY?
HE'S A MAN WHO SPENT TWO DECADES SUING EVERYONE HE CAME IN CONTACT WITH. SO I STRIPPED HIM OF HIS CONSTITUTIONAL RIGHT TO FILE LAWSUITS.
FOREVER.
YOU'RE ALLOWED TO DO THAT? TAKE AWAY PEOPLE'S CONSTITUTIONAL RIGHTS?

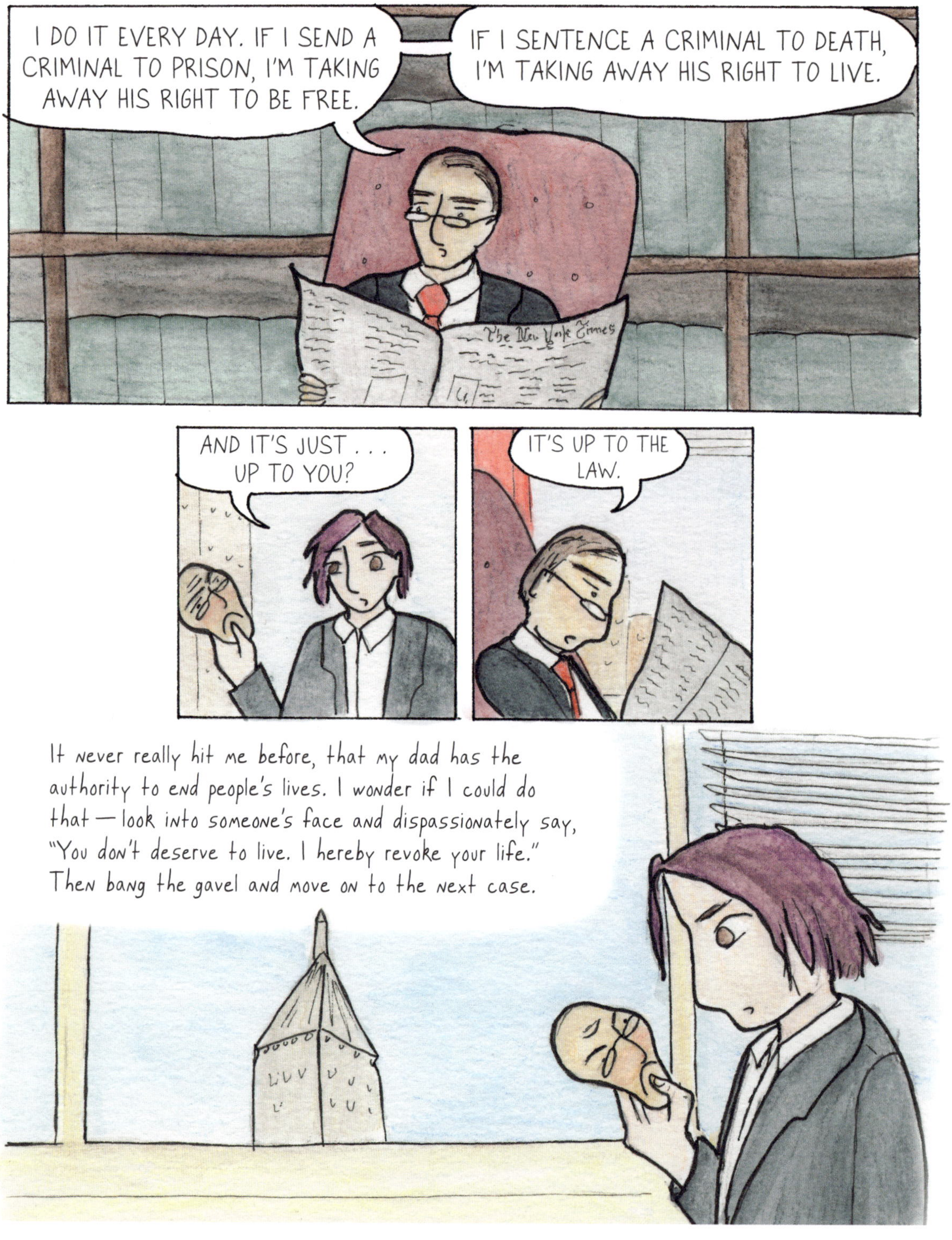
I DO IT EVERY DAY. IF I SEND A CRIMINAL TO PRISON, I'M TAKING AWAY HIS RIGHT TO BE FREE.
IF I SENTENCE A CRIMINAL TO DEATH, I'M TAKING AWAY HIS RIGHT TO LIVE.
AND IT'S JUST . . . UP TO YOU?
IT'S UP TO THE LAW.
It never really hit me before, that my dad has the authority to end people's lives. I wonder if I could do that — look into someone's face and dispassionately say, "You don't deserve to live. I hereby revoke your life." Then bang the gavel and move on to the next case.

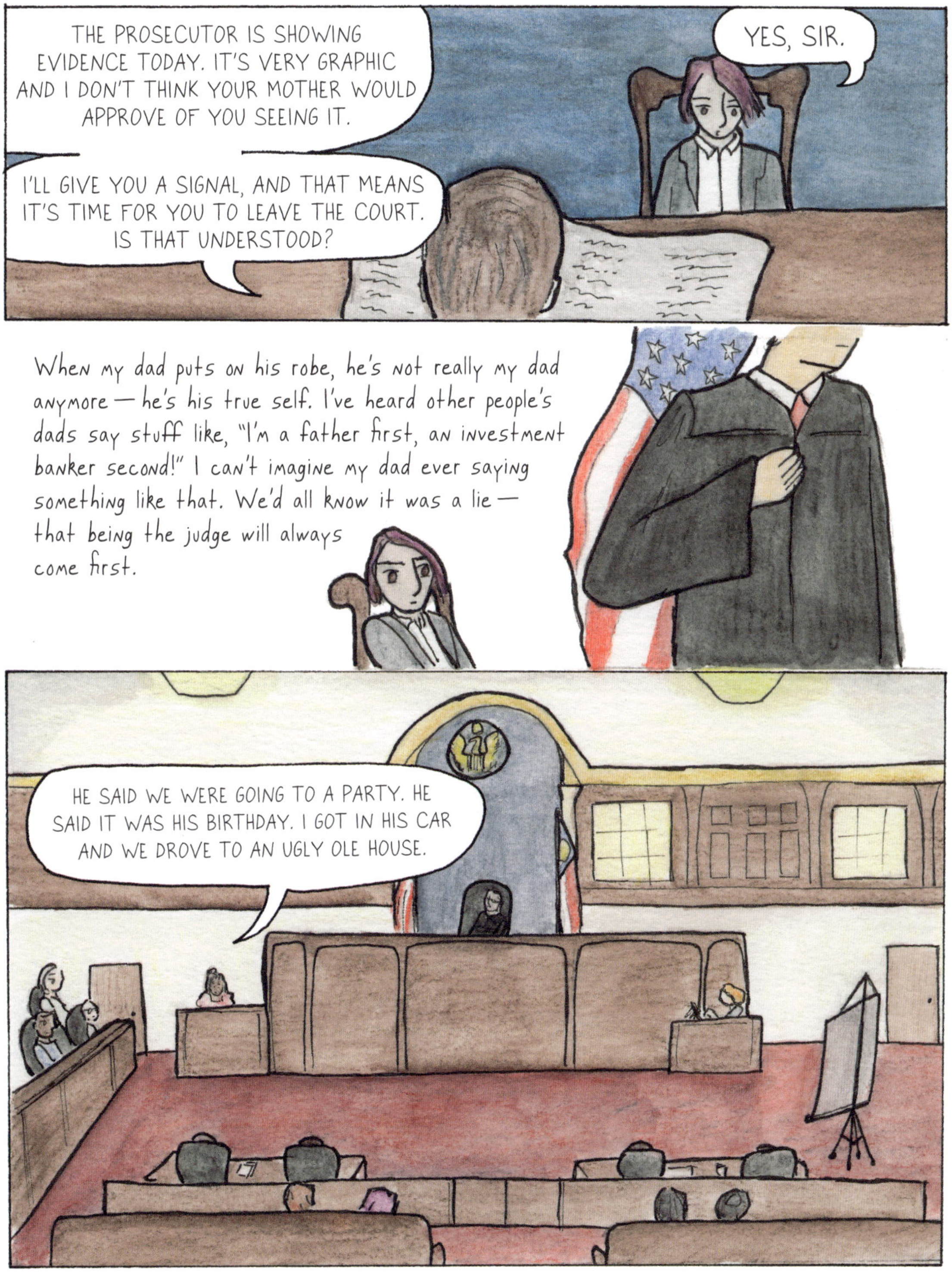
THE PROSECUTOR IS SHOWING EVIDENCE TODAY. IT'S VERY GRAPHIC AND I DON'T THINK YOUR MOTHER WOULD APPROVE OF YOU SEEING IT.
I'LL GIVE YOU A SIGNAL, AND THAT MEANS IT'S TIME FOR YOU TO LEAVE THE COURT. IS THAT UNDERSTOOD?
YES, SIR.
When my dad puts on his robe, he's not really my dad anymore — he's his true self. I've heard other people's dads say stuff like, "I'm a father first, an investment banker second!" I can't imagine my dad ever saying something like that. We'd all know it was a lie — that being the judge will always come first.
HE SAID WE WERE GOING TO A PARTY. HE SAID IT WAS HIS BIRTHDAY. I GOT IN HIS CAR AND WE DROVE TO AN UGLY OLE HOUSE.

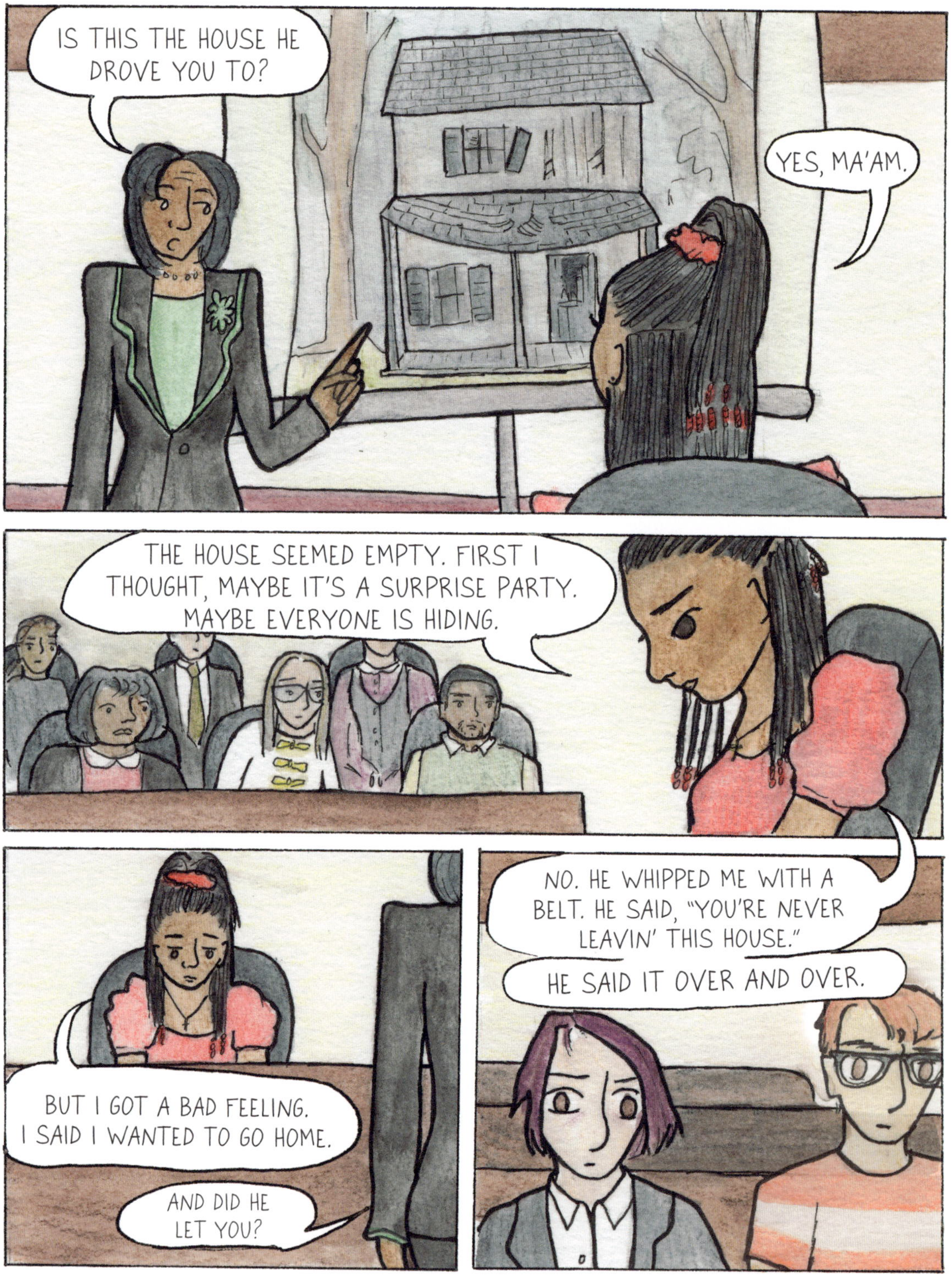
IS THIS THE HOUSE HE DROVE YOU TO?
YES, MA'AM.
THE HOUSE SEEMED EMPTY. FIRST I THOUGHT, MAYBE IT'S A SURPRISE PARTY. MAYBE EVERYONE IS HIDING.
BUT I GOT A BAD FEELING. I SAID I WANTED TO GO HOME.
AND DID HE LET YOU?
NO. HE WHIPPED ME WITH A BELT. HE SAID, "YOU'RE NEVER LEAVIN' THIS HOUSE."
HE SAID IT OVER AND OVER.

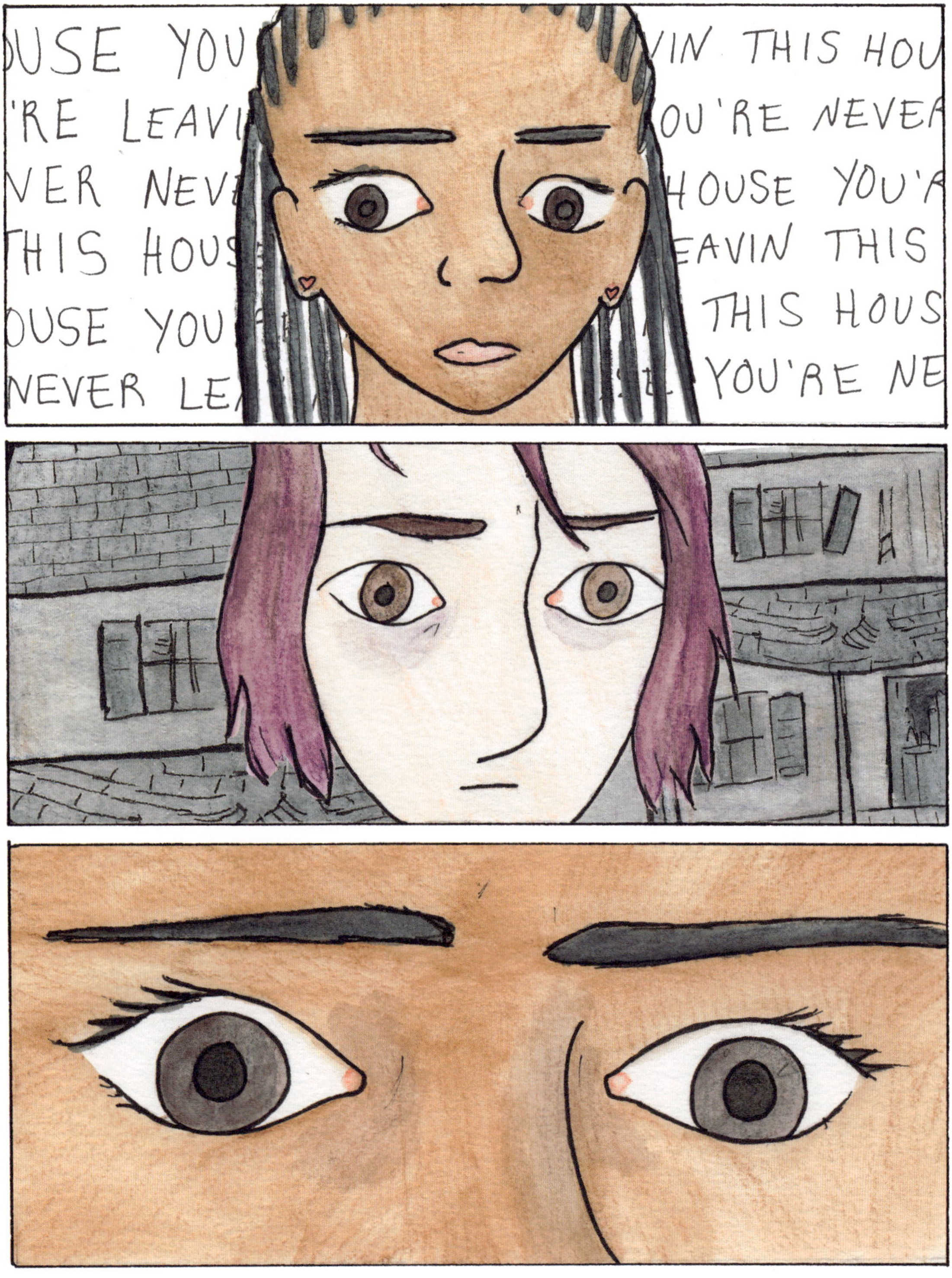
OUSE YOU
VIN THIS HOU
'RE LEAVI
OU'RE NEVER
VER NEVE
HOUSE YOU'
THIS HOUS
EAVIN THIS
OUSE YOU
THIS HOUS
NEVER LE
YOU'RE NE

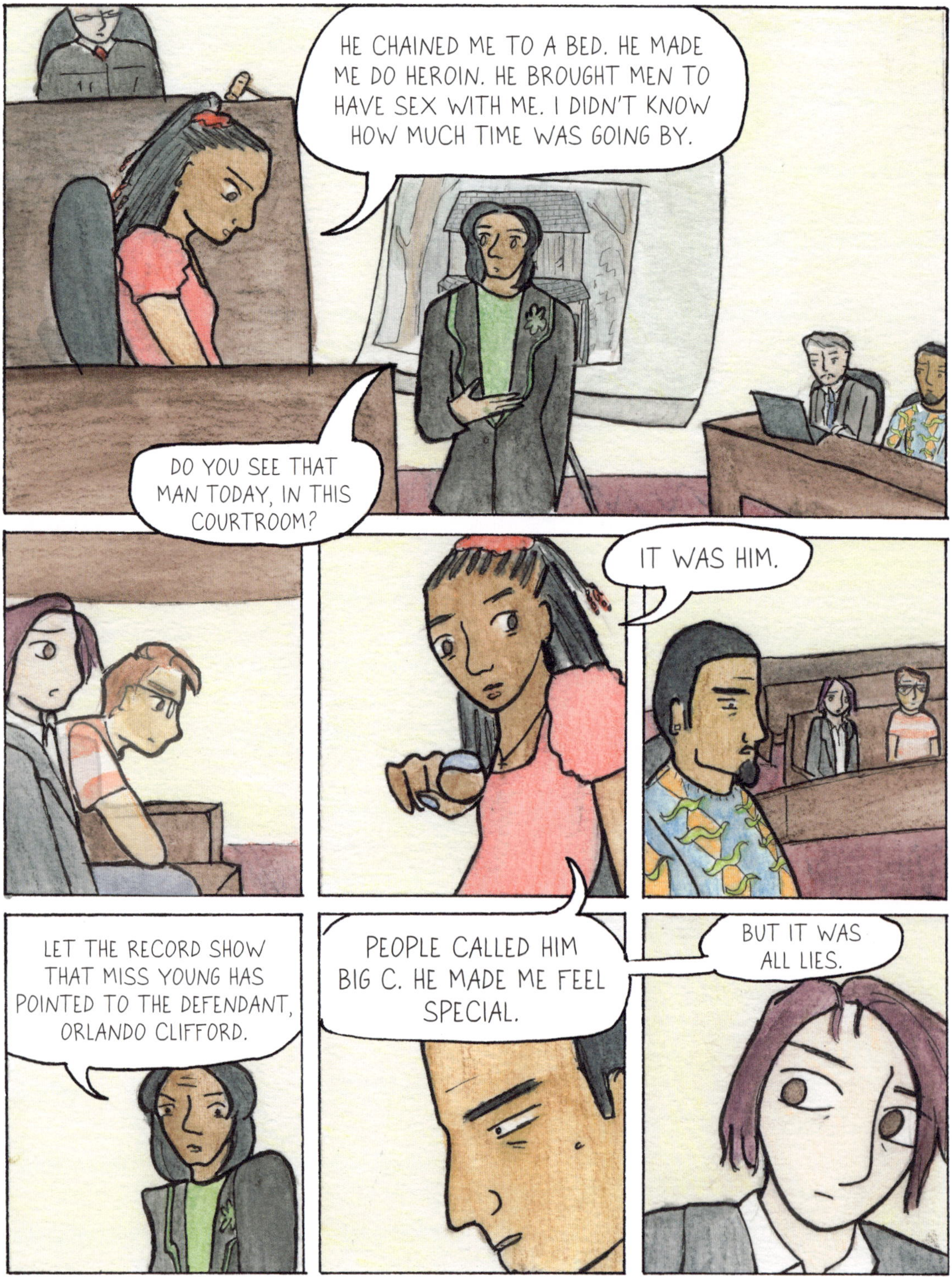
HE CHAINED ME TO A BED. HE MADE ME DO HEROIN. HE BROUGHT MEN TO HAVE SEX WITH ME. I DIDN'T KNOW HOW MUCH TIME WAS GOING BY.
DO YOU SEE THAT MAN TODAY, IN THIS COURTROOM?
IT WAS HIM.
LET THE RECORD SHOW THAT MISS YOUNG HAS POINTED TO THE DEFENDANT, ORLANDO CLIFFORD.
PEOPLE CALLED HIM BIG C. HE MADE ME FEEL SPECIAL.
BUT IT WAS ALL LIES.

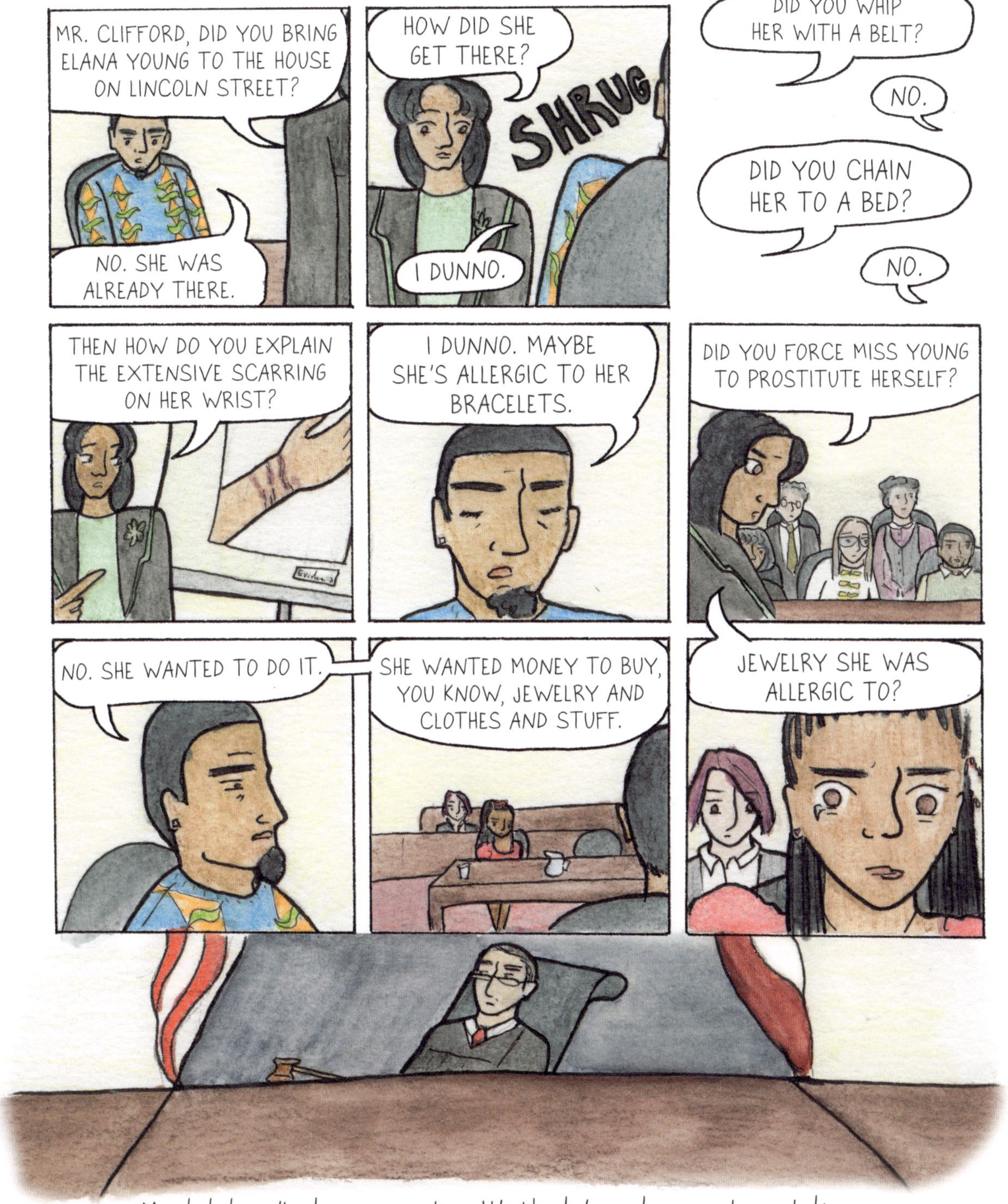
MR. CLIFFORD, DID YOU BRING ELANA YOUNG TO THE HOUSE ON LINCOLN STREET?
NO. SHE WAS ALREADY THERE.
HOW DID SHE GET THERE?
SHRUG
I DUNNO.
DID YOU WHIP HER WITH A BELT?
NO.
DID YOU CHAIN HER TO A BED?
NO.
THEN HOW DO YOU EXPLAIN THE EXTENSIVE SCARRING ON HER WRIST?
I DUNNO. MAYBE SHE'S ALLERGIC TO HER BRACELETS.
DID YOU FORCE MISS YOUNG TO PROSTITUTE HERSELF?
NO. SHE WANTED TO DO IT.
SHE WANTED MONEY TO BUY, YOU KNOW, JEWELRY AND CLOTHES AND STUFF.
JEWELRY SHE WAS ALLERGIC TO?

My dad doesn't show any emotion. It's like he's a chess master watching a game, and he can tell ten moves in advance who's going to win.

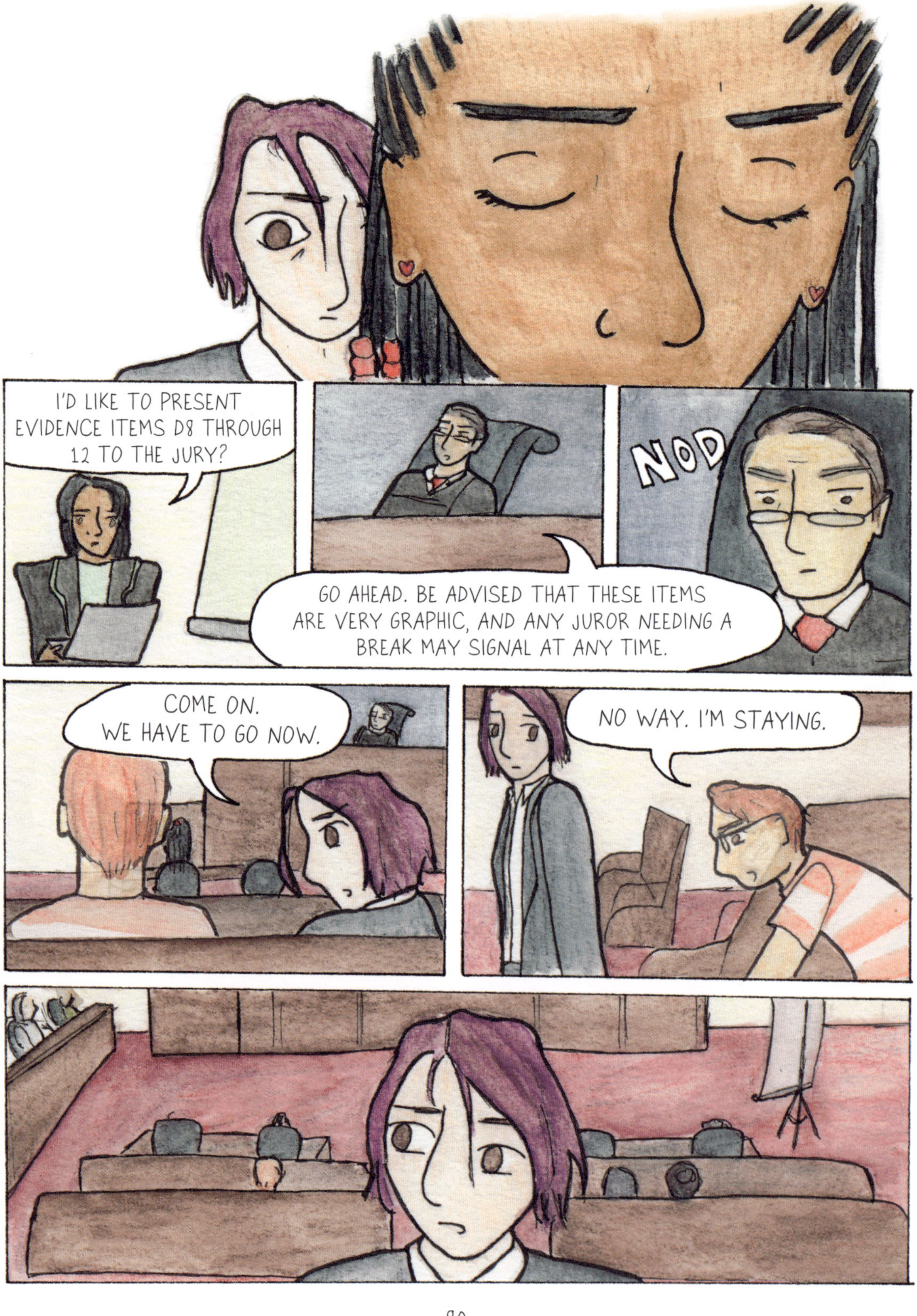
I'D LIKE TO PRESENT EVIDENCE ITEMS D8 THROUGH 12 TO THE JURY?
NOD
GO AHEAD. BE ADVISED THAT THESE ITEMS ARE VERY GRAPHIC, AND ANY JUROR NEEDING A BREAK MAY SIGNAL AT ANY TIME.
COME ON. WE HAVE TO GO NOW.
NO WAY. I'M STAYING.

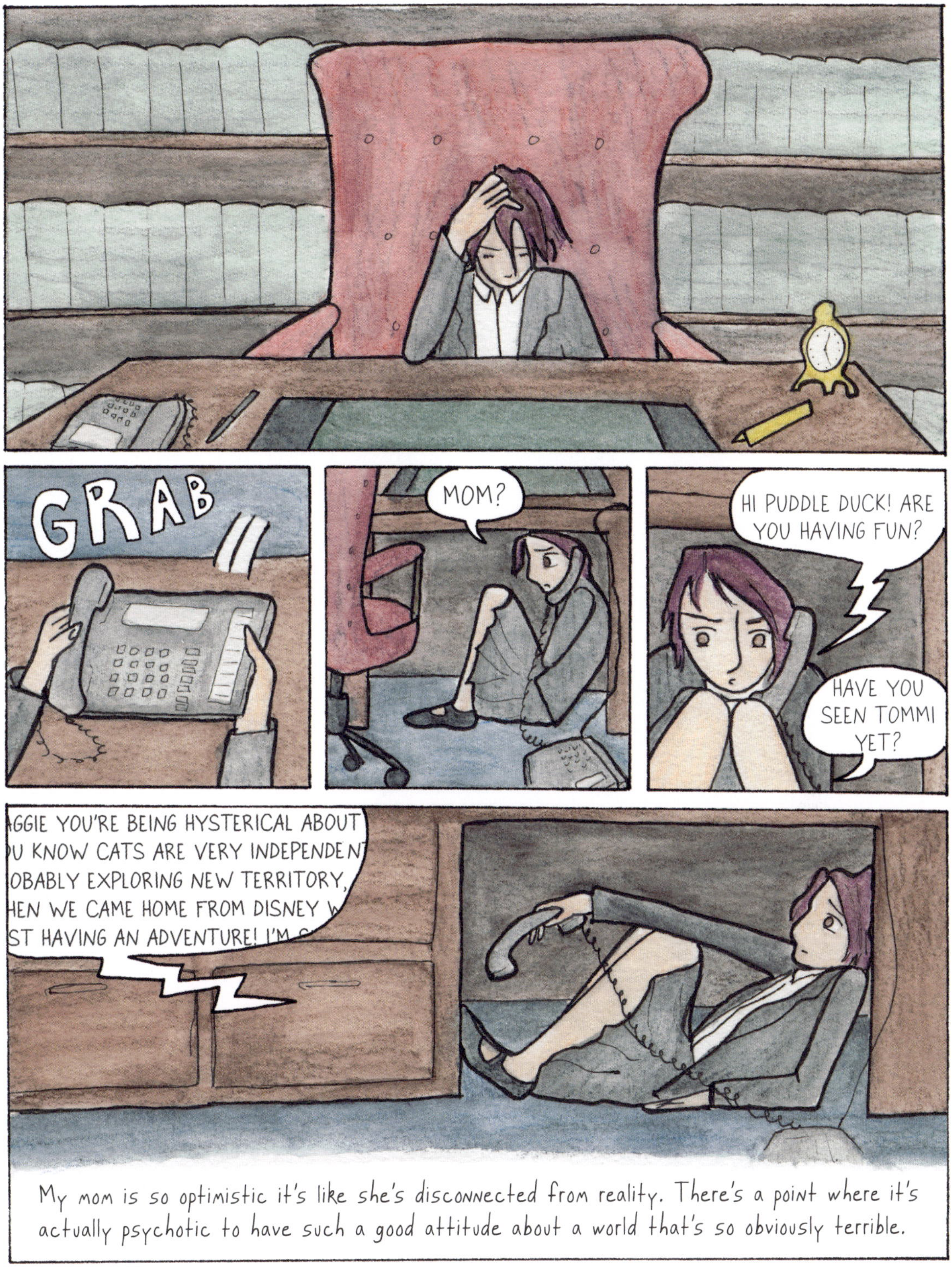
GRAB
MOM?
HI PUDDLE DUCK! ARE YOU HAVING FUN?
HAVE YOU SEEN TOMMI YET?
AGGIE YOU'RE BEING HYSTERICAL ABOUT
U KNOW CATS ARE VERY INDEPENDEN
OBABLY EXPLORING NEW TERRITORY,
HEN WE CAME HOME FROM DISNEY W
ST HAVING AN ADVENTURE! I'M
My mom is so optimistic it's like she's disconnected from reality. There's a point where it's actually psychotic to have such a good attitude about a world that's so obviously terrible.

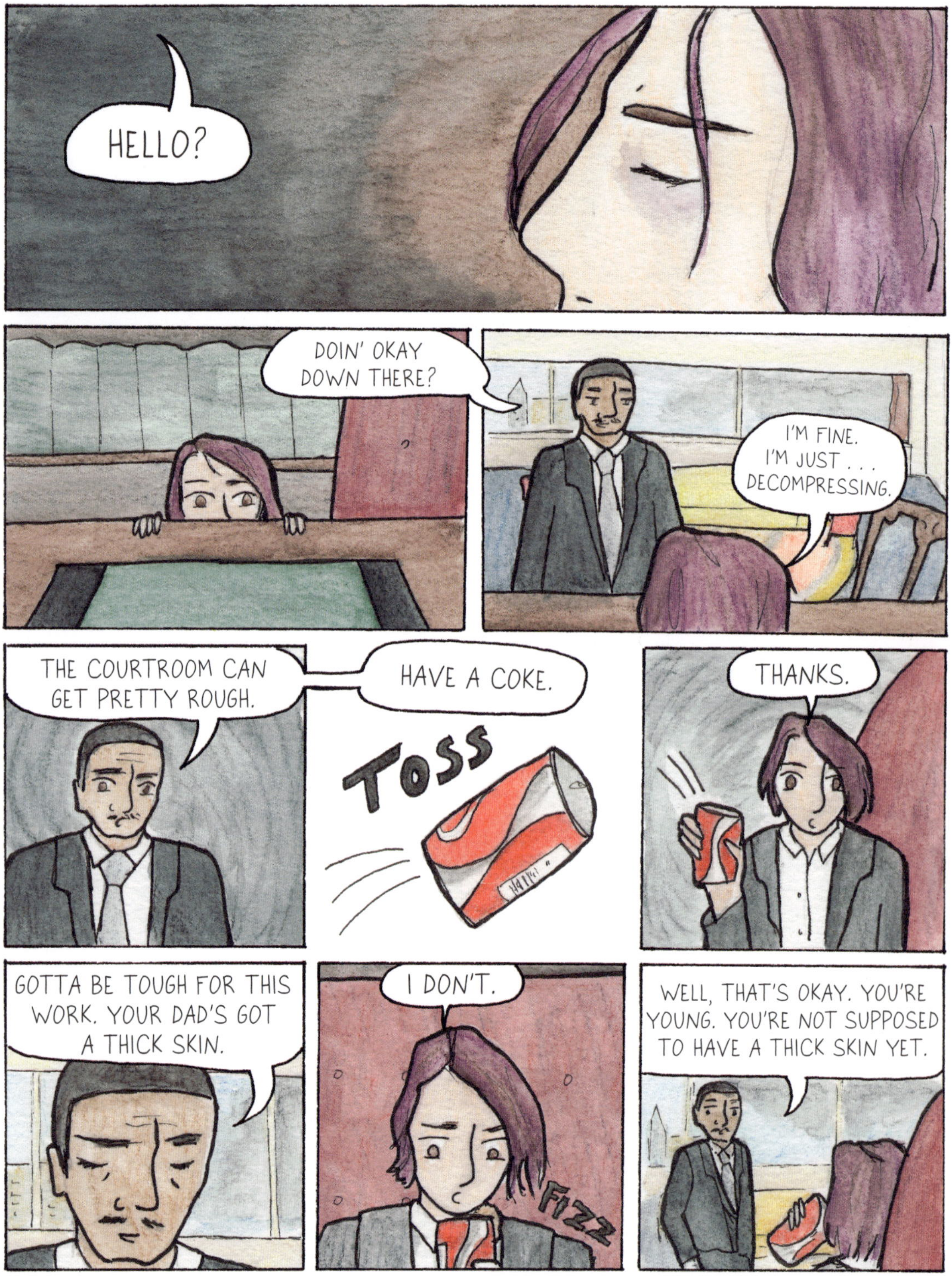
HELLO?
DOIN' OKAY DOWN THERE?
I'M FINE. I'M JUST . . . DECOMPRESSING.
THE COURTROOM CAN GET PRETTY ROUGH.
HAVE A COKE.
TOSS
THANKS.
GOTTA BE TOUGH FOR THIS WORK. YOUR DAD'S GOT A THICK SKIN.
I DON'T.
FIZZ
WELL, THAT'S OKAY. YOU'RE YOUNG. YOU'RE NOT SUPPOSED TO HAVE A THICK SKIN YET.

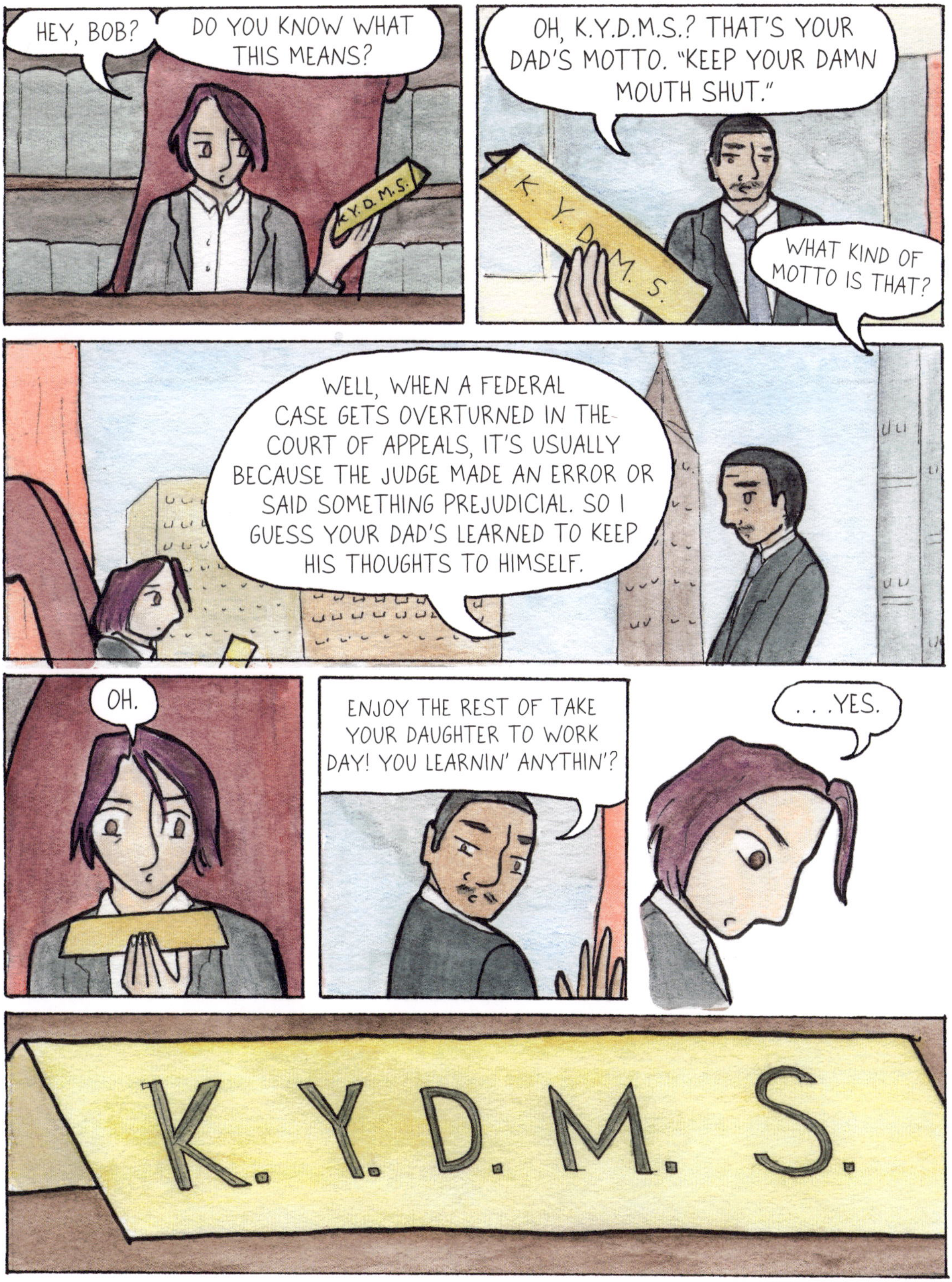
HEY, BOB?
DO YOU KNOW WHAT THIS MEANS?
K.Y.D.M.S.
OH, K.Y.D.M.S.? THAT'S YOUR DAD'S MOTTO. "KEEP YOUR DAMN MOUTH SHUT."
K.Y.D.M.S.
WHAT KIND OF MOTTO IS THAT?
WELL, WHEN A FEDERAL CASE GETS OVERTURNED IN THE COURT OF APPEALS, IT'S USUALLY BECAUSE THE JUDGE MADE AN ERROR OR SAID SOMETHING PREJUDICIAL. SO I GUESS YOUR DAD'S LEARNED TO KEEP HIS THOUGHTS TO HIMSELF.
OH.
ENJOY THE REST OF TAKE YOUR DAUGHTER TO WORK DAY! YOU LEARNIN' ANYTHIN'?
. . .YES.
K.Y.D.M.S.

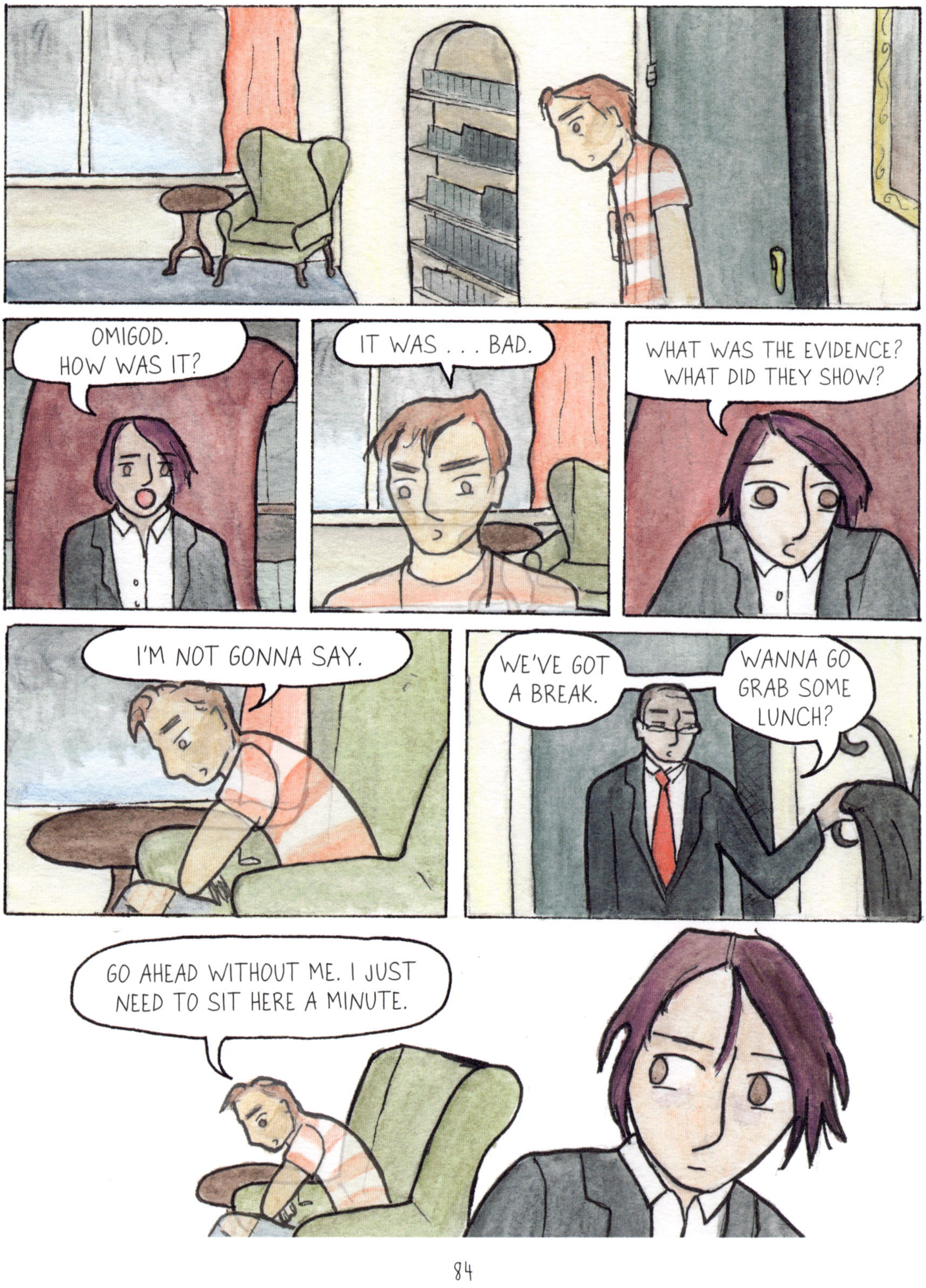
OMIGOD. HOW WAS IT?
IT WAS . . . BAD.
WHAT WAS THE EVIDENCE? WHAT DID THEY SHOW?
I'M NOT GONNA SAY.
WE'VE GOT A BREAK.
WANNA GO GRAB SOME LUNCH?
GO AHEAD WITHOUT ME. I JUST NEED TO SIT HERE A MINUTE.

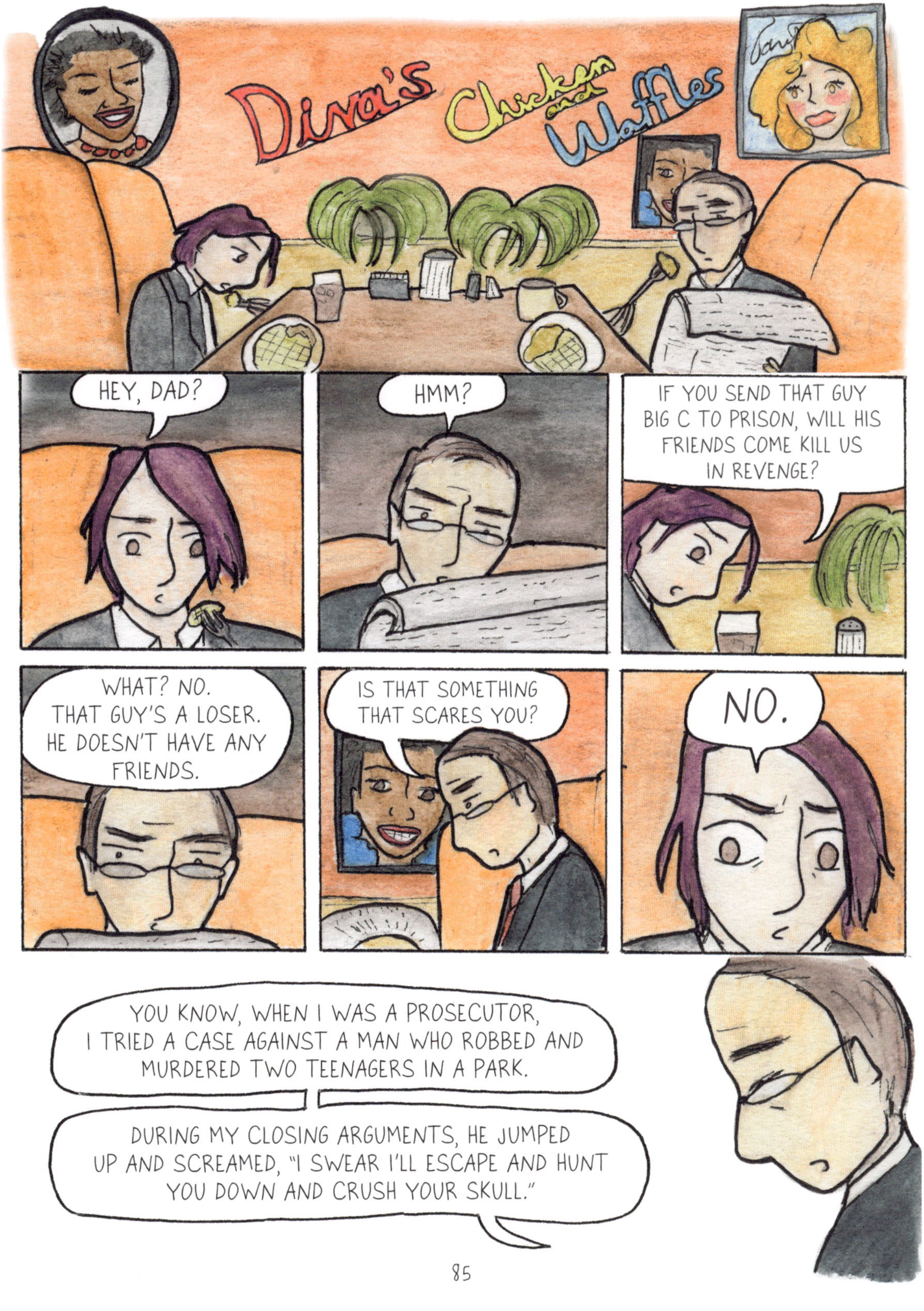
Diva's Chicken and Waffles
HEY, DAD?
HMM?
IF YOU SEND THAT GUY BIG C TO PRISON, WILL HIS FRIENDS COME KILL US IN REVENGE?
WHAT? NO. THAT GUY'S A LOSER. HE DOESN'T HAVE ANY FRIENDS.
IS THAT SOMETHING THAT SCARES YOU?
NO.
YOU KNOW, WHEN I WAS A PROSECUTOR, I TRIED A CASE AGAINST A MAN WHO ROBBED AND MURDERED TWO TEENAGERS IN A PARK.
DURING MY CLOSING ARGUMENTS, HE JUMPED UP AND SCREAMED, "I SWEAR I'LL ESCAPE AND HUNT YOU DOWN AND CRUSH YOUR SKULL."

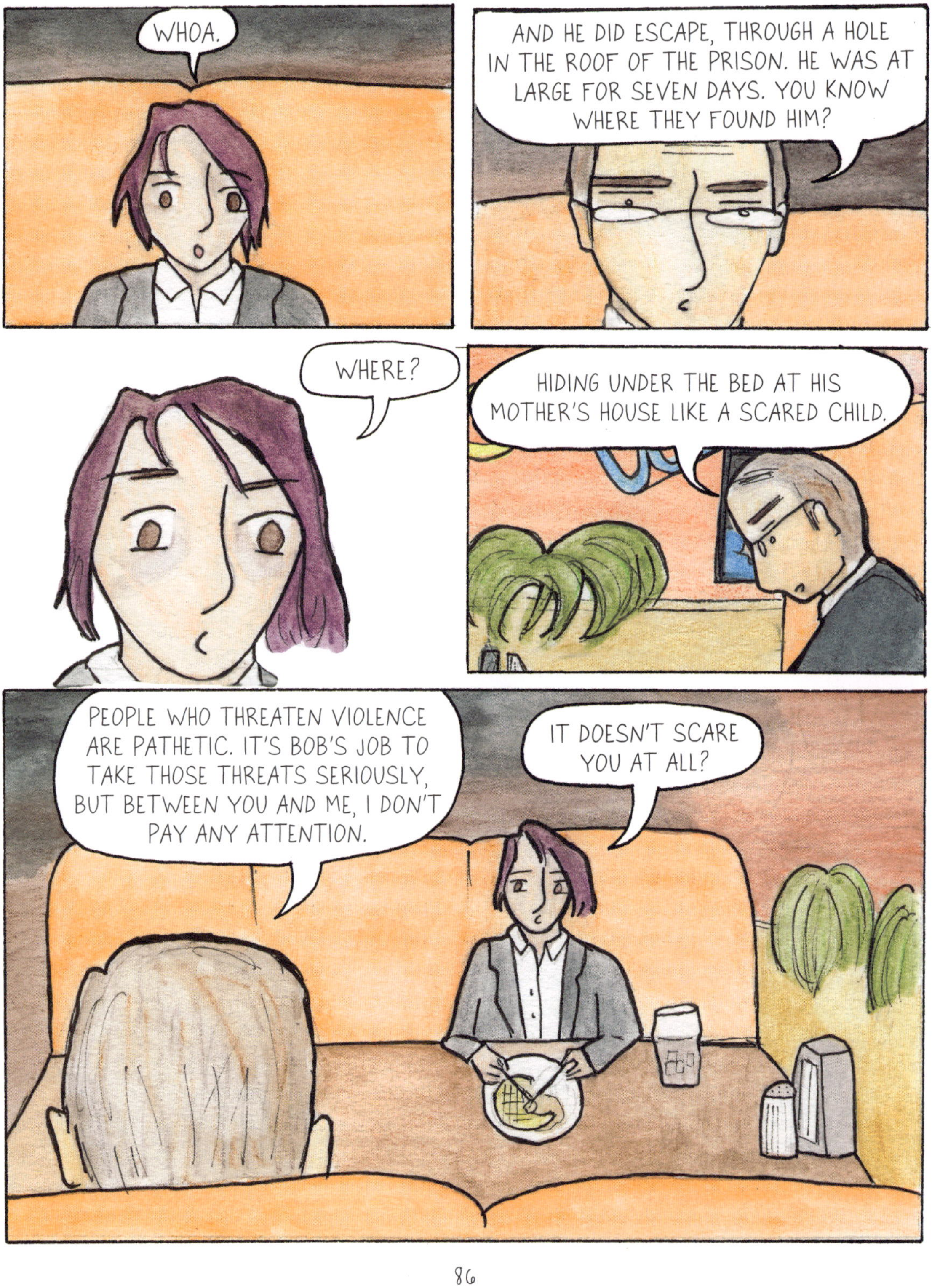
WHOA.
AND HE DID ESCAPE, THROUGH A HOLE IN THE ROOF OF THE PRISON. HE WAS AT LARGE FOR SEVEN DAYS. YOU KNOW WHERE THEY FOUND HIM?
WHERE?
HIDING UNDER THE BED AT HIS MOTHER'S HOUSE LIKE A SCARED CHILD.
PEOPLE WHO THREATEN VIOLENCE ARE PATHETIC. IT'S BOB'S JOB TO TAKE THOSE THREATS SERIOUSLY, BUT BETWEEN YOU AND ME, I DON'T PAY ANY ATTENTION.
IT DOESN'T SCARE YOU AT ALL?

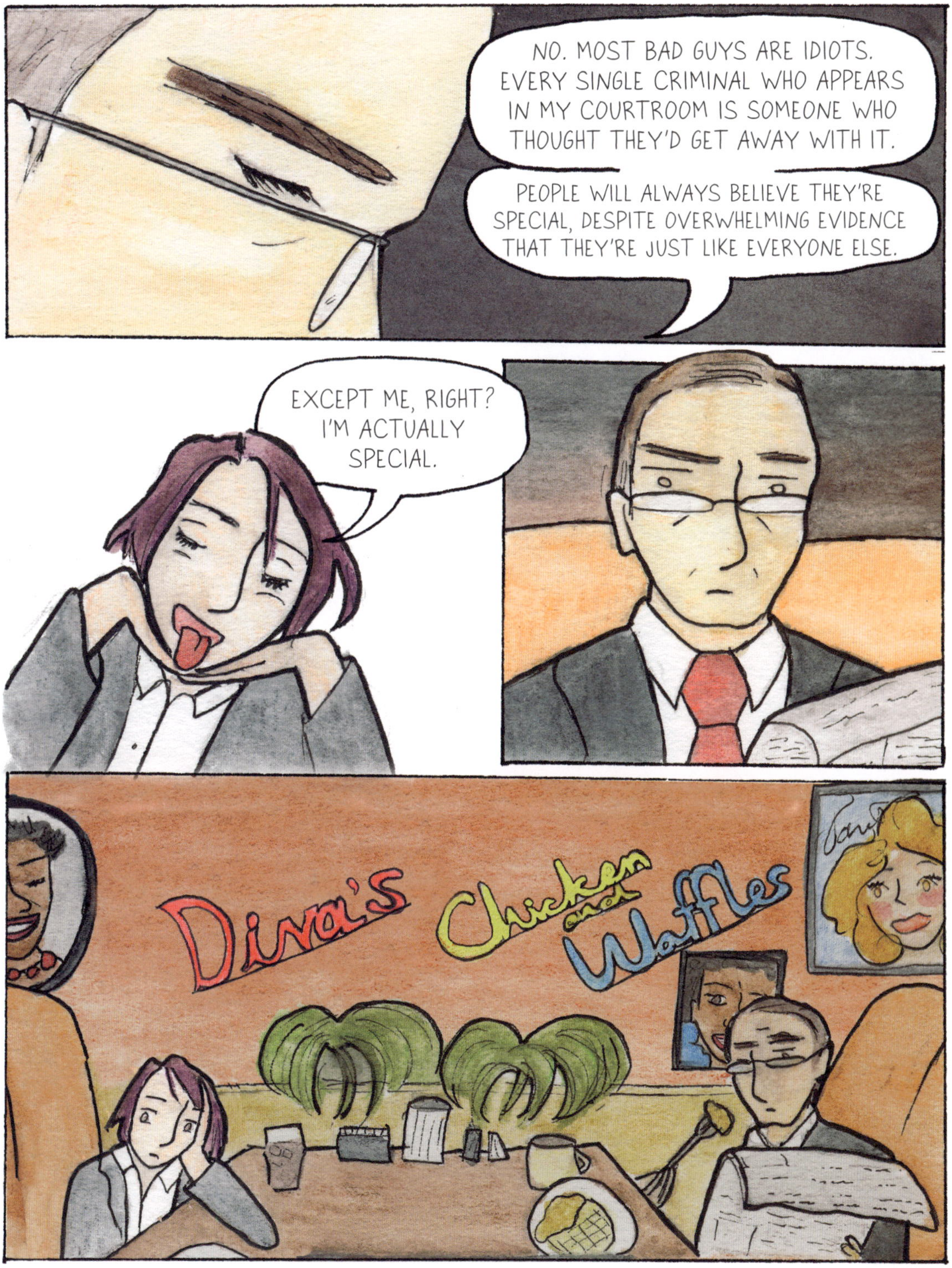
NO. MOST BAD GUYS ARE IDIOTS. EVERY SINGLE CRIMINAL WHO APPEARS IN MY COURTROOM IS SOMEONE WHO THOUGHT THEY'D GET AWAY WITH IT.
PEOPLE WILL ALWAYS BELIEVE THEY'RE SPECIAL, DESPITE OVERWHELMING EVIDENCE THAT THEY'RE JUST LIKE EVERYONE ELSE.
EXCEPT ME, RIGHT? I'M ACTUALLY SPECIAL.
Diva's Chicken and Waffles

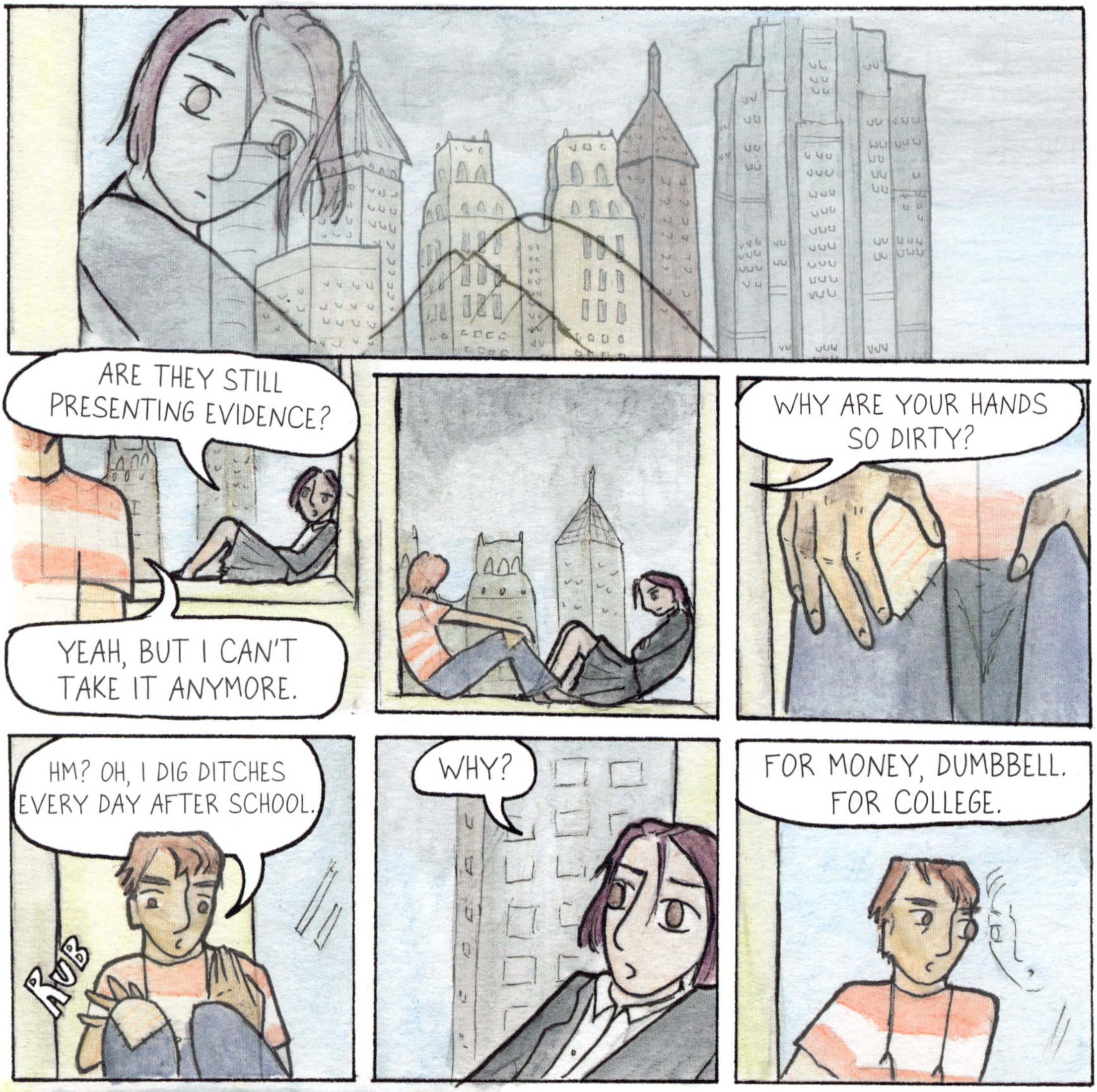
ARE THEY STILL PRESENTING EVIDENCE?
YEAH, BUT I CAN'T TAKE IT ANYMORE.
WHY ARE YOUR HANDS SO DIRTY?
HM? OH, I DIG DITCHES EVERY DAY AFTER SCHOOL.
RUB
WHY?
FOR MONEY, DUMBBELL. FOR COLLEGE.

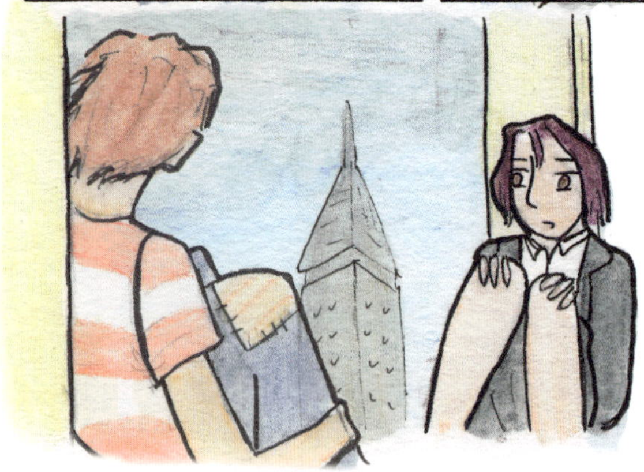

It kind of boggles my mind that there are people who literally have no money. I guess I had a dim impression that if someone was digging ditches for money, it was because they couldn't come up with a better idea. But of course it's not like I have a single idea of how to get money besides asking my dad. So if he didn't have any, I guess I'd just be lost.

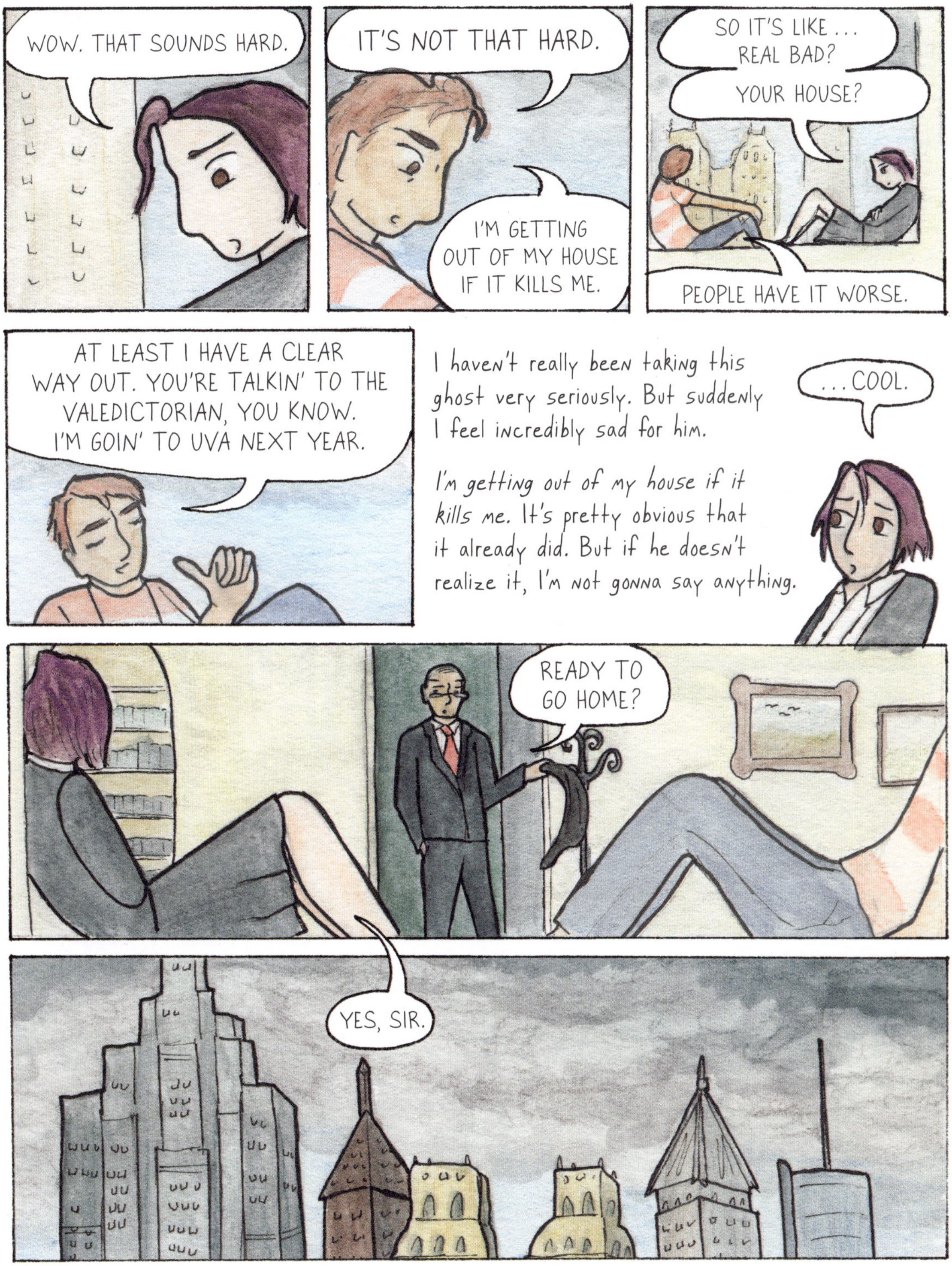
WOW. THAT SOUNDS HARD.
IT'S NOT THAT HARD.
I'M GETTING OUT OF MY HOUSE IF IT KILLS ME.
SO IT'S LIKE . . . REAL BAD?
YOUR HOUSE?
PEOPLE HAVE IT WORSE.
AT LEAST I HAVE A CLEAR WAY OUT. YOU'RE TALKIN' TO THE VALEDICTORIAN, YOU KNOW. I'M GOIN' TO UVA NEXT YEAR.
I haven't really been taking this ghost very seriously. But suddenly I feel incredibly sad for him.
I'm getting out of my house if it kills me. It's pretty obvious that it already did. But if he doesn't realize it, I'm not gonna say anything.
. . . COOL.
READY TO GO HOME?
YES, SIR.

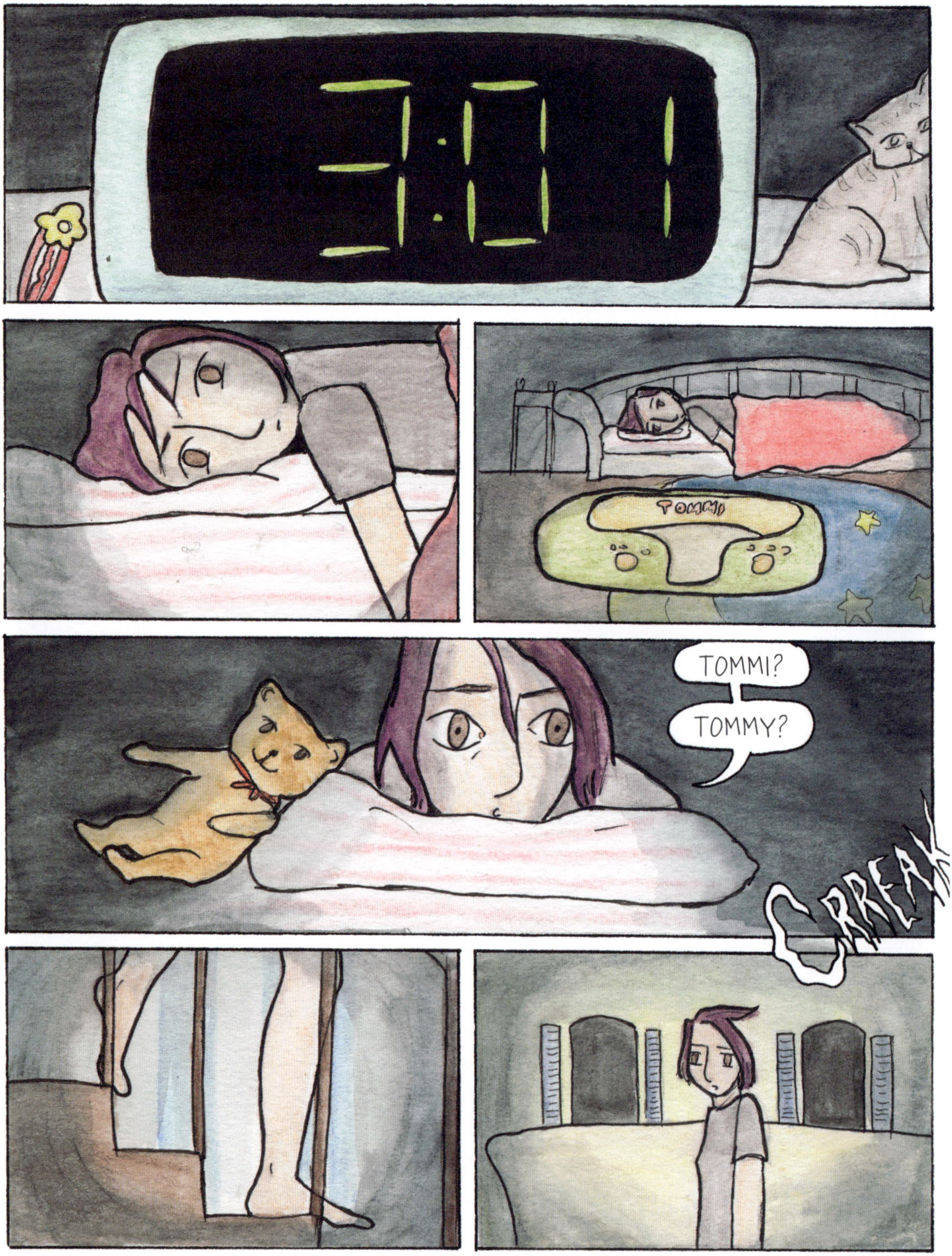
3:11
TOMMI
TOMMI?
TOMMY?
CRREAK

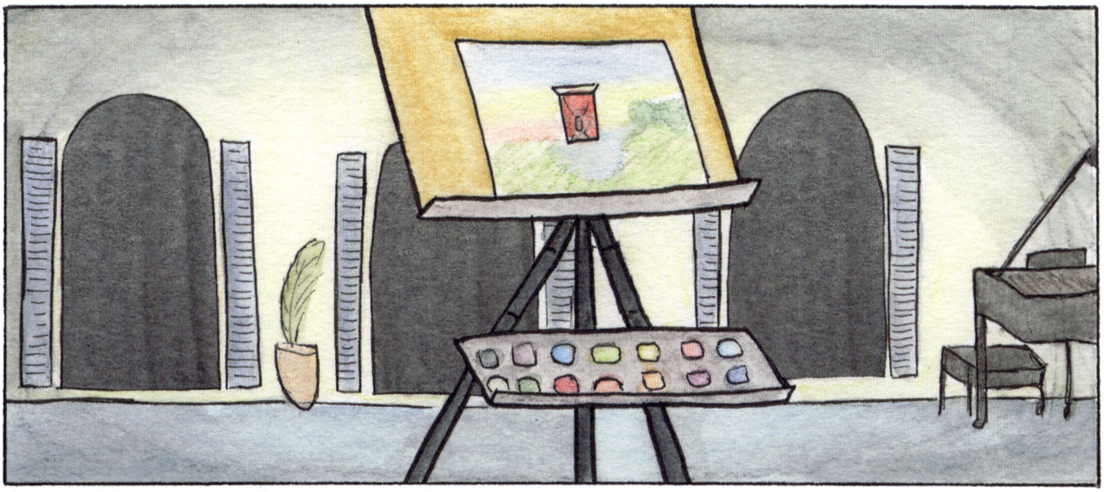

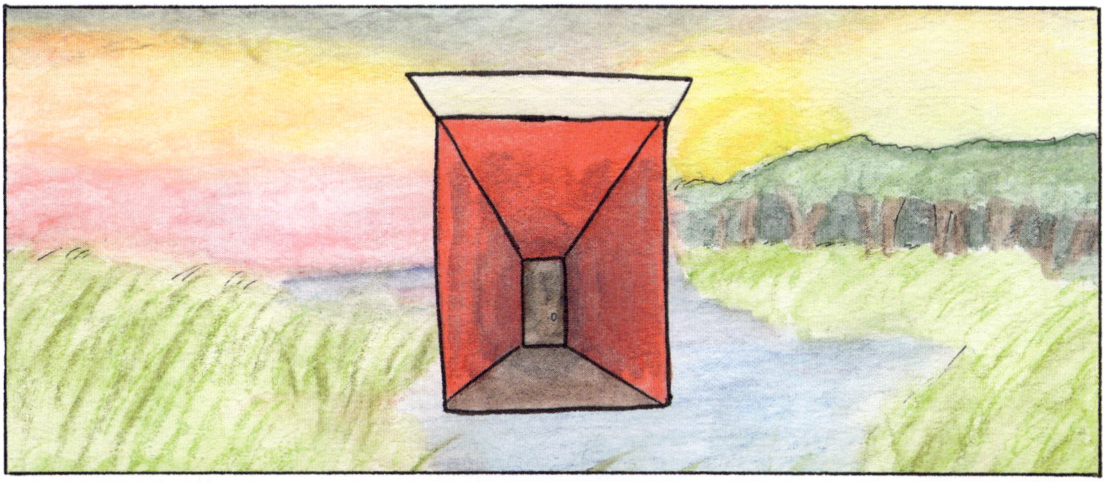

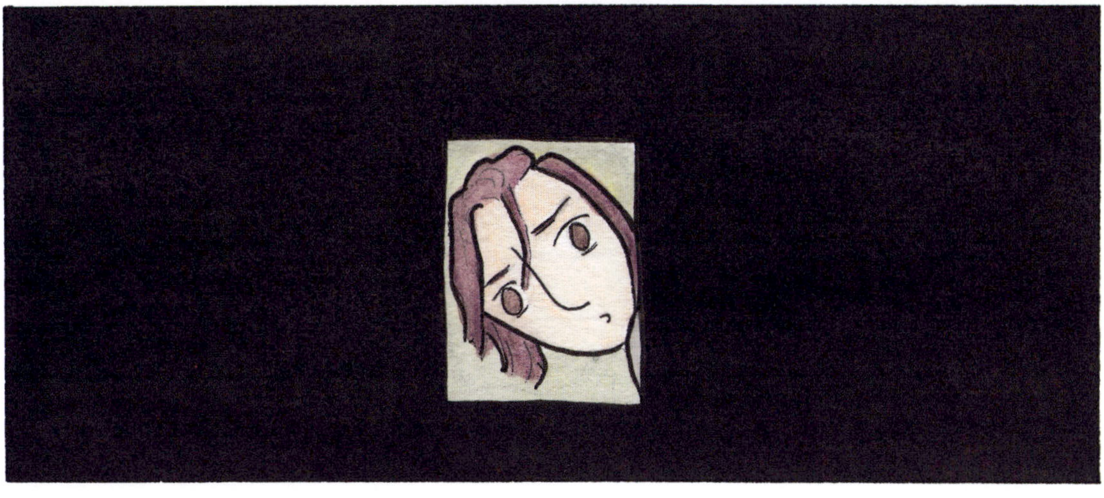

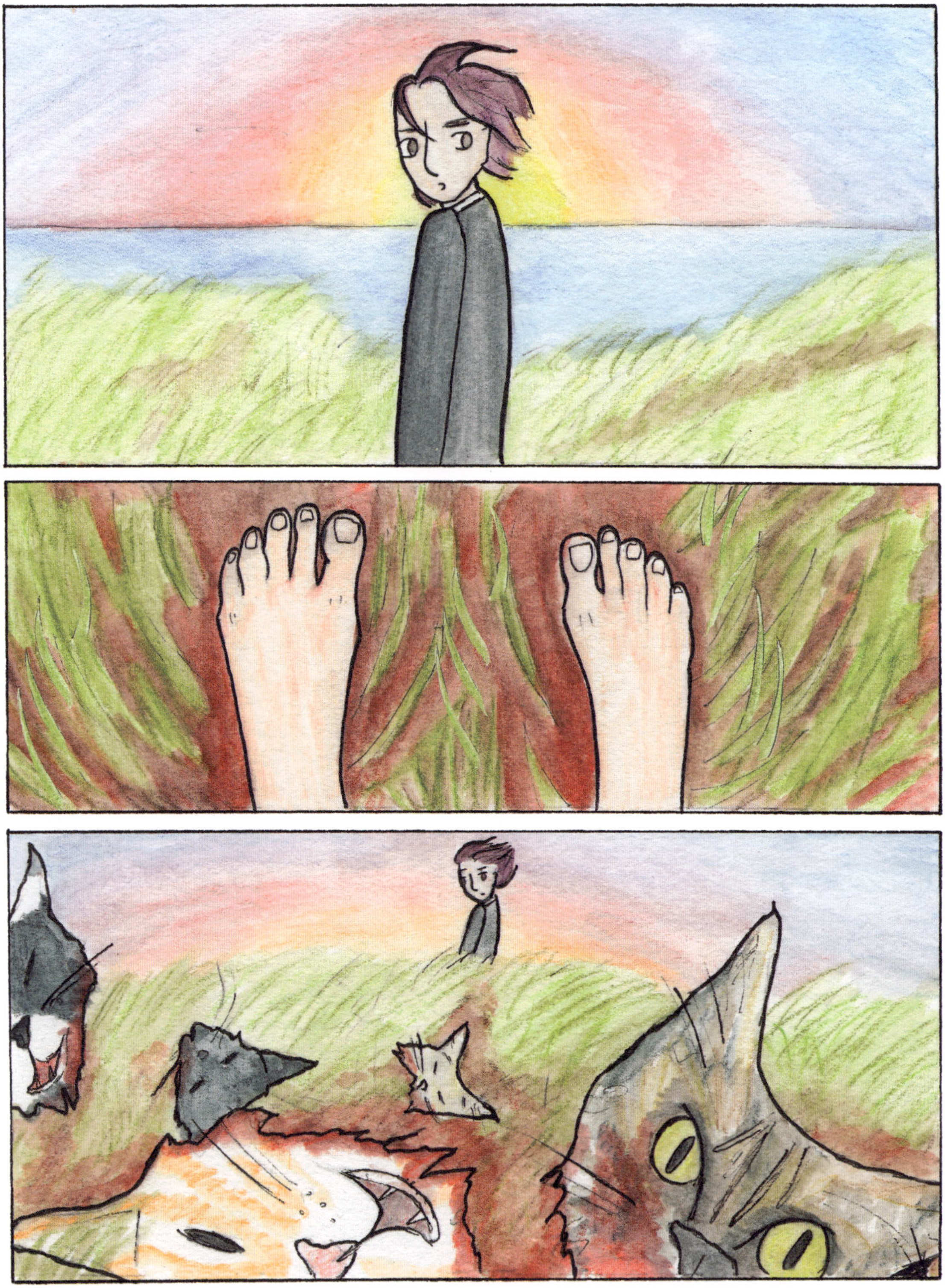

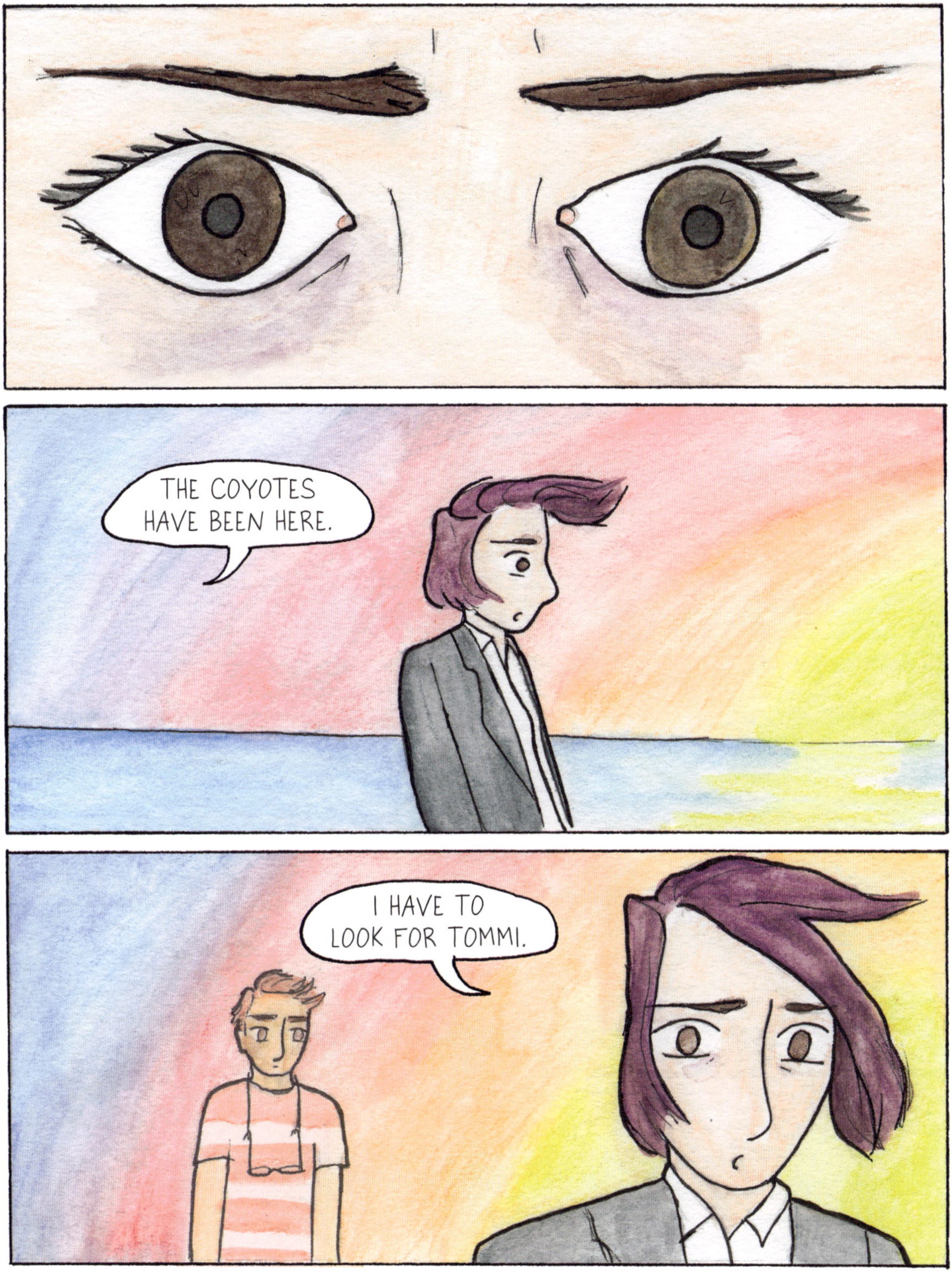
THE COYOTES HAVE BEEN HERE.
I HAVE TO LOOK FOR TOMMI.

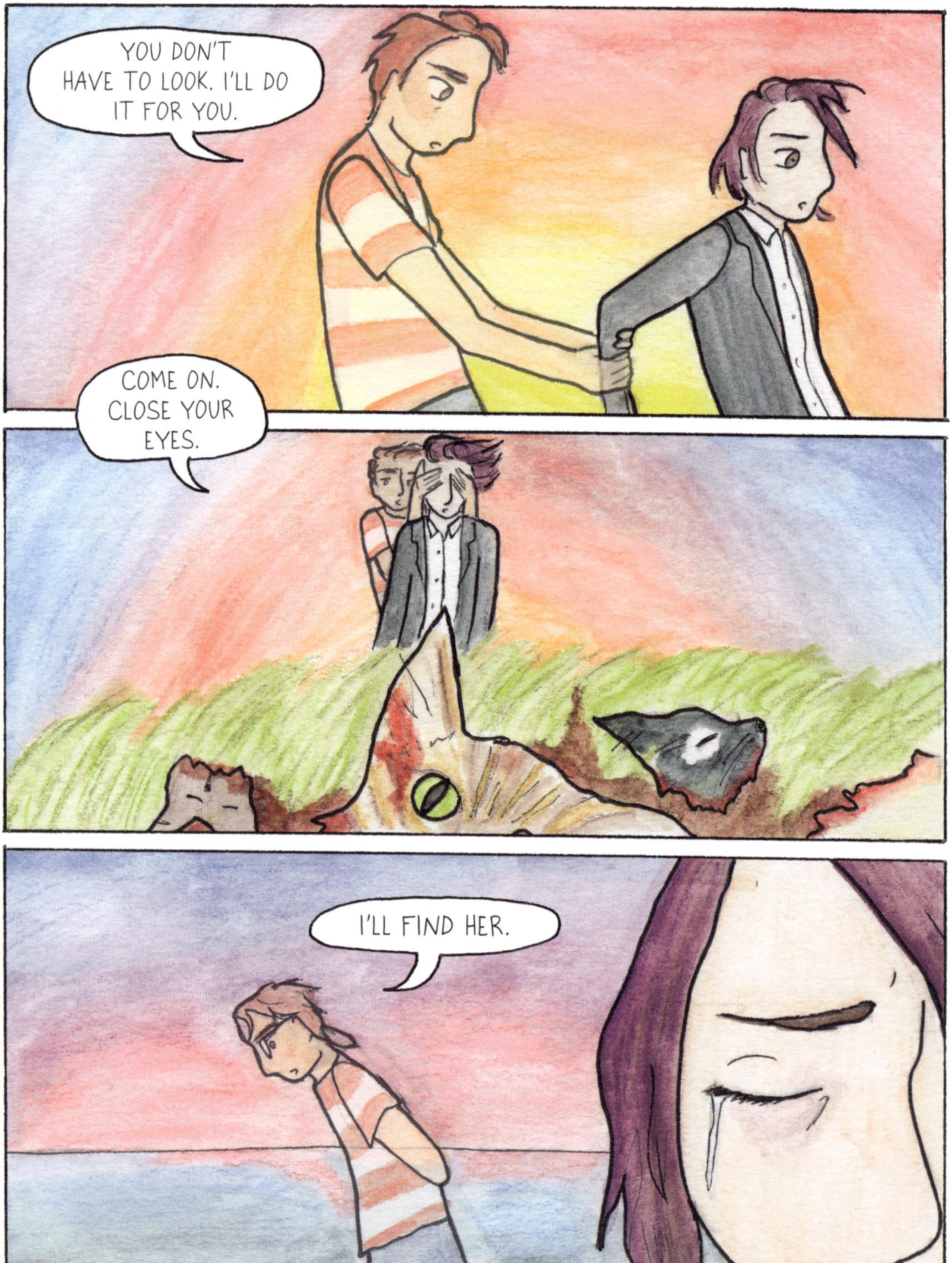
YOU DON'T HAVE TO LOOK. I'LL DO IT FOR YOU.
COME ON. CLOSE YOUR EYES.
I'LL FIND HER.

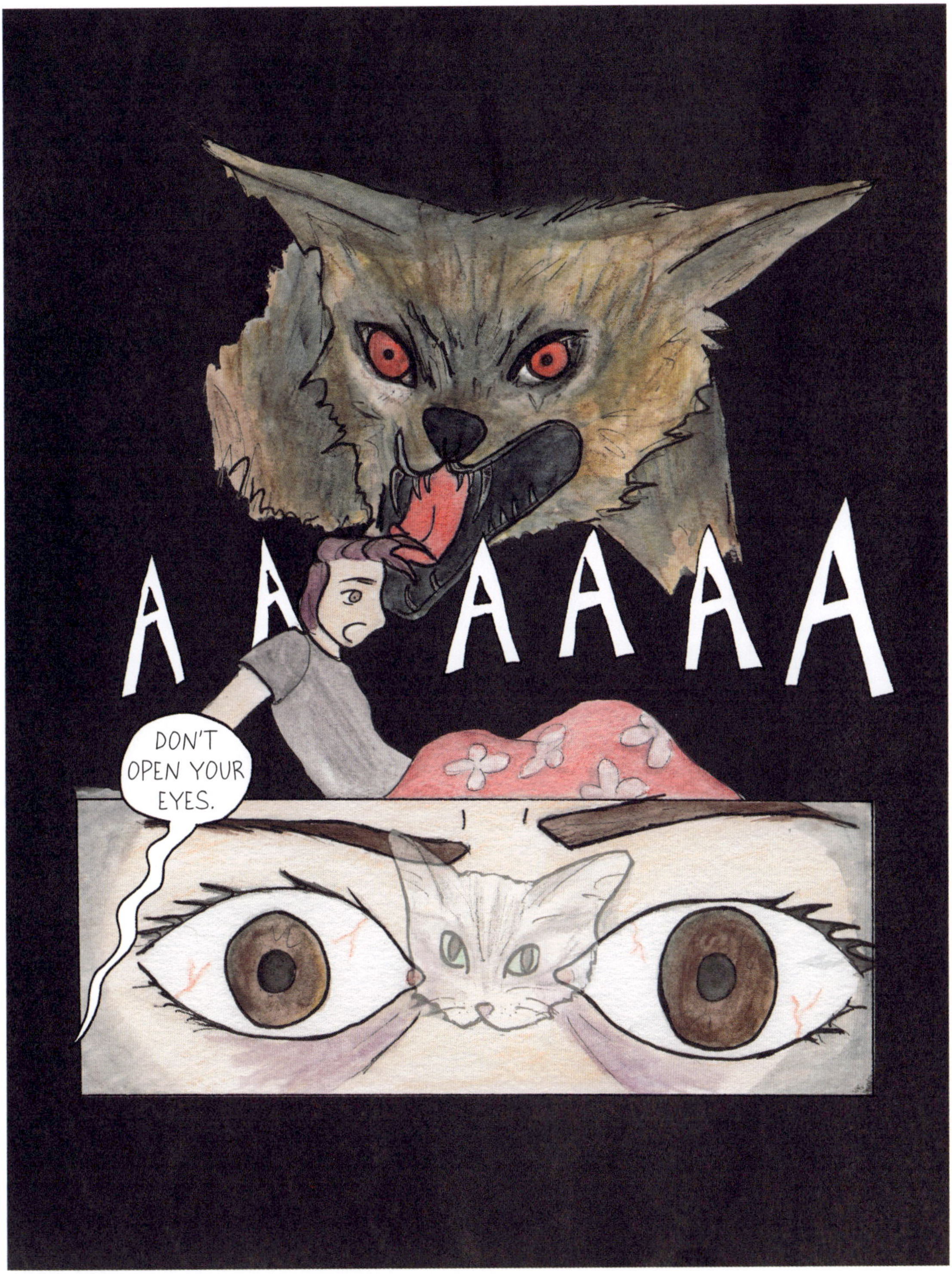
AAAAAA
DON'T OPEN YOUR EYES.

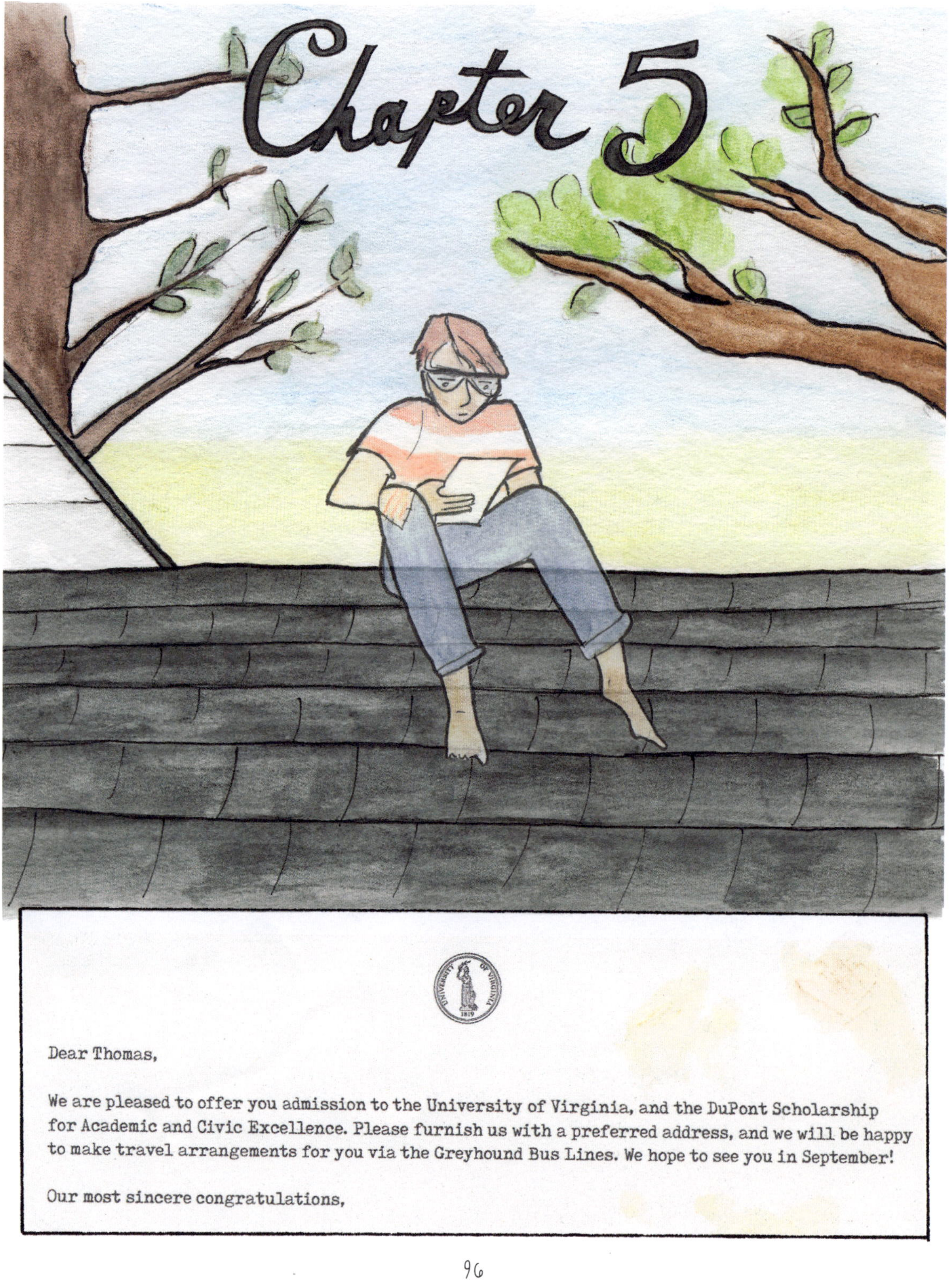
Chapter 5

Dear Thomas,

We are pleased to offer you admission to the University of Virginia, and the DuPont Scholarship for Academic and Civic Excellence. Please furnish us with a preferred address, and we will be happy to make travel arrangements for you via the Greyhound Bus Lines. We hope to see you in September!

Our most sincere congratulations,

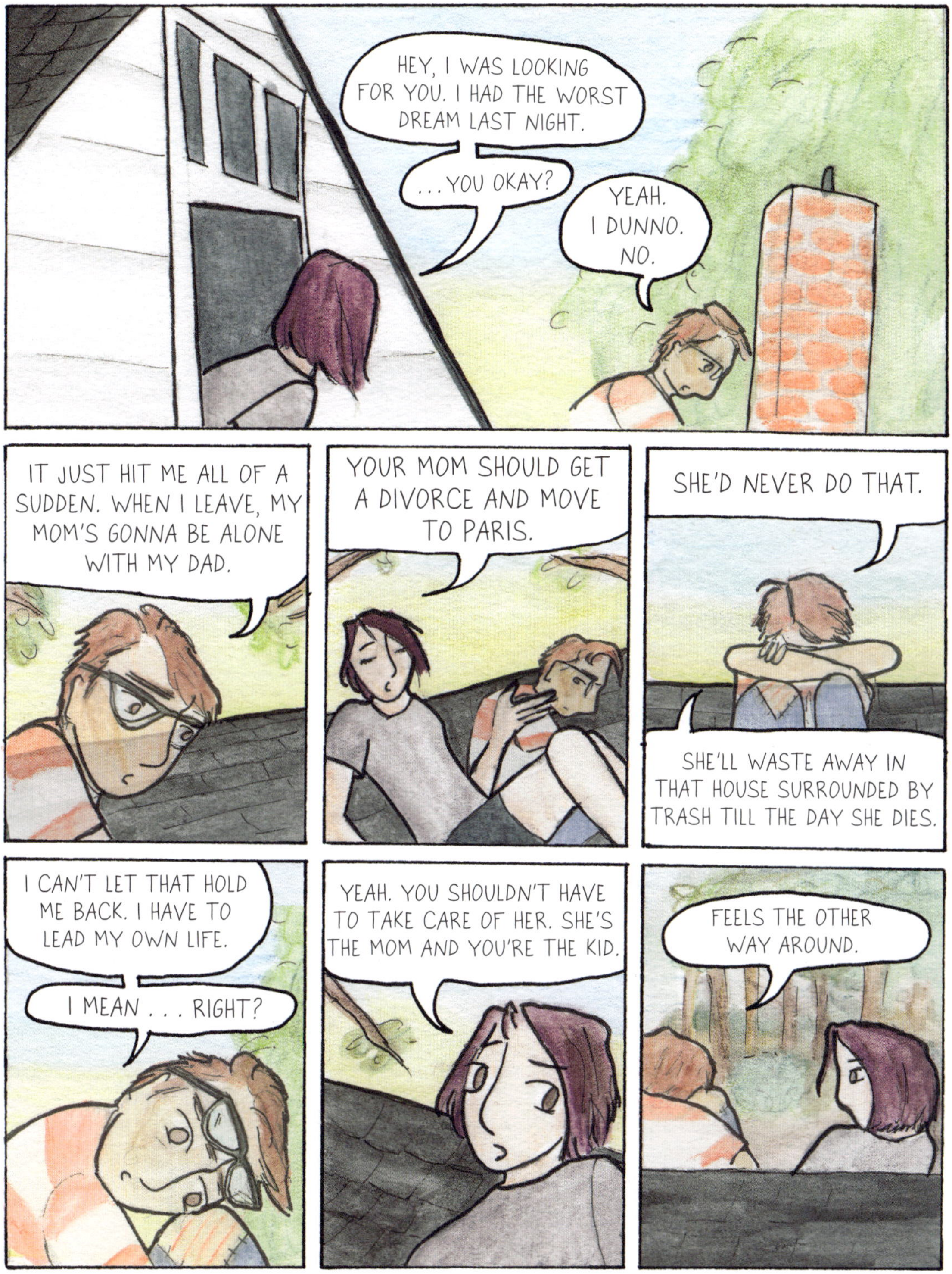
HEY, I WAS LOOKING FOR YOU. I HAD THE WORST DREAM LAST NIGHT.
. . . YOU OKAY?
YEAH. I DUNNO. NO.
IT JUST HIT ME ALL OF A SUDDEN. WHEN I LEAVE, MY MOM'S GONNA BE ALONE WITH MY DAD.
YOUR MOM SHOULD GET A DIVORCE AND MOVE TO PARIS.
SHE'D NEVER DO THAT.
SHE'LL WASTE AWAY IN THAT HOUSE SURROUNDED BY TRASH TILL THE DAY SHE DIES.
I CAN'T LET THAT HOLD ME BACK. I HAVE TO LEAD MY OWN LIFE.
I MEAN . . . RIGHT?
YEAH. YOU SHOULDN'T HAVE TO TAKE CARE OF HER. SHE'S THE MOM AND YOU'RE THE KID.
FEELS THE OTHER WAY AROUND.

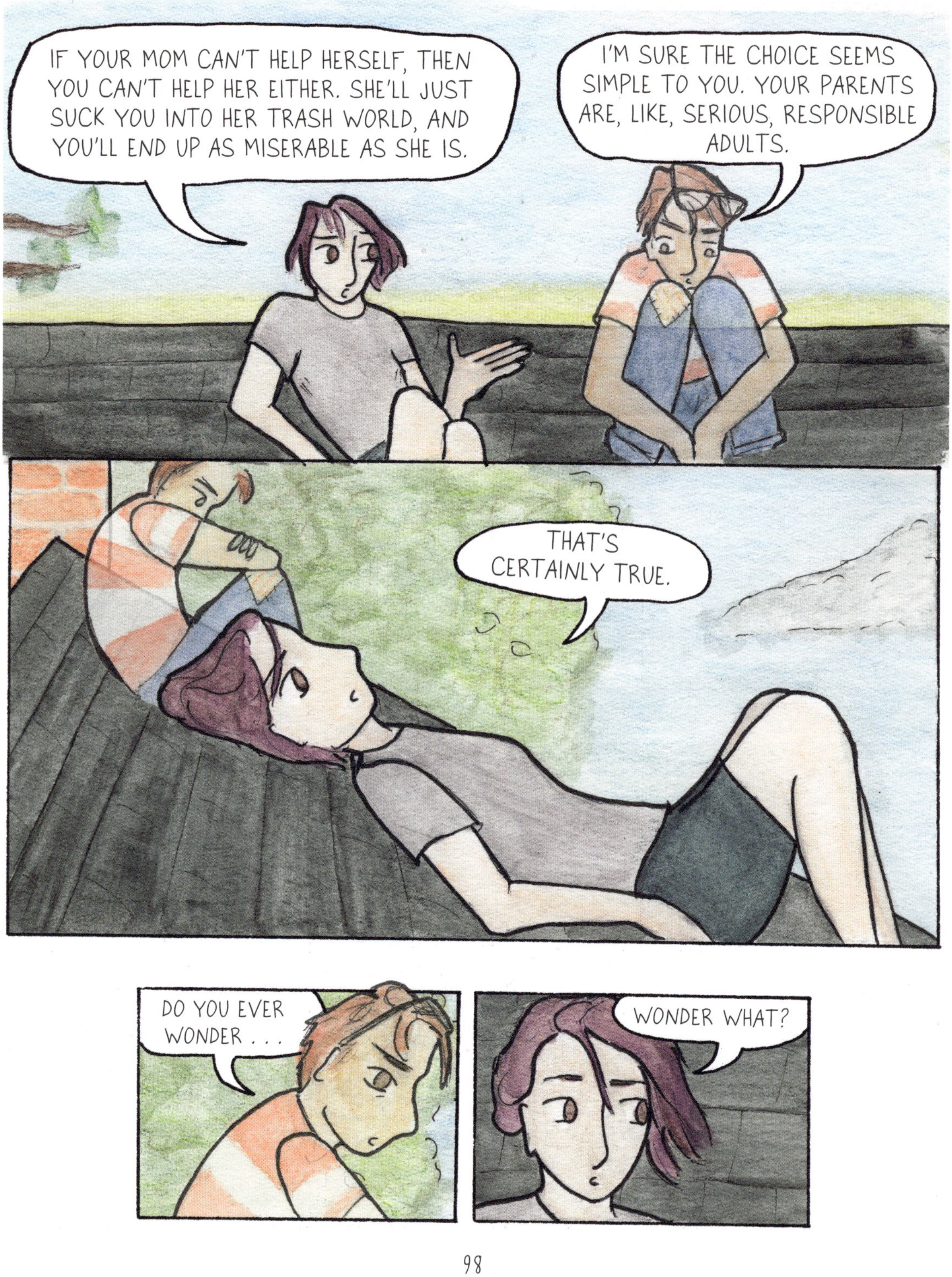
IF YOUR MOM CAN'T HELP HERSELF, THEN YOU CAN'T HELP HER EITHER. SHE'LL JUST SUCK YOU INTO HER TRASH WORLD, AND YOU'LL END UP AS MISERABLE AS SHE IS.
I'M SURE THE CHOICE SEEMS SIMPLE TO YOU. YOUR PARENTS ARE, LIKE, SERIOUS, RESPONSIBLE ADULTS.
THAT'S CERTAINLY TRUE.
DO YOU EVER WONDER . . .
WONDER WHAT?

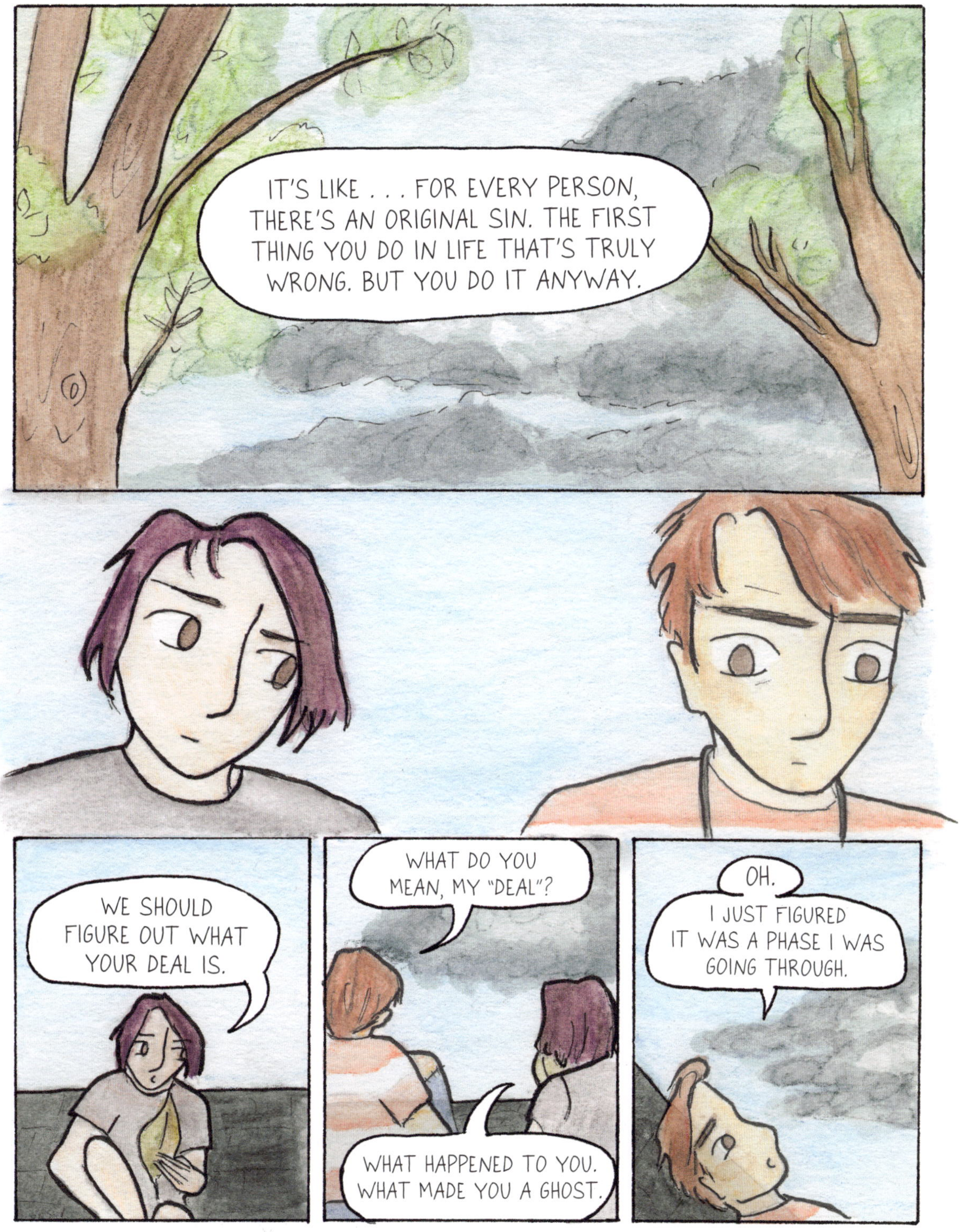
IT'S LIKE . . . FOR EVERY PERSON, THERE'S AN ORIGINAL SIN. THE FIRST THING YOU DO IN LIFE THAT'S TRULY WRONG. BUT YOU DO IT ANYWAY.
WE SHOULD FIGURE OUT WHAT YOUR DEAL IS.
WHAT DO YOU MEAN, MY "DEAL"?
WHAT HAPPENED TO YOU. WHAT MADE YOU A GHOST.
OH.
I JUST FIGURED IT WAS A PHASE I WAS GOING THROUGH.

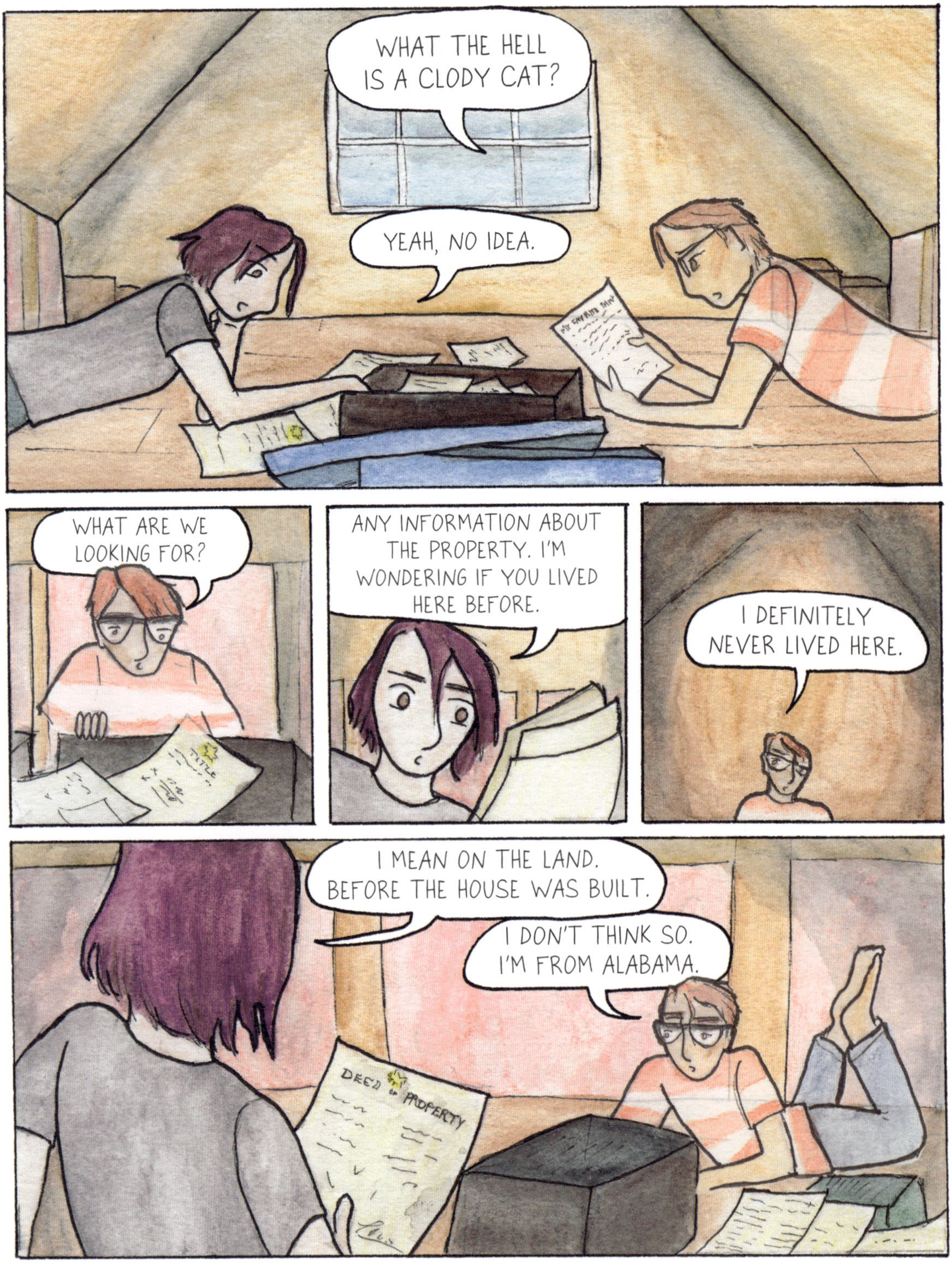
WHAT THE HELL IS A CLODY CAT?
YEAH, NO IDEA.
WHAT ARE WE LOOKING FOR?
ANY INFORMATION ABOUT THE PROPERTY. I'M WONDERING IF YOU LIVED HERE BEFORE.
I DEFINITELY NEVER LIVED HERE.
I MEAN ON THE LAND. BEFORE THE HOUSE WAS BUILT.
I DON'T THINK SO. I'M FROM ALABAMA.
DEED OF PROPERTY

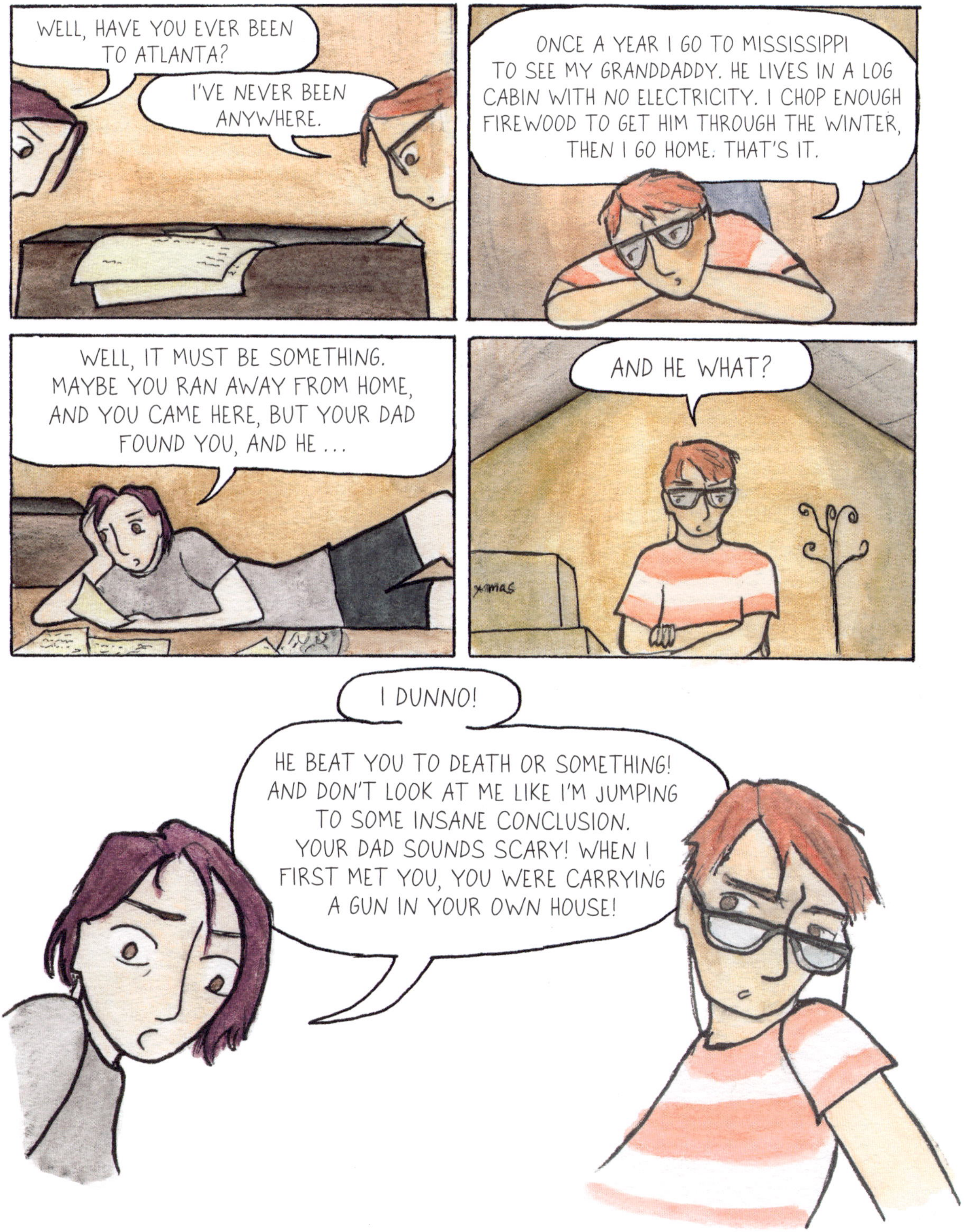
WELL, HAVE YOU EVER BEEN TO ATLANTA?
I'VE NEVER BEEN ANYWHERE.
ONCE A YEAR I GO TO MISSISSIPPI TO SEE MY GRANDDADDY. HE LIVES IN A LOG CABIN WITH NO ELECTRICITY. I CHOP ENOUGH FIREWOOD TO GET HIM THROUGH THE WINTER, THEN I GO HOME. THAT'S IT.
WELL, IT MUST BE SOMETHING. MAYBE YOU RAN AWAY FROM HOME, AND YOU CAME HERE, BUT YOUR DAD FOUND YOU, AND HE . . .
AND HE WHAT?
xmas
I DUNNO!
HE BEAT YOU TO DEATH OR SOMETHING! AND DON'T LOOK AT ME LIKE I'M JUMPING TO SOME INSANE CONCLUSION. YOUR DAD SOUNDS SCARY! WHEN I FIRST MET YOU, YOU WERE CARRYING A GUN IN YOUR OWN HOUSE!

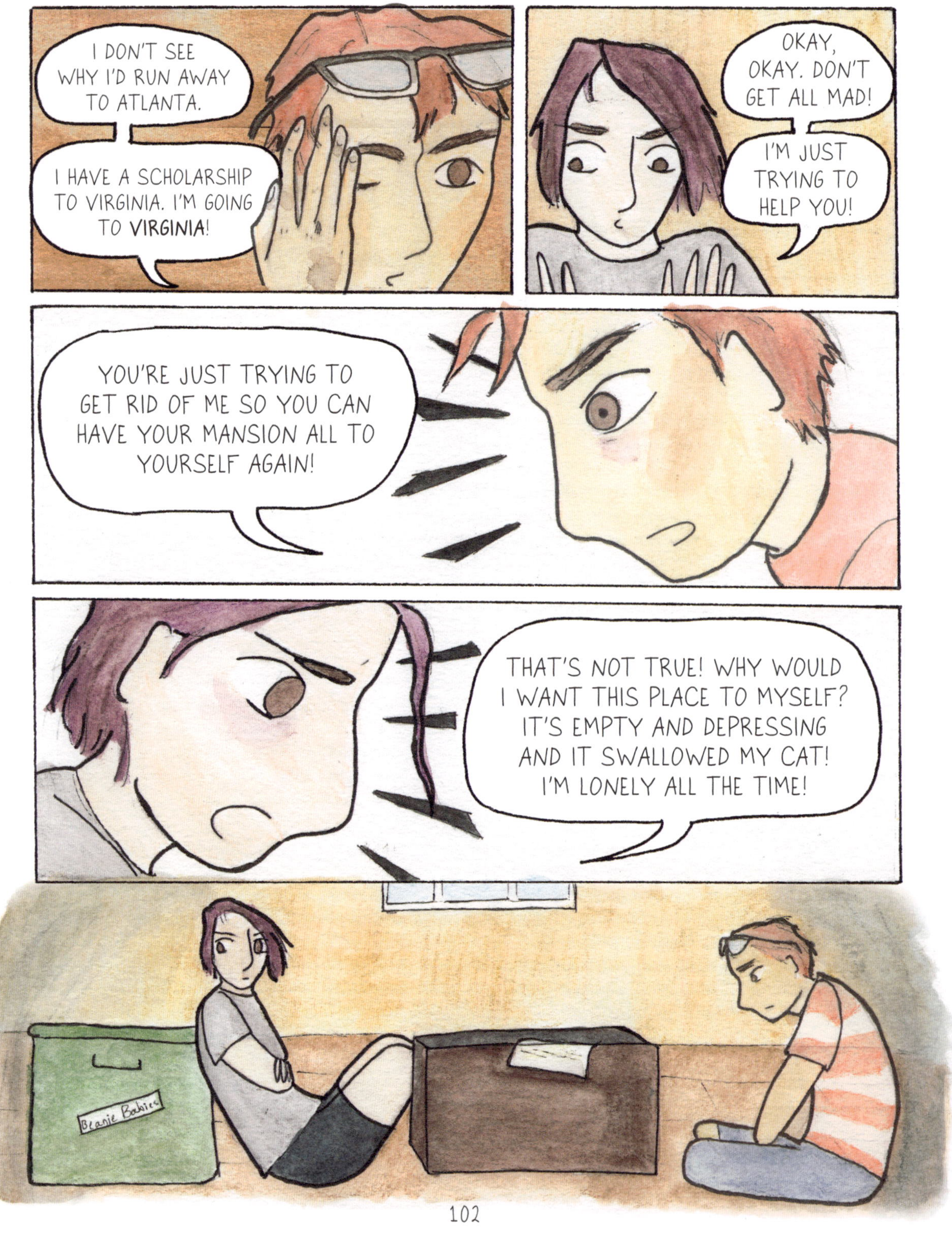
I DON'T SEE WHY I'D RUN AWAY TO ATLANTA.
I HAVE A SCHOLARSHIP TO VIRGINIA. I'M GOING TO **VIRGINIA**!
OKAY, OKAY. DON'T GET ALL MAD!
I'M JUST TRYING TO HELP YOU!
YOU'RE JUST TRYING TO GET RID OF ME SO YOU CAN HAVE YOUR MANSION ALL TO YOURSELF AGAIN!
THAT'S NOT TRUE! WHY WOULD I WANT THIS PLACE TO MYSELF? IT'S EMPTY AND DEPRESSING AND IT SWALLOWED MY CAT! I'M LONELY ALL THE TIME!
Beanie Babies

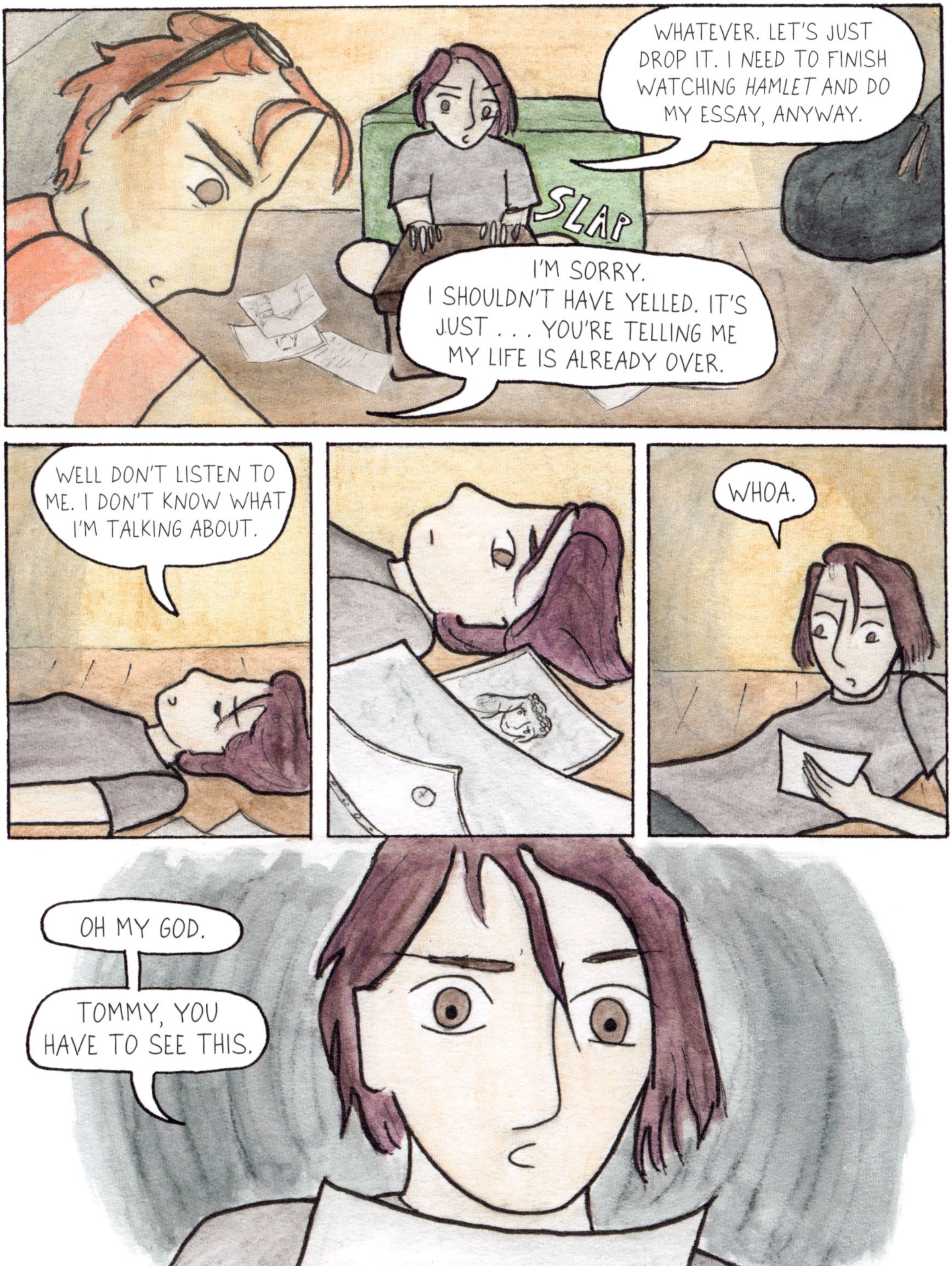
WHATEVER. LET'S JUST DROP IT. I NEED TO FINISH WATCHING *HAMLET* AND DO MY ESSAY, ANYWAY.
SLAP
I'M SORRY. I SHOULDN'T HAVE YELLED. IT'S JUST . . . YOU'RE TELLING ME MY LIFE IS ALREADY OVER.
WELL DON'T LISTEN TO ME. I DON'T KNOW WHAT I'M TALKING ABOUT.
WHOA.
OH MY GOD.
TOMMY, YOU HAVE TO SEE THIS.

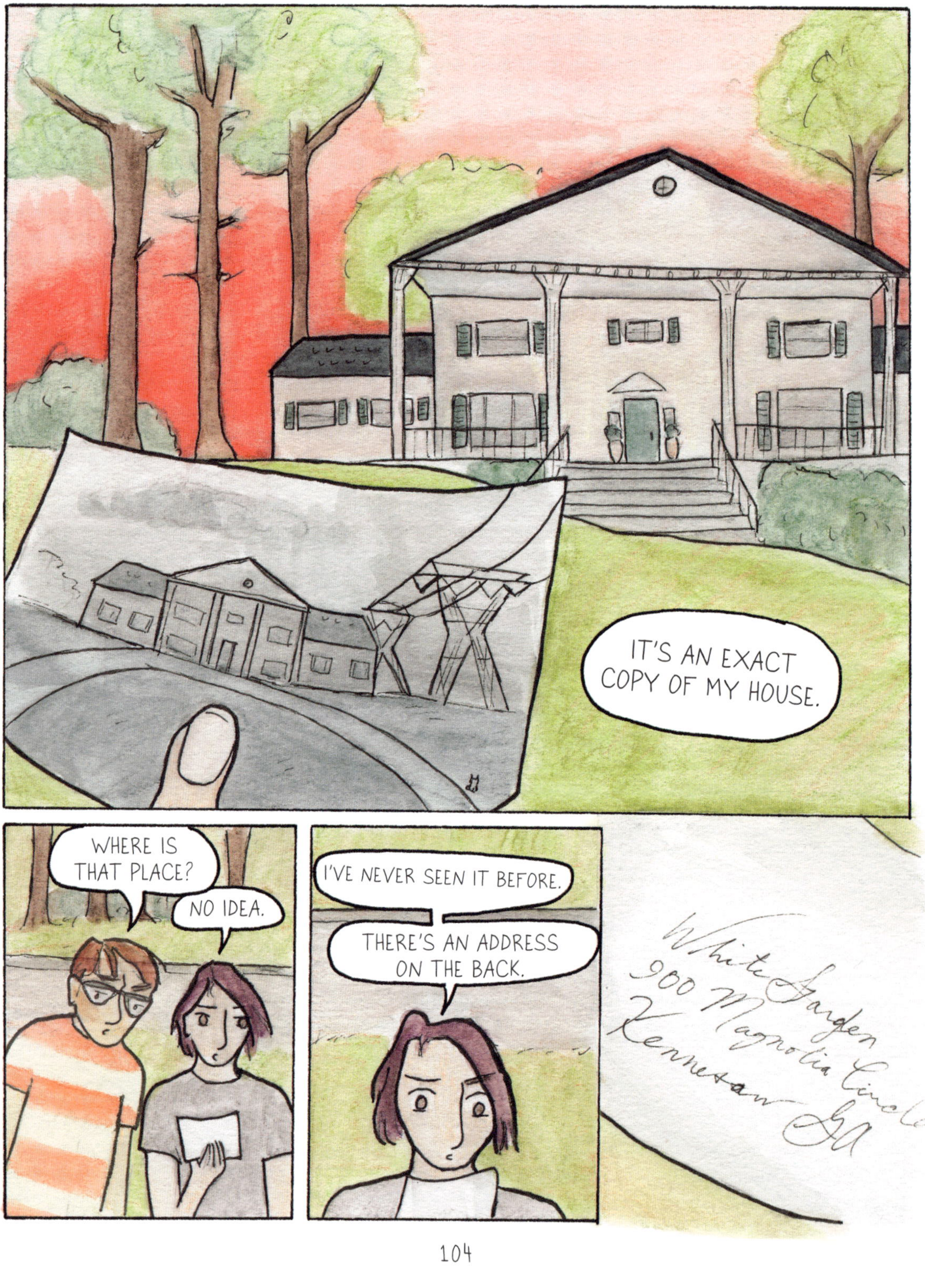
IT'S AN EXACT COPY OF MY HOUSE.
WHERE IS THAT PLACE?
NO IDEA.
I'VE NEVER SEEN IT BEFORE.
THERE'S AN ADDRESS ON THE BACK.
White Garden
900 Magnolia Circl
Kennesaw GA

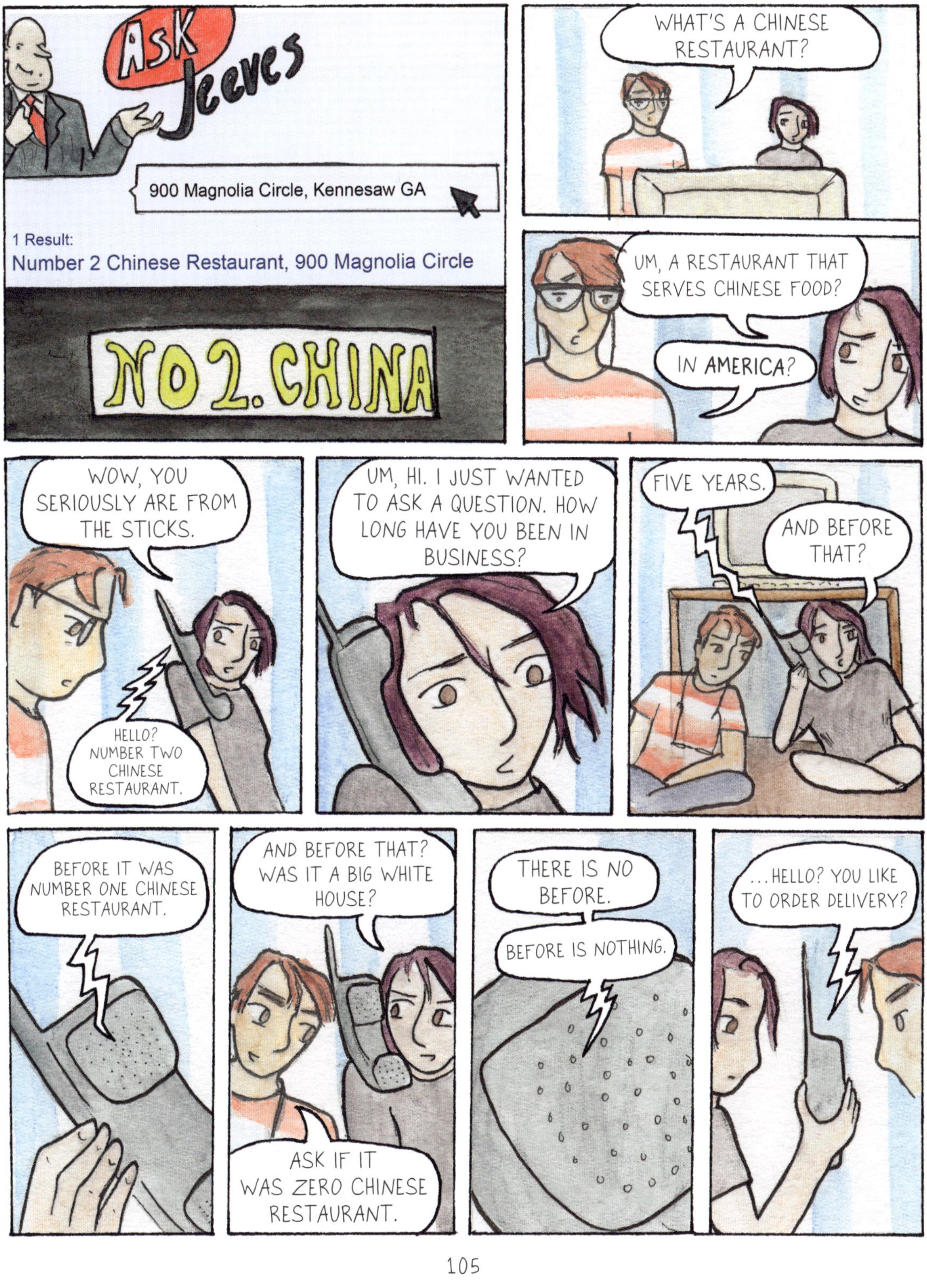
Ask Jeeves
900 Magnolia Circle, Kennesaw GA
1 Result:
Number 2 Chinese Restaurant, 900 Magnolia Circle
NO 2. CHINA
WHAT'S A CHINESE RESTAURANT?
UM, A RESTAURANT THAT SERVES CHINESE FOOD?
IN AMERICA?
WOW, YOU SERIOUSLY ARE FROM THE STICKS.
HELLO? NUMBER TWO CHINESE RESTAURANT.
UM, HI. I JUST WANTED TO ASK A QUESTION. HOW LONG HAVE YOU BEEN IN BUSINESS?
FIVE YEARS.
AND BEFORE THAT?
BEFORE IT WAS NUMBER ONE CHINESE RESTAURANT.
AND BEFORE THAT? WAS IT A BIG WHITE HOUSE?
ASK IF IT WAS ZERO CHINESE RESTAURANT.
THERE IS NO BEFORE.
BEFORE IS NOTHING.
...HELLO? YOU LIKE TO ORDER DELIVERY?

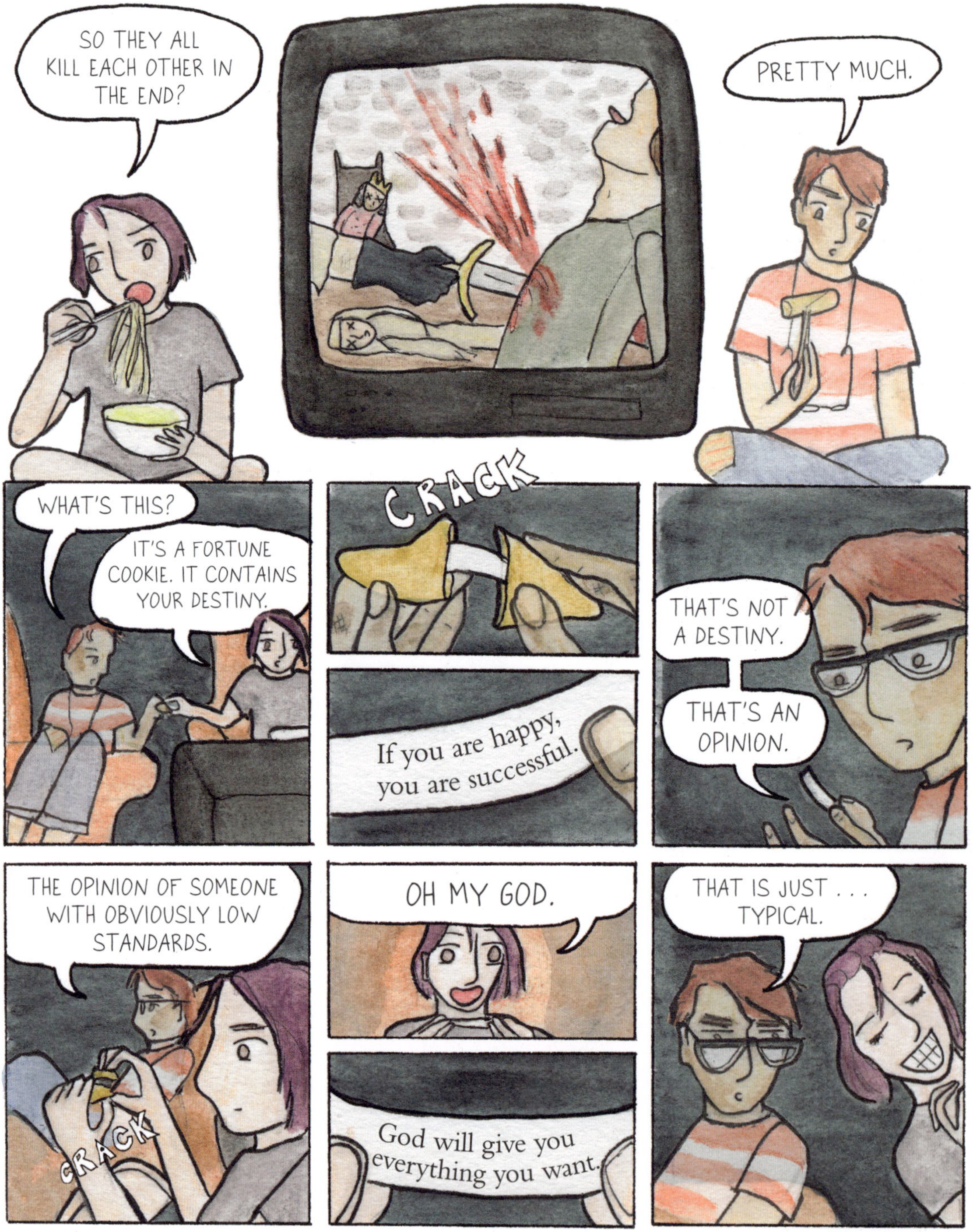
SO THEY ALL KILL EACH OTHER IN THE END?
PRETTY MUCH.
WHAT'S THIS?
IT'S A FORTUNE COOKIE. IT CONTAINS YOUR DESTINY.
CRACK
If you are happy, you are successful.
THAT'S NOT A DESTINY.
THAT'S AN OPINION.
THE OPINION OF SOMEONE WITH OBVIOUSLY LOW STANDARDS.
CRACK
OH MY GOD.
God will give you everything you want.
THAT IS JUST . . . TYPICAL.

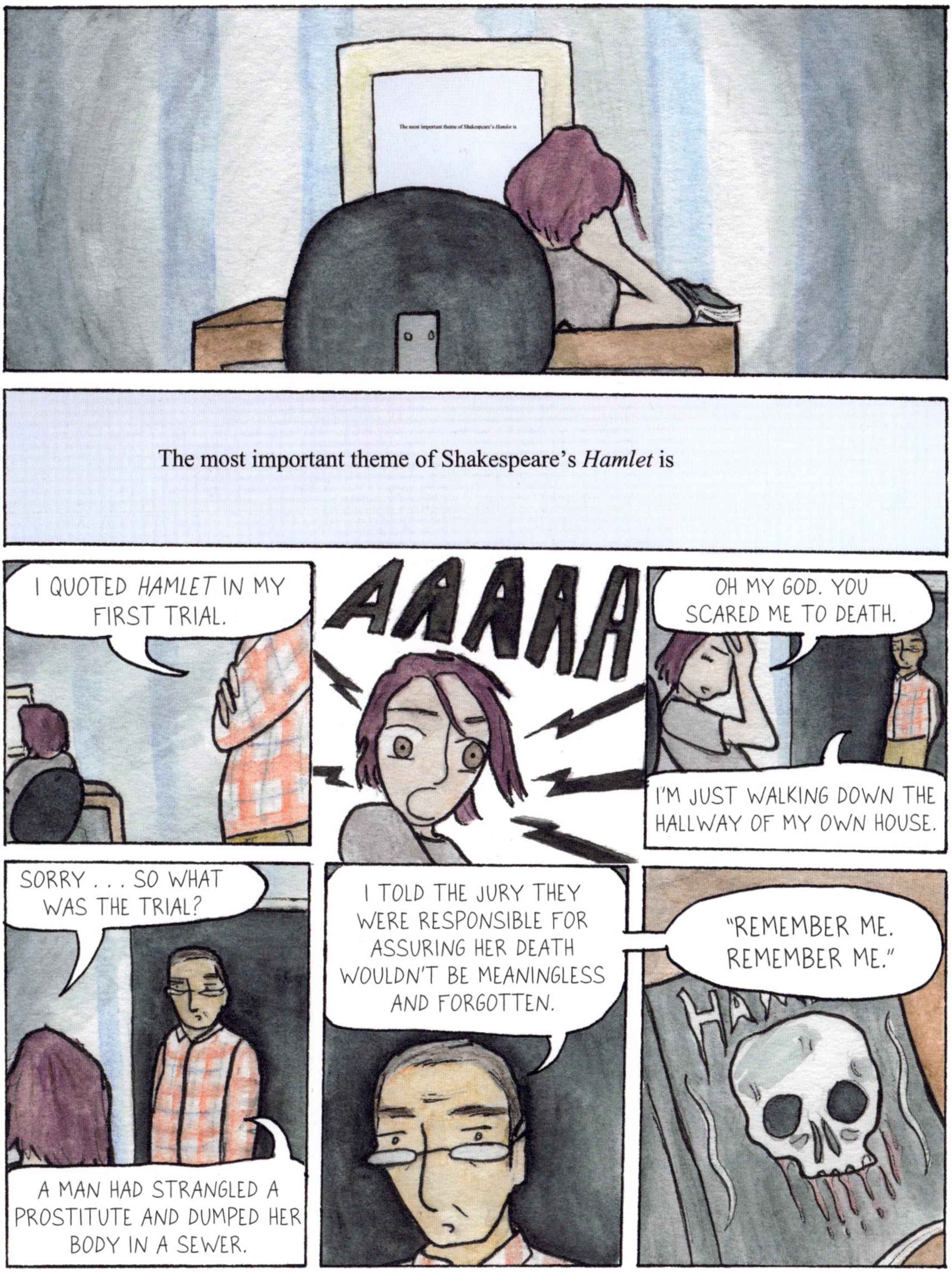
The most important theme of Shakespeare's *Hamlet* is
The most important theme of Shakespeare's *Hamlet* is
I QUOTED *HAMLET* IN MY FIRST TRIAL.
AAAAA
OH MY GOD. YOU SCARED ME TO DEATH.
I'M JUST WALKING DOWN THE HALLWAY OF MY OWN HOUSE.
SORRY . . . SO WHAT WAS THE TRIAL?
A MAN HAD STRANGLED A PROSTITUTE AND DUMPED HER BODY IN A SEWER.
I TOLD THE JURY THEY WERE RESPONSIBLE FOR ASSURING HER DEATH WOULDN'T BE MEANINGLESS AND FORGOTTEN.
"REMEMBER ME. REMEMBER ME."

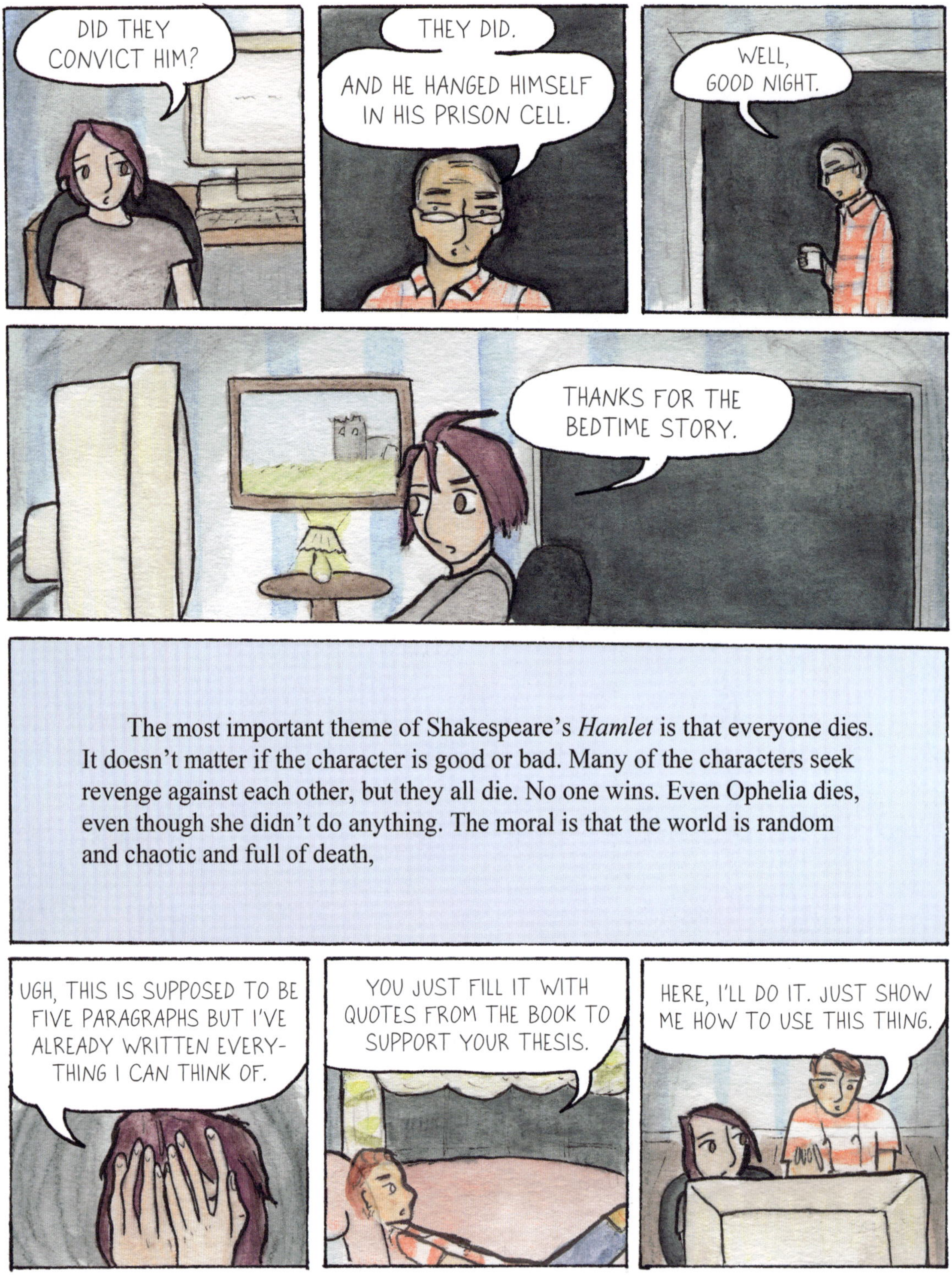
DID THEY CONVICT HIM?
THEY DID.
AND HE HANGED HIMSELF IN HIS PRISON CELL.
WELL, GOOD NIGHT.
THANKS FOR THE BEDTIME STORY.
The most important theme of Shakespeare's *Hamlet* is that everyone dies. It doesn't matter if the character is good or bad. Many of the characters seek revenge against each other, but they all die. No one wins. Even Ophelia dies, even though she didn't do anything. The moral is that the world is random and chaotic and full of death,
UGH, THIS IS SUPPOSED TO BE FIVE PARAGRAPHS BUT I'VE ALREADY WRITTEN EVERY-THING I CAN THINK OF.
YOU JUST FILL IT WITH QUOTES FROM THE BOOK TO SUPPORT YOUR THESIS.
HERE, I'LL DO IT. JUST SHOW ME HOW TO USE THIS THING.

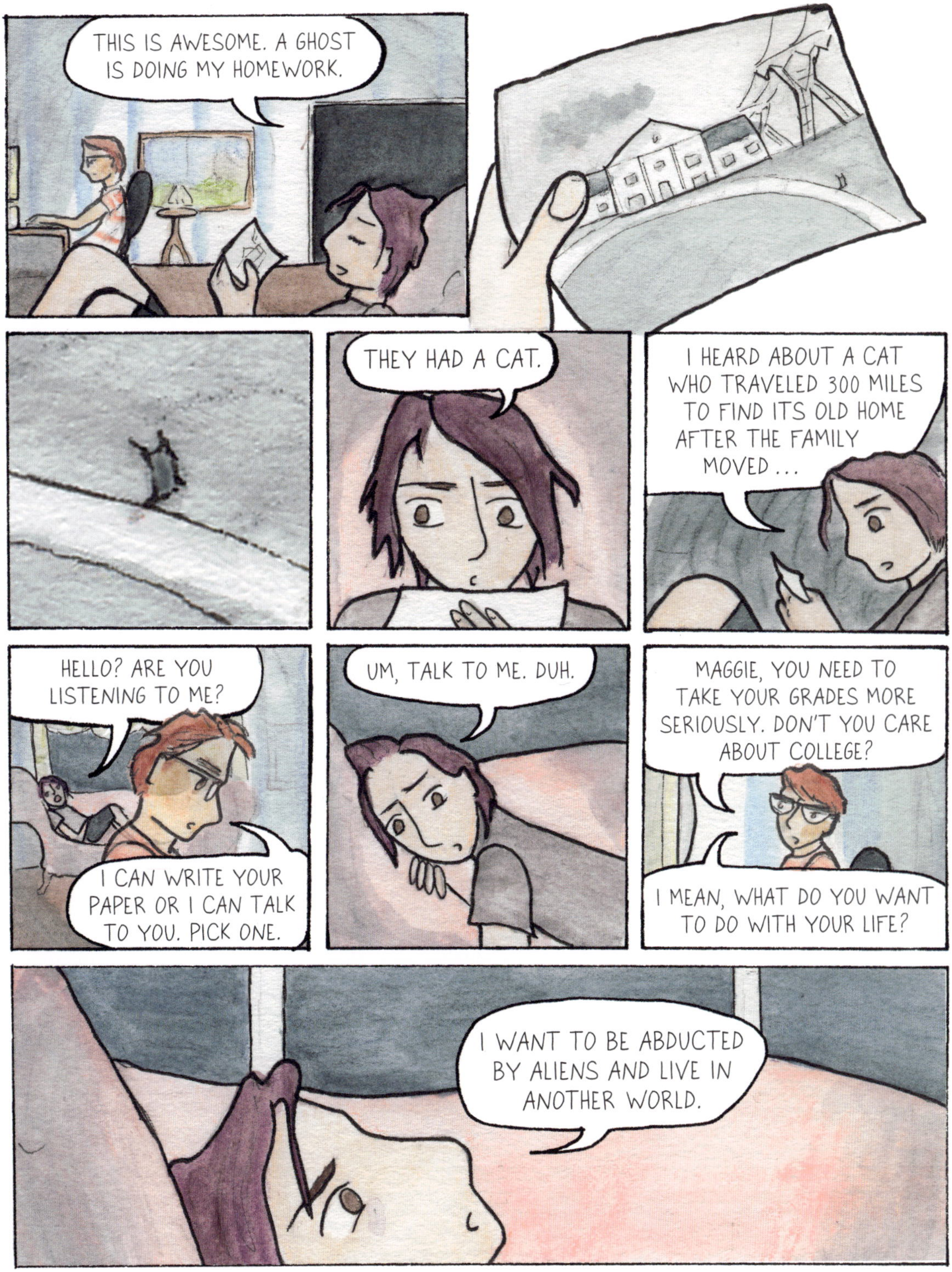
THIS IS AWESOME. A GHOST IS DOING MY HOMEWORK.
THEY HAD A CAT.
I HEARD ABOUT A CAT WHO TRAVELED 300 MILES TO FIND ITS OLD HOME AFTER THE FAMILY MOVED...
HELLO? ARE YOU LISTENING TO ME?
I CAN WRITE YOUR PAPER OR I CAN TALK TO YOU. PICK ONE.
UM, TALK TO ME. DUH.
MAGGIE, YOU NEED TO TAKE YOUR GRADES MORE SERIOUSLY. DON'T YOU CARE ABOUT COLLEGE?
I MEAN, WHAT DO YOU WANT TO DO WITH YOUR LIFE?
I WANT TO BE ABDUCTED BY ALIENS AND LIVE IN ANOTHER WORLD.

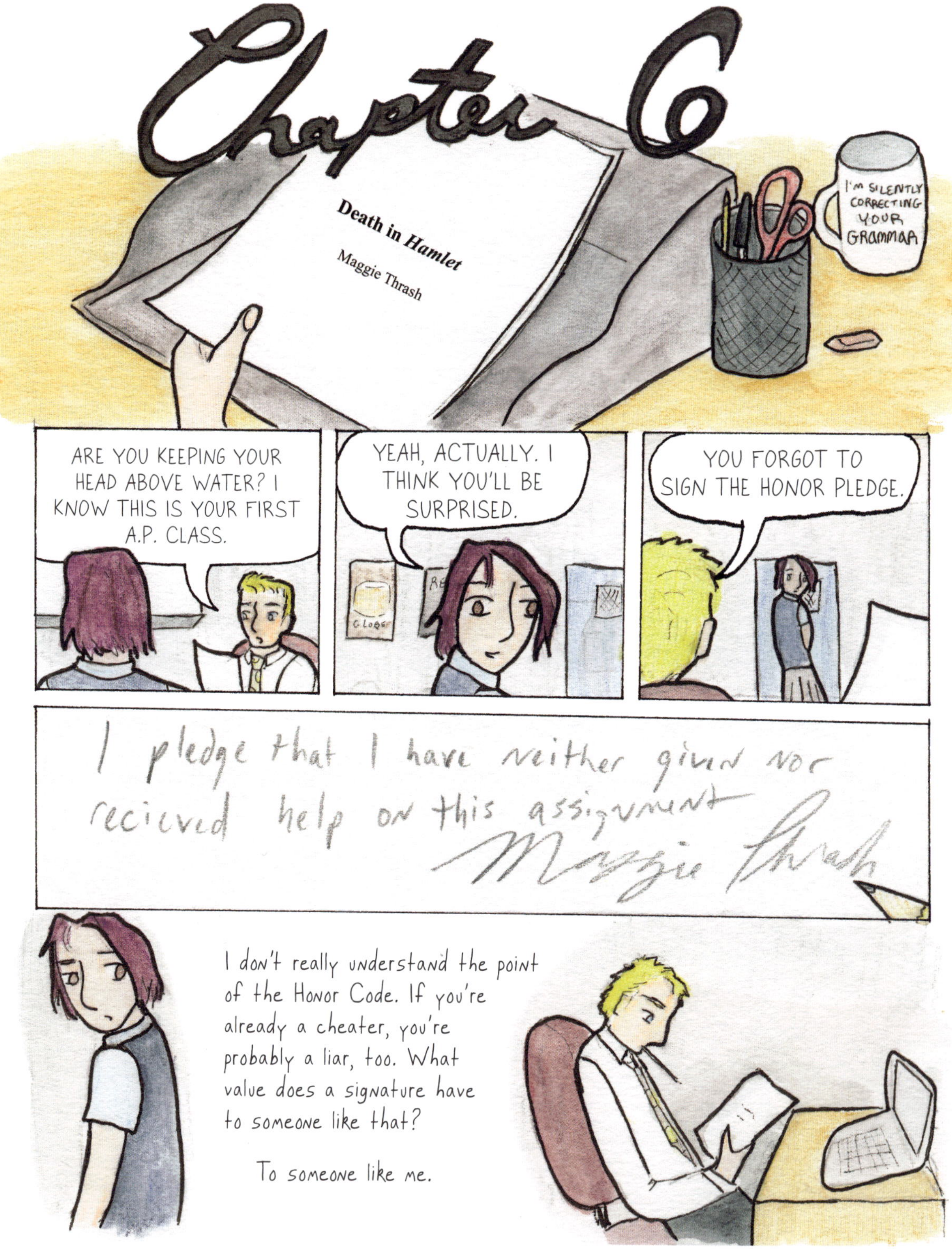
Chapter 6
Death in Hamlet
Maggie Thrash
I'M SILENTLY CORRECTING YOUR GRAMMAR
ARE YOU KEEPING YOUR HEAD ABOVE WATER? I KNOW THIS IS YOUR FIRST A.P. CLASS.
YEAH, ACTUALLY. I THINK YOU'LL BE SURPRISED.
YOU FORGOT TO SIGN THE HONOR PLEDGE.
I pledge that I have neither given nor recieved help on this assignment
Maggie Thrash
I don't really understand the point of the Honor Code. If you're already a cheater, you're probably a liar, too. What value does a signature have to someone like that?
To someone like me.

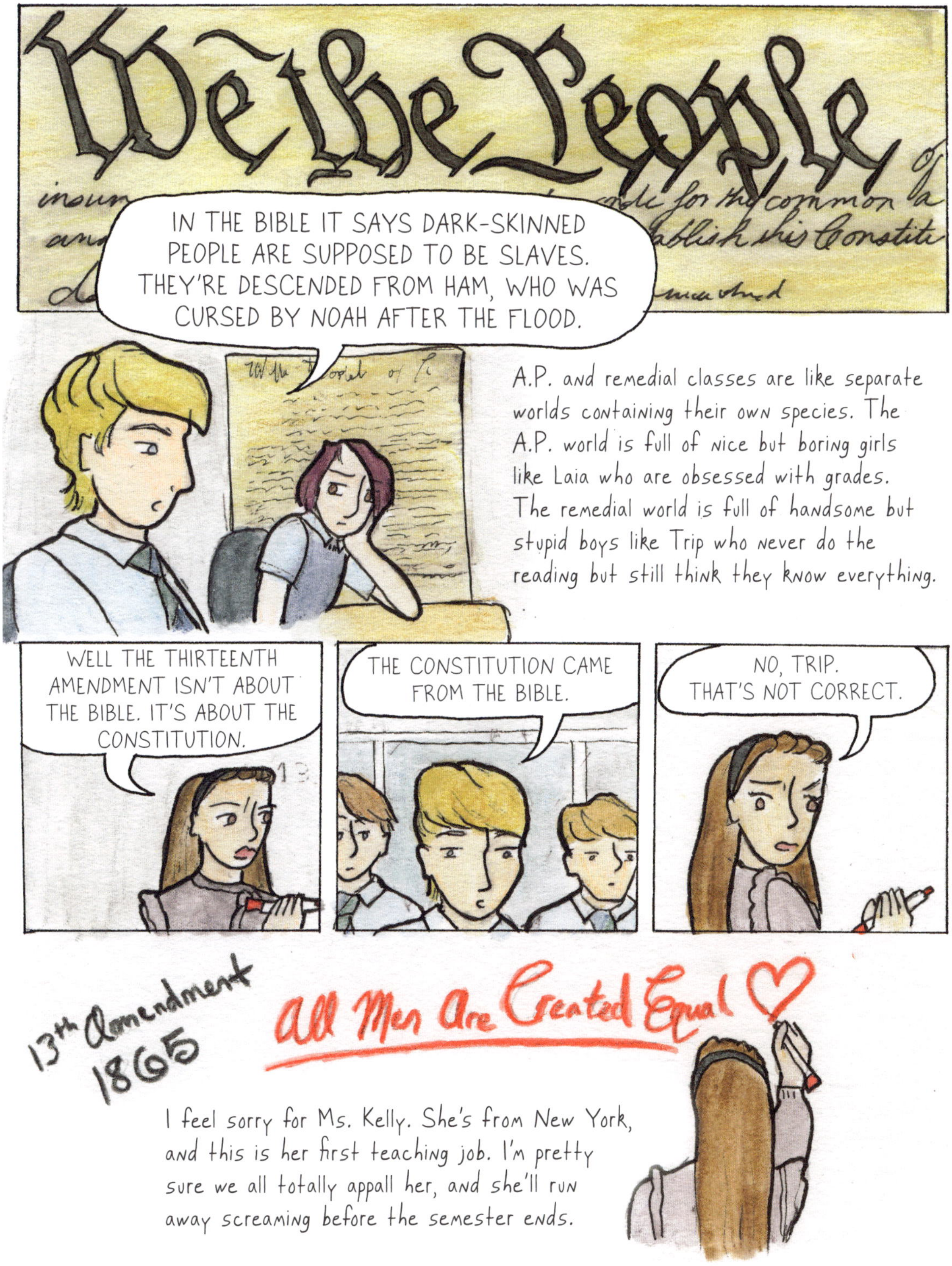
We the People
IN THE BIBLE IT SAYS DARK-SKINNED PEOPLE ARE SUPPOSED TO BE SLAVES. THEY'RE DESCENDED FROM HAM, WHO WAS CURSED BY NOAH AFTER THE FLOOD.
A.P. and remedial classes are like separate worlds containing their own species. The A.P. world is full of nice but boring girls like Laia who are obsessed with grades. The remedial world is full of handsome but stupid boys like Trip who never do the reading but still think they know everything.
WELL THE THIRTEENTH AMENDMENT ISN'T ABOUT THE BIBLE. IT'S ABOUT THE CONSTITUTION.
THE CONSTITUTION CAME FROM THE BIBLE.
NO, TRIP. THAT'S NOT CORRECT.
13th Amendment 1865
All Men Are Created Equal
I feel sorry for Ms. Kelly. She's from New York, and this is her first teaching job. I'm pretty sure we all totally appall her, and she'll run away screaming before the semester ends.

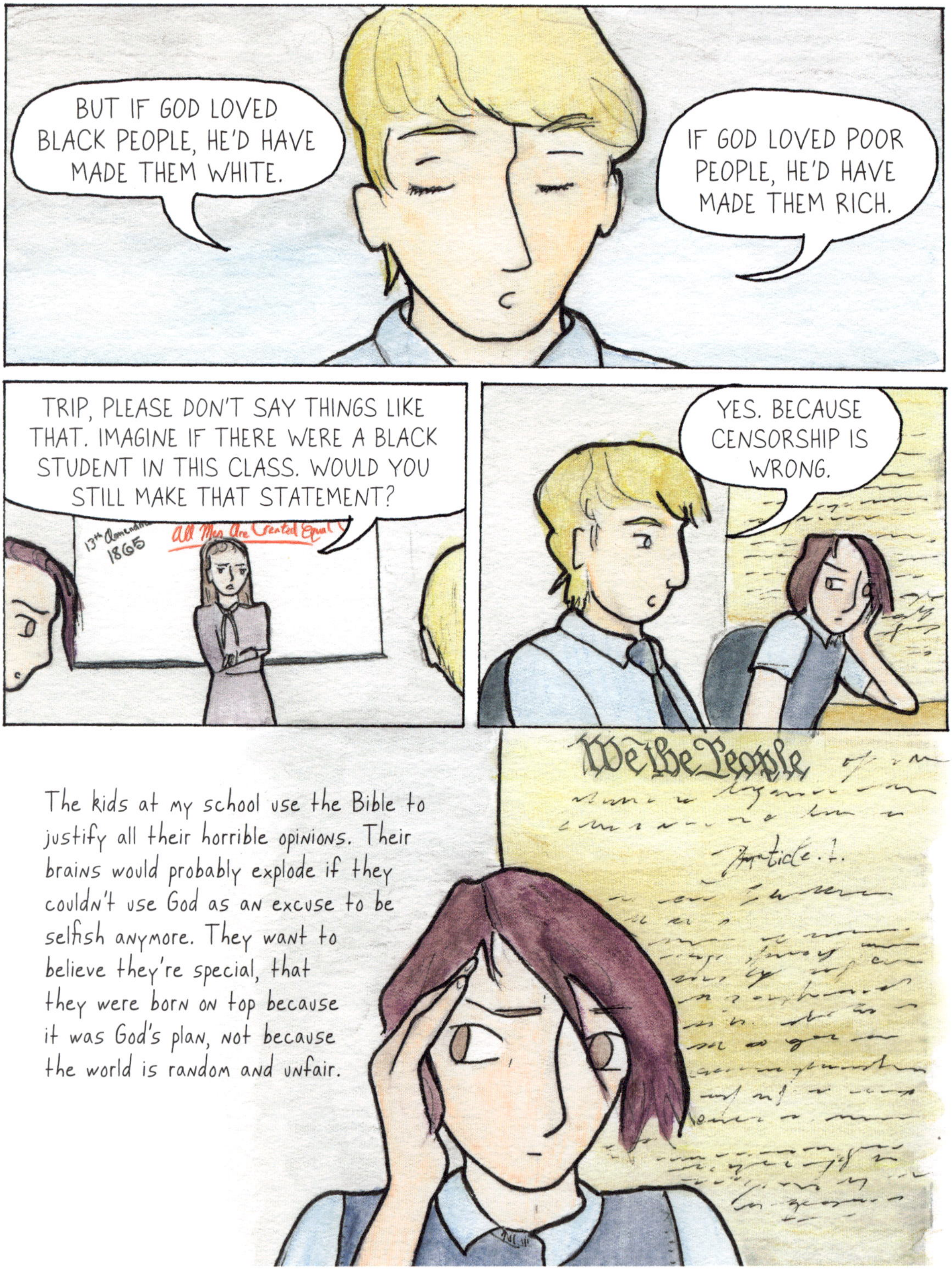
BUT IF GOD LOVED BLACK PEOPLE, HE'D HAVE MADE THEM WHITE.
IF GOD LOVED POOR PEOPLE, HE'D HAVE MADE THEM RICH.
TRIP, PLEASE DON'T SAY THINGS LIKE THAT. IMAGINE IF THERE WERE A BLACK STUDENT IN THIS CLASS. WOULD YOU STILL MAKE THAT STATEMENT?
13th Amendment 1865
All Men Are Created Equal
YES. BECAUSE CENSORSHIP IS WRONG.
We the People
Article. 1.
The kids at my school use the Bible to justify all their horrible opinions. Their brains would probably explode if they couldn't use God as an excuse to be selfish anymore. They want to believe they're special, that they were born on top because it was God's plan, not because the world is random and unfair.

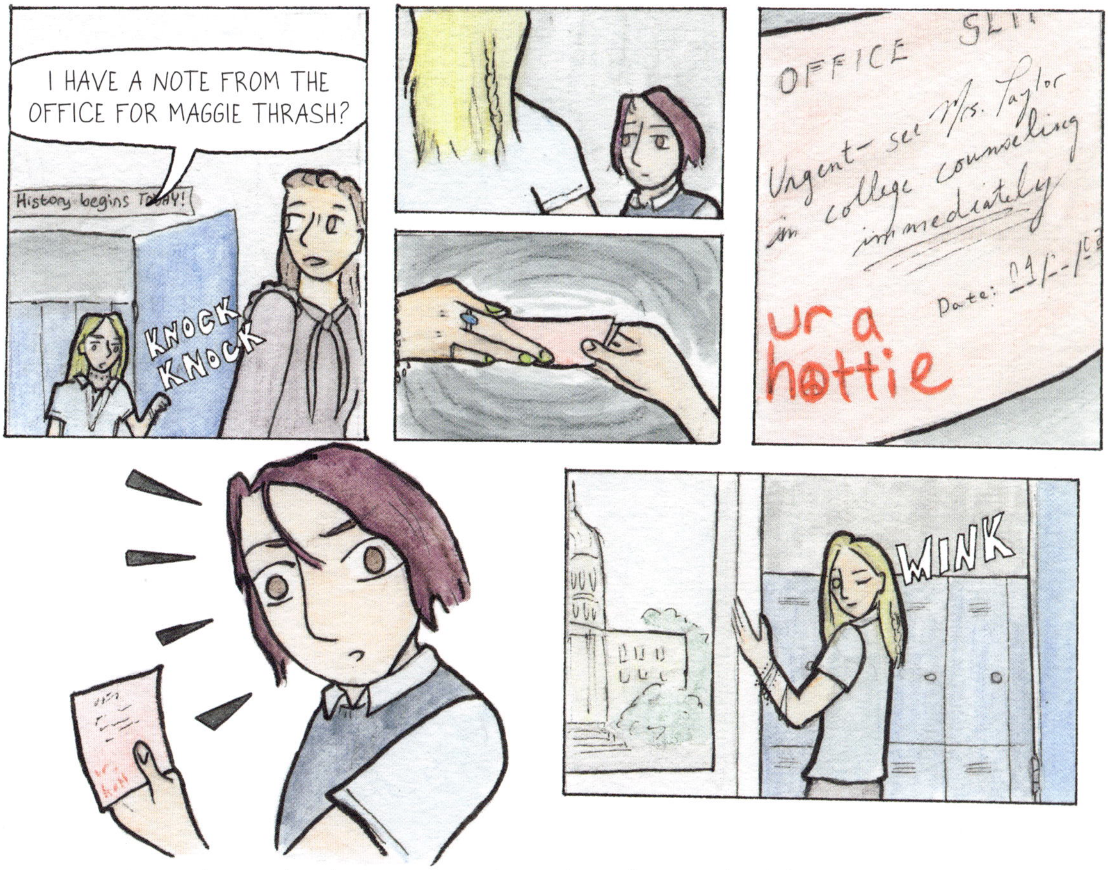
I HAVE A NOTE FROM THE OFFICE FOR MAGGIE THRASH?
History begins TODAY!
KNOCK KNOCK
OFFICE
Urgent- see Mrs. Taylor in college counseling immediately
Date:
ur a hottie
WINK

I barely know who that girl is. I think she's the girl who did LSD at prom and spent the summer in rehab in Utah. Is she . . . GAY? It's totally possible that she is and I just never heard about it, because if you try to be gay at this school, everyone just ignores you to death until you shut up about it.

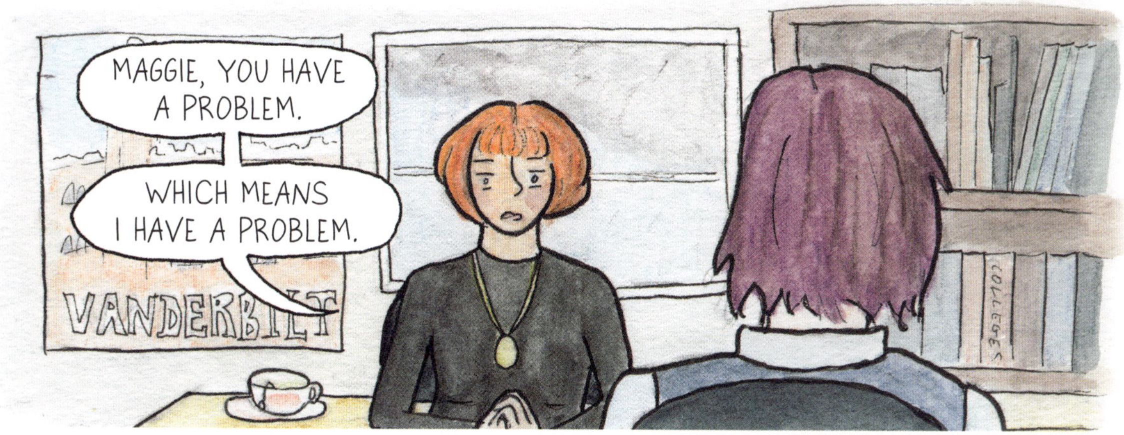
MAGGIE, YOU HAVE A PROBLEM.
WHICH MEANS I HAVE A PROBLEM.
VANDERBILT
COLLEGES

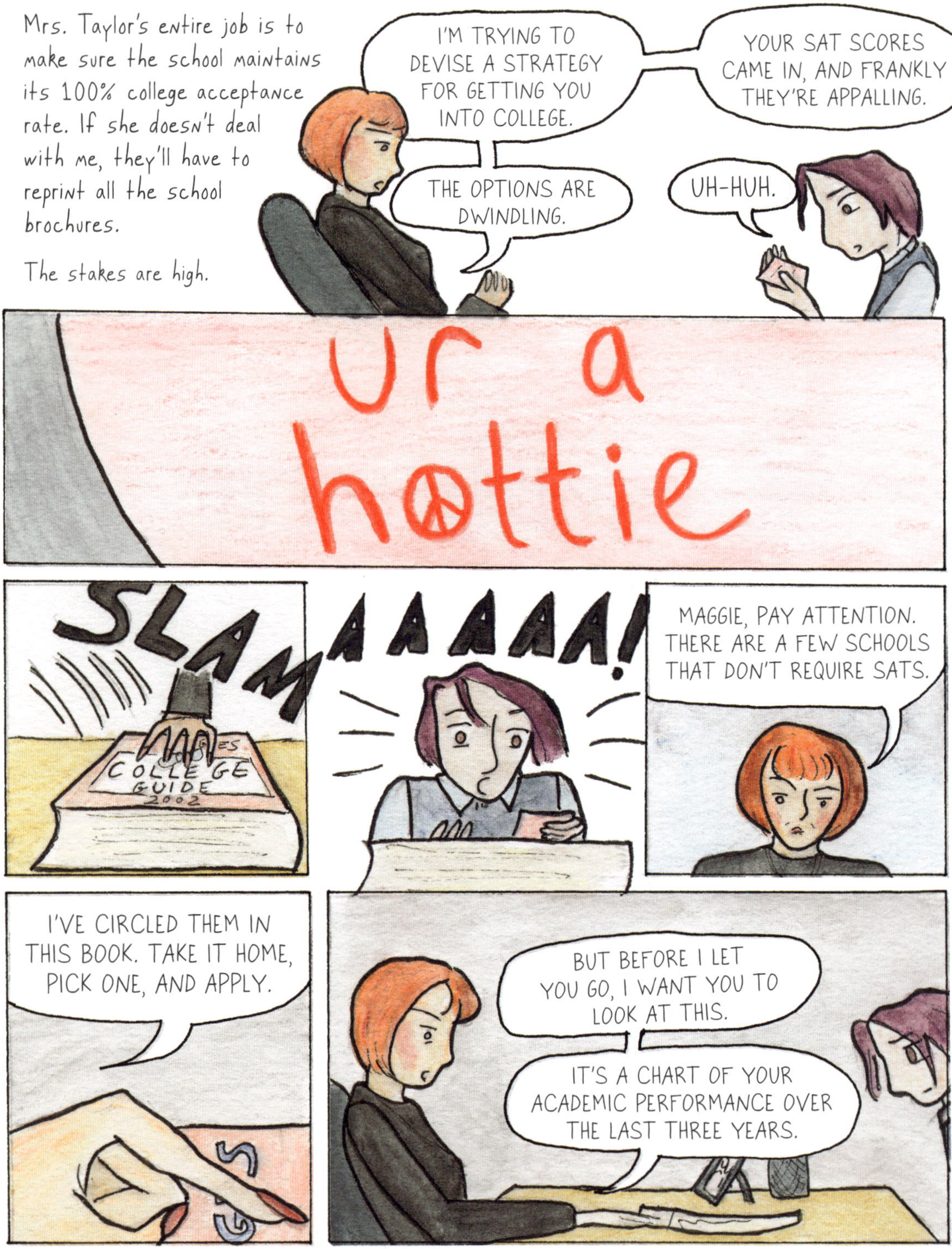
Mrs. Taylor's entire job is to make sure the school maintains its 100% college acceptance rate. If she doesn't deal with me, they'll have to reprint all the school brochures.
The stakes are high.
I'M TRYING TO DEVISE A STRATEGY FOR GETTING YOU INTO COLLEGE.
YOUR SAT SCORES CAME IN, AND FRANKLY THEY'RE APPALLING.
THE OPTIONS ARE DWINDLING.
UH-HUH.
ur a hottie
SLAM
COLLEGE GUIDE 2002
AAAAA!
MAGGIE, PAY ATTENTION. THERE ARE A FEW SCHOOLS THAT DON'T REQUIRE SATS.
I'VE CIRCLED THEM IN THIS BOOK. TAKE IT HOME, PICK ONE, AND APPLY.
BUT BEFORE I LET YOU GO, I WANT YOU TO LOOK AT THIS.
IT'S A CHART OF YOUR ACADEMIC PERFORMANCE OVER THE LAST THREE YEARS.

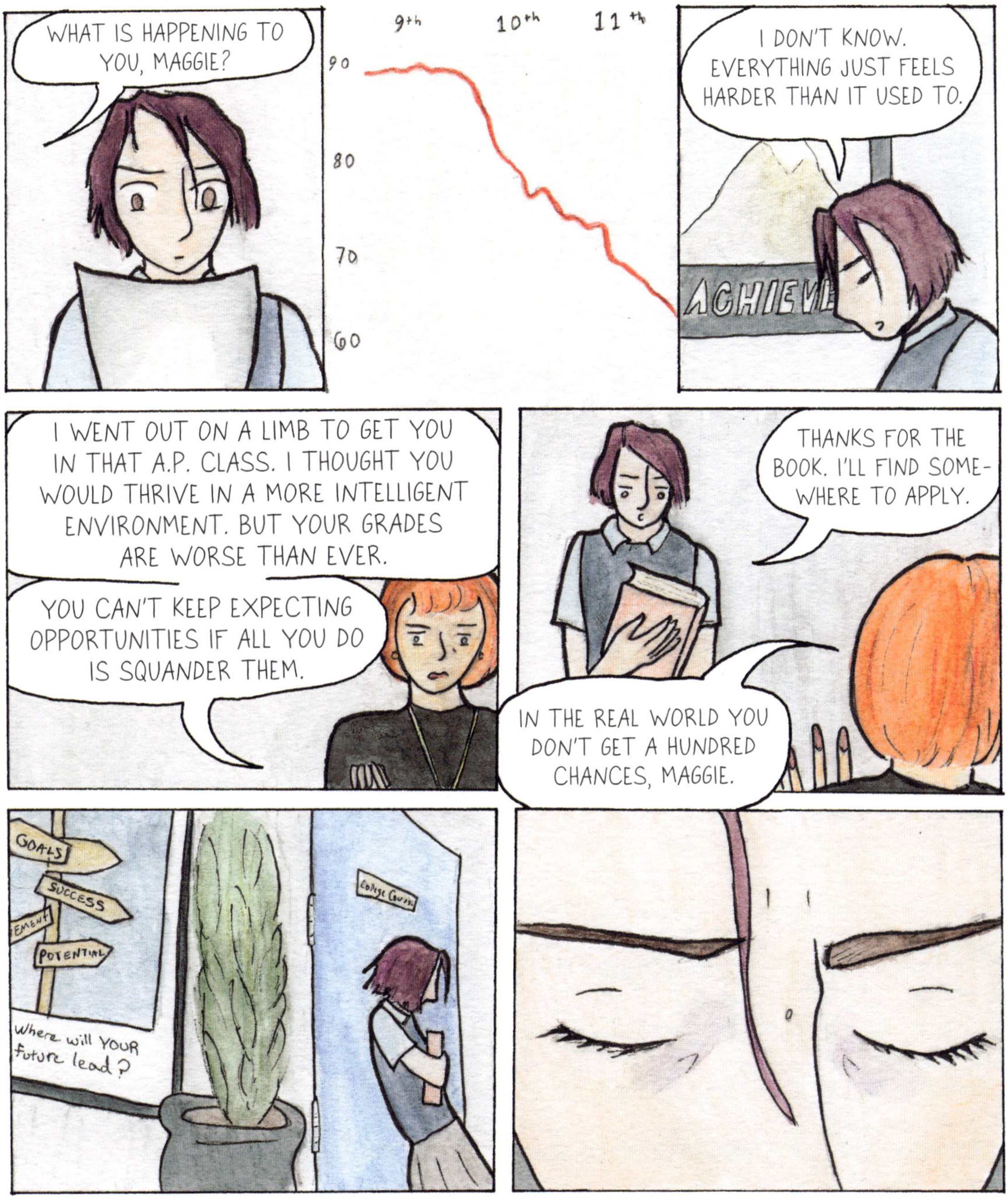
WHAT IS HAPPENING TO YOU, MAGGIE?
9th
10th
11th
90
80
70
60
I DON'T KNOW. EVERYTHING JUST FEELS HARDER THAN IT USED TO.
ACHIEVE
I WENT OUT ON A LIMB TO GET YOU IN THAT A.P. CLASS. I THOUGHT YOU WOULD THRIVE IN A MORE INTELLIGENT ENVIRONMENT. BUT YOUR GRADES ARE WORSE THAN EVER.
YOU CAN'T KEEP EXPECTING OPPORTUNITIES IF ALL YOU DO IS SQUANDER THEM.
THANKS FOR THE BOOK. I'LL FIND SOMEWHERE TO APPLY.
IN THE REAL WORLD YOU DON'T GET A HUNDRED CHANCES, MAGGIE.
GOALS
SUCCESS
POTENTIAL
Where will YOUR future lead?

I don't know why I'm so upset. I don't even like Mrs. Taylor. But I guess there's just nothing worse than having to look at a chart showing how much you've declined in quality.

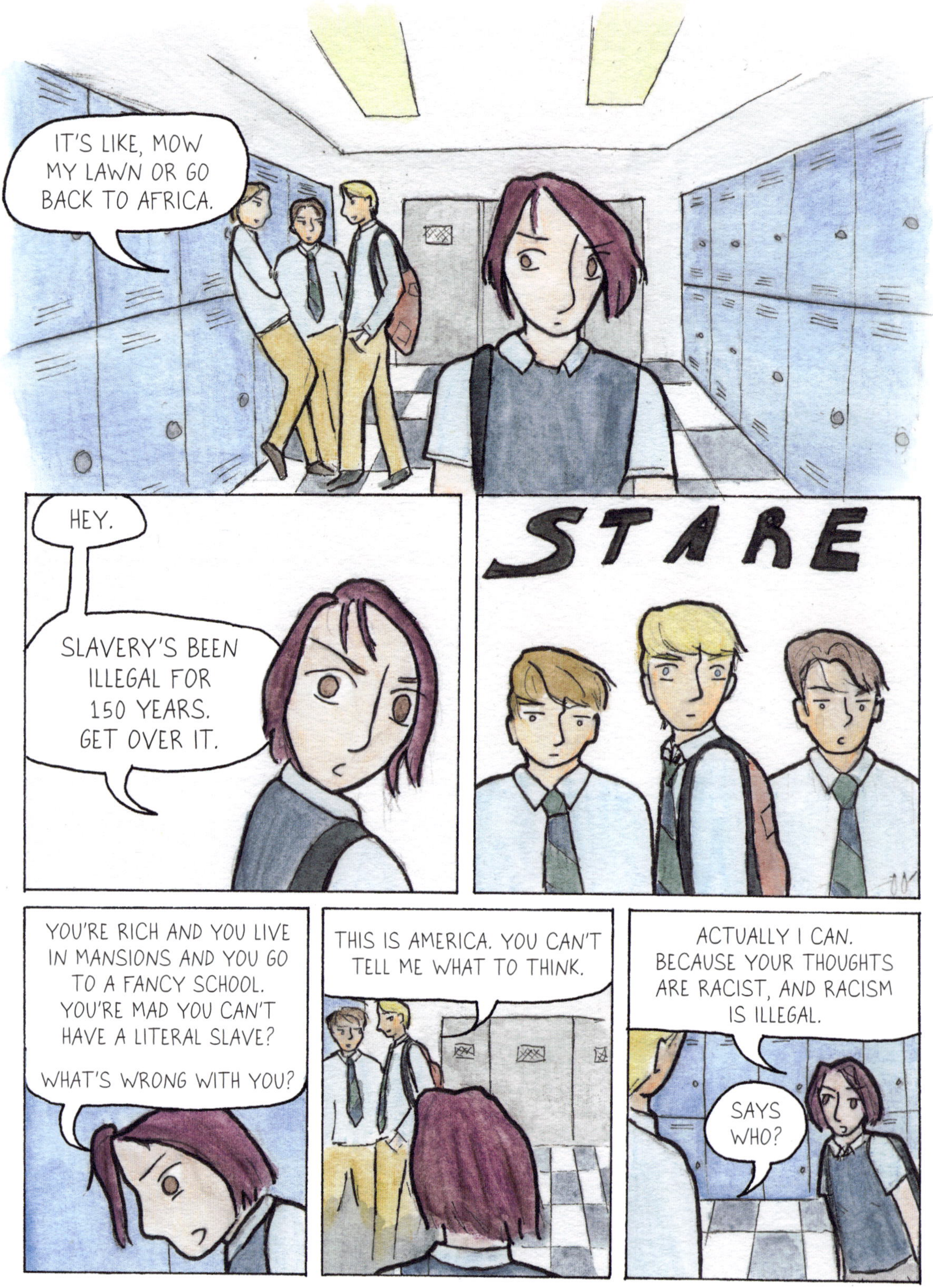
IT'S LIKE, MOW MY LAWN OR GO BACK TO AFRICA.
HEY.
SLAVERY'S BEEN ILLEGAL FOR 150 YEARS. GET OVER IT.
STARE
YOU'RE RICH AND YOU LIVE IN MANSIONS AND YOU GO TO A FANCY SCHOOL. YOU'RE MAD YOU CAN'T HAVE A LITERAL SLAVE?
WHAT'S WRONG WITH YOU?
THIS IS AMERICA. YOU CAN'T TELL ME WHAT TO THINK.
ACTUALLY I CAN. BECAUSE YOUR THOUGHTS ARE RACIST, AND RACISM IS ILLEGAL.
SAYS WHO?

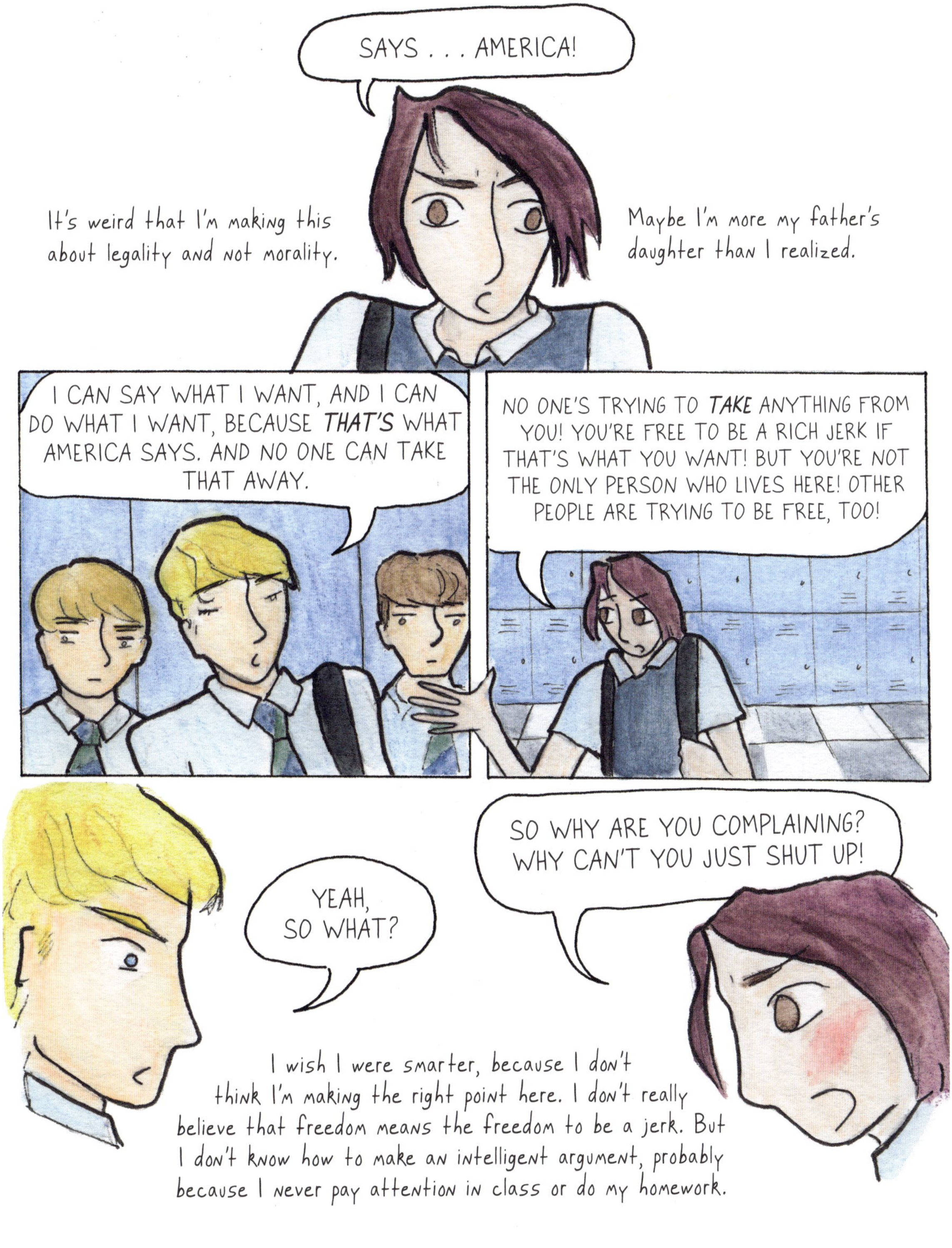

SAYS . . . AMERICA!
It's weird that I'm making this about legality and not morality.
Maybe I'm more my father's daughter than I realized.
I CAN SAY WHAT I WANT, AND I CAN DO WHAT I WANT, BECAUSE *THAT'S* WHAT AMERICA SAYS. AND NO ONE CAN TAKE THAT AWAY.
NO ONE'S TRYING TO *TAKE* ANYTHING FROM YOU! YOU'RE FREE TO BE A RICH JERK IF THAT'S WHAT YOU WANT! BUT YOU'RE NOT THE ONLY PERSON WHO LIVES HERE! OTHER PEOPLE ARE TRYING TO BE FREE, TOO!
YEAH, SO WHAT?
SO WHY ARE YOU COMPLAINING? WHY CAN'T YOU JUST SHUT UP!
I wish I were smarter, because I don't think I'm making the right point here. I don't really believe that freedom means the freedom to be a jerk. But I don't know how to make an intelligent argument, probably because I never pay attention in class or do my homework.

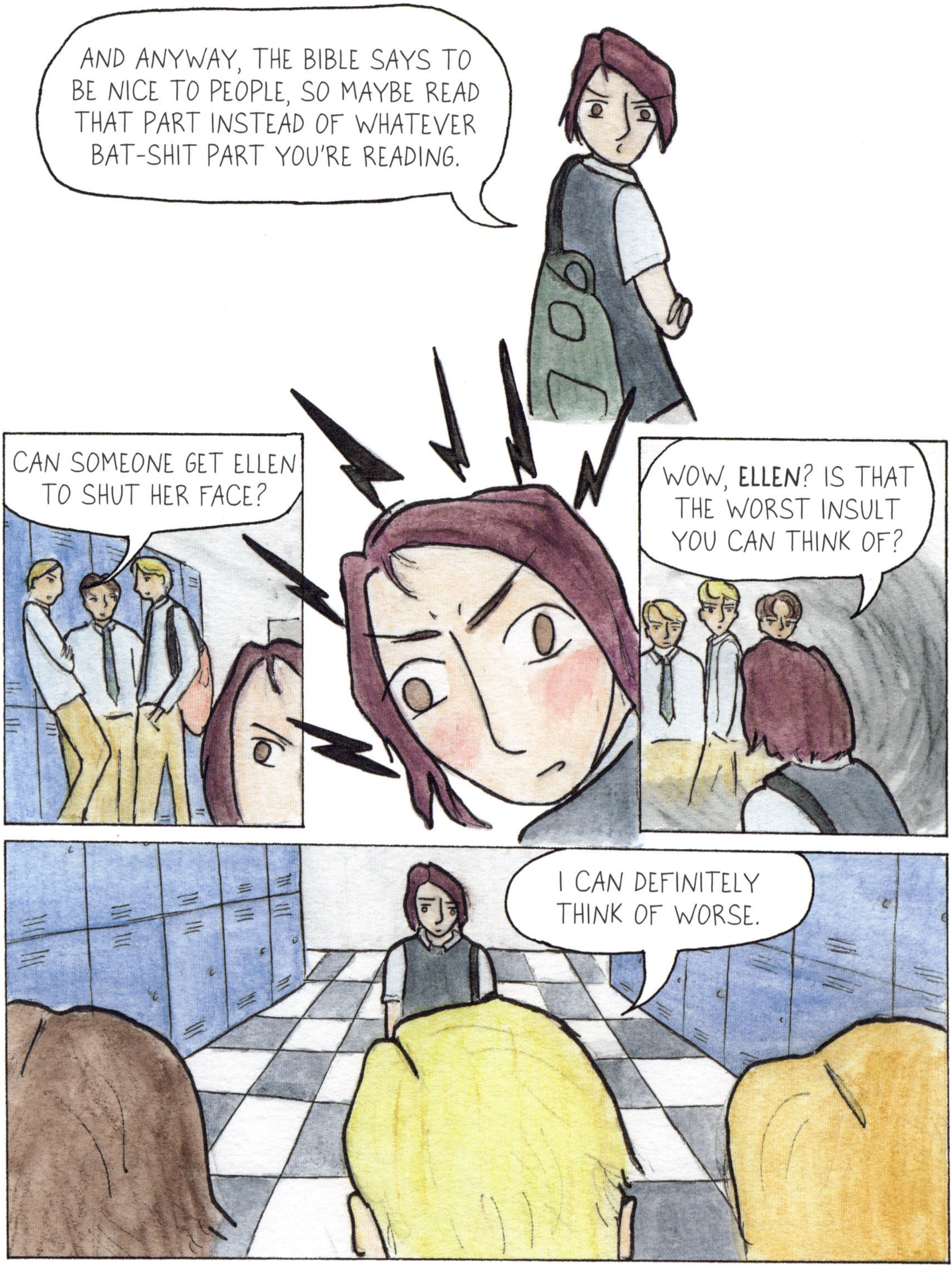
AND ANYWAY, THE BIBLE SAYS TO BE NICE TO PEOPLE, SO MAYBE READ THAT PART INSTEAD OF WHATEVER BAT-SHIT PART YOU'RE READING.
CAN SOMEONE GET ELLEN TO SHUT HER FACE?
WOW, **ELLEN**? IS THAT THE WORST INSULT YOU CAN THINK OF?
I CAN DEFINITELY THINK OF WORSE.

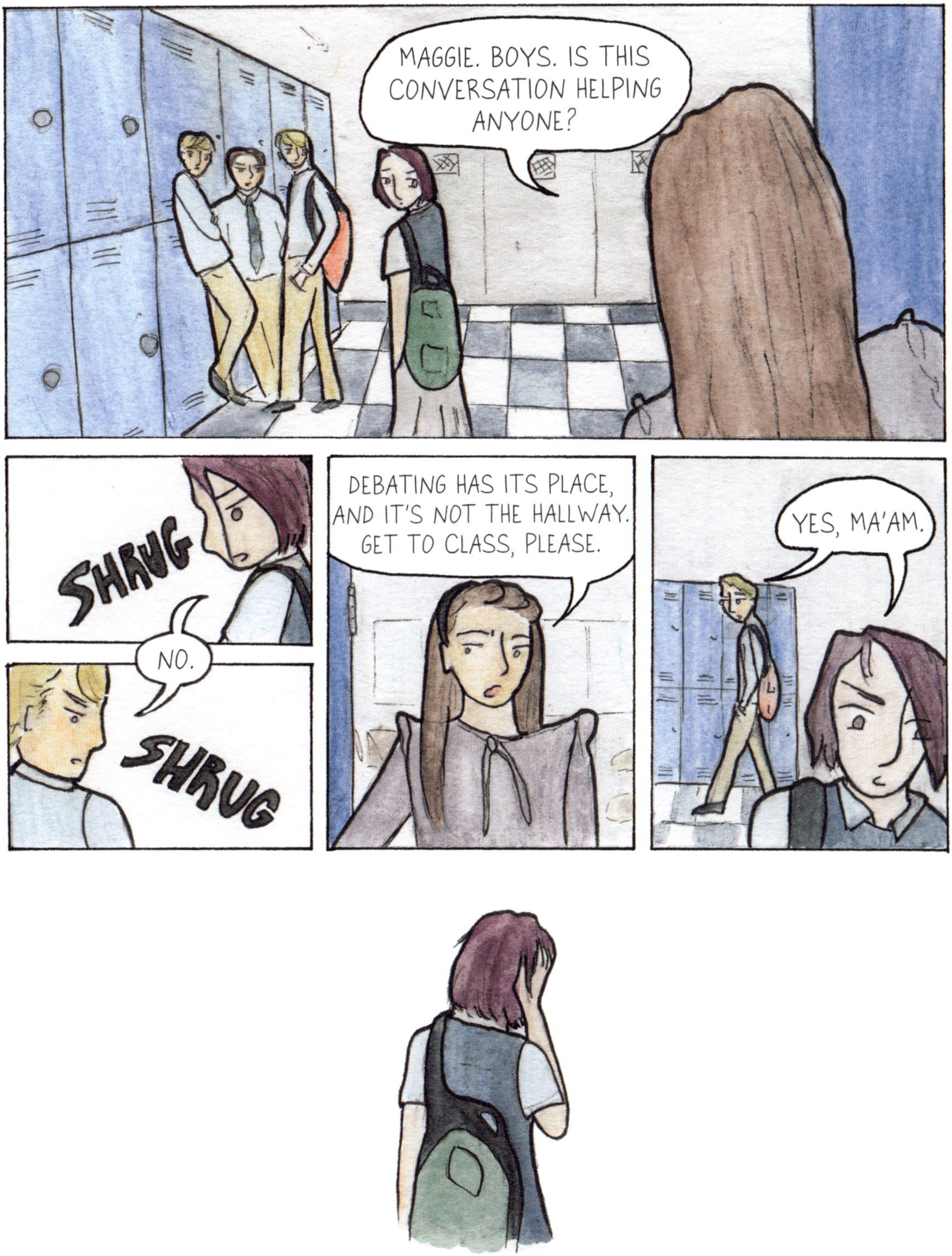
MAGGIE. BOYS. IS THIS CONVERSATION HELPING ANYONE?
SHRUG
NO.
SHRUG
DEBATING HAS ITS PLACE, AND IT'S NOT THE HALLWAY. GET TO CLASS, PLEASE.
YES, MA'AM.

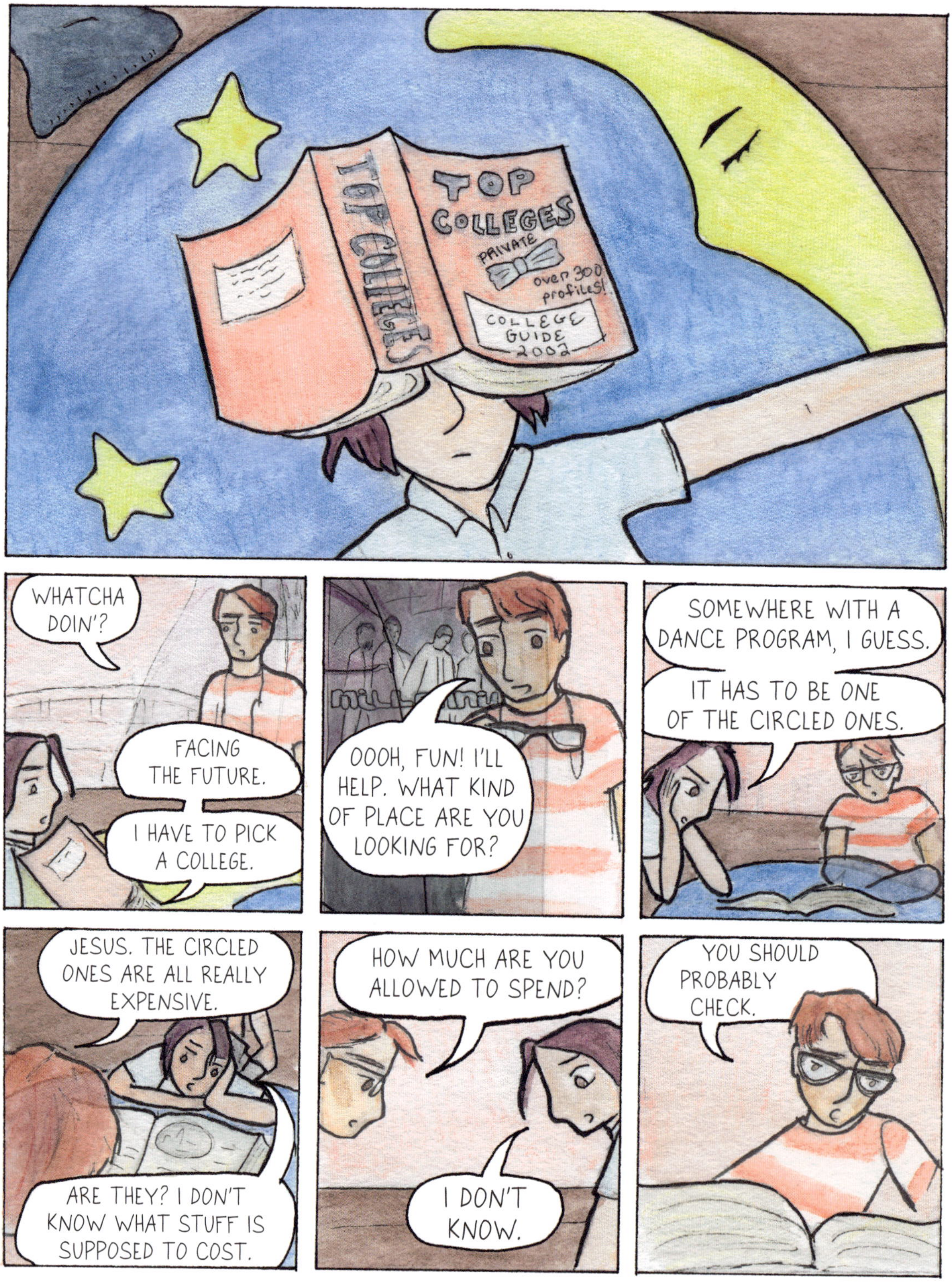
TOP COLLEGES
TOP COLLEGES
PRIVATE
over 300 profiles!
COLLEGE GUIDE 2002
WHATCHA DOIN'?
FACING THE FUTURE.
I HAVE TO PICK A COLLEGE.
OOOH, FUN! I'LL HELP. WHAT KIND OF PLACE ARE YOU LOOKING FOR?
SOMEWHERE WITH A DANCE PROGRAM, I GUESS.
IT HAS TO BE ONE OF THE CIRCLED ONES.
JESUS. THE CIRCLED ONES ARE ALL REALLY EXPENSIVE.
ARE THEY? I DON'T KNOW WHAT STUFF IS SUPPOSED TO COST.
HOW MUCH ARE YOU ALLOWED TO SPEND?
I DON'T KNOW.
YOU SHOULD PROBABLY CHECK.

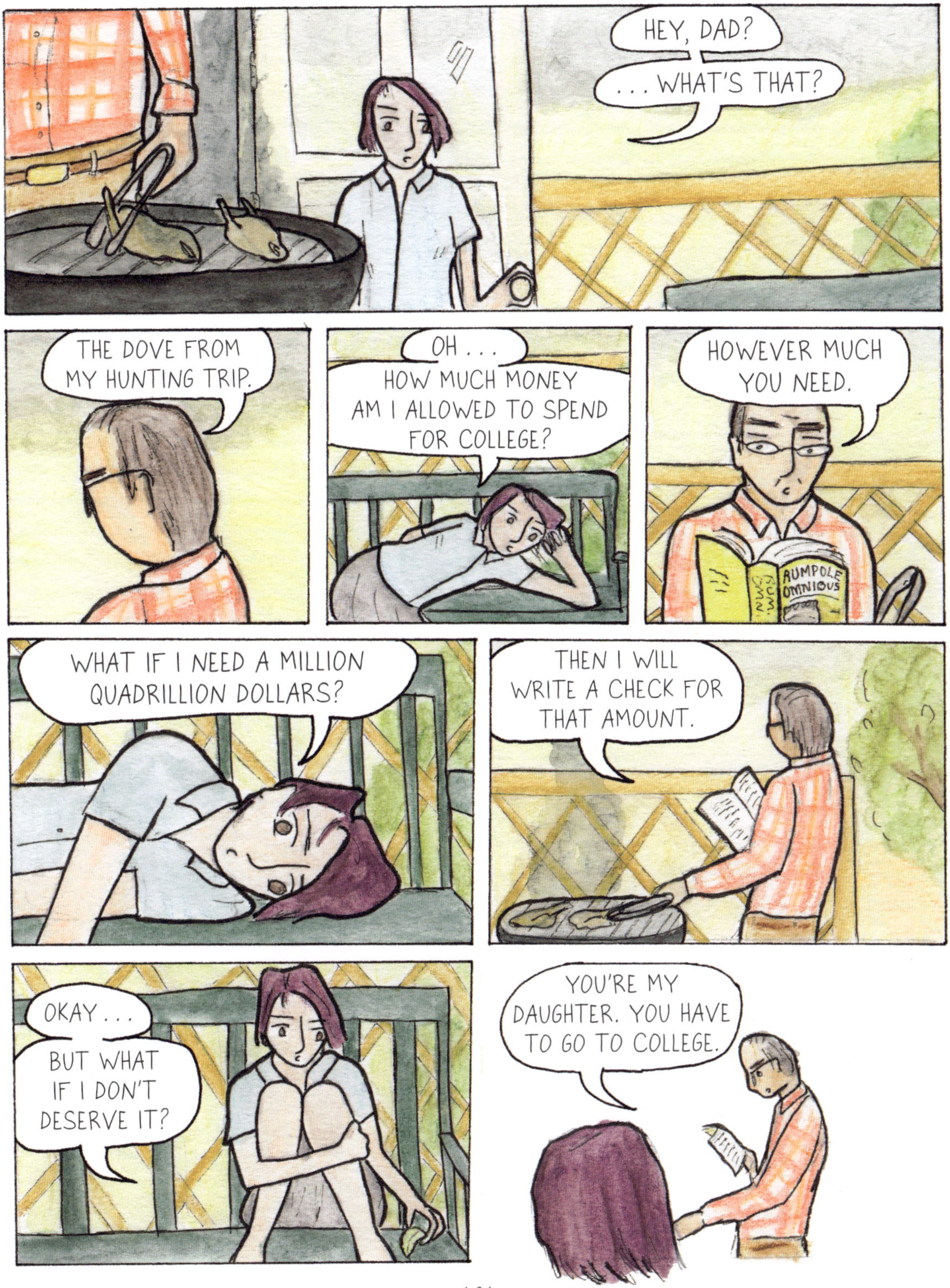
HEY, DAD?
. . . WHAT'S THAT?
THE DOVE FROM MY HUNTING TRIP.
OH . . .
HOW MUCH MONEY AM I ALLOWED TO SPEND FOR COLLEGE?
HOWEVER MUCH YOU NEED.
RUMPOLE OMNIBUS
WHAT IF I NEED A MILLION QUADRILLION DOLLARS?
THEN I WILL WRITE A CHECK FOR THAT AMOUNT.
OKAY . . .
BUT WHAT IF I DON'T DESERVE IT?
YOU'RE MY DAUGHTER. YOU HAVE TO GO TO COLLEGE.

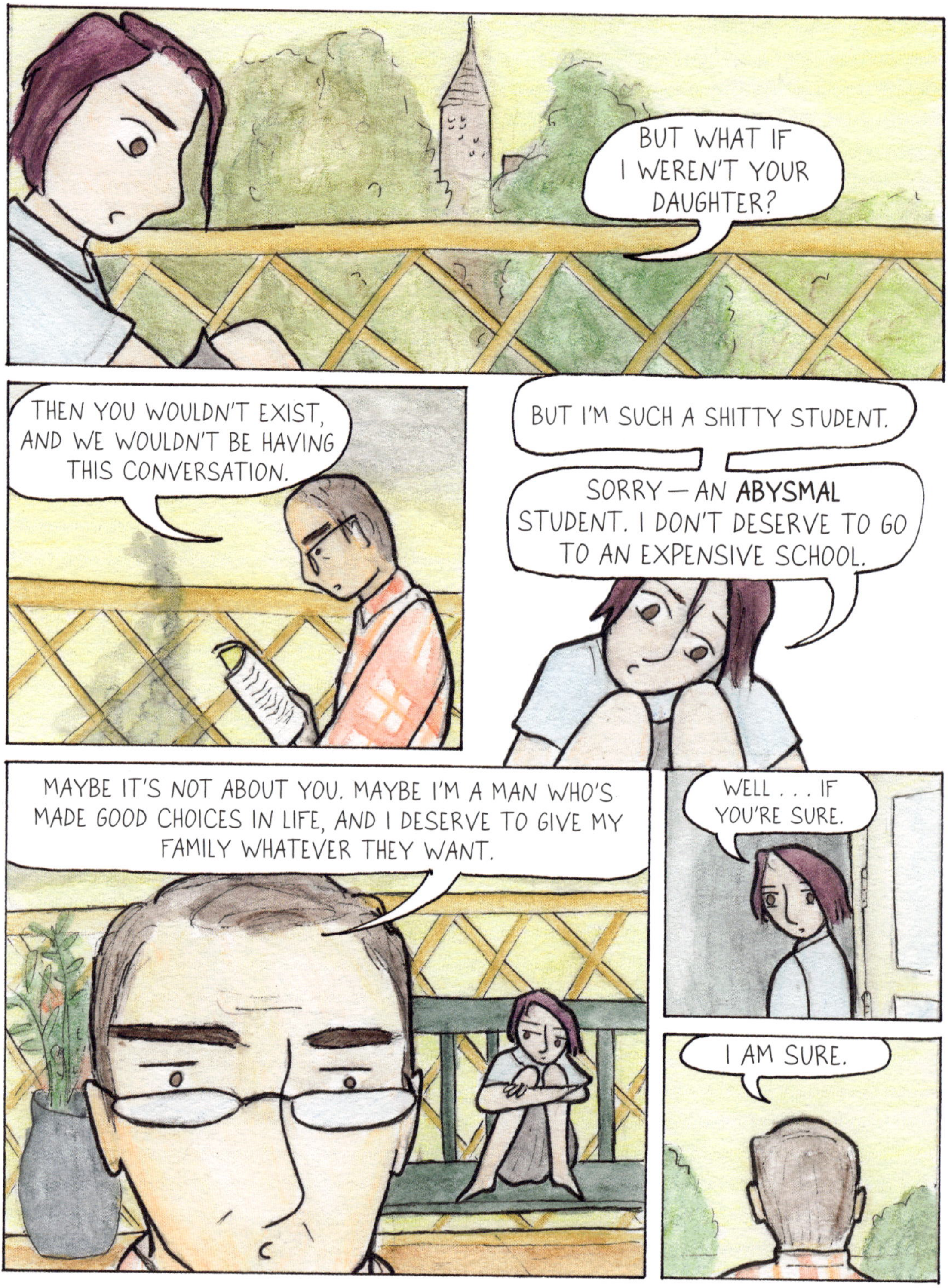
BUT WHAT IF I WEREN'T YOUR DAUGHTER?
THEN YOU WOULDN'T EXIST, AND WE WOULDN'T BE HAVING THIS CONVERSATION.
BUT I'M SUCH A SHITTY STUDENT.
SORRY — AN **ABYSMAL** STUDENT. I DON'T DESERVE TO GO TO AN EXPENSIVE SCHOOL.
MAYBE IT'S NOT ABOUT YOU. MAYBE I'M A MAN WHO'S MADE GOOD CHOICES IN LIFE, AND I DESERVE TO GIVE MY FAMILY WHATEVER THEY WANT.
WELL . . . IF YOU'RE SURE.
I AM SURE.

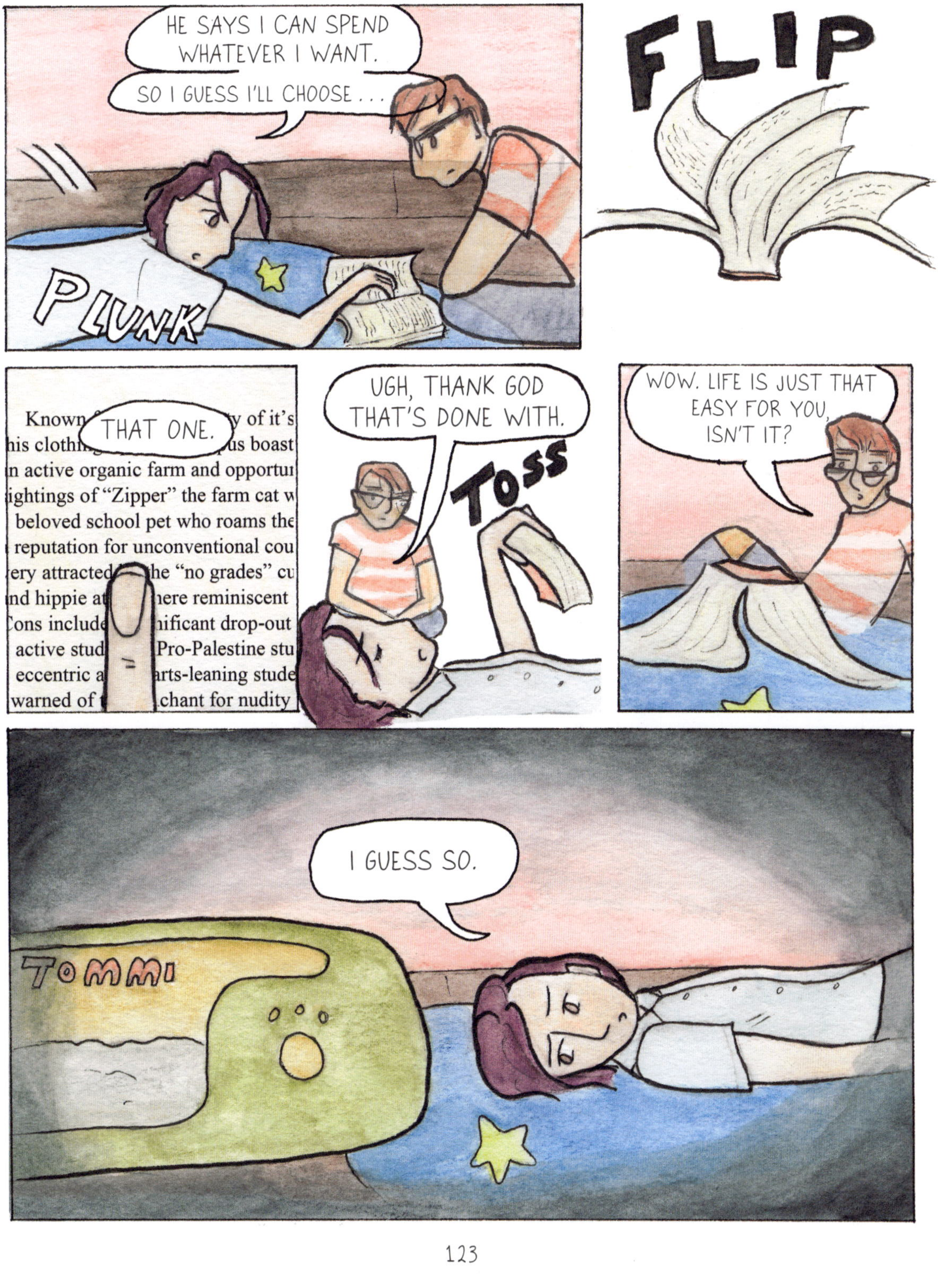
HE SAYS I CAN SPEND WHATEVER I WANT.
SO I GUESS I'LL CHOOSE . . .
PLUNK
FLIP
THAT ONE.
UGH, THANK GOD THAT'S DONE WITH.
TOSS
WOW. LIFE IS JUST THAT EASY FOR YOU, ISN'T IT?
I GUESS SO.
TOMMI

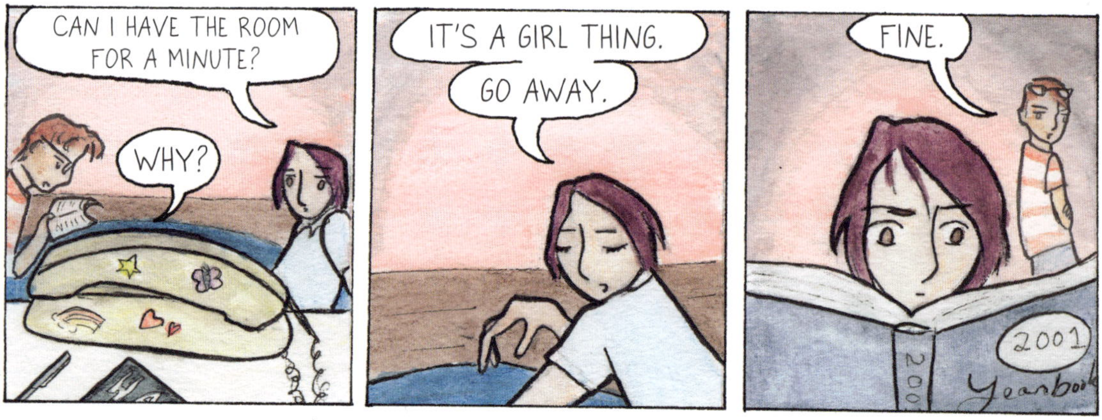
CAN I HAVE THE ROOM FOR A MINUTE?
WHY?
IT'S A GIRL THING.
GO AWAY.
FINE.
2001
Yearbook

Sometimes I get a random surge of courage. Or maybe it's not courage, maybe it's just a feeling that the universe is pointless, so you may as well do whatever weird idea pops into your brain.

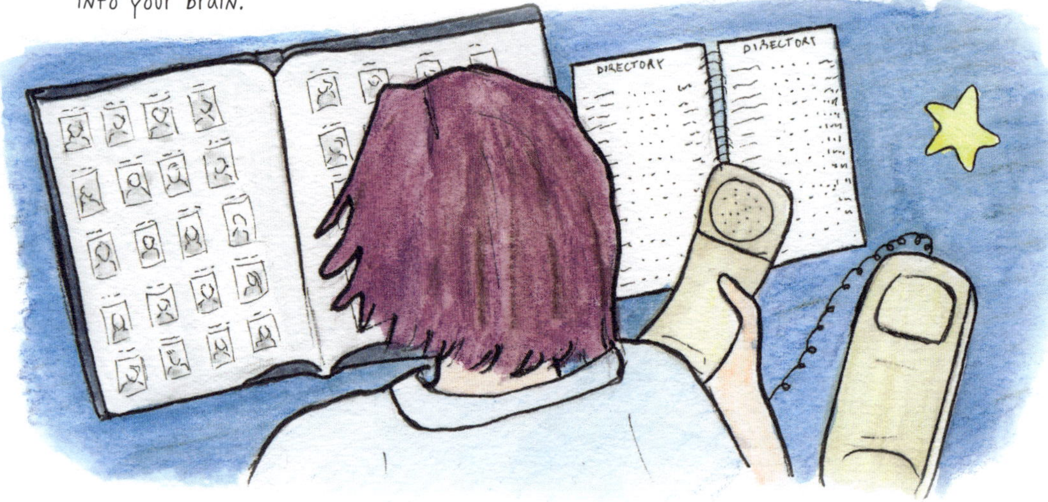
DIRECTORY
DIRECTORY

Sometimes it works out, sometimes it's a huge mistake.

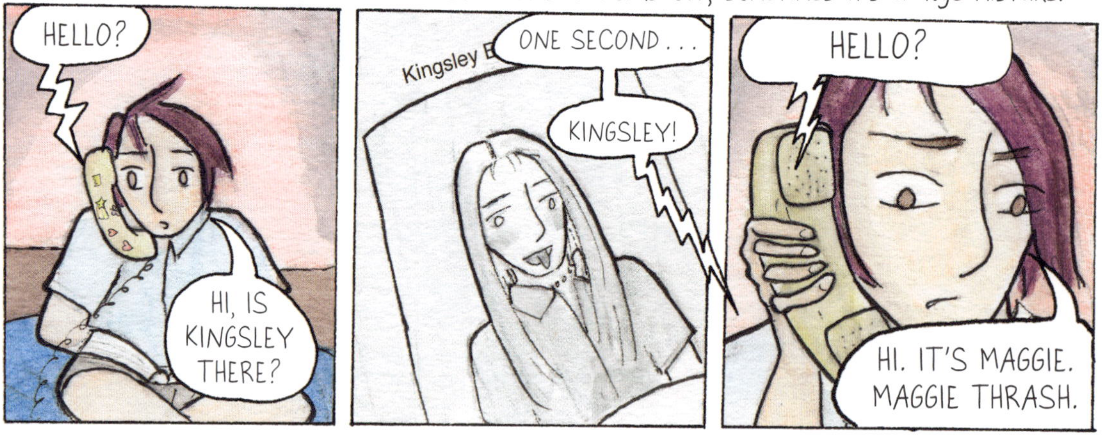
HELLO?
HI, IS KINGSLEY THERE?
ONE SECOND . . .
KINGSLEY!
HELLO?
HI. IT'S MAGGIE. MAGGIE THRASH.

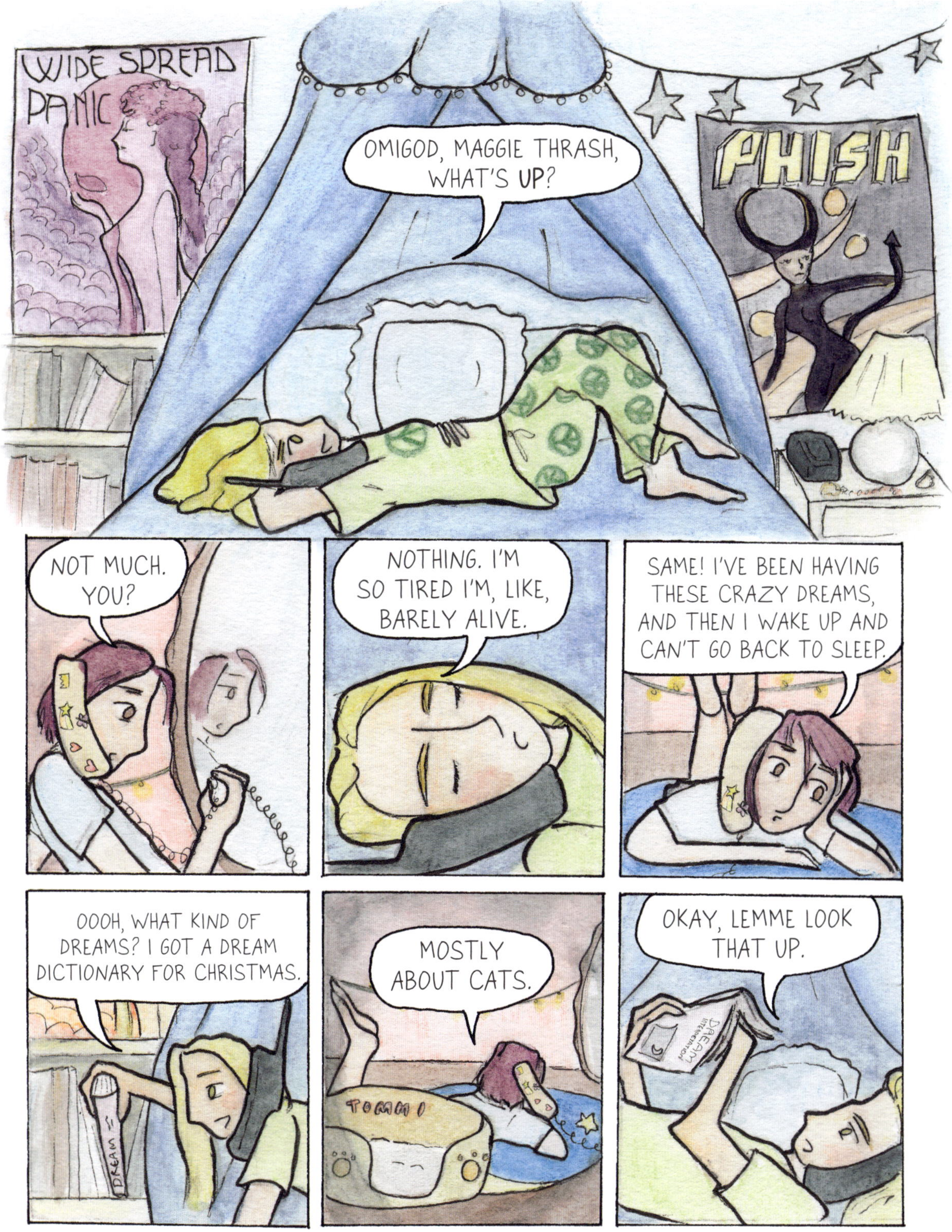
WIDE SPREAD PANIC
PHISH
OMIGOD, MAGGIE THRASH, WHAT'S UP?
NOT MUCH. YOU?
NOTHING. I'M SO TIRED I'M, LIKE, BARELY ALIVE.
SAME! I'VE BEEN HAVING THESE CRAZY DREAMS, AND THEN I WAKE UP AND CAN'T GO BACK TO SLEEP.
OOOH, WHAT KIND OF DREAMS? I GOT A DREAM DICTIONARY FOR CHRISTMAS.
DREAM
MOSTLY ABOUT CATS.
TOMMI
OKAY, LEMME LOOK THAT UP.
DREAM

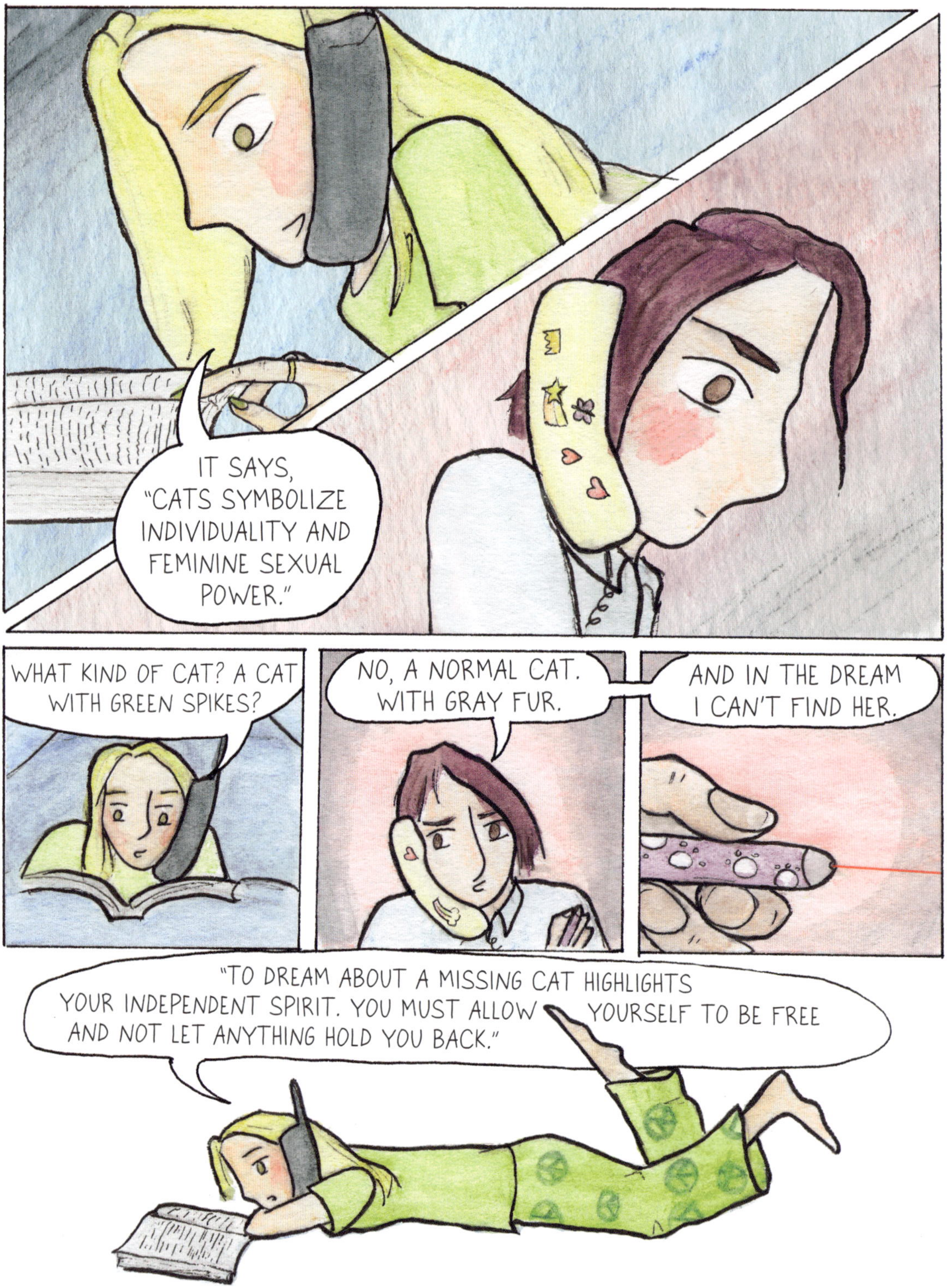
IT SAYS, "CATS SYMBOLIZE INDIVIDUALITY AND FEMININE SEXUAL POWER."
WHAT KIND OF CAT? A CAT WITH GREEN SPIKES?
NO, A NORMAL CAT. WITH GRAY FUR.
AND IN THE DREAM I CAN'T FIND HER.
"TO DREAM ABOUT A MISSING CAT HIGHLIGHTS YOUR INDEPENDENT SPIRIT. YOU MUST ALLOW YOURSELF TO BE FREE AND NOT LET ANYTHING HOLD YOU BACK."

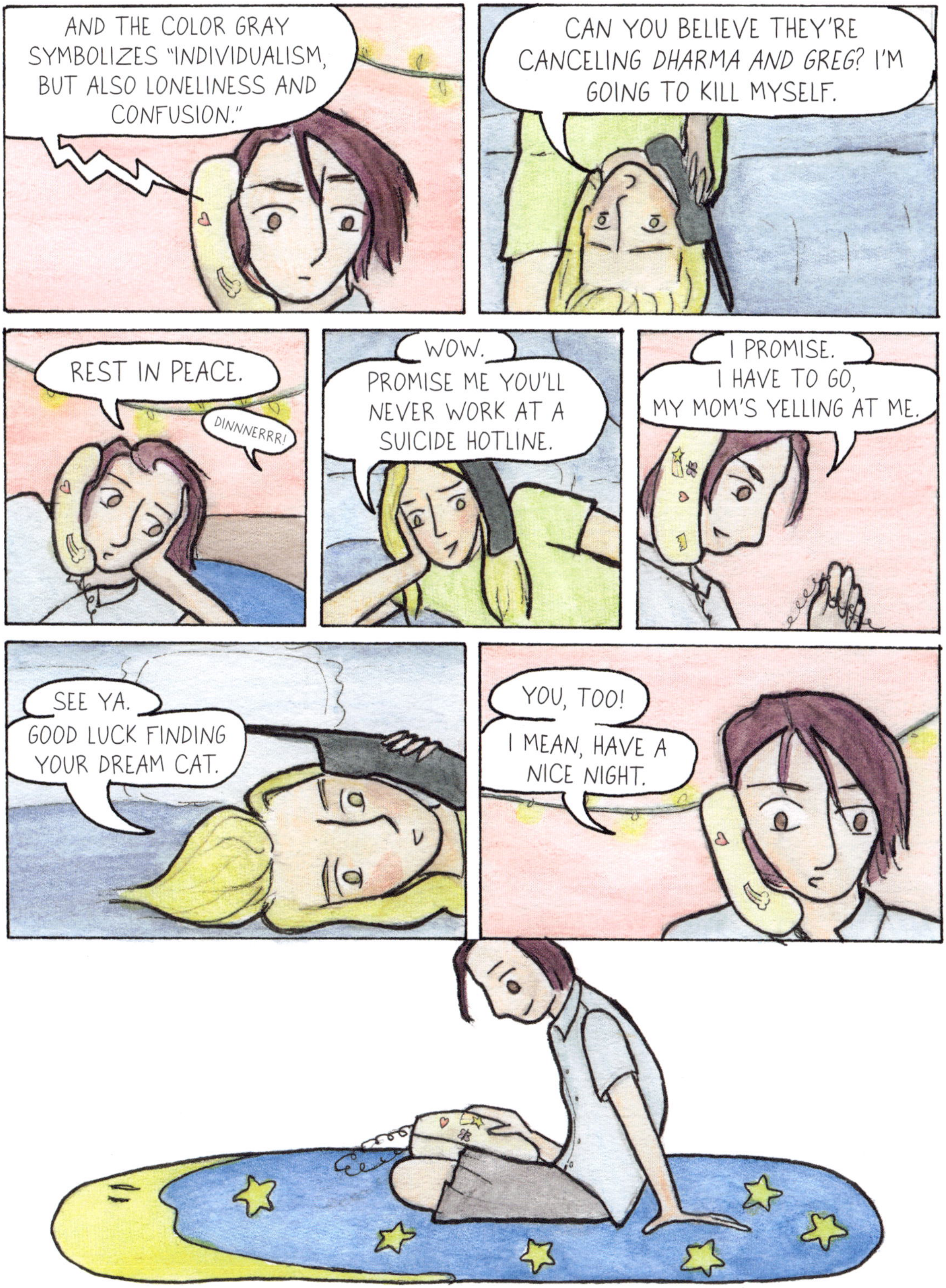
AND THE COLOR GRAY SYMBOLIZES "INDIVIDUALISM, BUT ALSO LONELINESS AND CONFUSION."
CAN YOU BELIEVE THEY'RE CANCELING *DHARMA AND GREG*? I'M GOING TO KILL MYSELF.
REST IN PEACE.
DINNNERRR!
WOW.
PROMISE ME YOU'LL NEVER WORK AT A SUICIDE HOTLINE.
I PROMISE.
I HAVE TO GO, MY MOM'S YELLING AT ME.
SEE YA.
GOOD LUCK FINDING YOUR DREAM CAT.
YOU, TOO!
I MEAN, HAVE A NICE NIGHT.

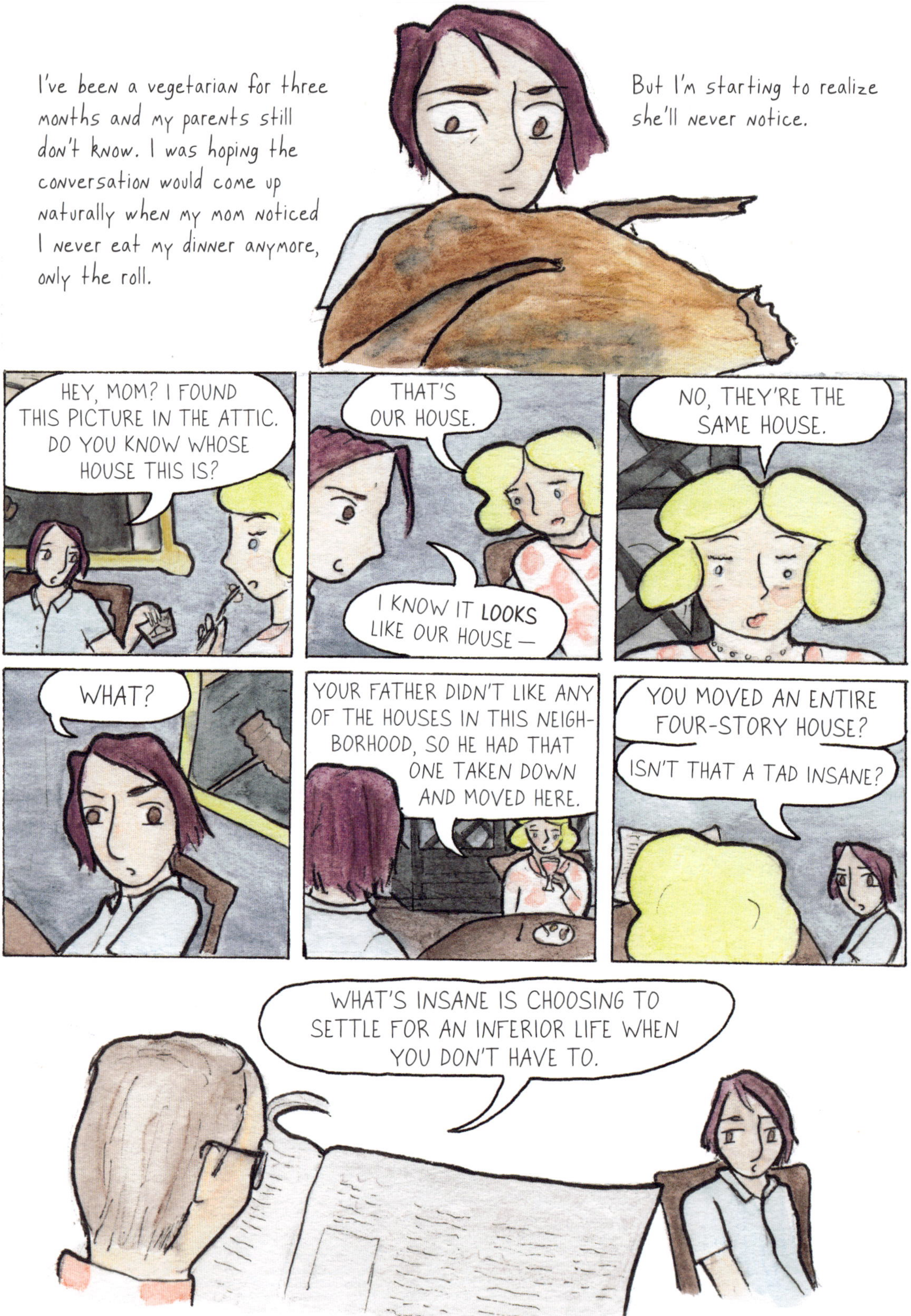
I've been a vegetarian for three months and my parents still don't know. I was hoping the conversation would come up naturally when my mom noticed I never eat my dinner anymore, only the roll.
But I'm starting to realize she'll never notice.
HEY, MOM? I FOUND THIS PICTURE IN THE ATTIC. DO YOU KNOW WHOSE HOUSE THIS IS?
THAT'S OUR HOUSE.
I KNOW IT **LOOKS** LIKE OUR HOUSE —
NO, THEY'RE THE SAME HOUSE.
WHAT?
YOUR FATHER DIDN'T LIKE ANY OF THE HOUSES IN THIS NEIGHBORHOOD, SO HE HAD THAT ONE TAKEN DOWN AND MOVED HERE.
YOU MOVED AN ENTIRE FOUR-STORY HOUSE?
ISN'T THAT A TAD INSANE?
WHAT'S INSANE IS CHOOSING TO SETTLE FOR AN INFERIOR LIFE WHEN YOU DON'T HAVE TO.

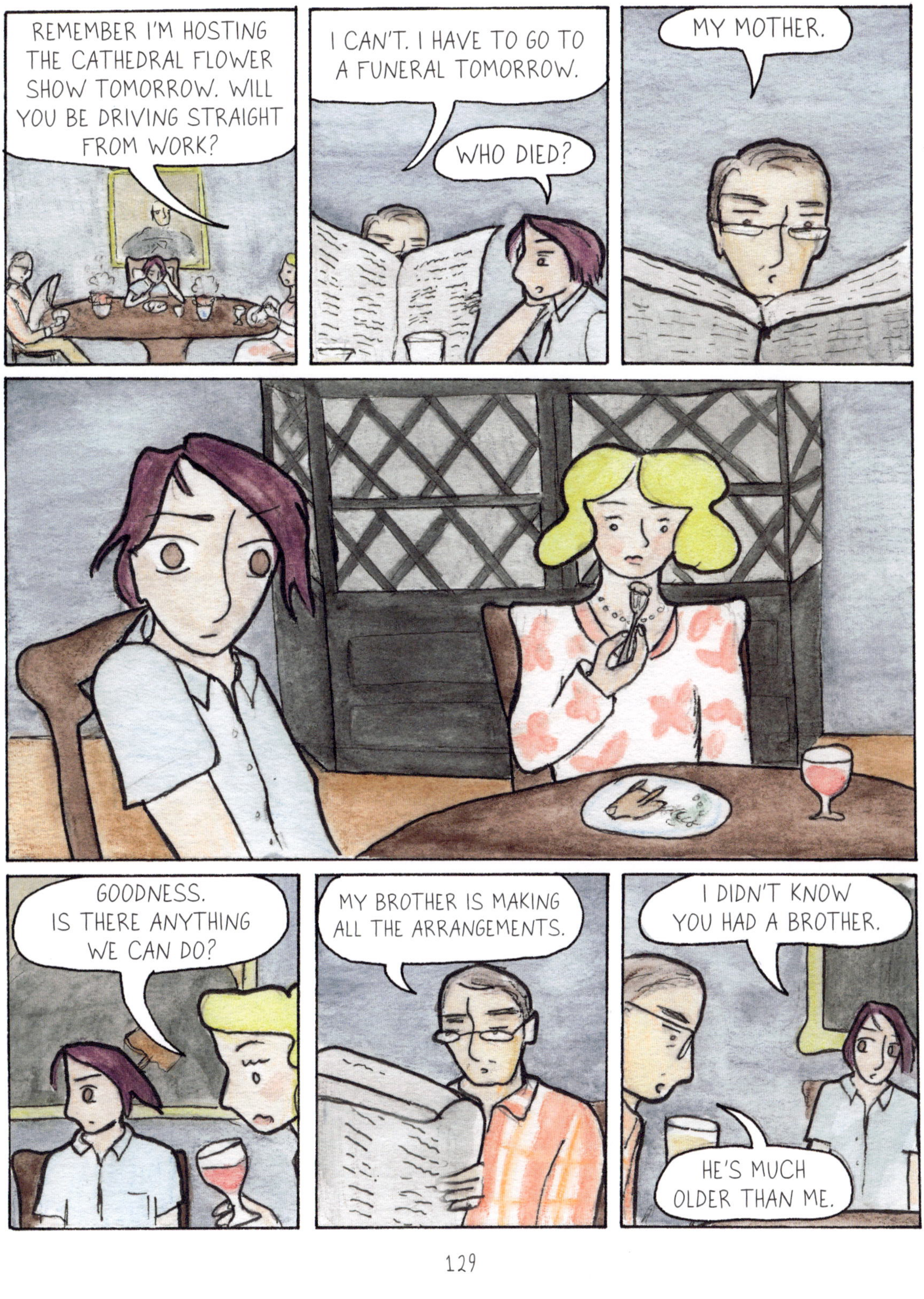
REMEMBER I'M HOSTING THE CATHEDRAL FLOWER SHOW TOMORROW. WILL YOU BE DRIVING STRAIGHT FROM WORK?
I CAN'T. I HAVE TO GO TO A FUNERAL TOMORROW.
WHO DIED?
MY MOTHER.
GOODNESS. IS THERE ANYTHING WE CAN DO?
MY BROTHER IS MAKING ALL THE ARRANGEMENTS.
I DIDN'T KNOW YOU HAD A BROTHER.
HE'S MUCH OLDER THAN ME.

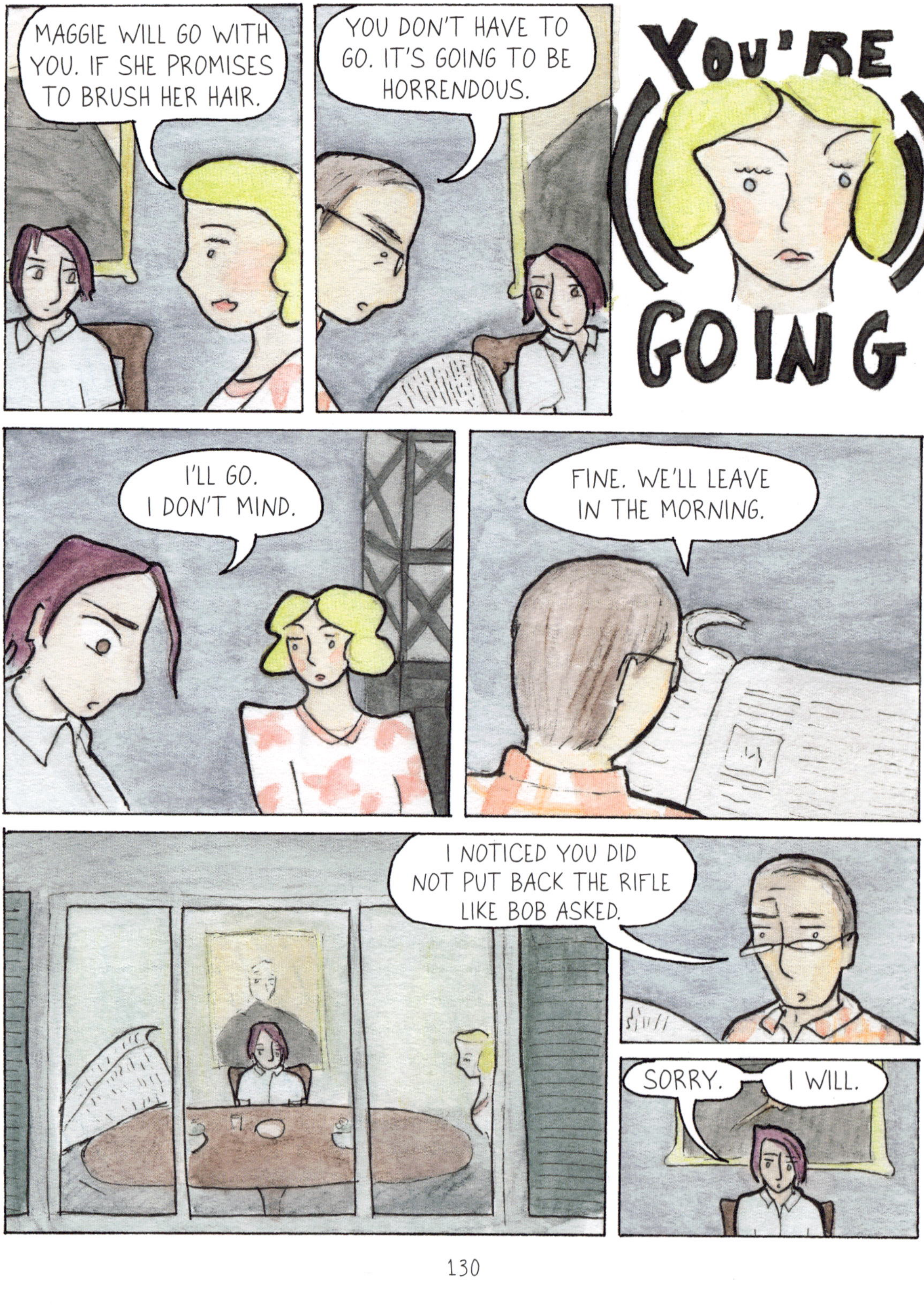

MAGGIE WILL GO WITH YOU. IF SHE PROMISES TO BRUSH HER HAIR.
YOU DON'T HAVE TO GO. IT'S GOING TO BE HORRENDOUS.
YOU'RE GOING
I'LL GO. I DON'T MIND.
FINE. WE'LL LEAVE IN THE MORNING.
I NOTICED YOU DID NOT PUT BACK THE RIFLE LIKE BOB ASKED.
SORRY.
I WILL.

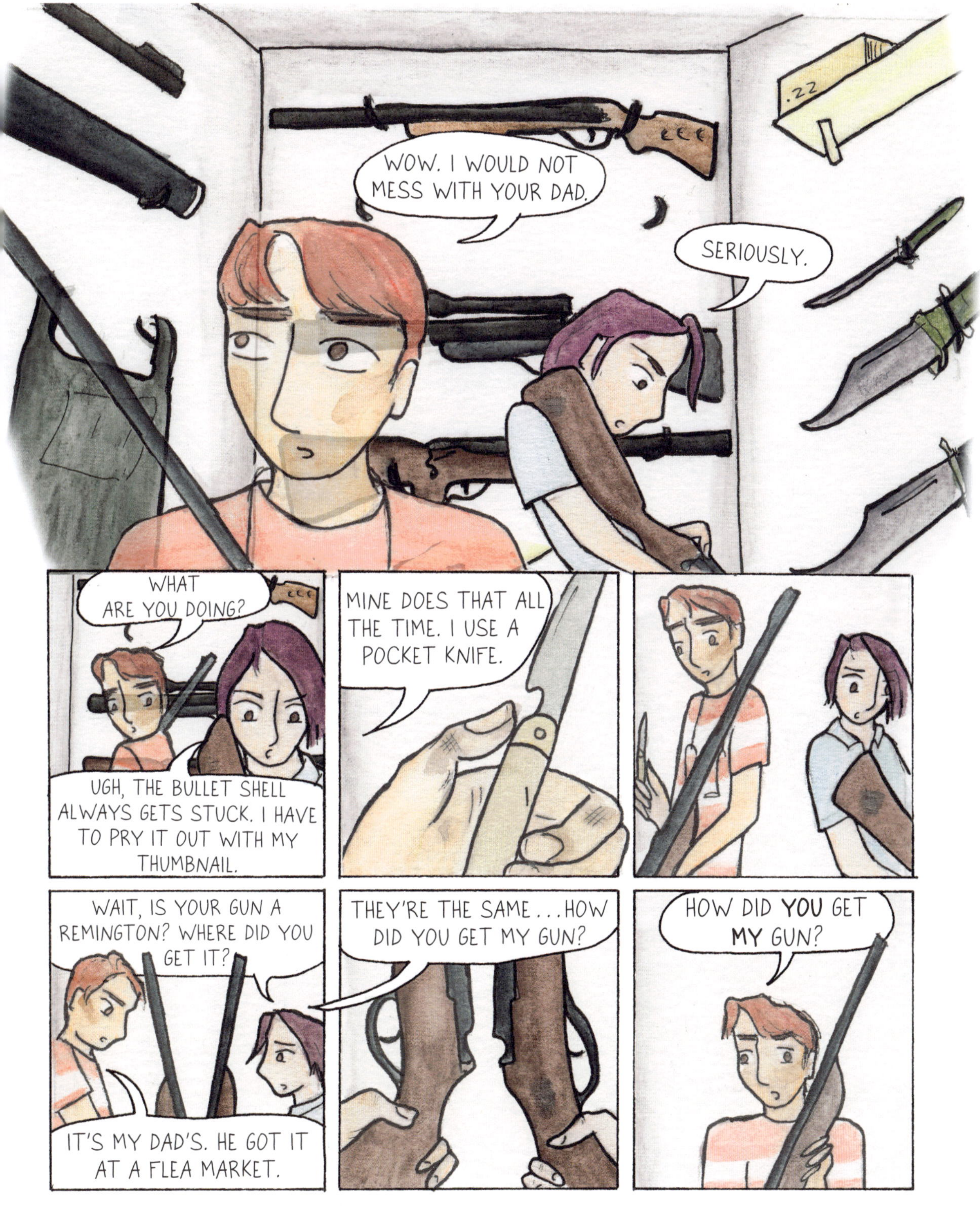

WOW. I WOULD NOT MESS WITH YOUR DAD.
SERIOUSLY.
WHAT ARE YOU DOING?
UGH, THE BULLET SHELL ALWAYS GETS STUCK. I HAVE TO PRY IT OUT WITH MY THUMBNAIL.
MINE DOES THAT ALL THE TIME. I USE A POCKET KNIFE.
WAIT, IS YOUR GUN A REMINGTON? WHERE DID YOU GET IT?
IT'S MY DAD'S. HE GOT IT AT A FLEA MARKET.
THEY'RE THE SAME . . . HOW DID YOU GET MY GUN?
HOW DID **YOU** GET **MY** GUN?

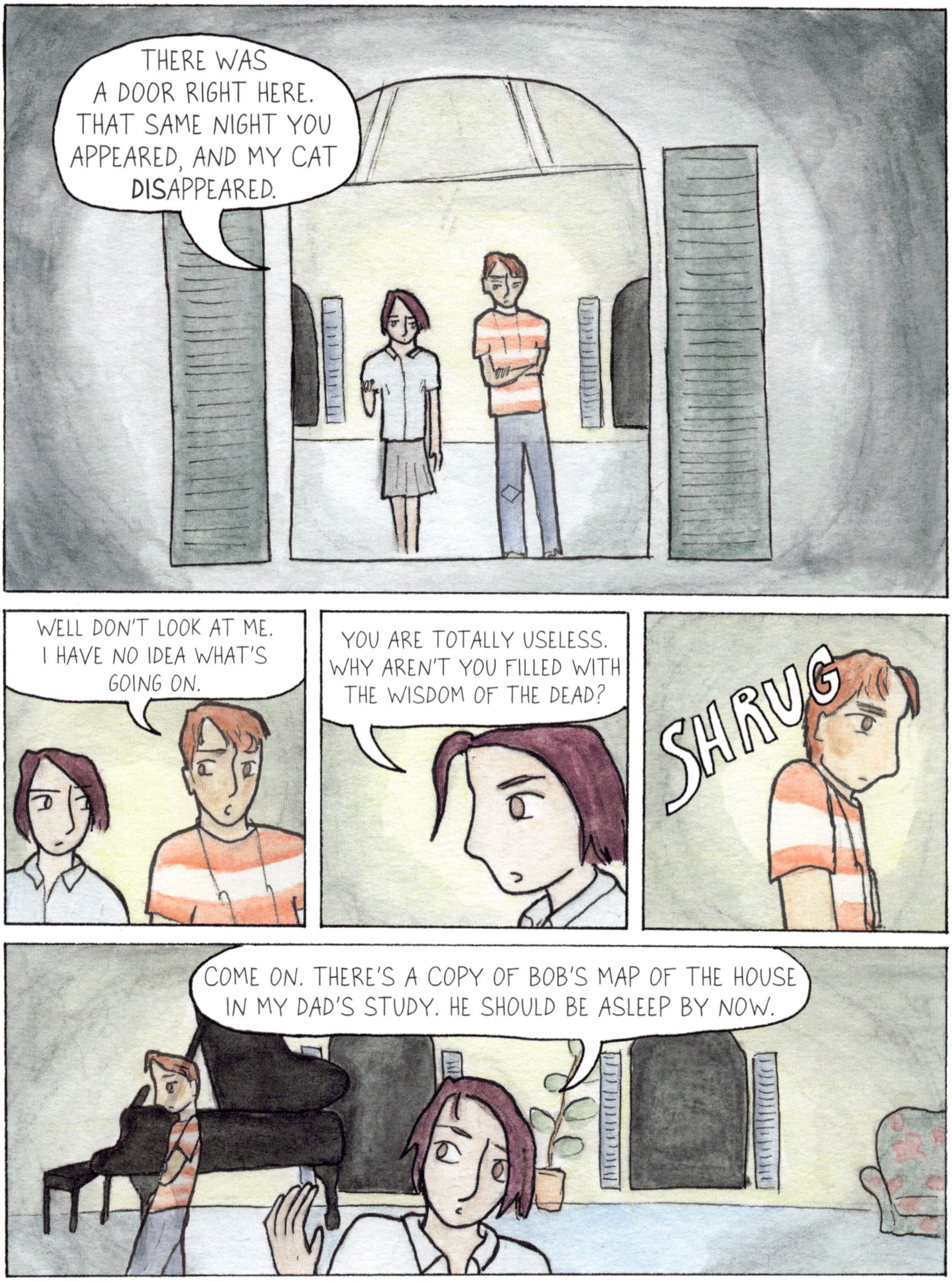
THERE WAS A DOOR RIGHT HERE. THAT SAME NIGHT YOU APPEARED, AND MY CAT **DIS**APPEARED.
WELL DON'T LOOK AT ME. I HAVE NO IDEA WHAT'S GOING ON.
YOU ARE TOTALLY USELESS. WHY AREN'T YOU FILLED WITH THE WISDOM OF THE DEAD?
SHRUG
COME ON. THERE'S A COPY OF BOB'S MAP OF THE HOUSE IN MY DAD'S STUDY. HE SHOULD BE ASLEEP BY NOW.

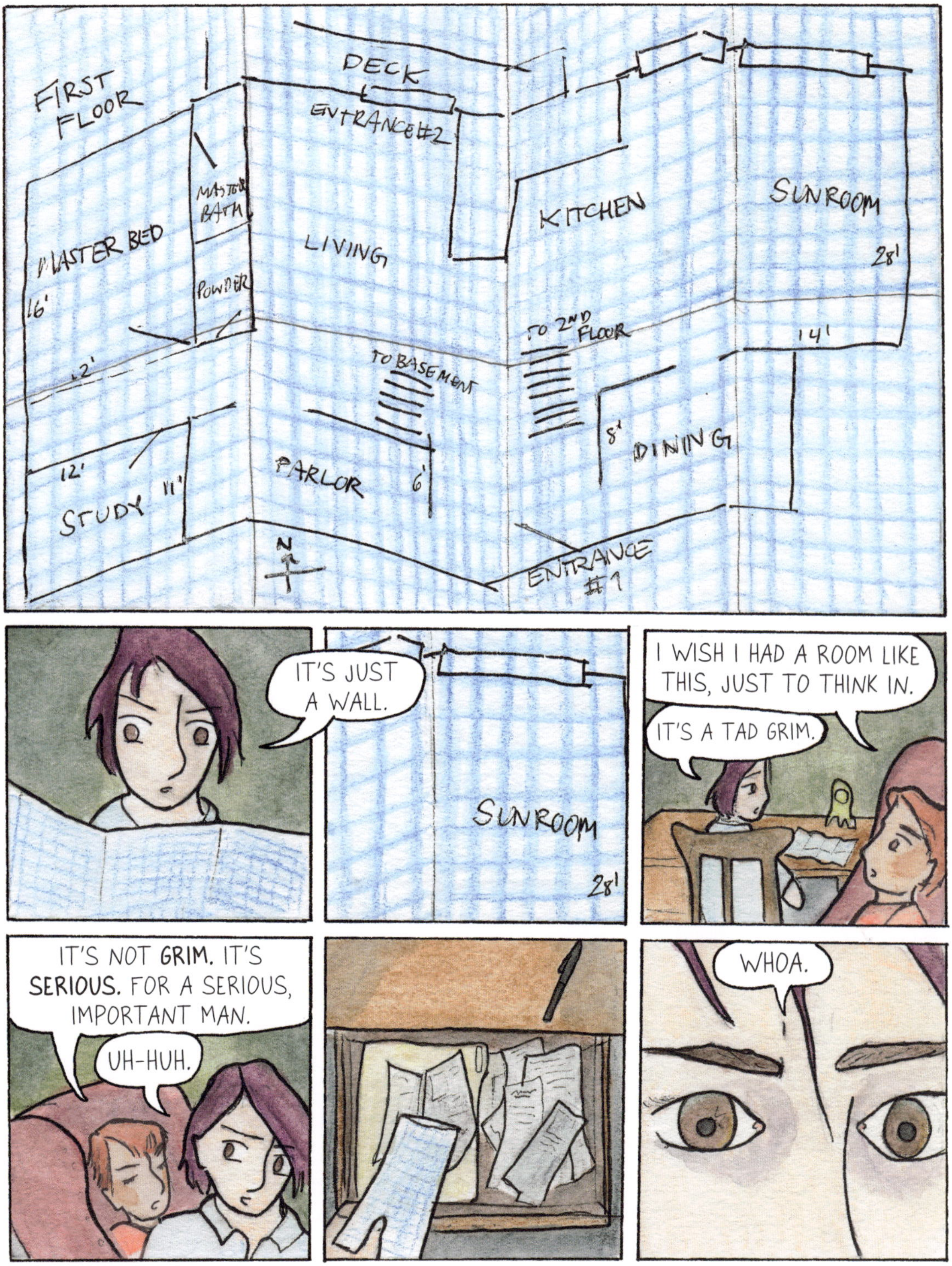
FIRST FLOOR
DECK
ENTRANCE #2
MASTER BATH
MASTER BED
16'
POWDER
LIVING
KITCHEN
SUNROOM
28'
TO 2ND FLOOR
14'
12'
TO BASEMENT
8'
DINING
12'
STUDY 11'
PARLOR
6'
N
ENTRANCE #1
IT'S JUST A WALL.
SUNROOM
28'
I WISH I HAD A ROOM LIKE THIS, JUST TO THINK IN.
IT'S A TAD GRIM.
IT'S NOT GRIM. IT'S SERIOUS. FOR A SERIOUS, IMPORTANT MAN.
UH-HUH.
WHOA.

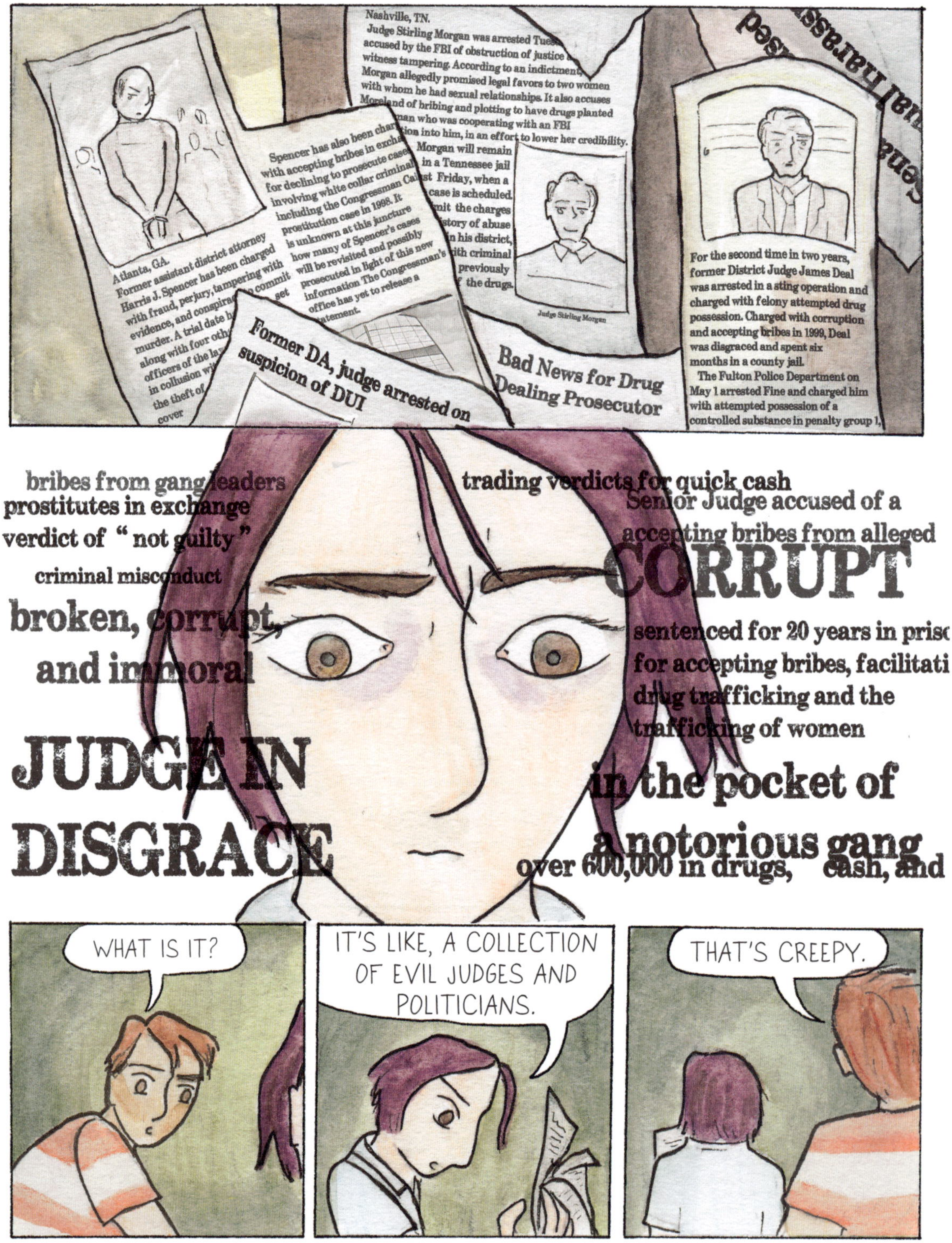
Nashville, TN.
Judge Stirling Morgan was arrested
accused by the FBI of obstruction of justice
witness tampering. According to an indictment,
Morgan allegedly promised legal favors to two women
with whom he had sexual relationships. It also accuses
Morgan will remain
in a Tennessee jail
Judge Stirling Morgan
Spencer has also been
with accepting bribes in
for declining to prosecute
involving white collar
including the Congressman
prostitution case in 1998. It
is unknown at this juncture
how many of Spencer's cases
will be revisited and possibly
prosecuted in light of this new
information The Congressman's
office has yet to release a
Atlanta, GA.
Former assistant district attorney
Harris J. Spencer has been charged
with fraud, perjury, tampering with
Former DA, judge arrested on suspicion of DUI
Bad News for Drug Dealing Prosecutor
For the second time in two years, former District Judge James Deal was arrested in a sting operation and charged with felony attempted drug possession. Charged with corruption and accepting bribes in 1999, Deal was disgraced and spent six months in a county jail.
The Fulton Police Department on May 1 arrested Fine and charged him with attempted possession of a controlled substance in penalty group 1,
bribes from gang leaders
prostitutes in exchange
verdict of "not guilty"
criminal misconduct
broken, corrupt,
and immoral
JUDGE IN DISGRACE
trading verdicts for quick cash
Senior Judge accused of a
accepting bribes from alleged
CORRUPT
for accepting bribes, facilitati
drug trafficking and the
trafficking of women
in the pocket of
a notorious gang
over 600,000 in drugs, cash, and
WHAT IS IT?
IT'S LIKE, A COLLECTION OF EVIL JUDGES AND POLITICIANS.
THAT'S CREEPY.

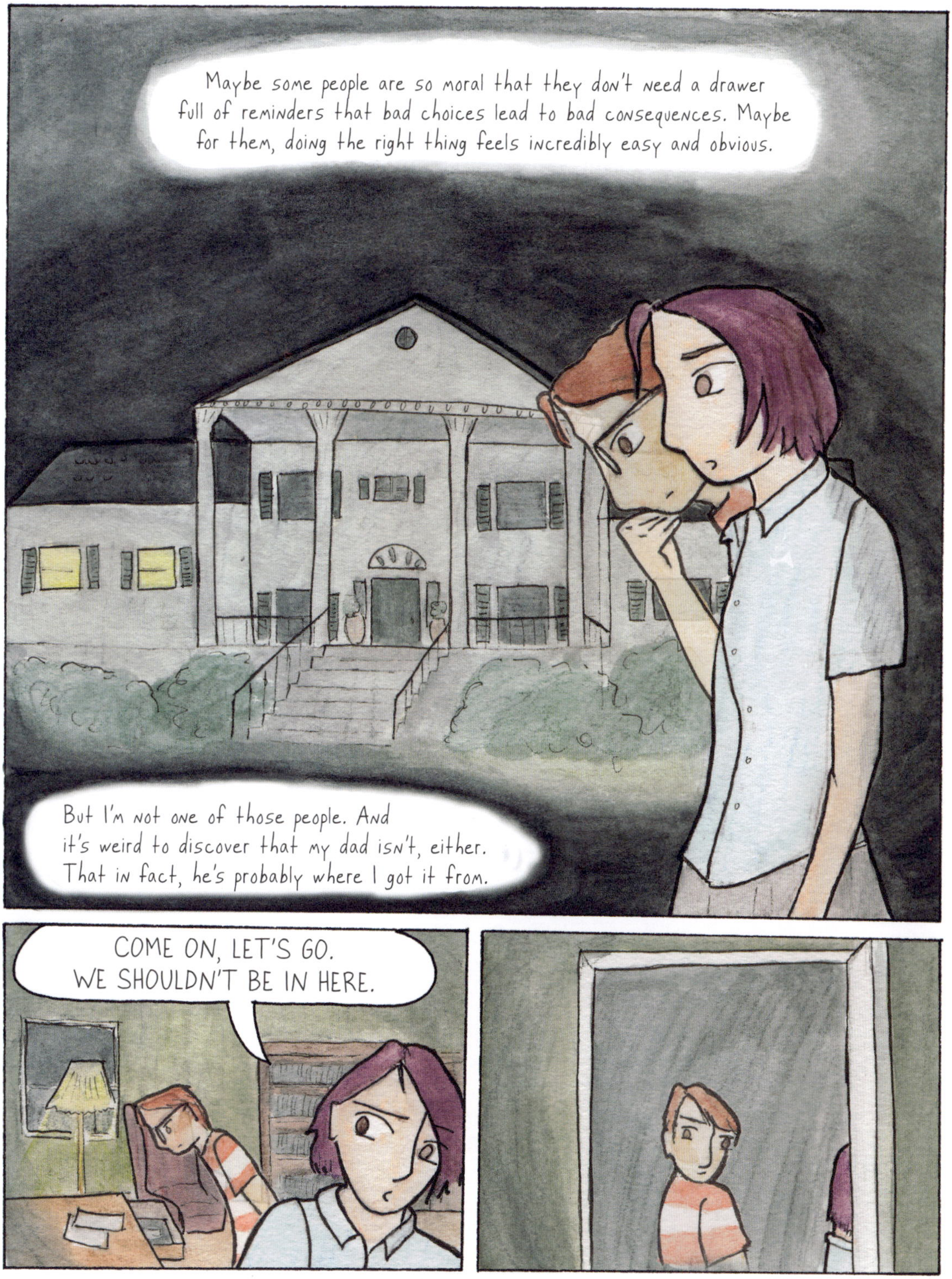
Maybe some people are so moral that they don't need a drawer full of reminders that bad choices lead to bad consequences. Maybe for them, doing the right thing feels incredibly easy and obvious.
But I'm not one of those people. And it's weird to discover that my dad isn't, either. That in fact, he's probably where I got it from.
COME ON, LET'S GO. WE SHOULDN'T BE IN HERE.

# Chapter 7

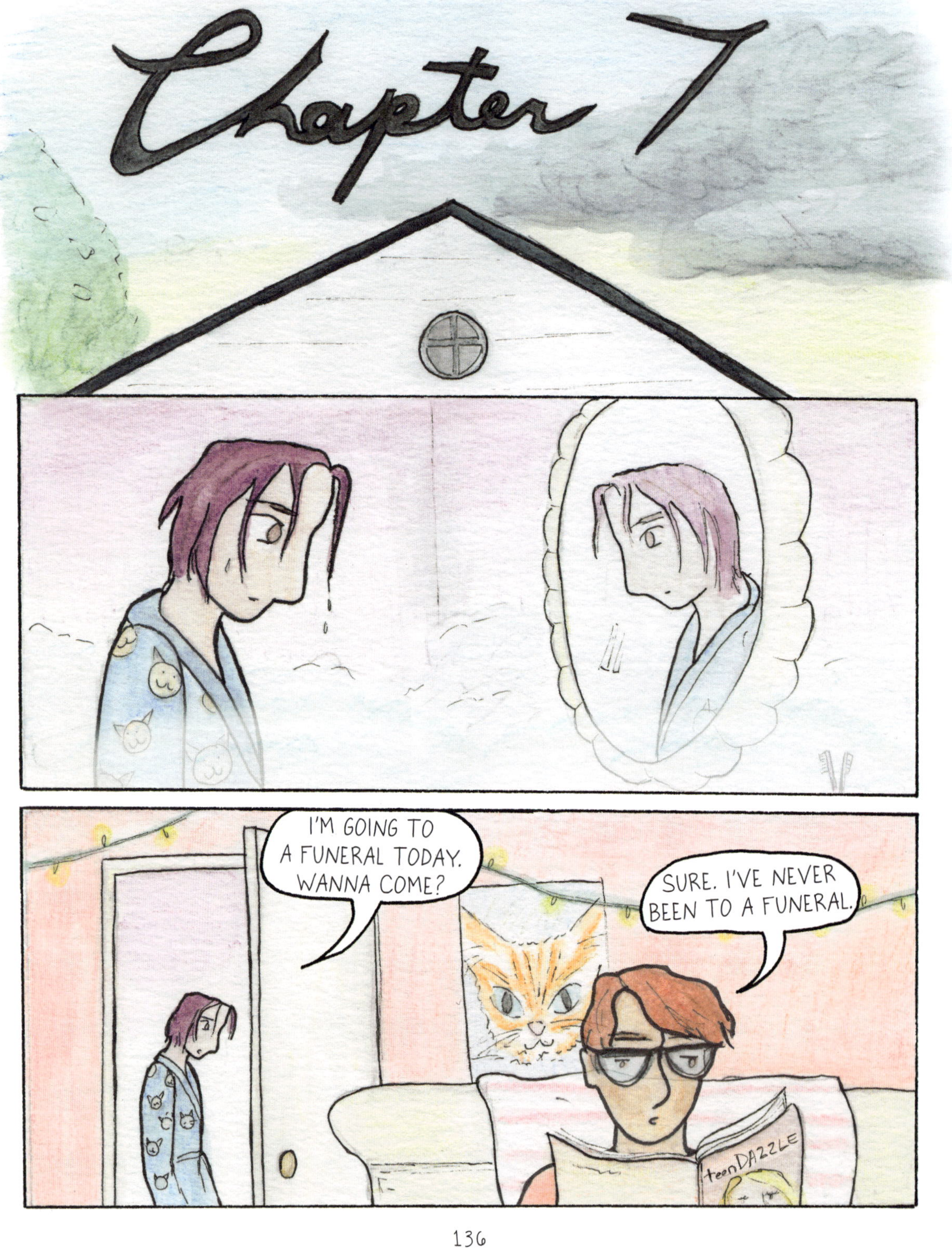

I'M GOING TO A FUNERAL TODAY. WANNA COME?
SURE. I'VE NEVER BEEN TO A FUNERAL.
teenDAZZLE

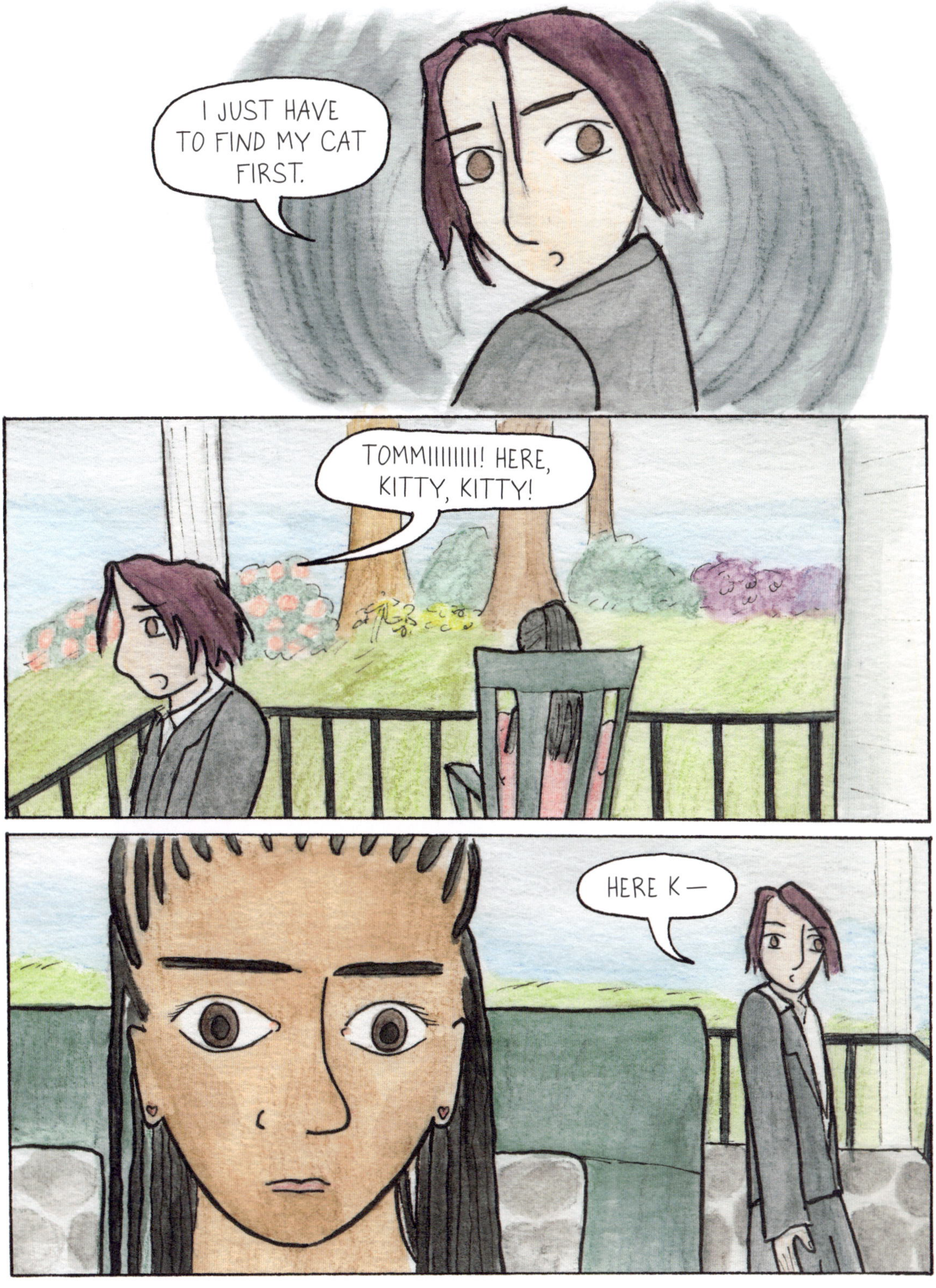
I JUST HAVE TO FIND MY CAT FIRST.
TOMMIIIIIIIII! HERE, KITTY, KITTY!
HERE K—

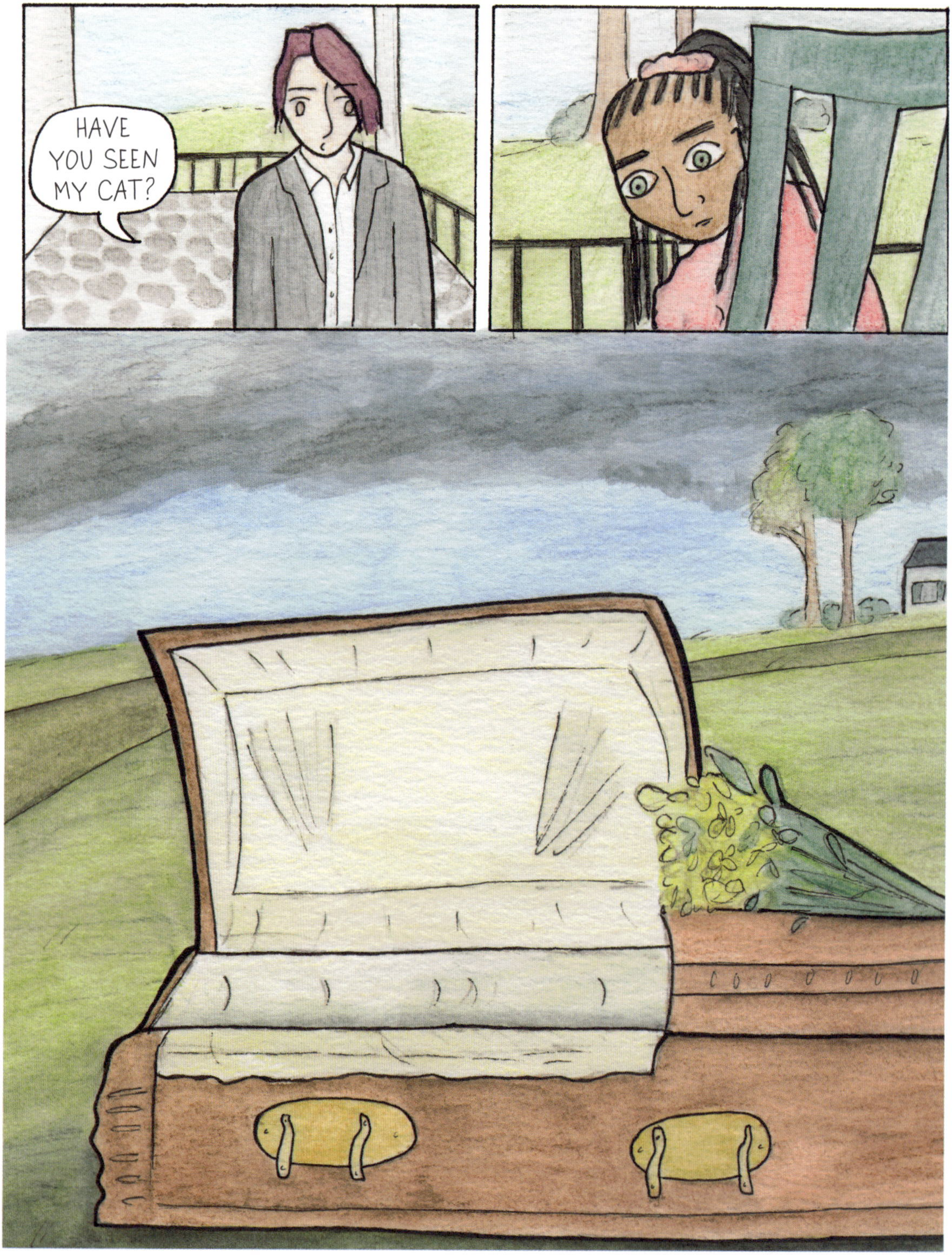
HAVE YOU SEEN MY CAT?

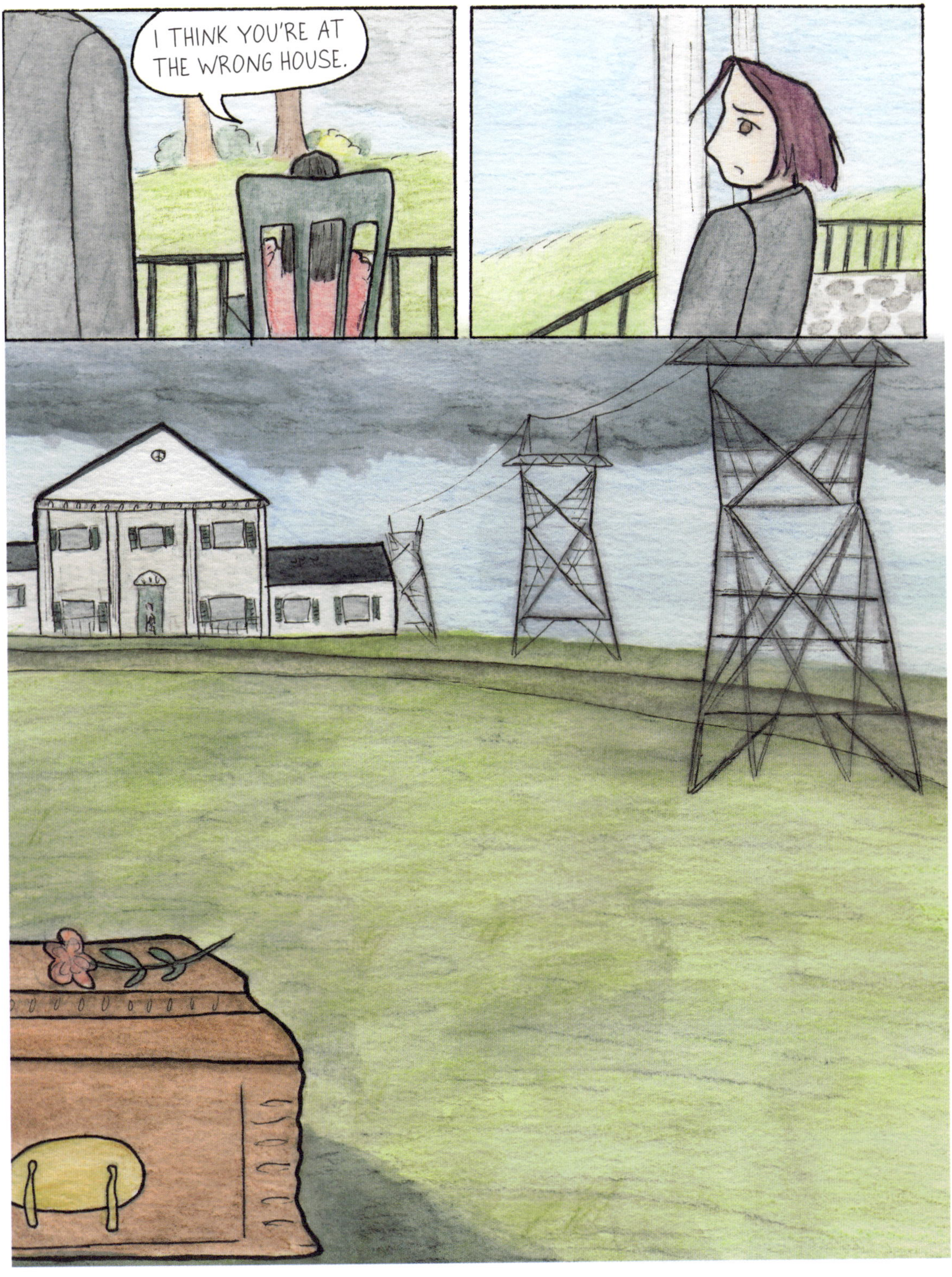
I THINK YOU'RE AT THE WRONG HOUSE.

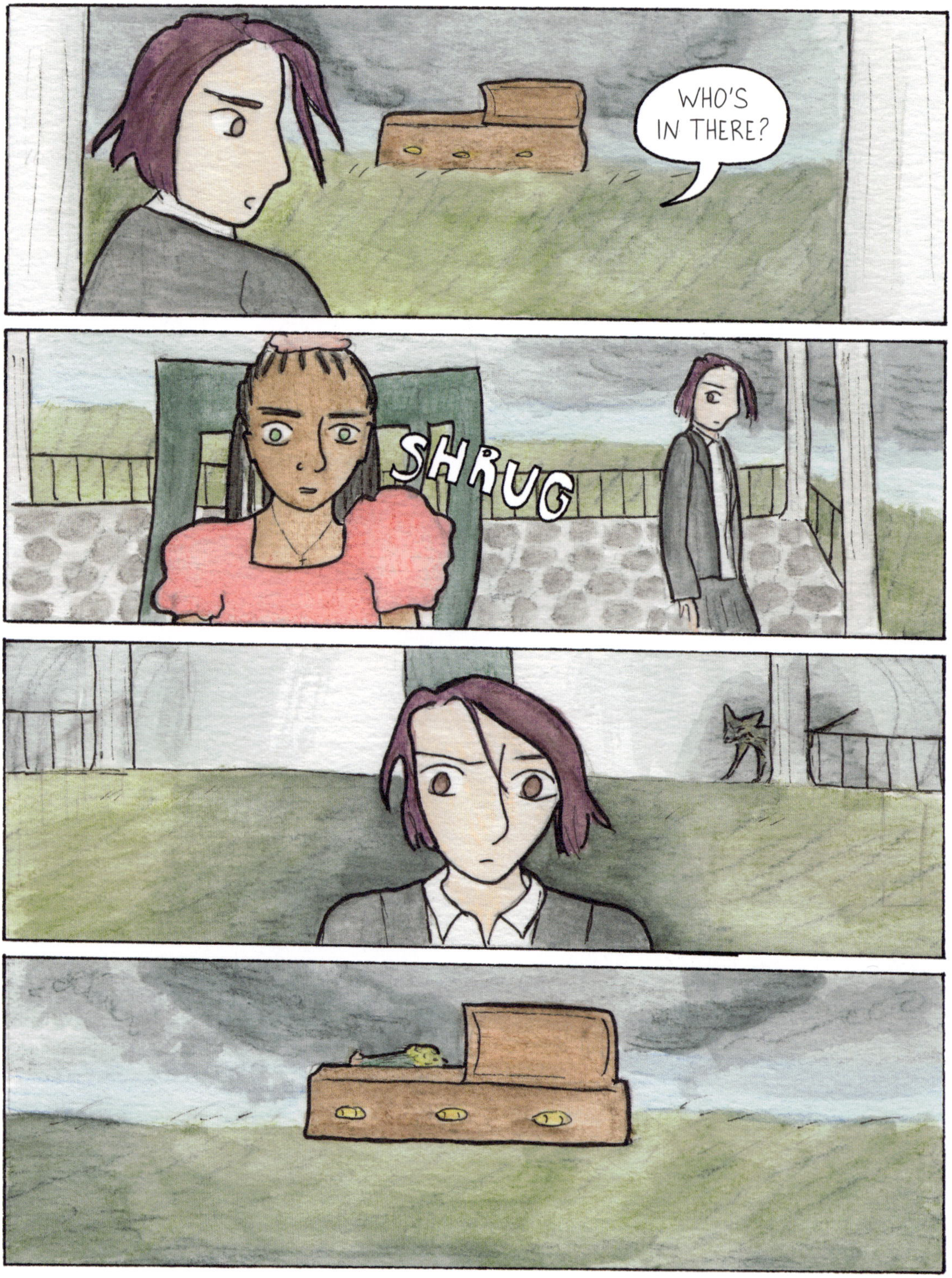
WHO'S IN THERE?
SHRUG

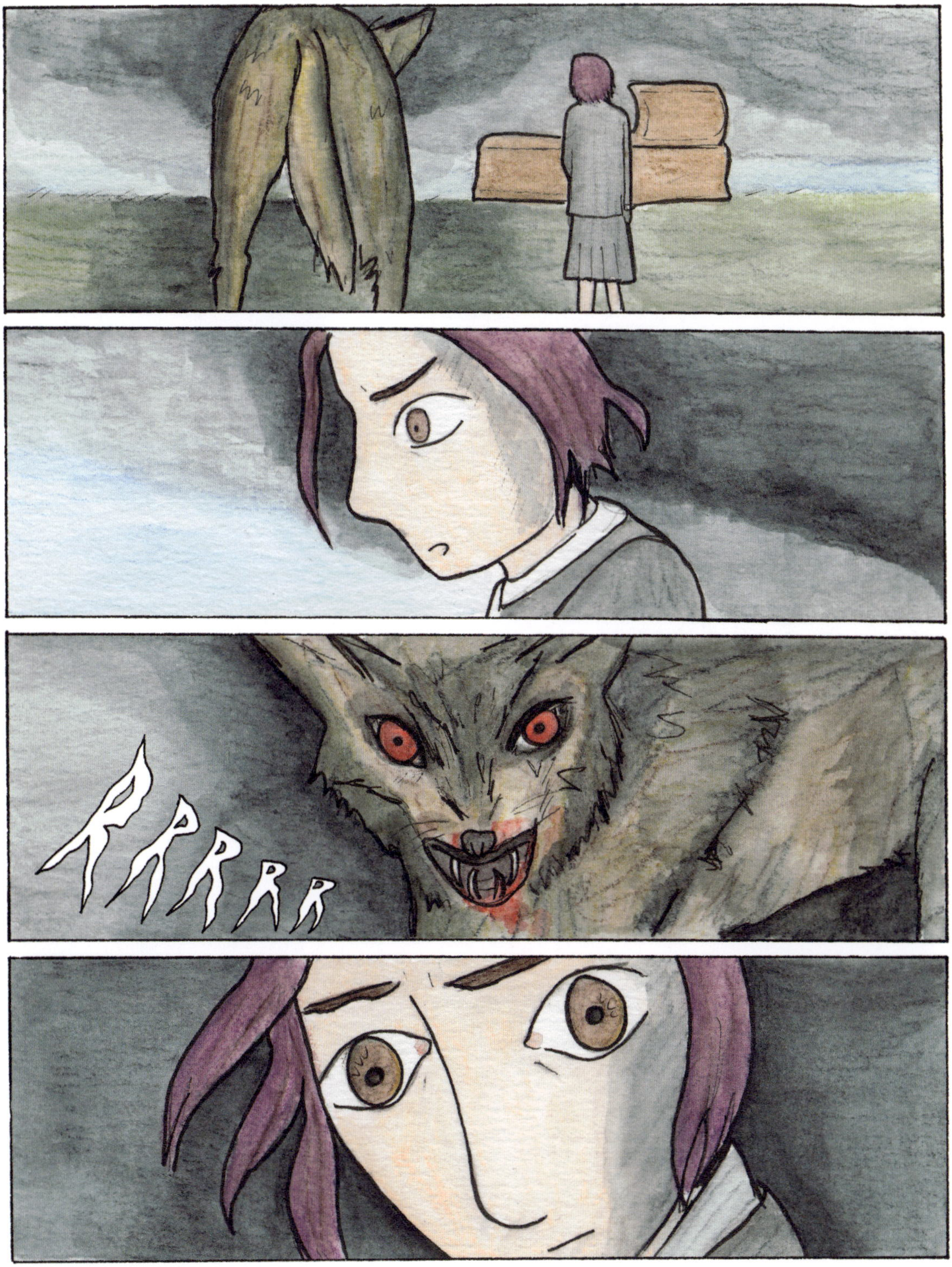
RRRRR

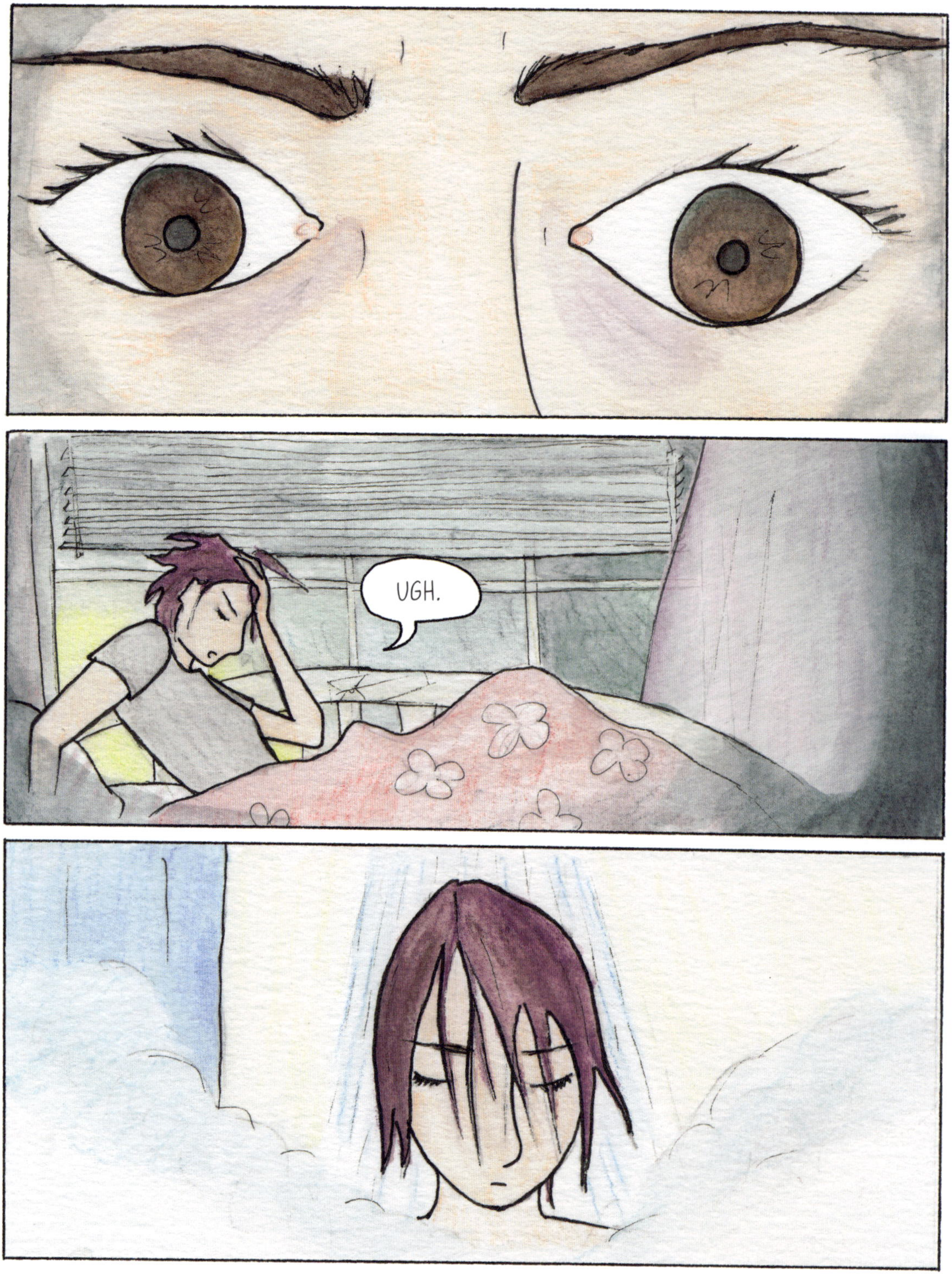
UGH.

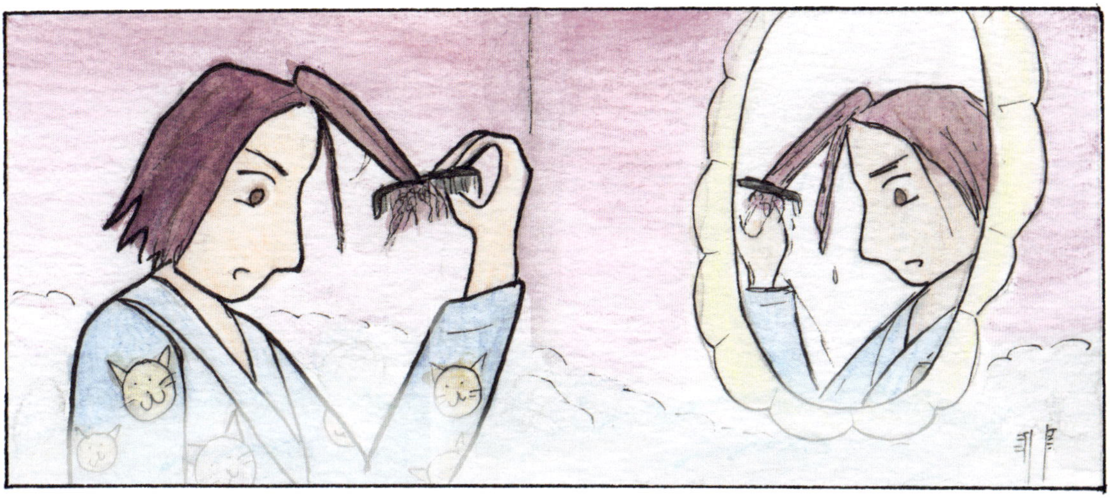

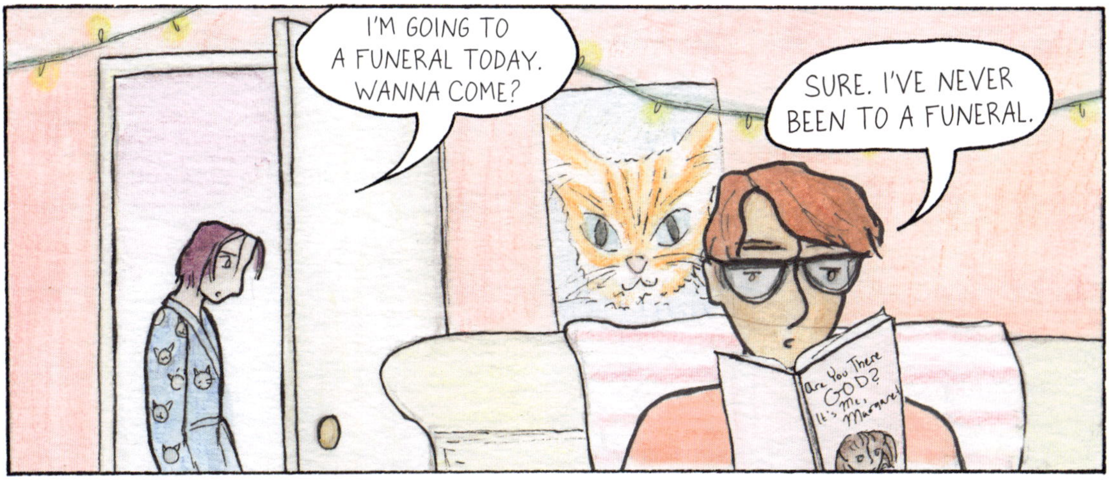
I'M GOING TO A FUNERAL TODAY. WANNA COME?
SURE. I'VE NEVER BEEN TO A FUNERAL.
Are You There GOD? It's Me, Margaret

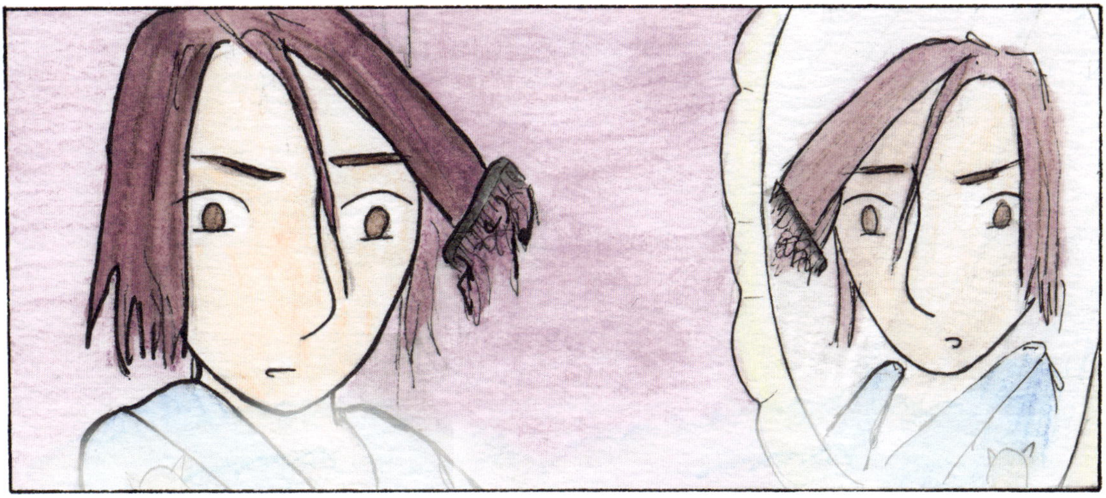

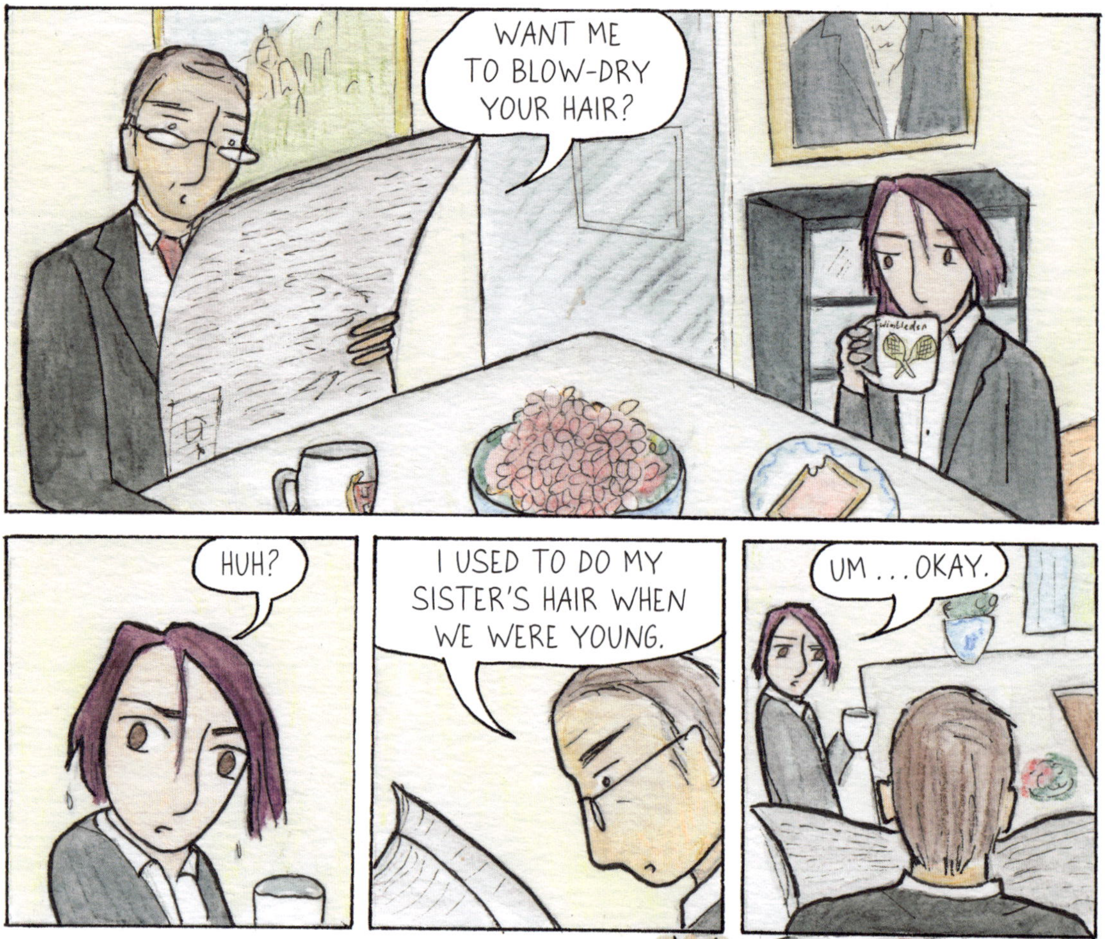
WANT ME TO BLOW-DRY YOUR HAIR?
HUH?
I USED TO DO MY SISTER'S HAIR WHEN WE WERE YOUNG.
UM . . . OKAY.

Who knew my dad could do girls' hair? It's weird to see him filling such a maternal role, and to know that his sister saw this side of him every day, while I'm seeing it for the first time in my life.

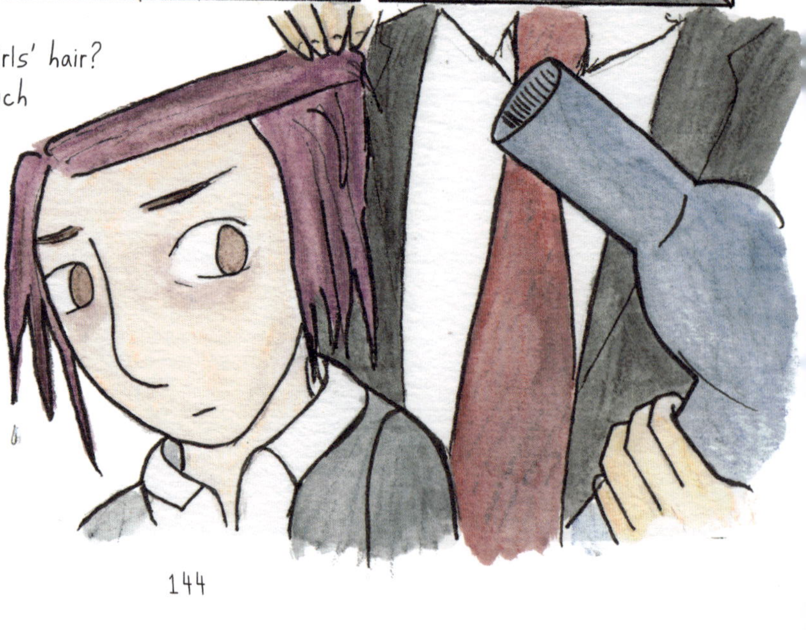

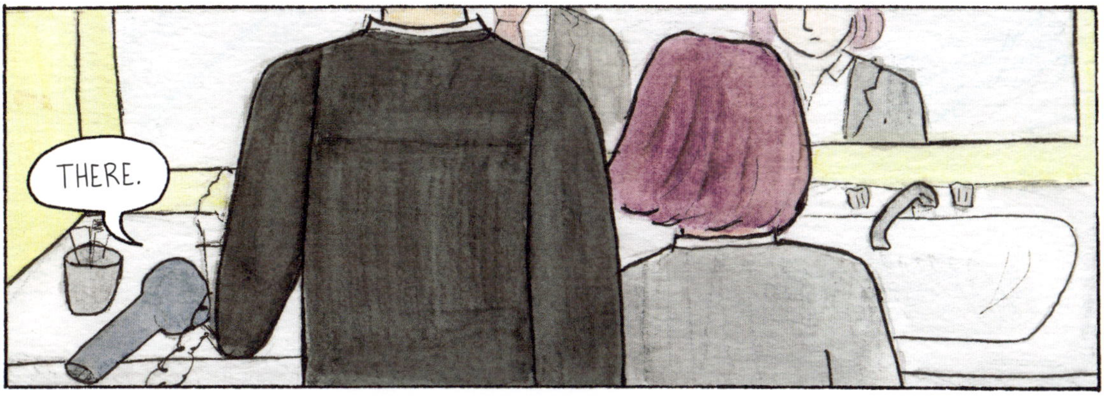
THERE.

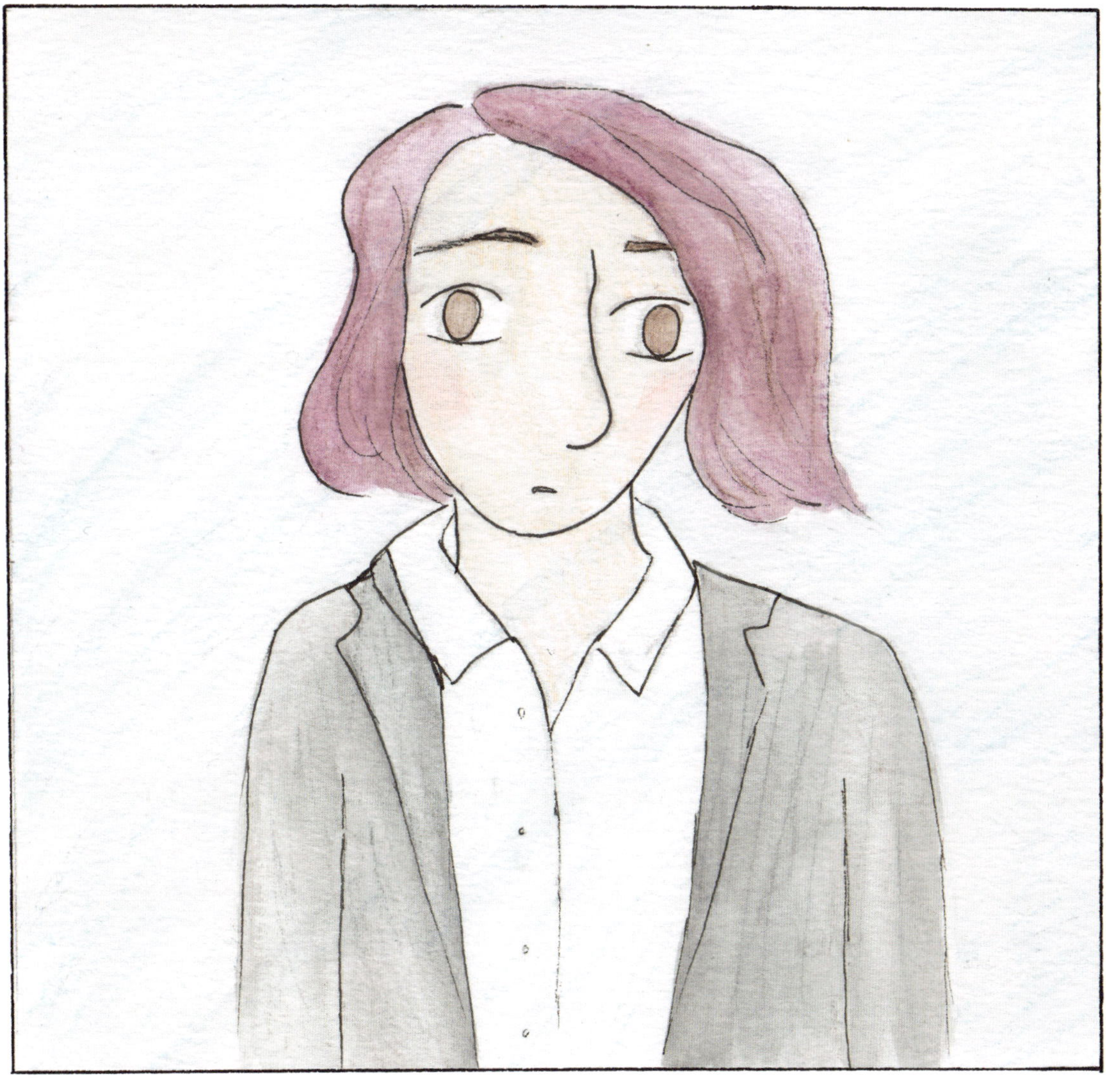

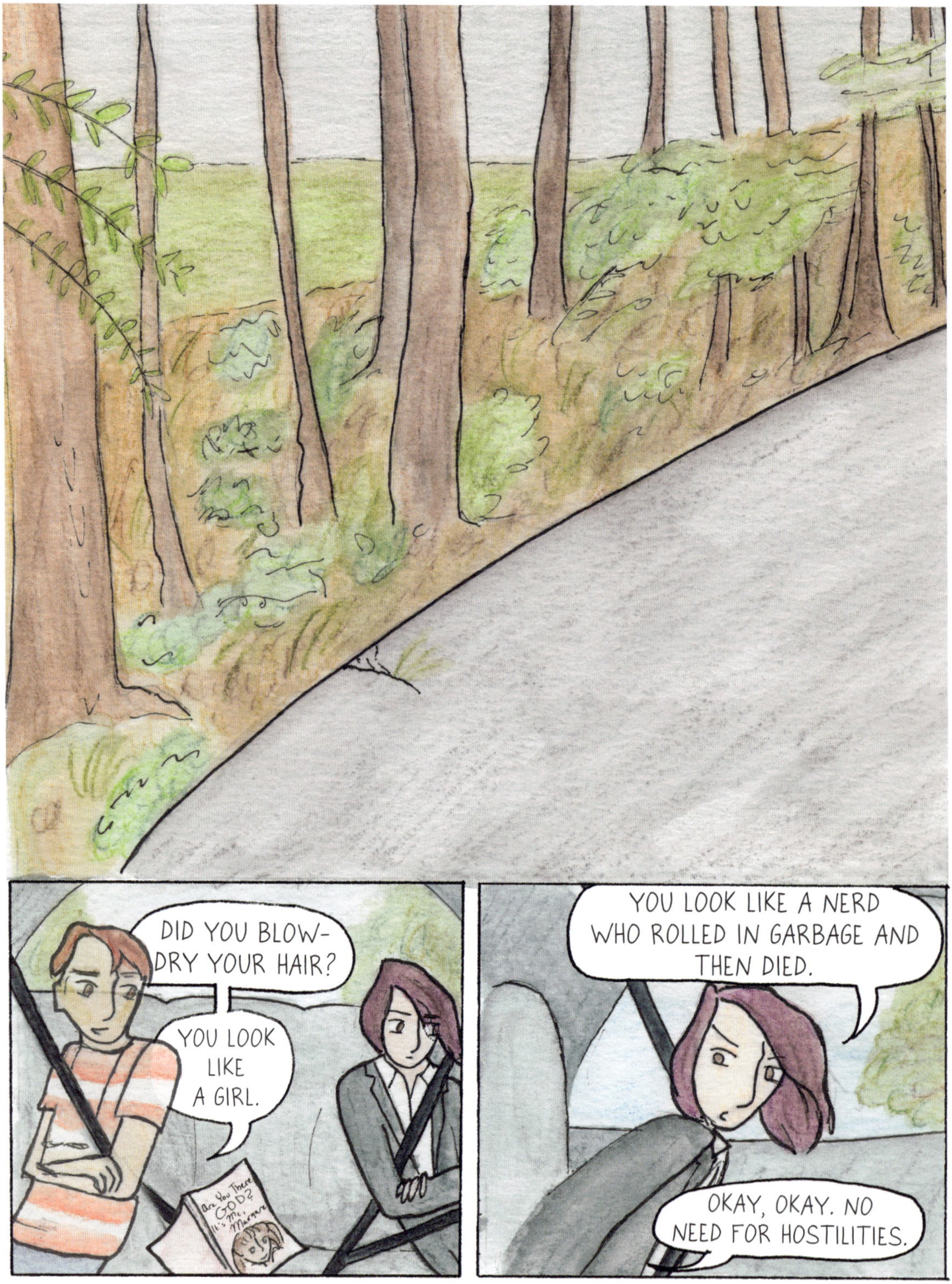
DID YOU BLOW-DRY YOUR HAIR?
YOU LOOK LIKE A GIRL.
YOU LOOK LIKE A NERD WHO ROLLED IN GARBAGE AND THEN DIED.
OKAY, OKAY. NO NEED FOR HOSTILITIES.

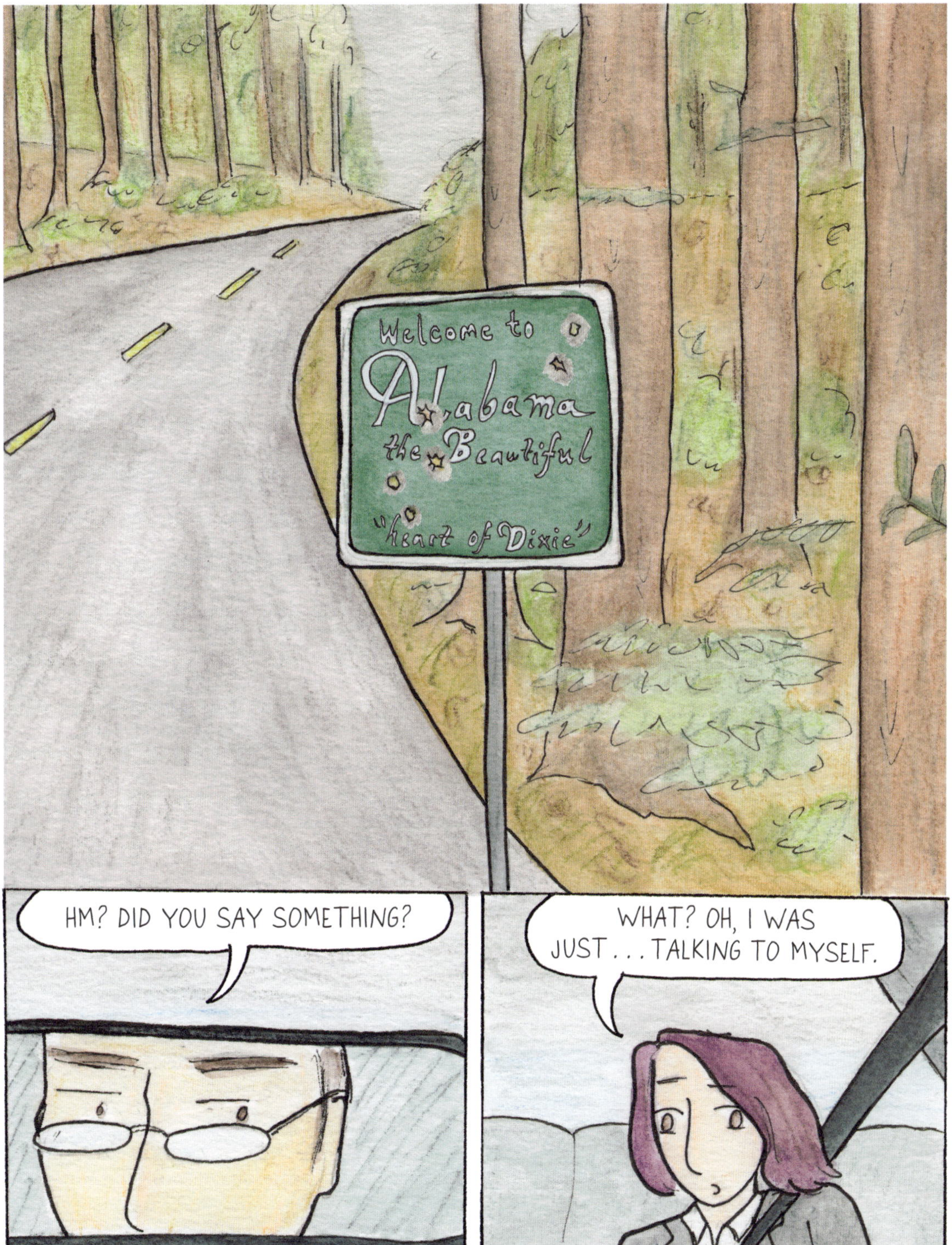
Welcome to
Alabama
the Beautiful
"heart of Dixie"
HM? DID YOU SAY SOMETHING?
WHAT? OH, I WAS JUST . . . TALKING TO MYSELF.

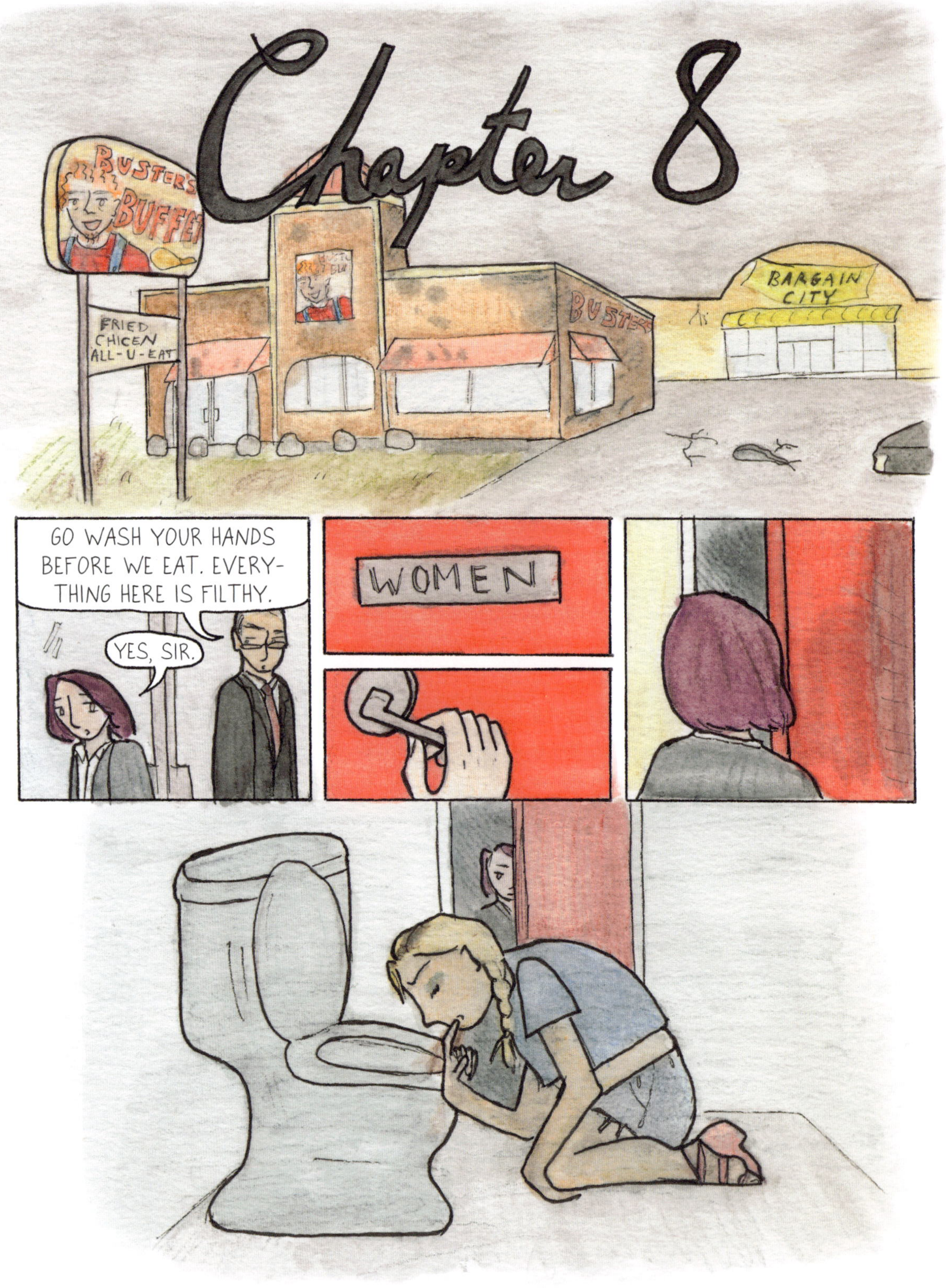
Chapter 8
BUSTER'S BUFFET
FRIED CHICEN ALL-U-EAT
BUSTERS
BARGAIN CITY
GO WASH YOUR HANDS BEFORE WE EAT. EVERYTHING HERE IS FILTHY.
YES, SIR.
WOMEN

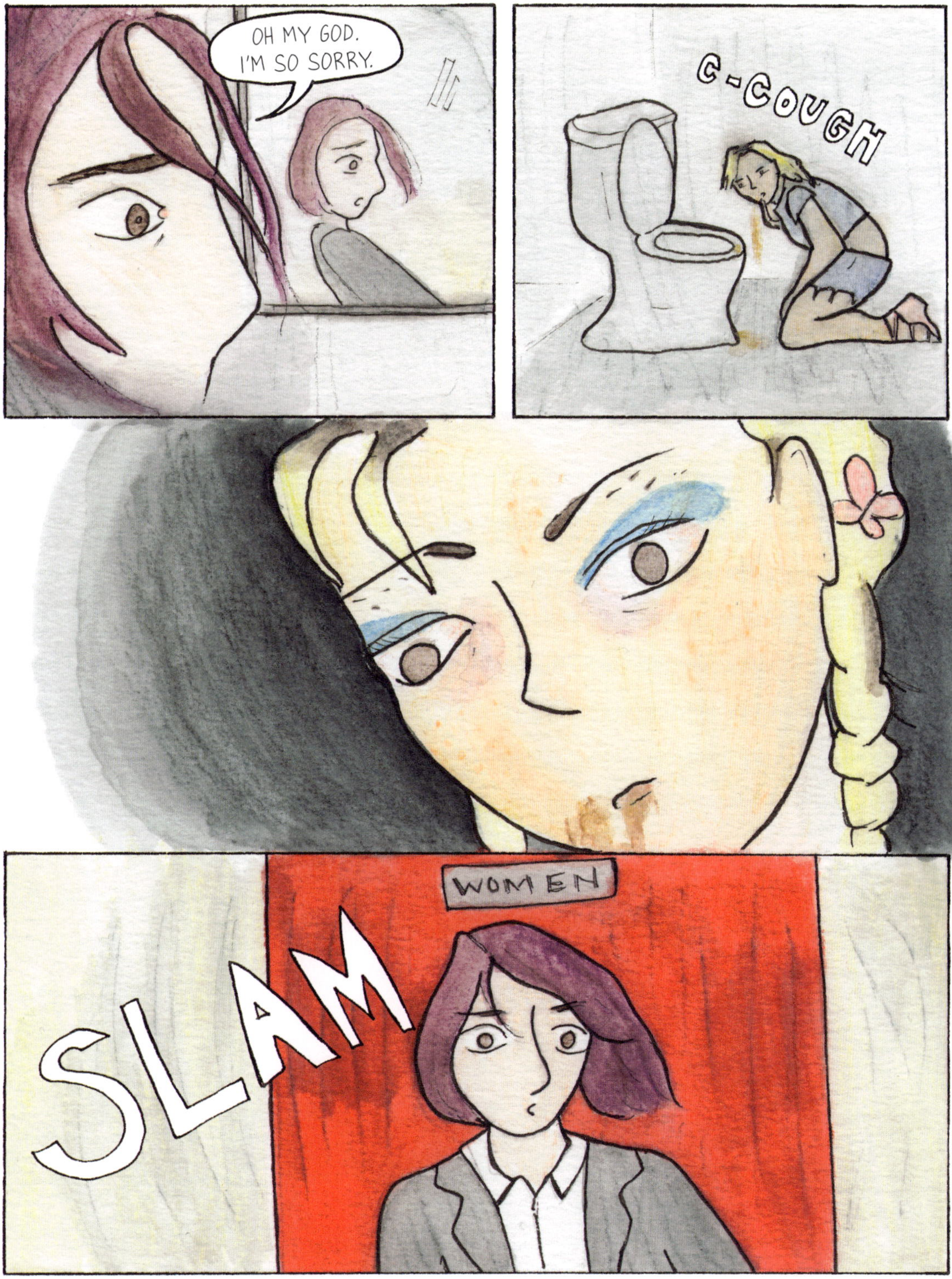
OH MY GOD. I'M SO SORRY.
C-COUGH
WOMEN
SLAM

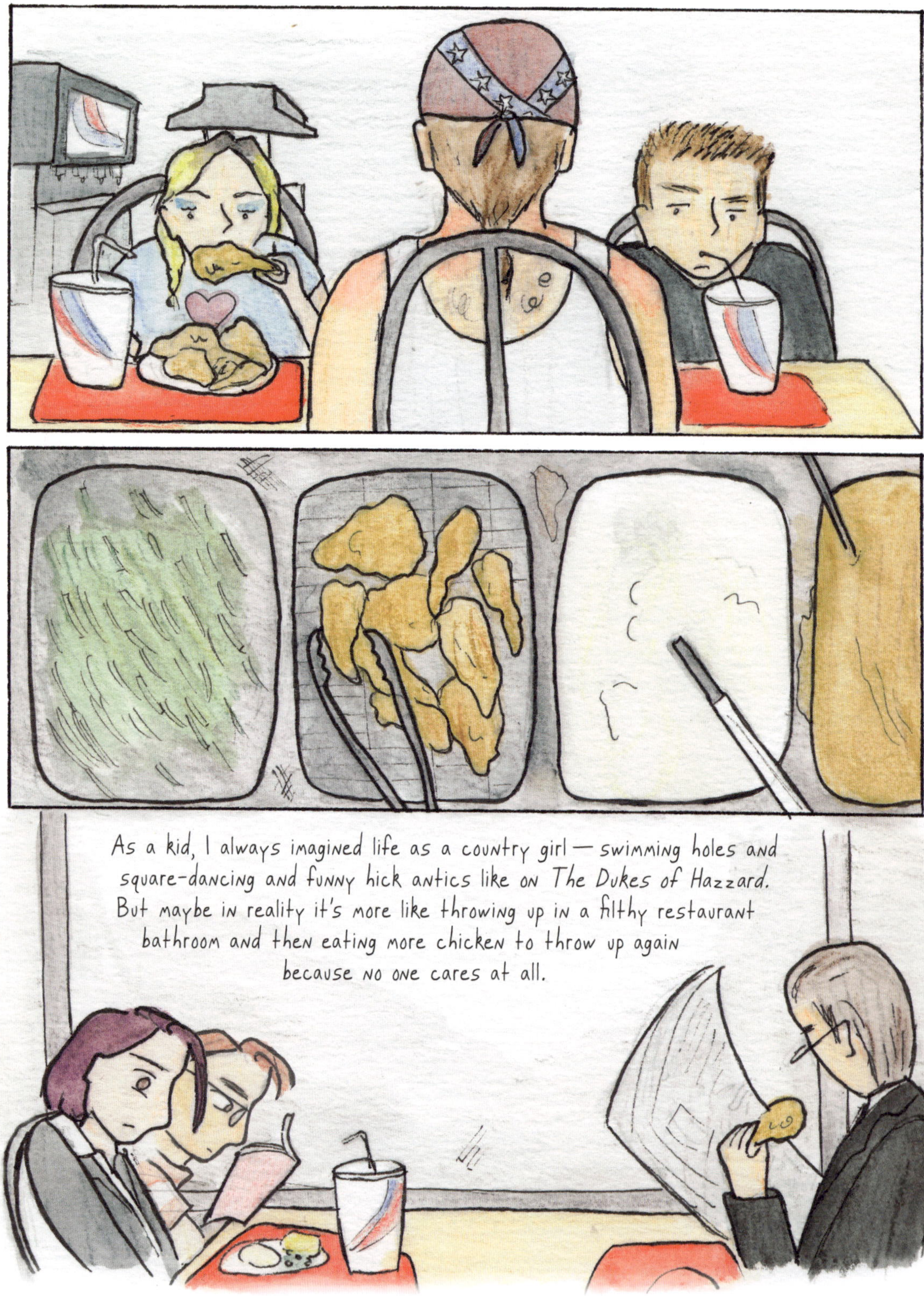
As a kid, I always imagined life as a country girl — swimming holes and square-dancing and funny hick antics like on *The Dukes of Hazzard.* But maybe in reality it's more like throwing up in a filthy restaurant bathroom and then eating more chicken to throw up again because no one cares at all.

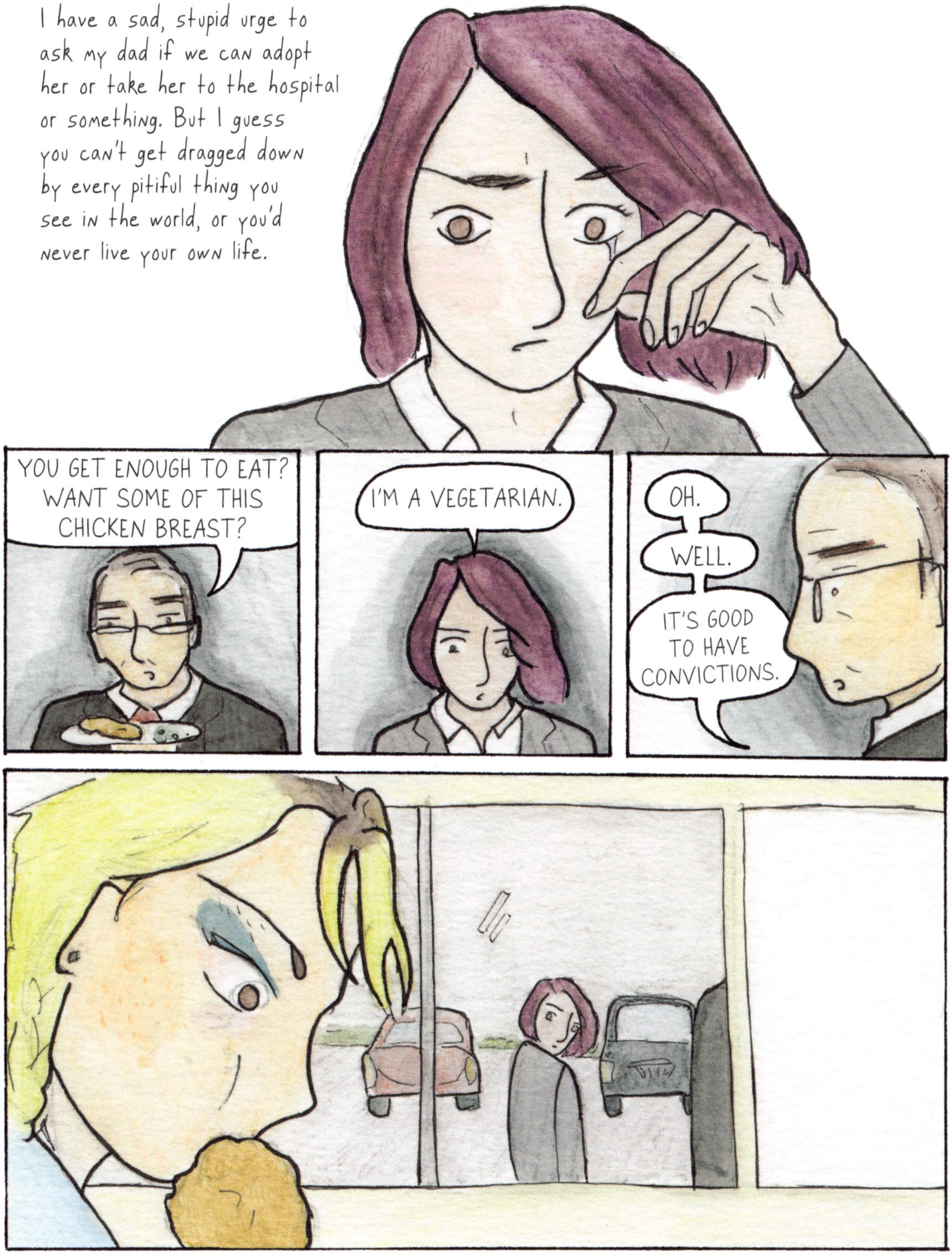
I have a sad, stupid urge to ask my dad if we can adopt her or take her to the hospital or something. But I guess you can't get dragged down by every pitiful thing you see in the world, or you'd never live your own life.
YOU GET ENOUGH TO EAT? WANT SOME OF THIS CHICKEN BREAST?
I'M A VEGETARIAN.
OH.
WELL.
IT'S GOOD TO HAVE CONVICTIONS.

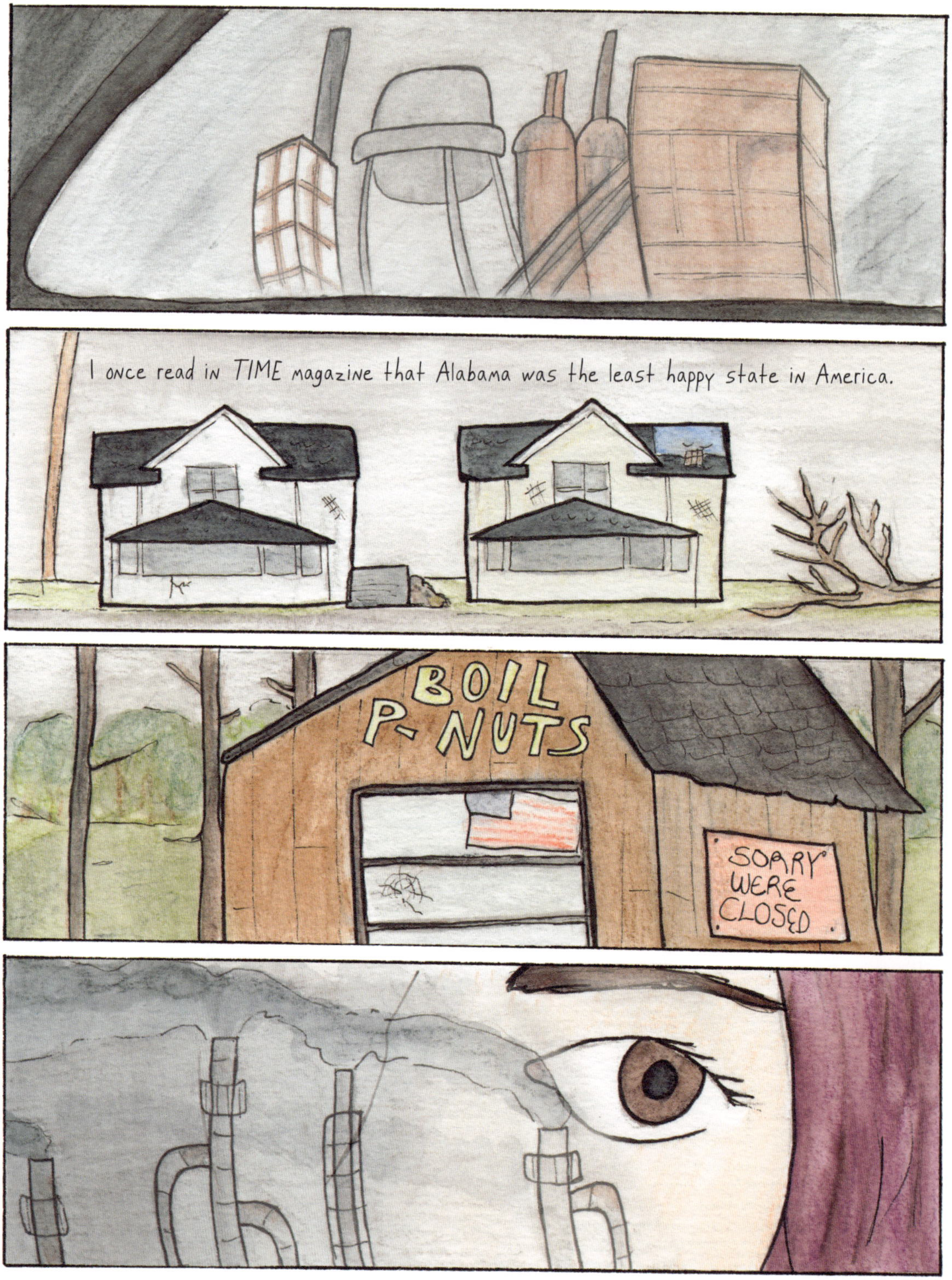
I once read in TIME magazine that Alabama was the least happy state in America.
BOIL P-NUTS
SORRY WERE CLOSED

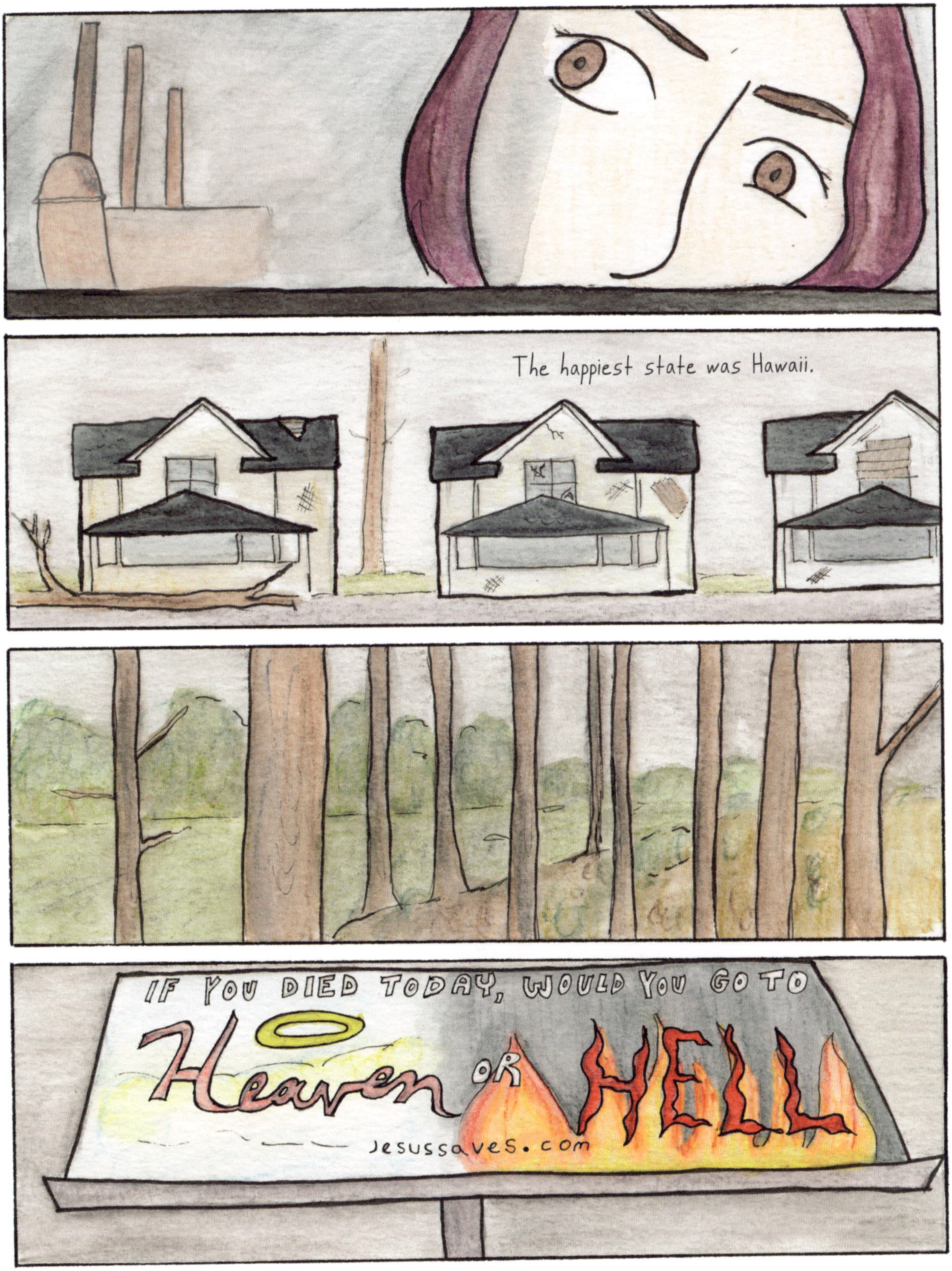
The happiest state was Hawaii.
IF YOU DIED TODAY, WOULD YOU GO TO
Heaven OR HELL
jesussaves.com

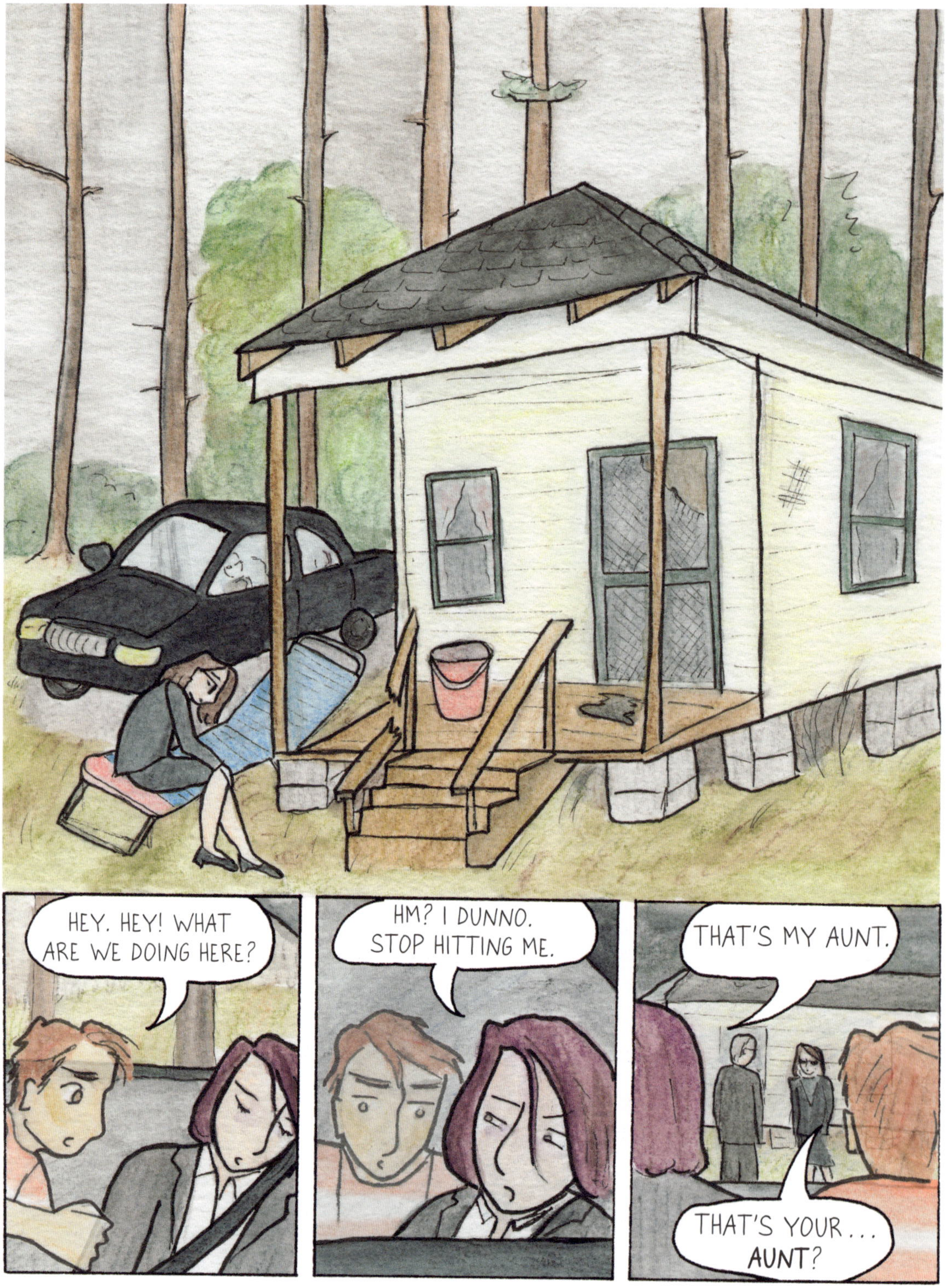
HEY. HEY! WHAT ARE WE DOING HERE?
HM? I DUNNO. STOP HITTING ME.
THAT'S MY AUNT.
THAT'S YOUR . . . **AUNT**?

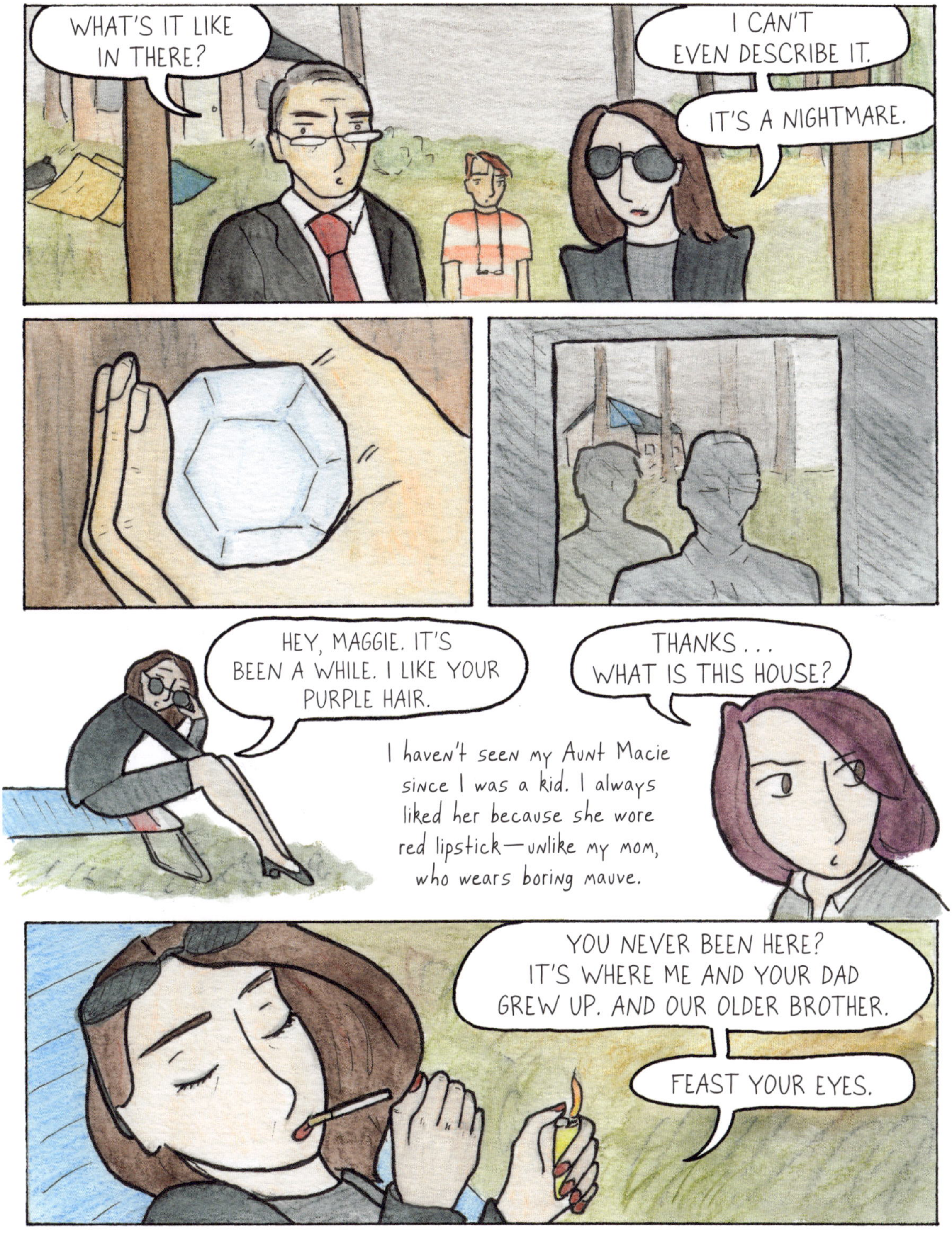

WHAT'S IT LIKE IN THERE?
I CAN'T EVEN DESCRIBE IT.
IT'S A NIGHTMARE.
HEY, MAGGIE. IT'S BEEN A WHILE. I LIKE YOUR PURPLE HAIR.
I haven't seen my Aunt Macie since I was a kid. I always liked her because she wore red lipstick—unlike my mom, who wears boring mauve.
THANKS... WHAT IS THIS HOUSE?
YOU NEVER BEEN HERE? IT'S WHERE ME AND YOUR DAD GREW UP. AND OUR OLDER BROTHER.
FEAST YOUR EYES.

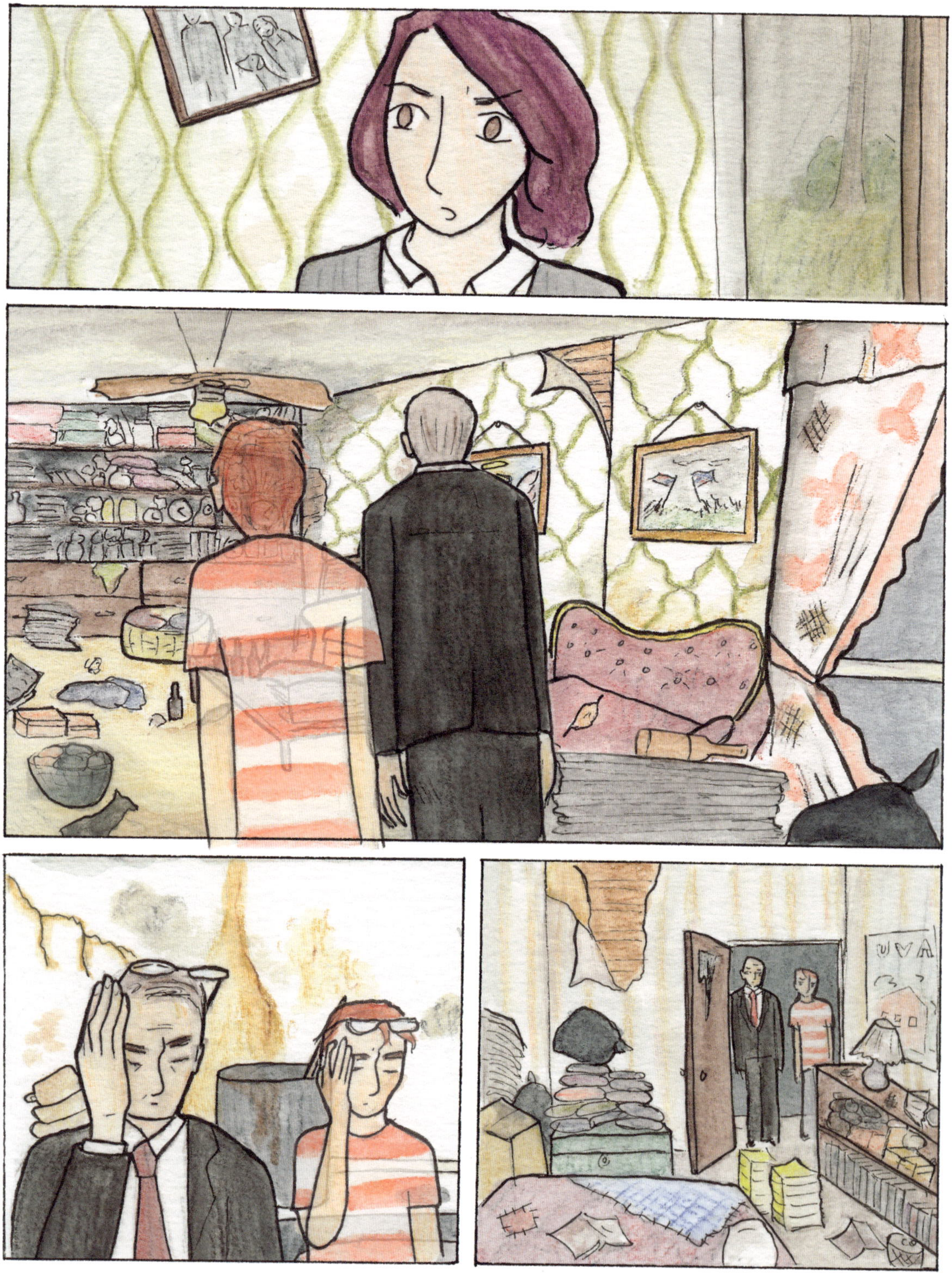
UVA

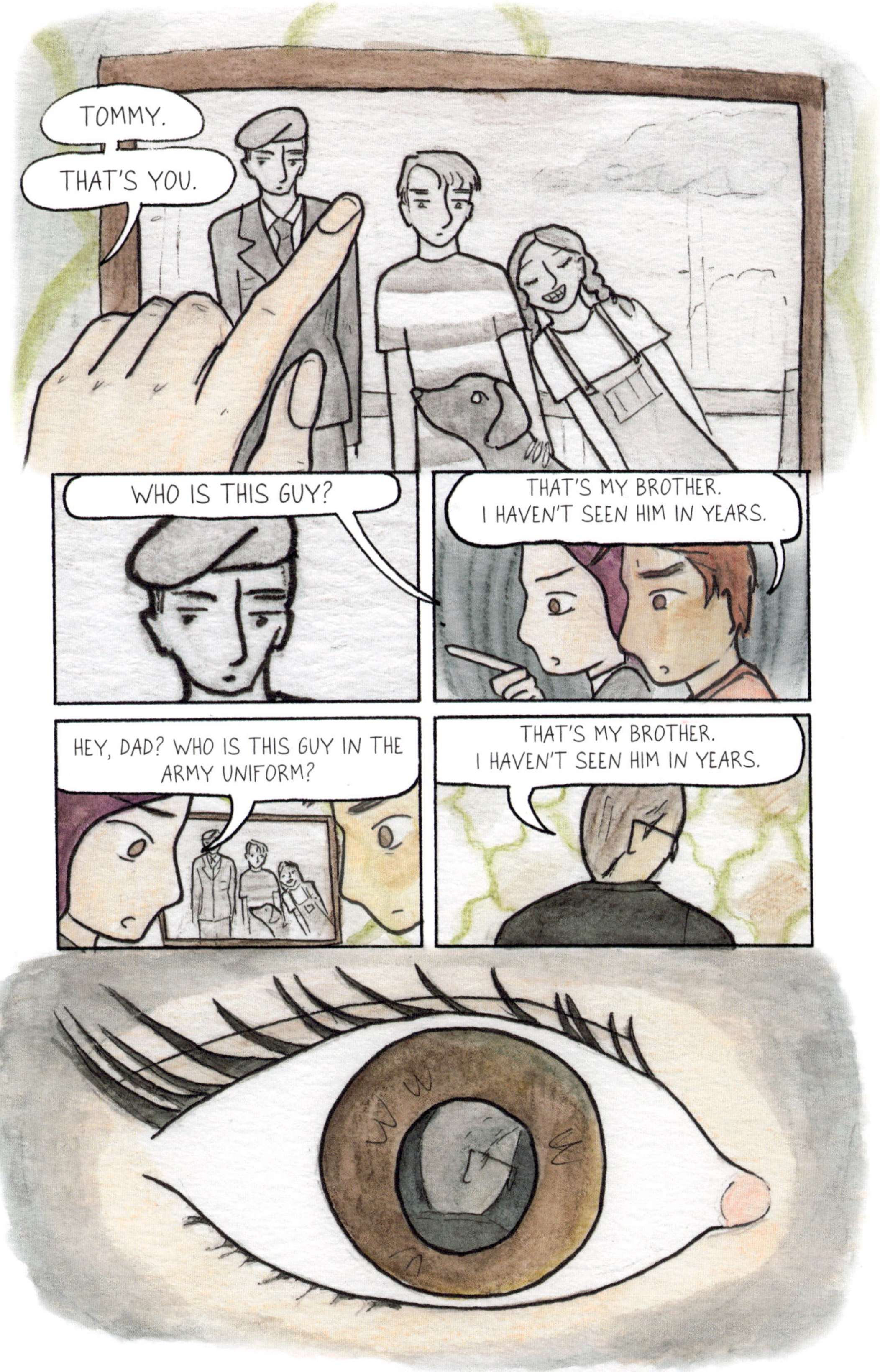
TOMMY.
THAT'S YOU.
WHO IS THIS GUY?
THAT'S MY BROTHER. I HAVEN'T SEEN HIM IN YEARS.
HEY, DAD? WHO IS THIS GUY IN THE ARMY UNIFORM?
THAT'S MY BROTHER. I HAVEN'T SEEN HIM IN YEARS.

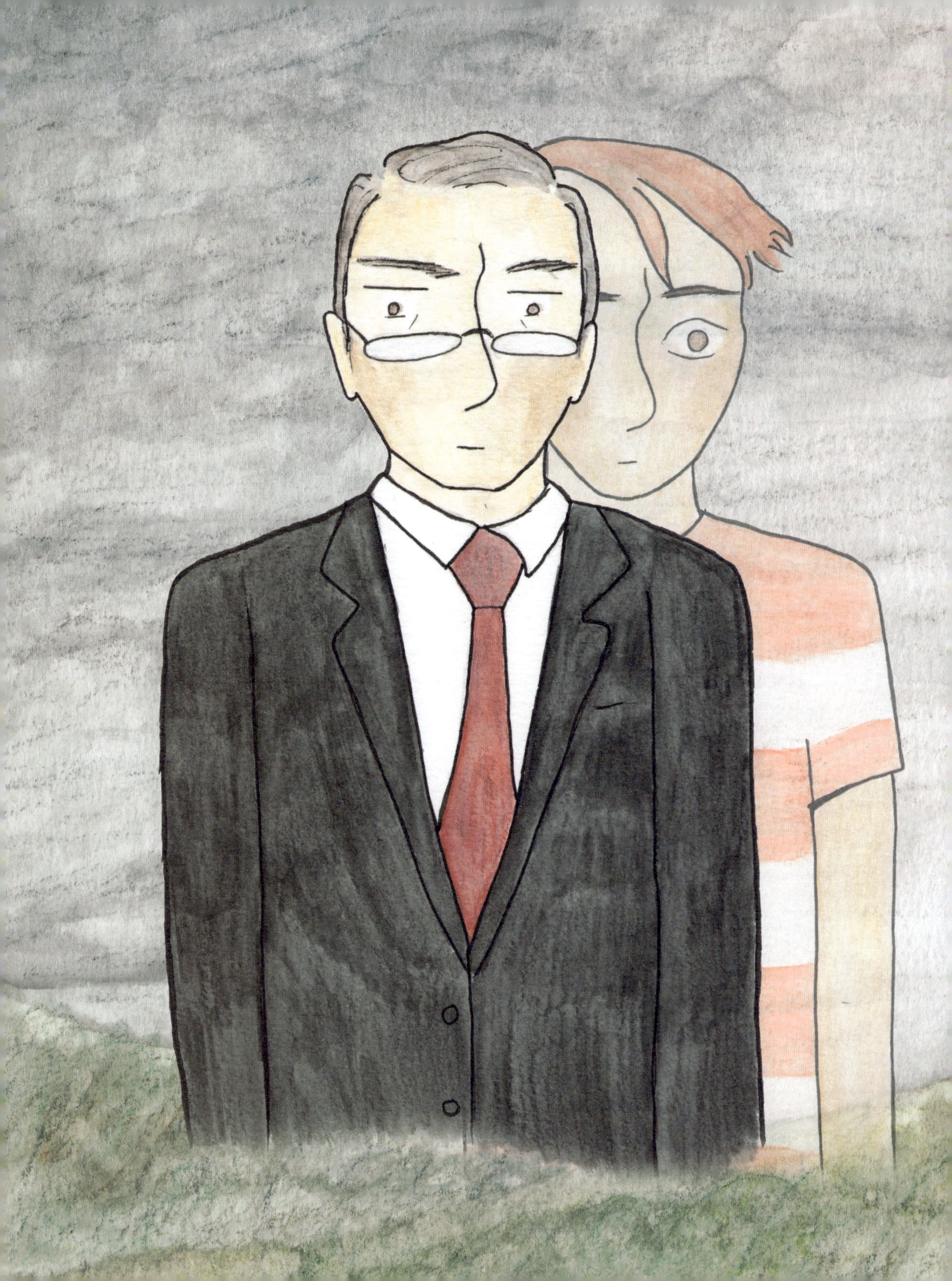

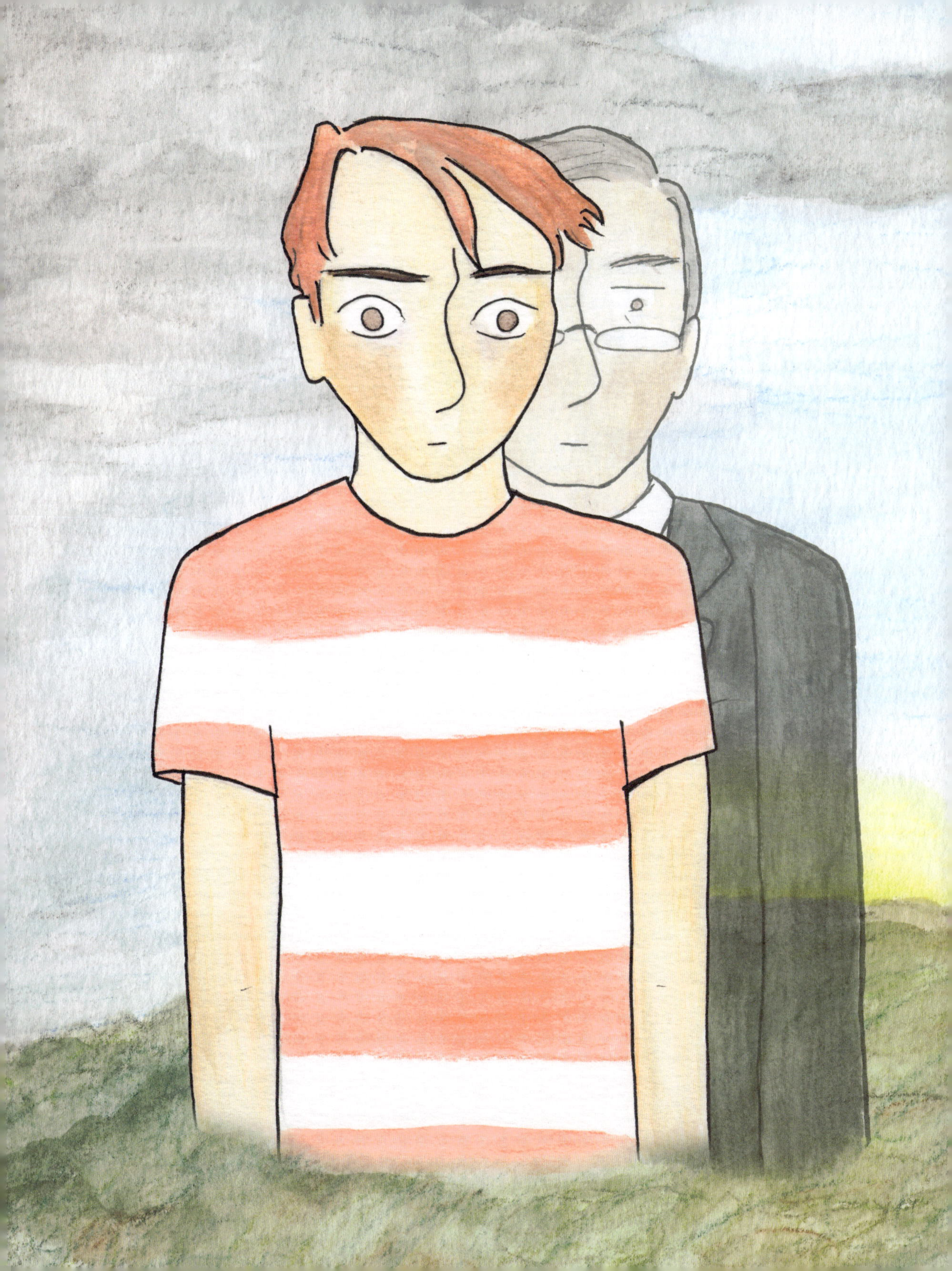

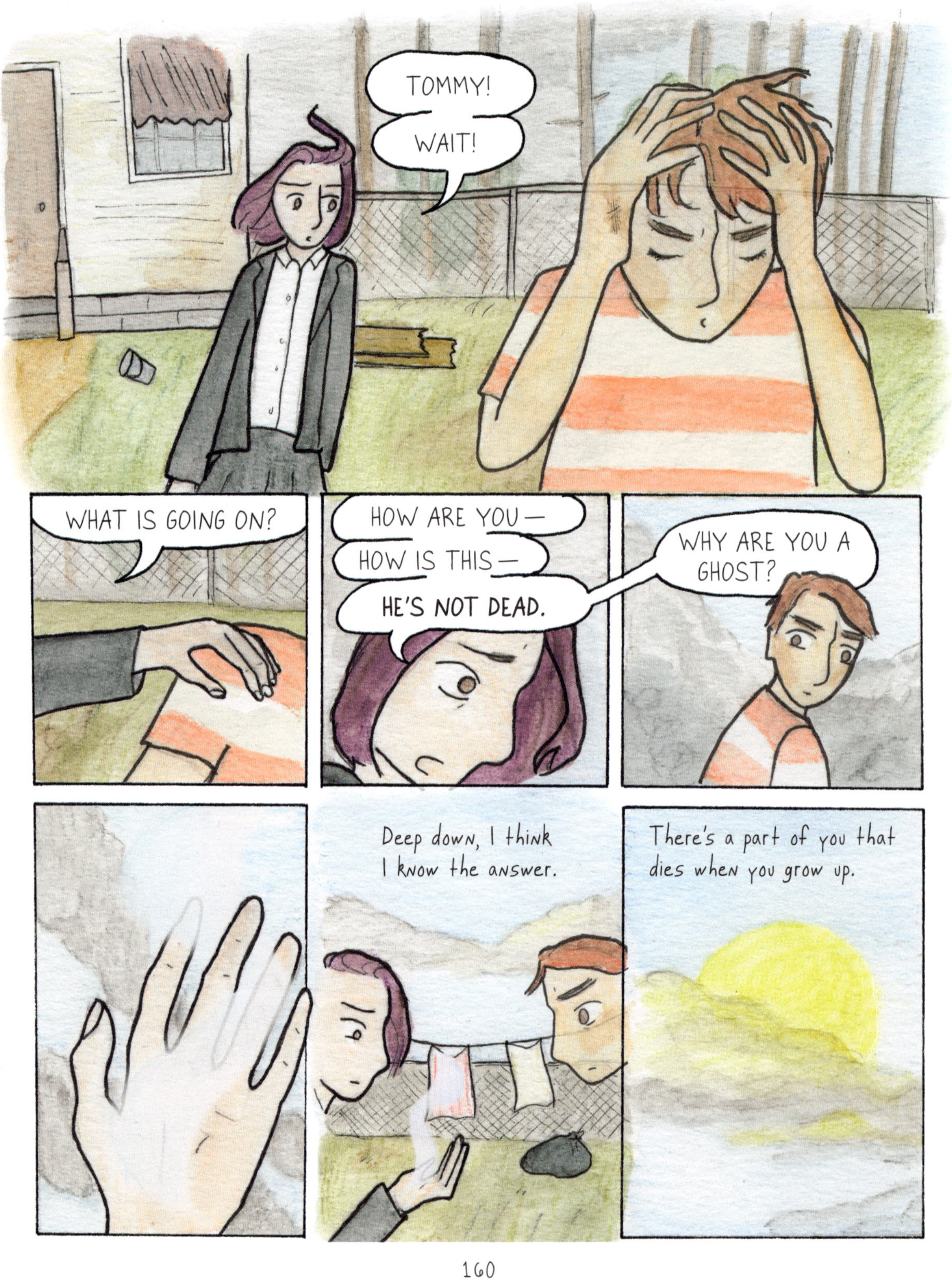
TOMMY!
WAIT!
WHAT IS GOING ON?
HOW ARE YOU—
HOW IS THIS—
HE'S NOT DEAD.
WHY ARE YOU A GHOST?
Deep down, I think I know the answer.
There's a part of you that dies when you grow up.

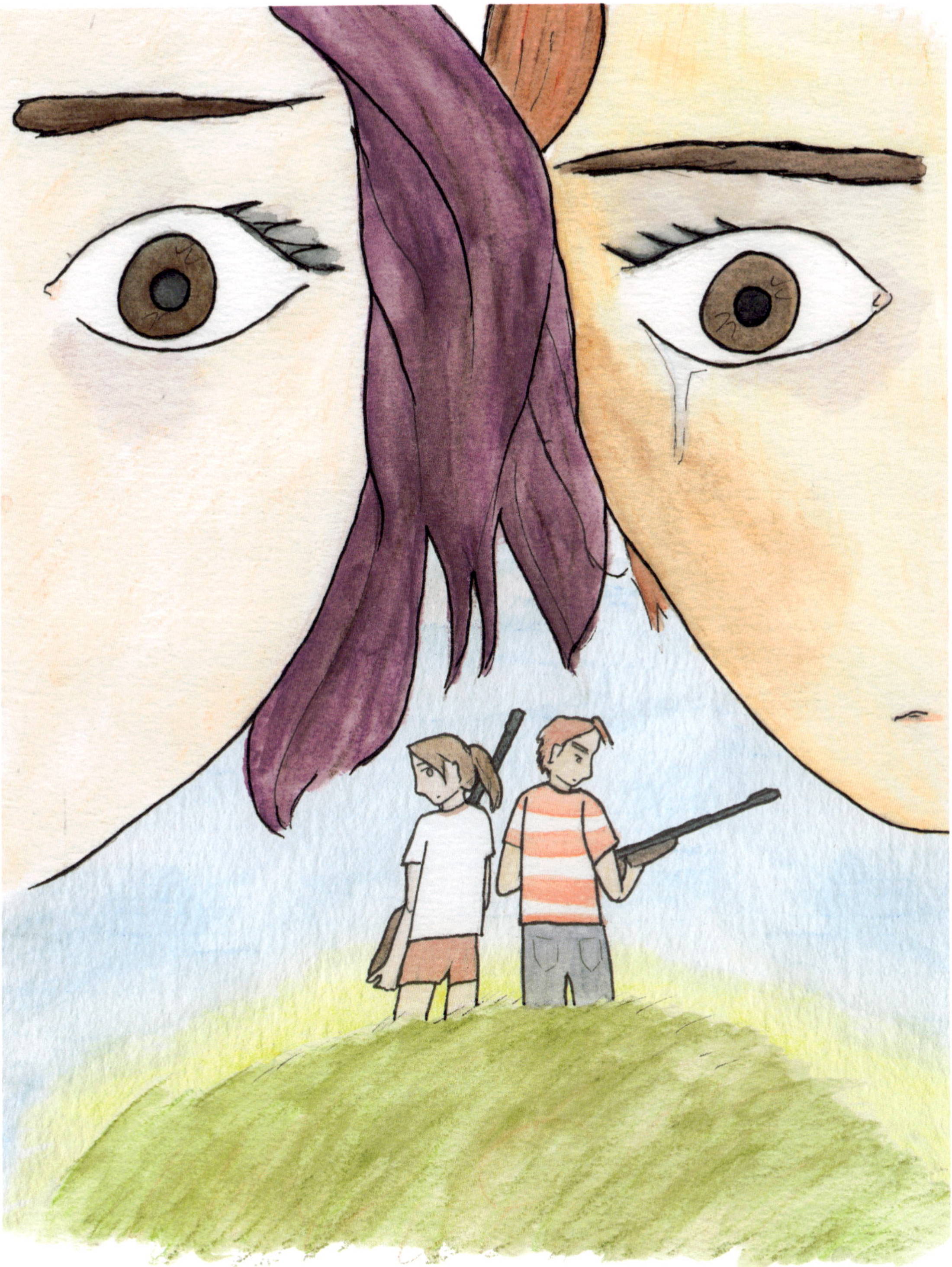

A ghost you have to leave behind.

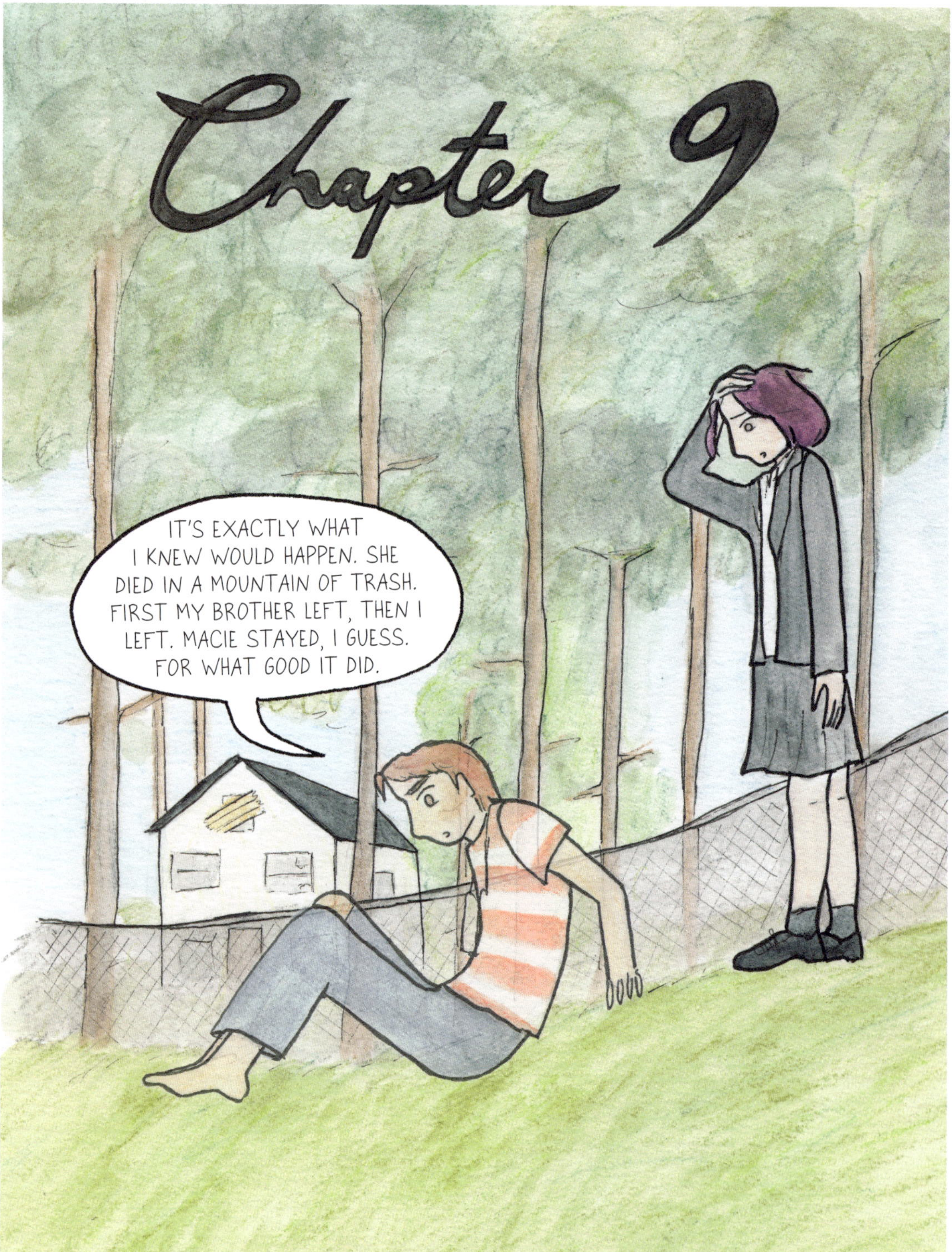
Chapter 9
IT'S EXACTLY WHAT I KNEW WOULD HAPPEN. SHE DIED IN A MOUNTAIN OF TRASH. FIRST MY BROTHER LEFT, THEN I LEFT. MACIE STAYED, I GUESS. FOR WHAT GOOD IT DID.

Maybe it's harder for girls to abandon people. Or just easier for girls to get trapped in other people's trash. I don't know what I would have done in my dad's situation. Would I have left like he did, or stayed like his sister? And I don't know which of those choices is weak or strong.

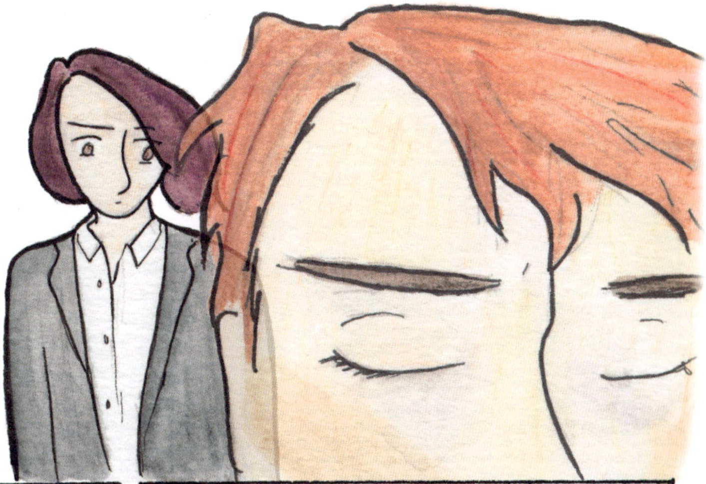

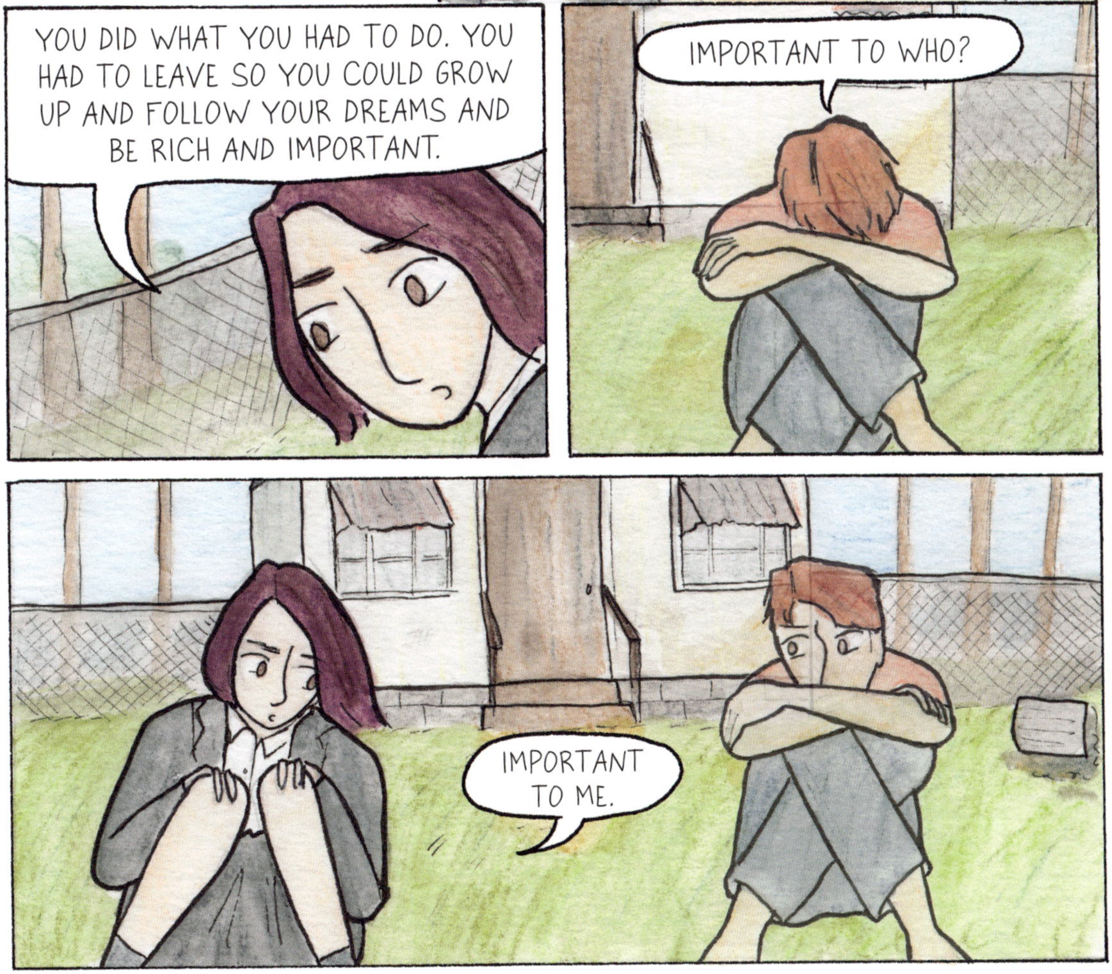
YOU DID WHAT YOU HAD TO DO. YOU HAD TO LEAVE SO YOU COULD GROW UP AND FOLLOW YOUR DREAMS AND BE RICH AND IMPORTANT.
IMPORTANT TO WHO?
IMPORTANT TO ME.

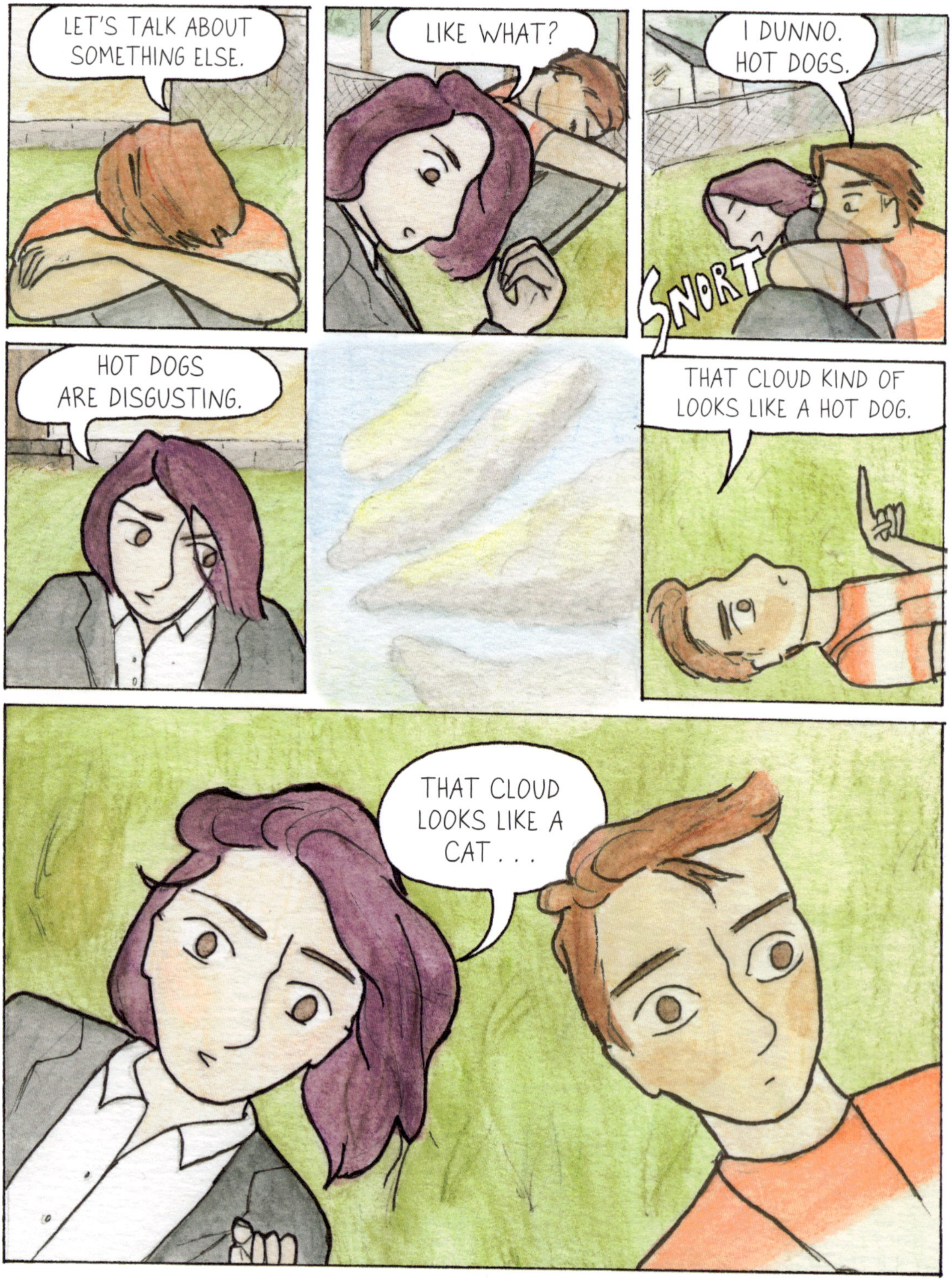
LET'S TALK ABOUT SOMETHING ELSE.
LIKE WHAT?
I DUNNO. HOT DOGS.
SNORT
HOT DOGS ARE DISGUSTING.
THAT CLOUD KIND OF LOOKS LIKE A HOT DOG.
THAT CLOUD LOOKS LIKE A CAT . . .

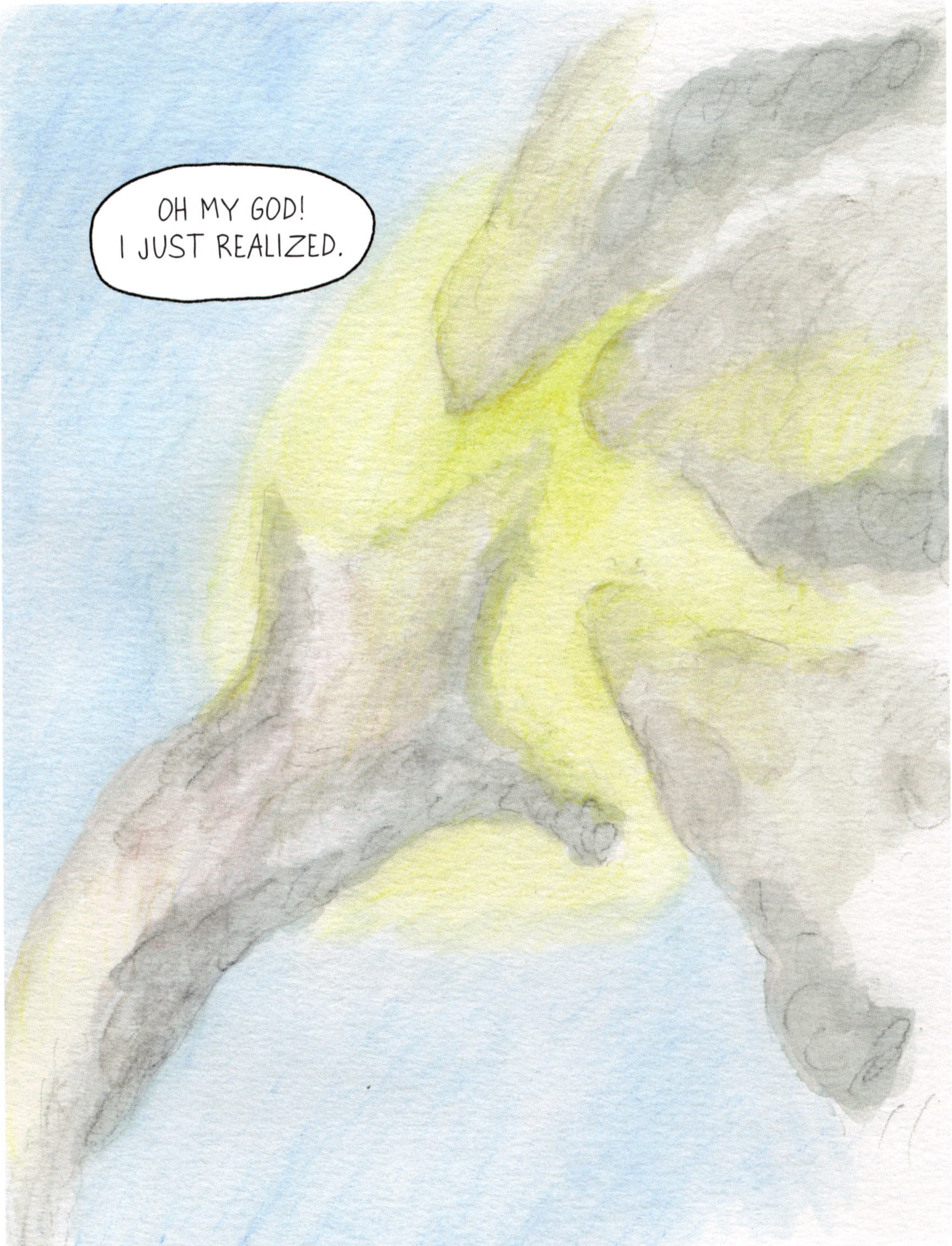
OH MY GOD!
I JUST REALIZED.

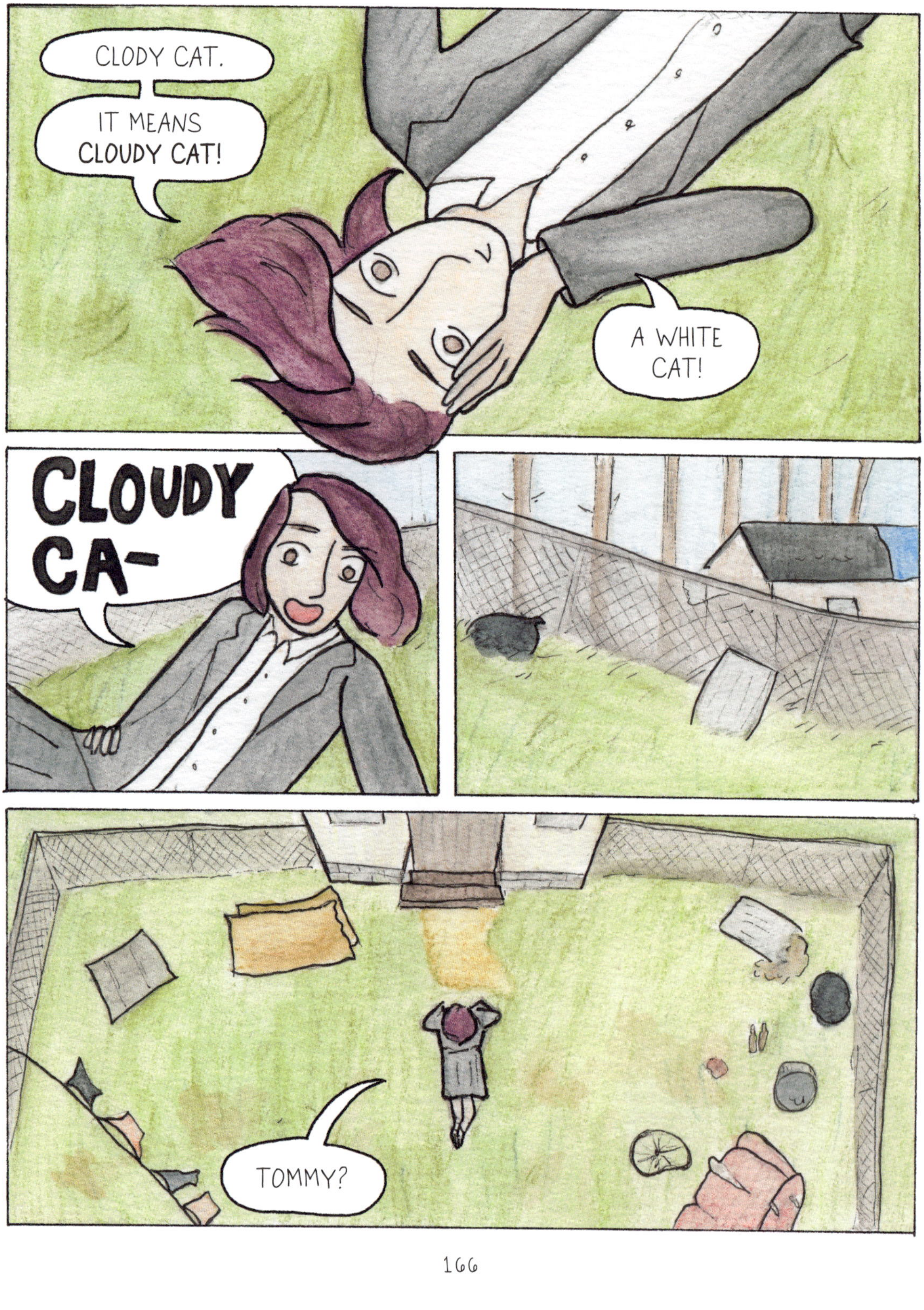

CLODY CAT.
IT MEANS CLOUDY CAT!
A WHITE CAT!
CLOUDY CA-
TOMMY?

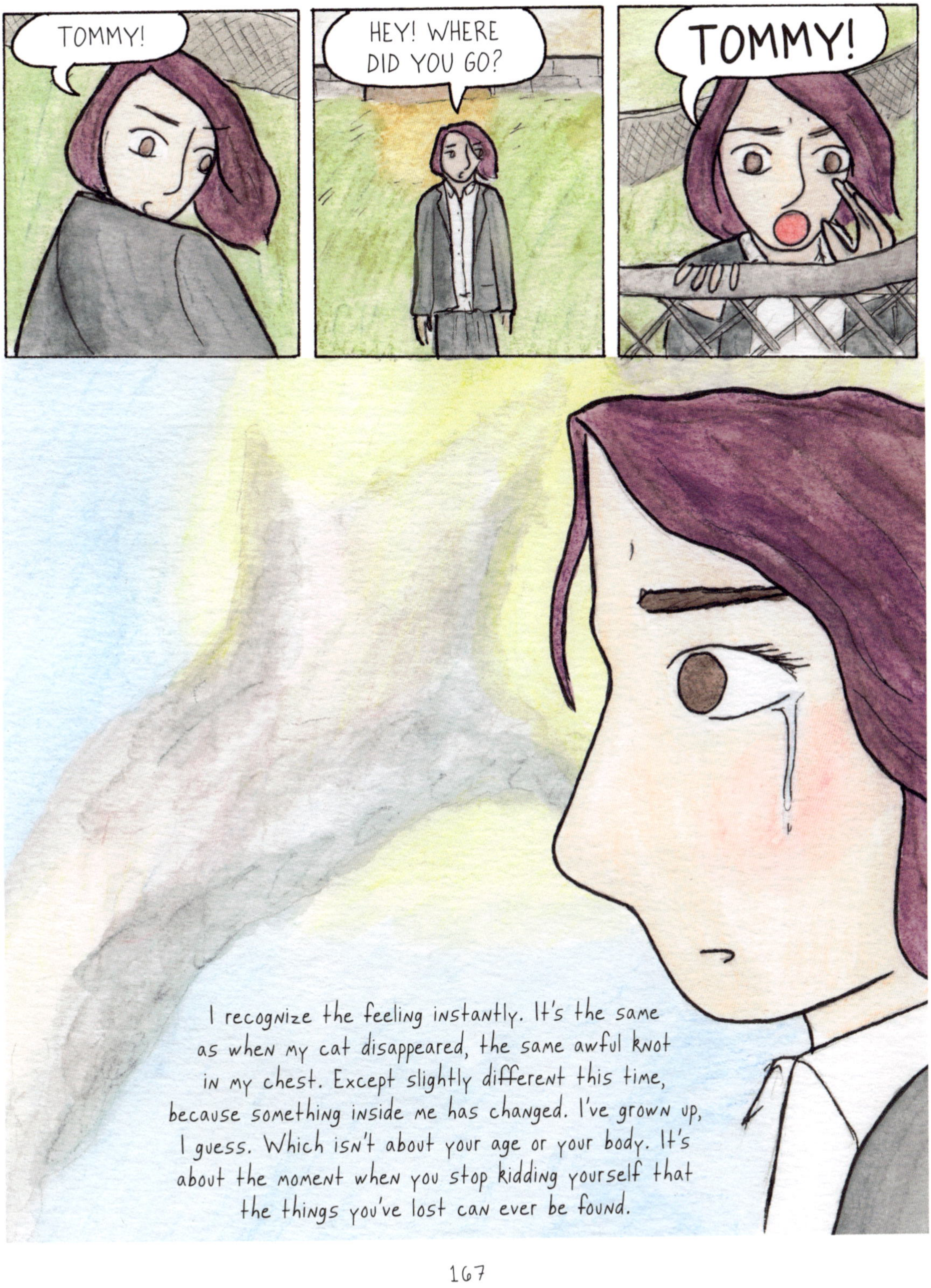
TOMMY!
HEY! WHERE DID YOU GO?
TOMMY!
I recognize the feeling instantly. It's the same as when my cat disappeared, the same awful knot in my chest. Except slightly different this time, because something inside me has changed. I've grown up, I guess. Which isn't about your age or your body. It's about the moment when you stop kidding yourself that the things you've lost can ever be found.

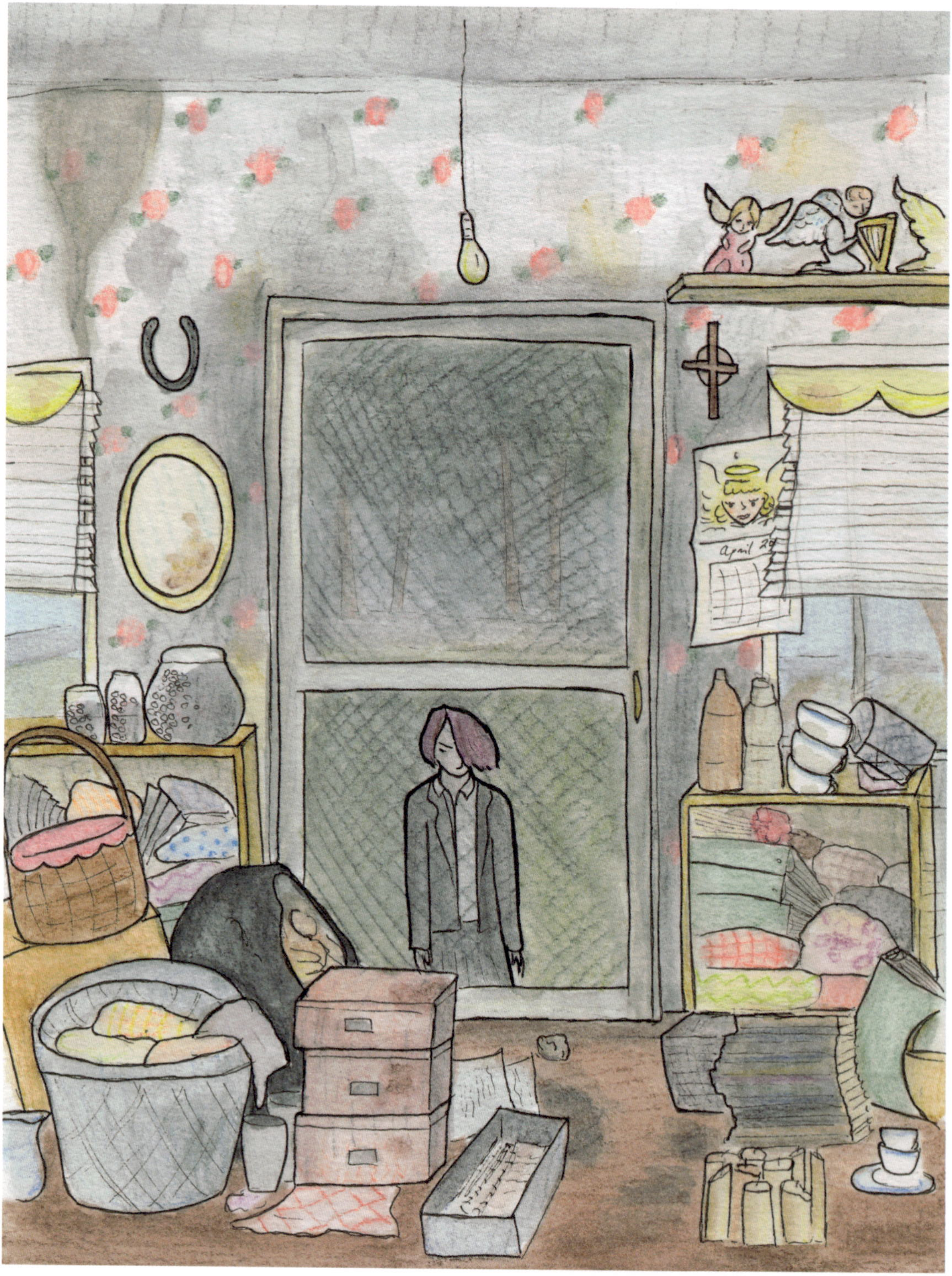
April 2

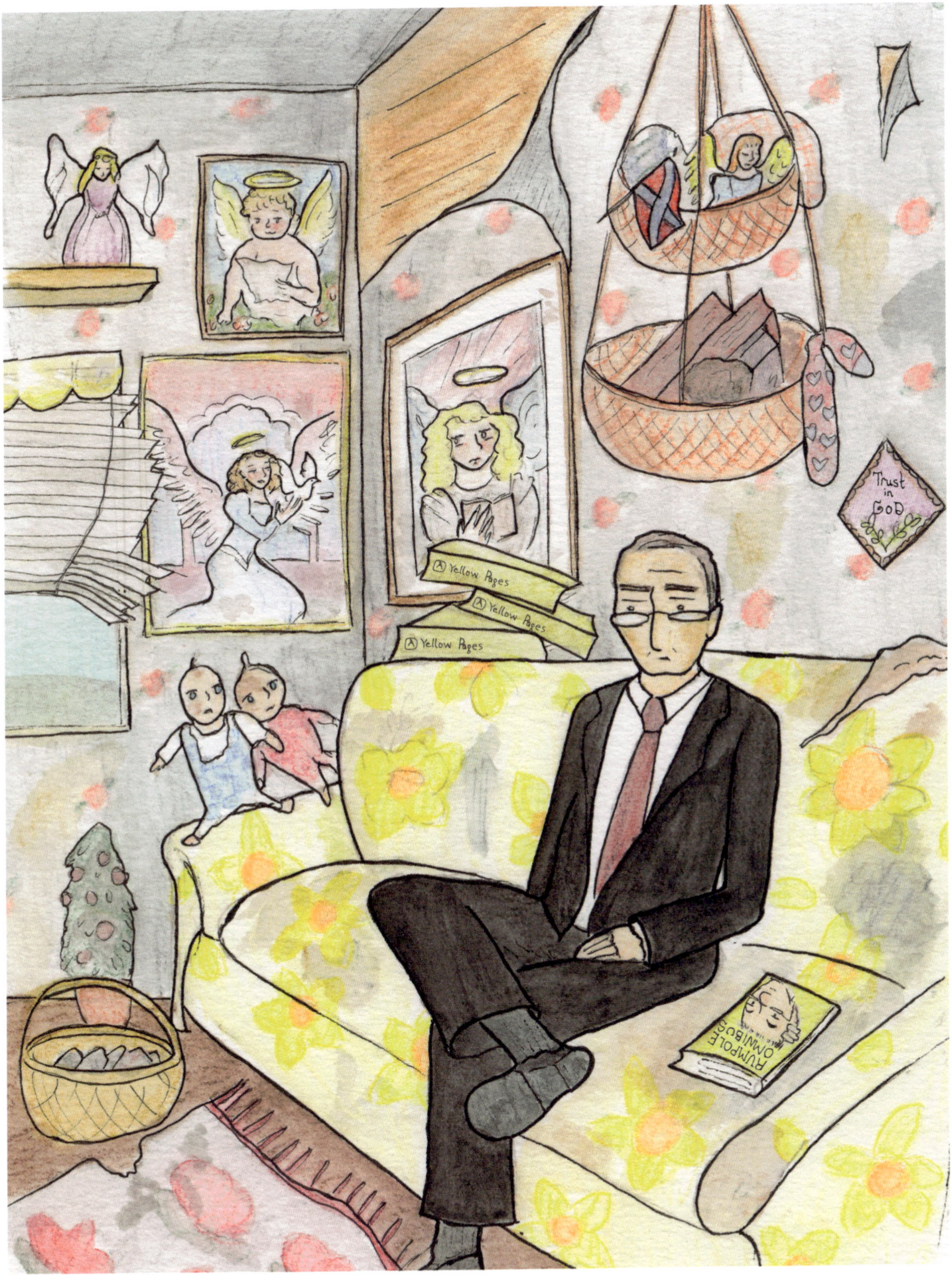
Trust in GOD
Yellow Pages
Yellow Pages
Yellow Pages
RUMPOLE OMNIBUS

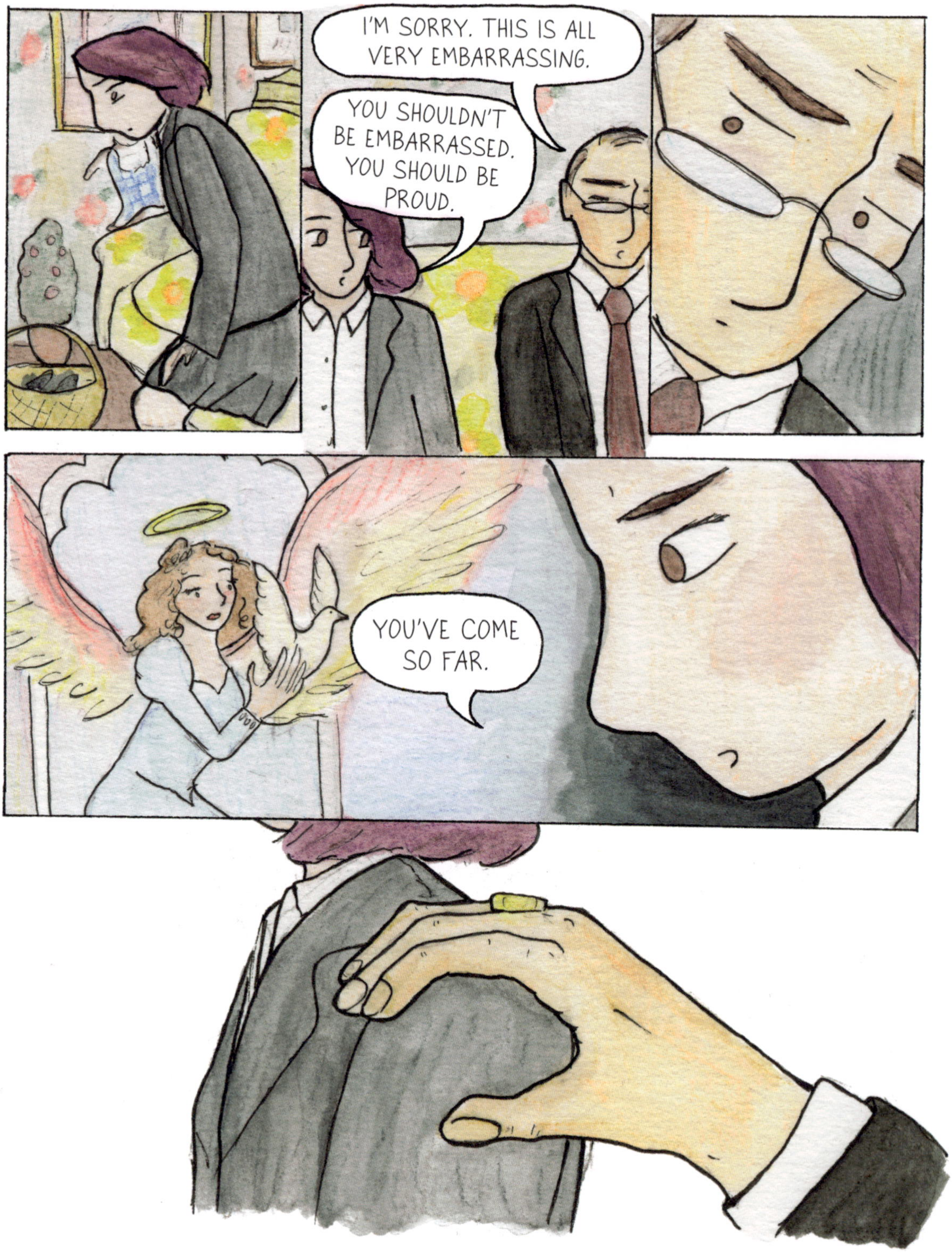
I'M SORRY. THIS IS ALL VERY EMBARRASSING.
YOU SHOULDN'T BE EMBARRASSED. YOU SHOULD BE PROUD.
YOU'VE COME SO FAR.

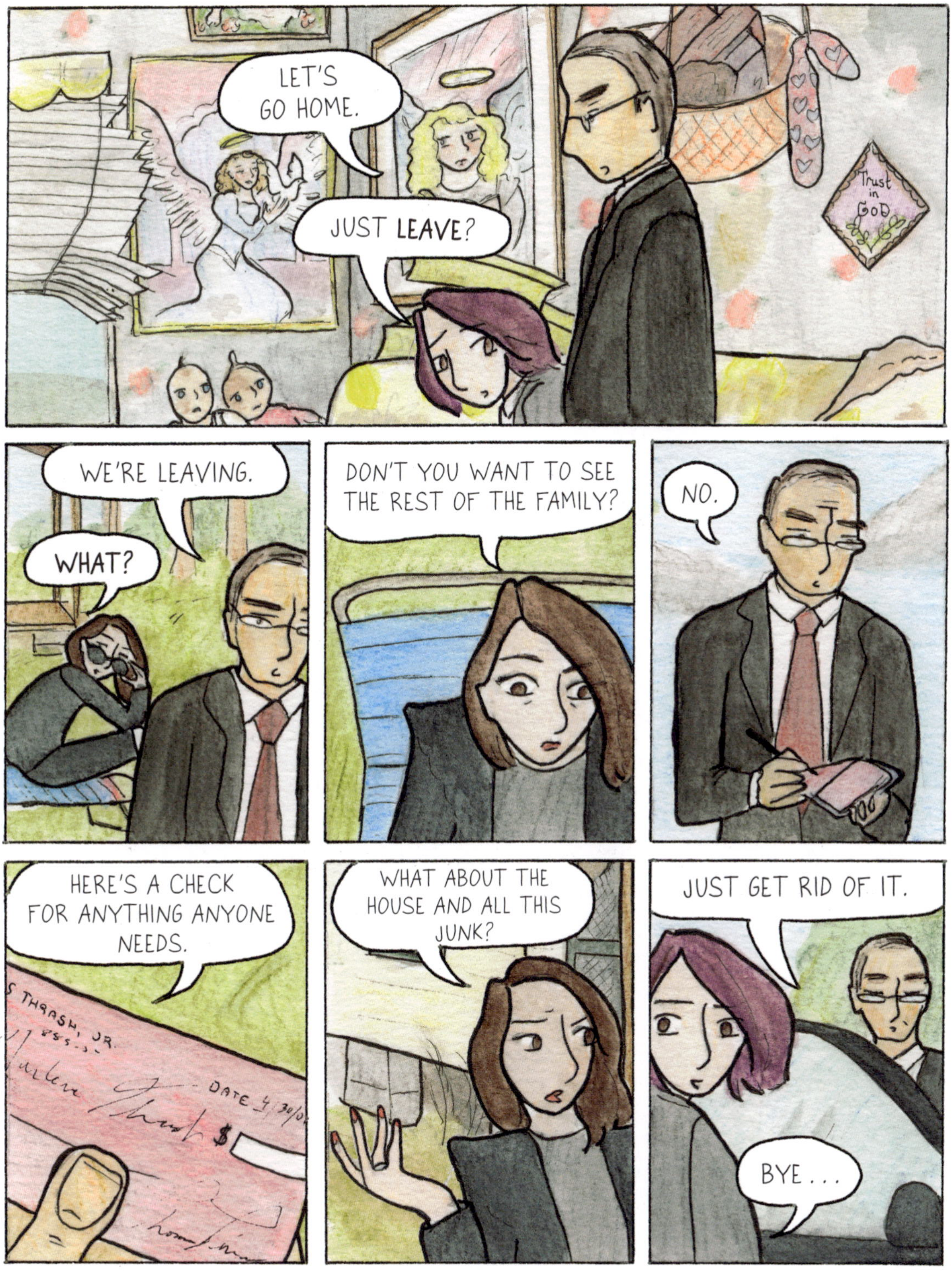
LET'S GO HOME.
JUST LEAVE?
Trust in GOD
WE'RE LEAVING.
WHAT?
DON'T YOU WANT TO SEE THE REST OF THE FAMILY?
NO.
HERE'S A CHECK FOR ANYTHING ANYONE NEEDS.
WHAT ABOUT THE HOUSE AND ALL THIS JUNK?
JUST GET RID OF IT.
BYE . . .

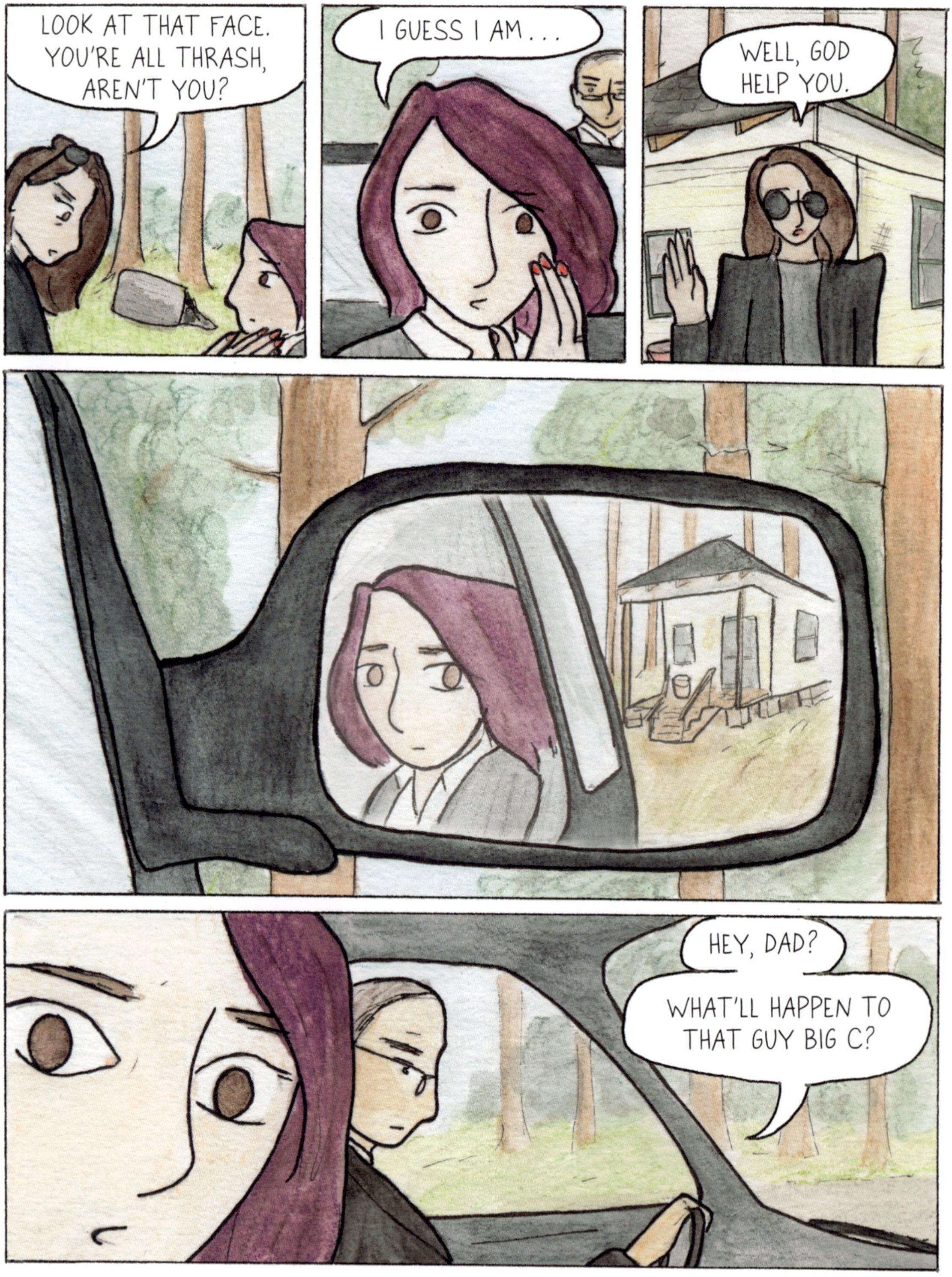
LOOK AT THAT FACE. YOU'RE ALL THRASH, AREN'T YOU?
I GUESS I AM . . .
WELL, GOD HELP YOU.
HEY, DAD?
WHAT'LL HAPPEN TO THAT GUY BIG C?

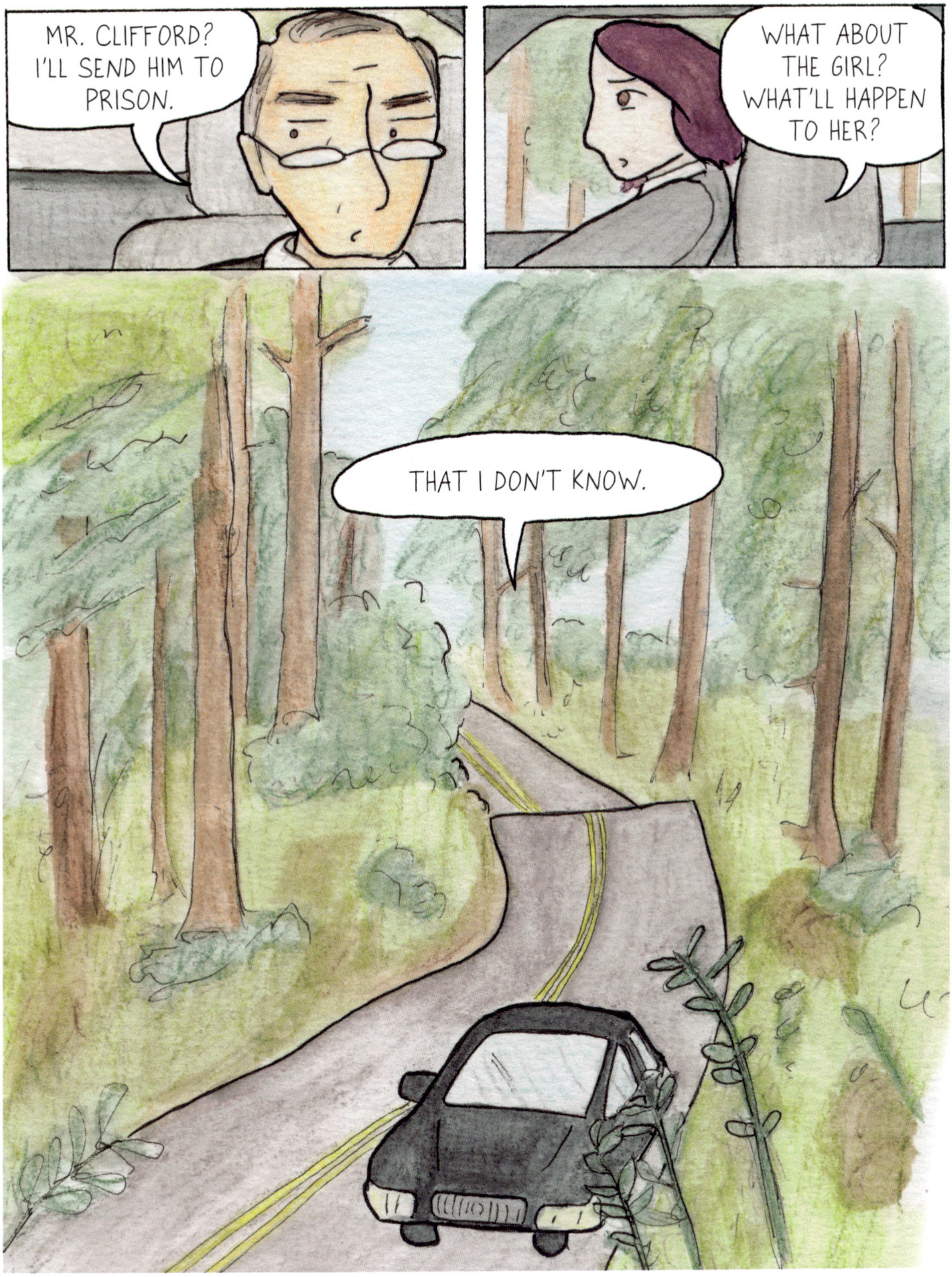
MR. CLIFFORD? I'LL SEND HIM TO PRISON.
WHAT ABOUT THE GIRL? WHAT'LL HAPPEN TO HER?
THAT I DON'T KNOW.

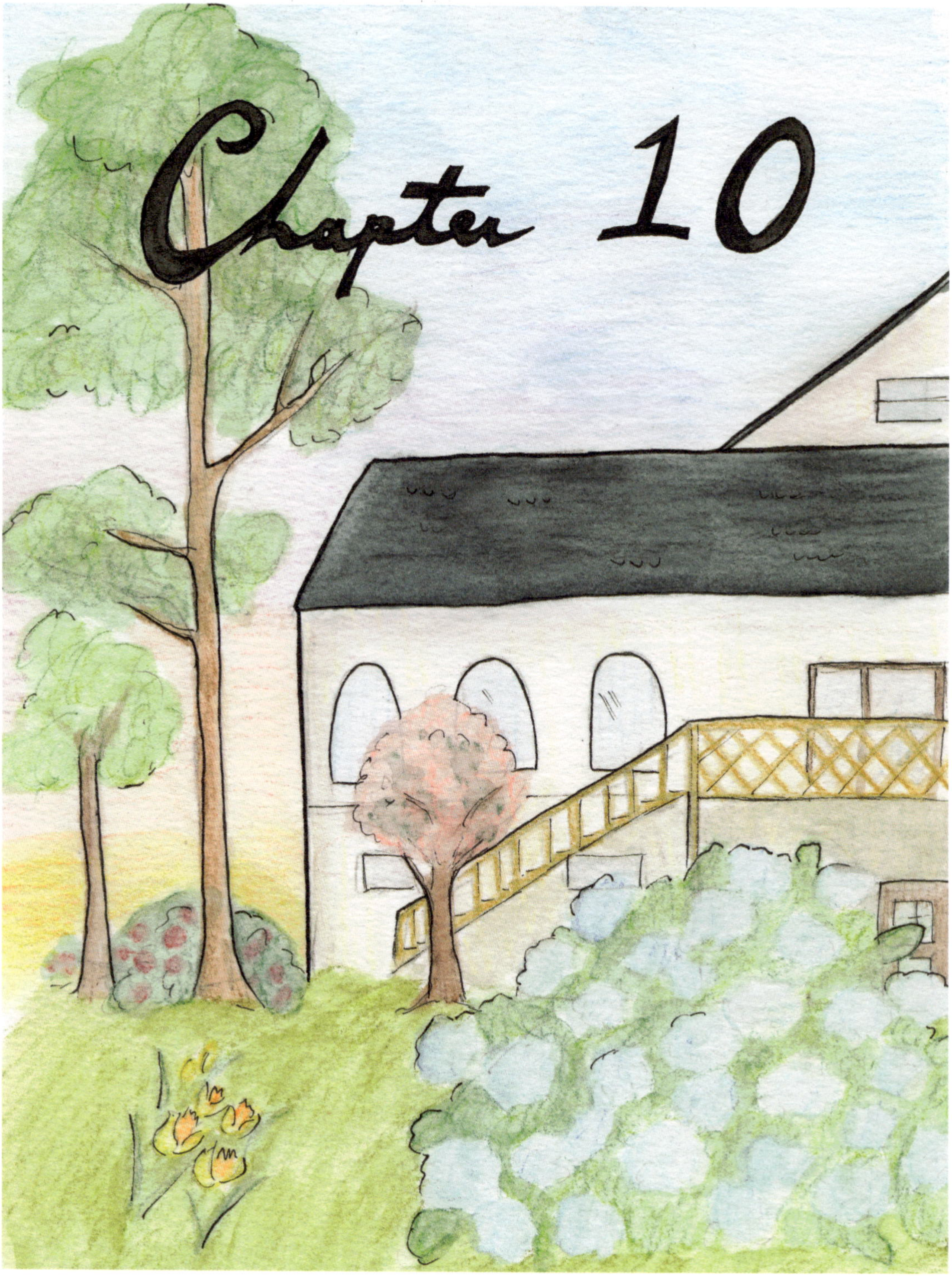
Chapter 10

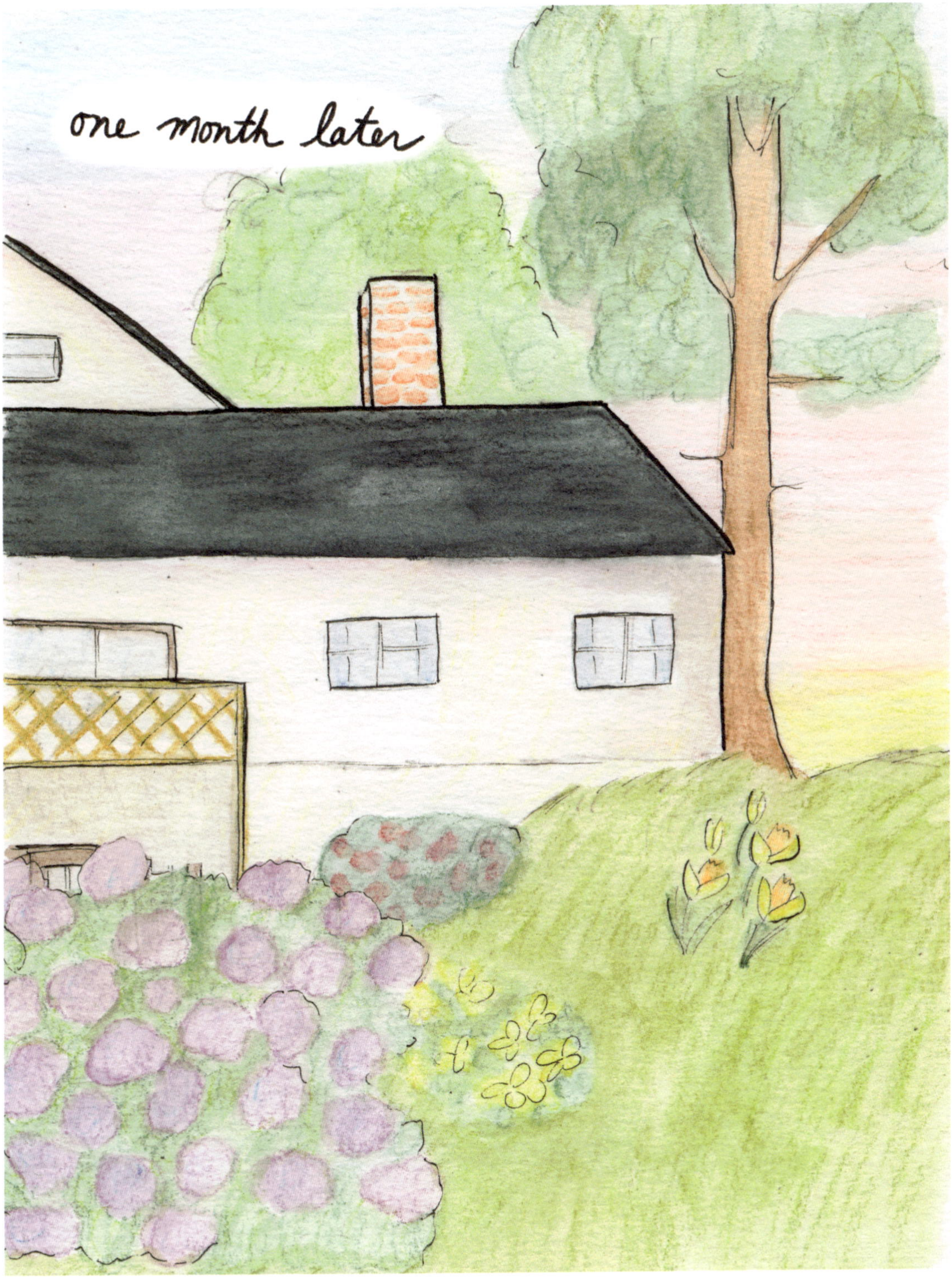
one month later

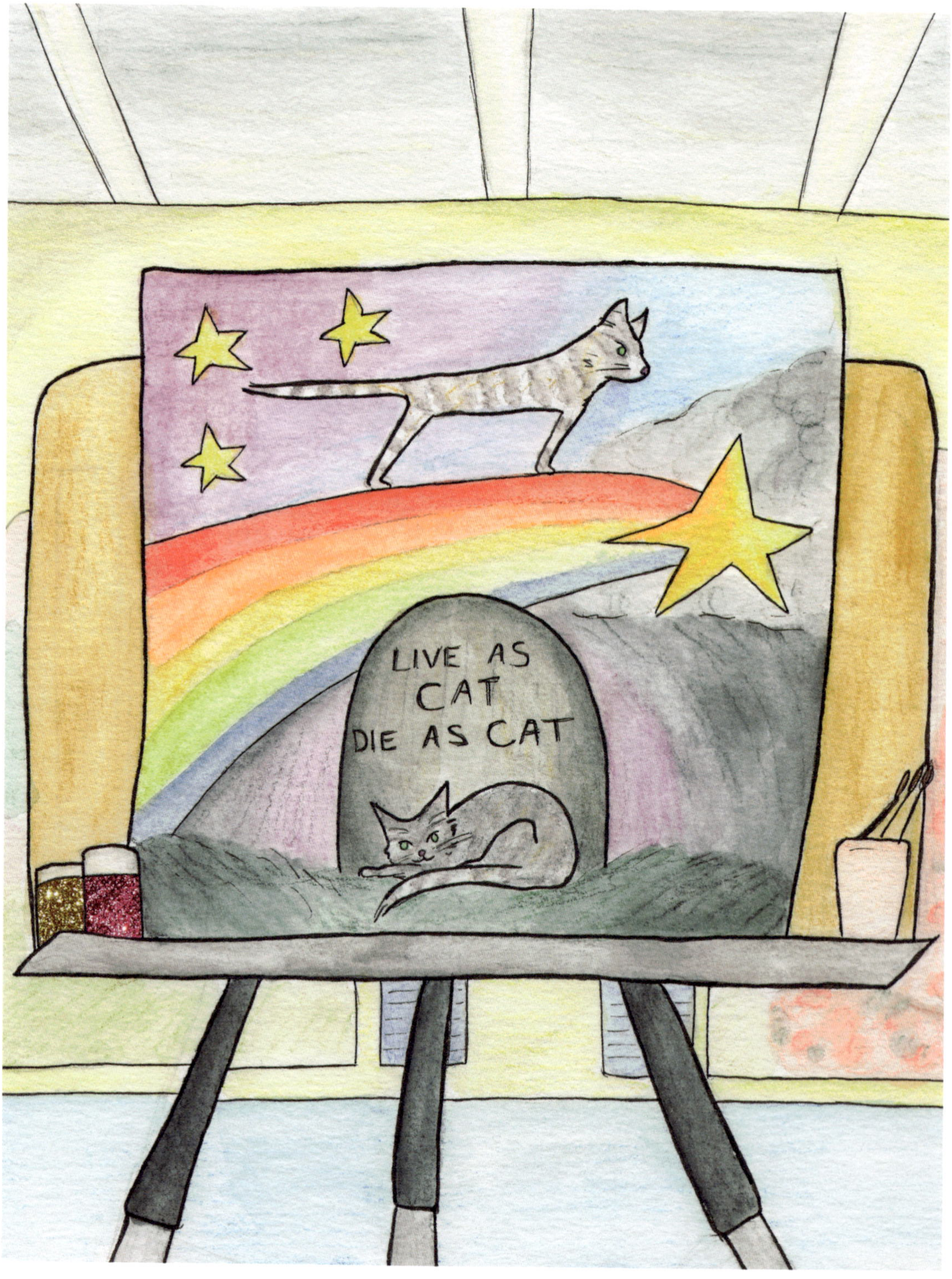
LIVE AS
CAT
DIE AS CAT

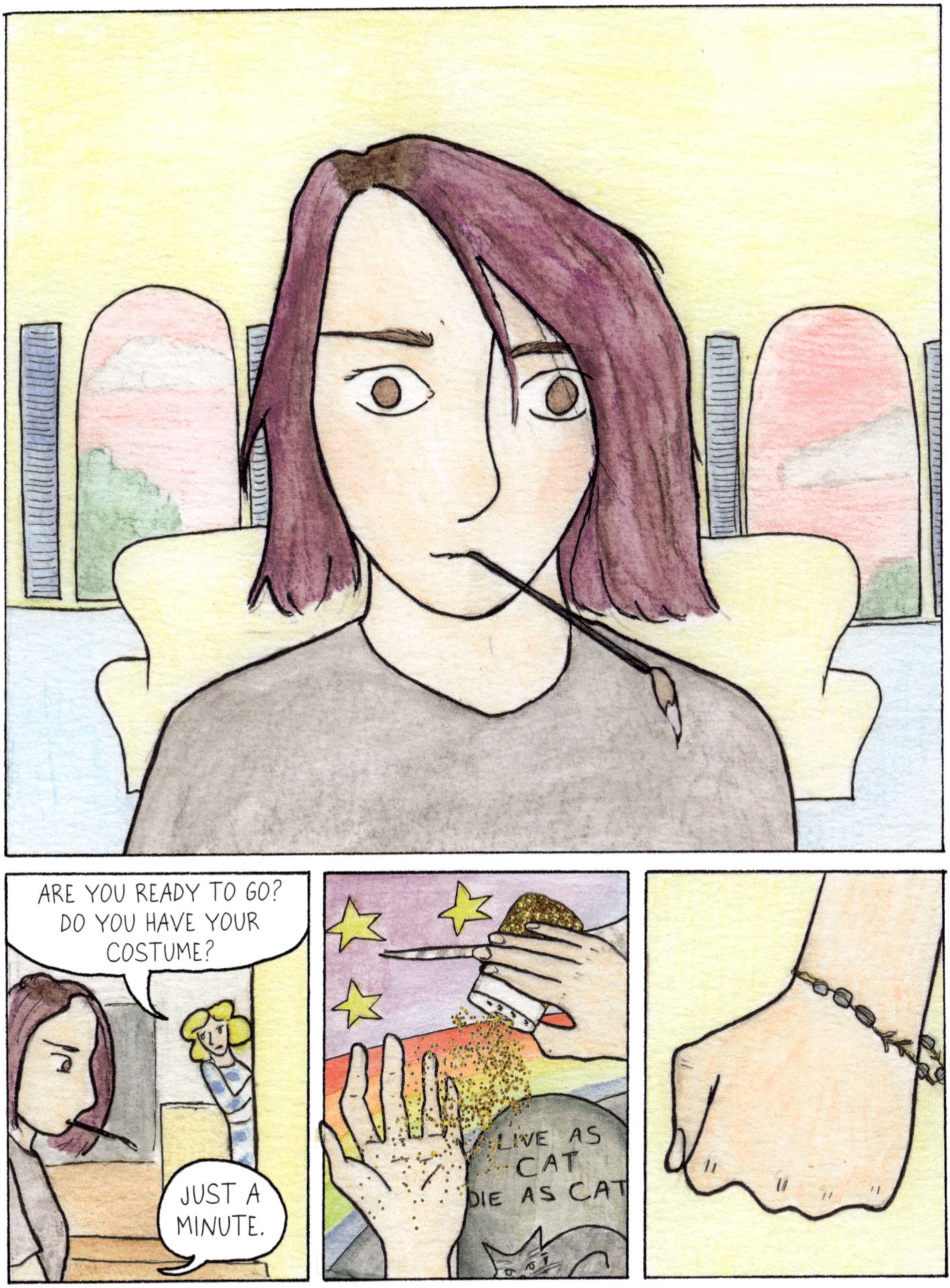
ARE YOU READY TO GO? DO YOU HAVE YOUR COSTUME?
JUST A MINUTE.
LIVE AS CAT DIE AS CAT

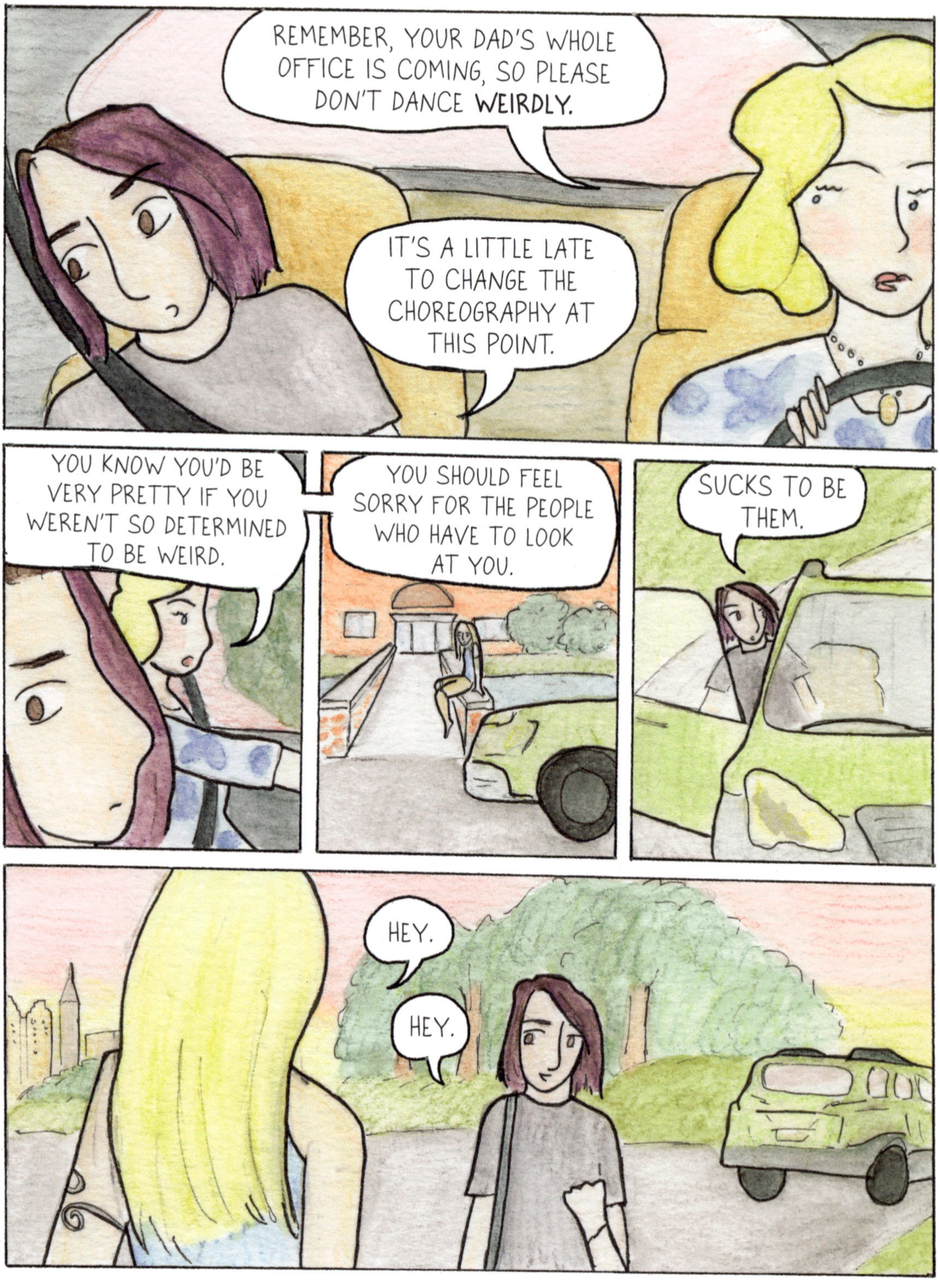
REMEMBER, YOUR DAD'S WHOLE OFFICE IS COMING, SO PLEASE DON'T DANCE **WEIRDLY.**
IT'S A LITTLE LATE TO CHANGE THE CHOREOGRAPHY AT THIS POINT.
YOU KNOW YOU'D BE VERY PRETTY IF YOU WEREN'T SO DETERMINED TO BE WEIRD.
YOU SHOULD FEEL SORRY FOR THE PEOPLE WHO HAVE TO LOOK AT YOU.
SUCKS TO BE THEM.
HEY.
HEY.

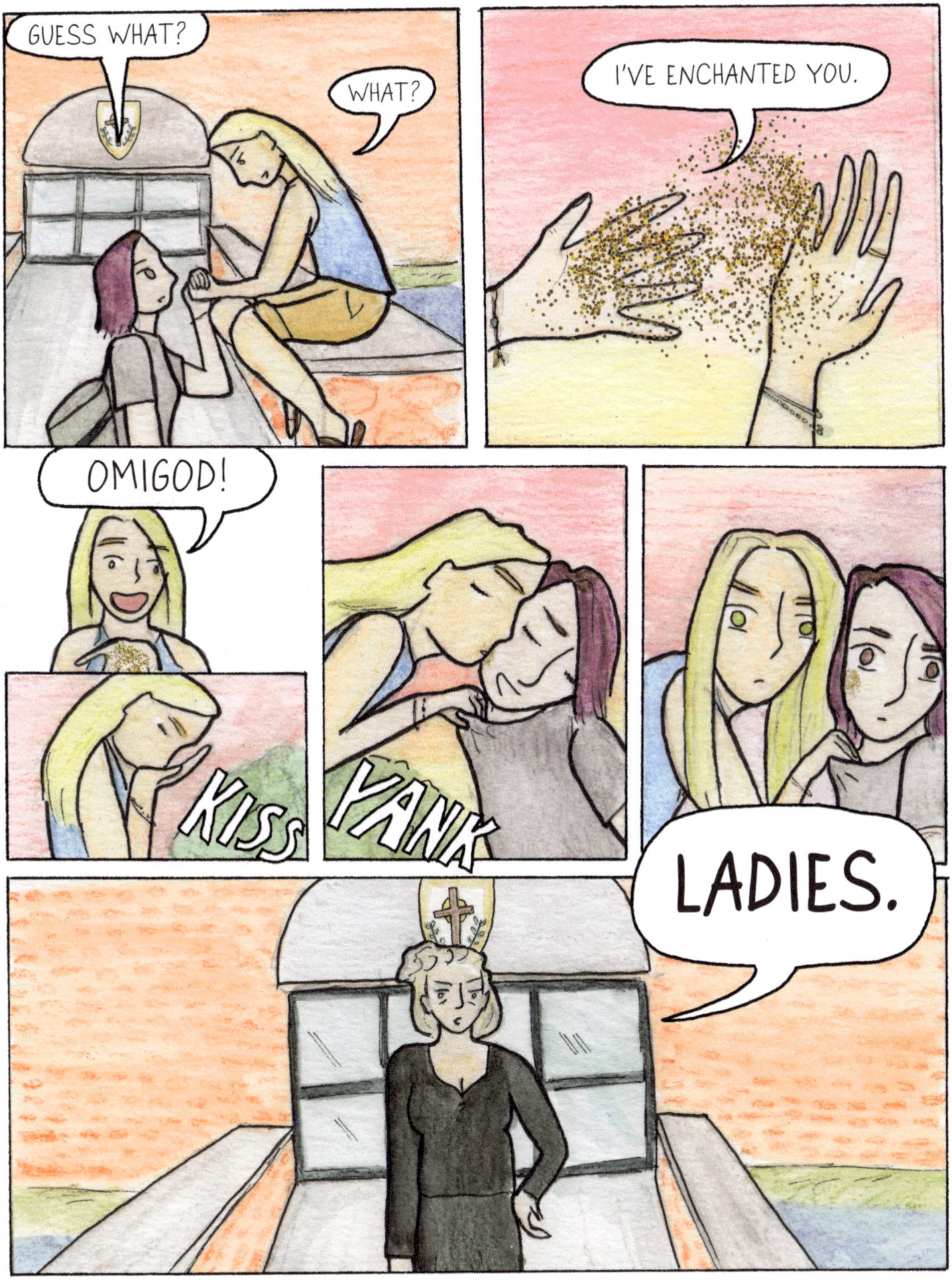
GUESS WHAT?
WHAT?
I'VE ENCHANTED YOU.
OMIGOD!
KISS
YANK
LADIES.

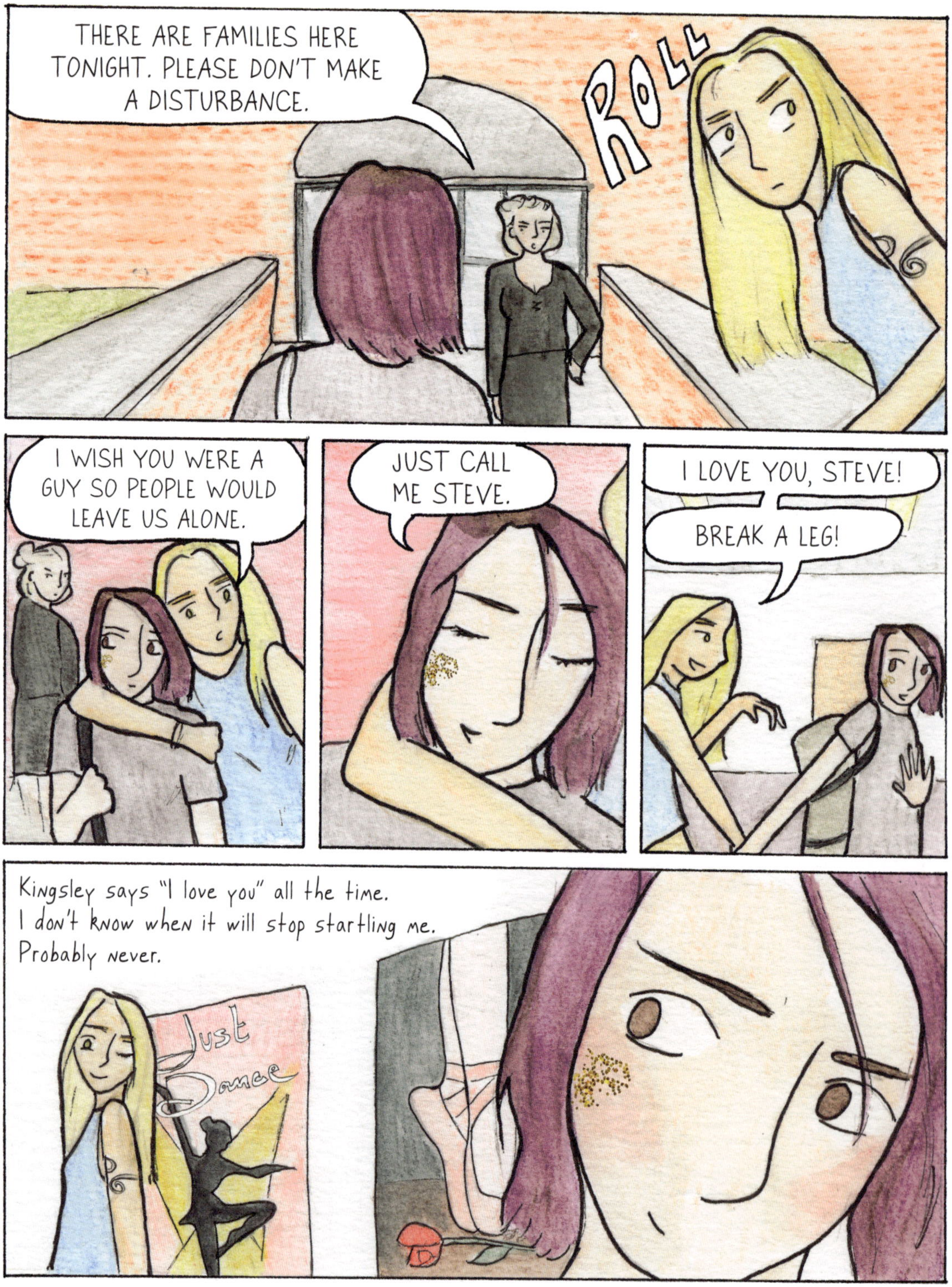
THERE ARE FAMILIES HERE TONIGHT. PLEASE DON'T MAKE A DISTURBANCE.
ROLL
I WISH YOU WERE A GUY SO PEOPLE WOULD LEAVE US ALONE.
JUST CALL ME STEVE.
I LOVE YOU, STEVE!
BREAK A LEG!
Kingsley says "I love you" all the time.
I don't know when it will stop startling me.
Probably never.
Just Dance

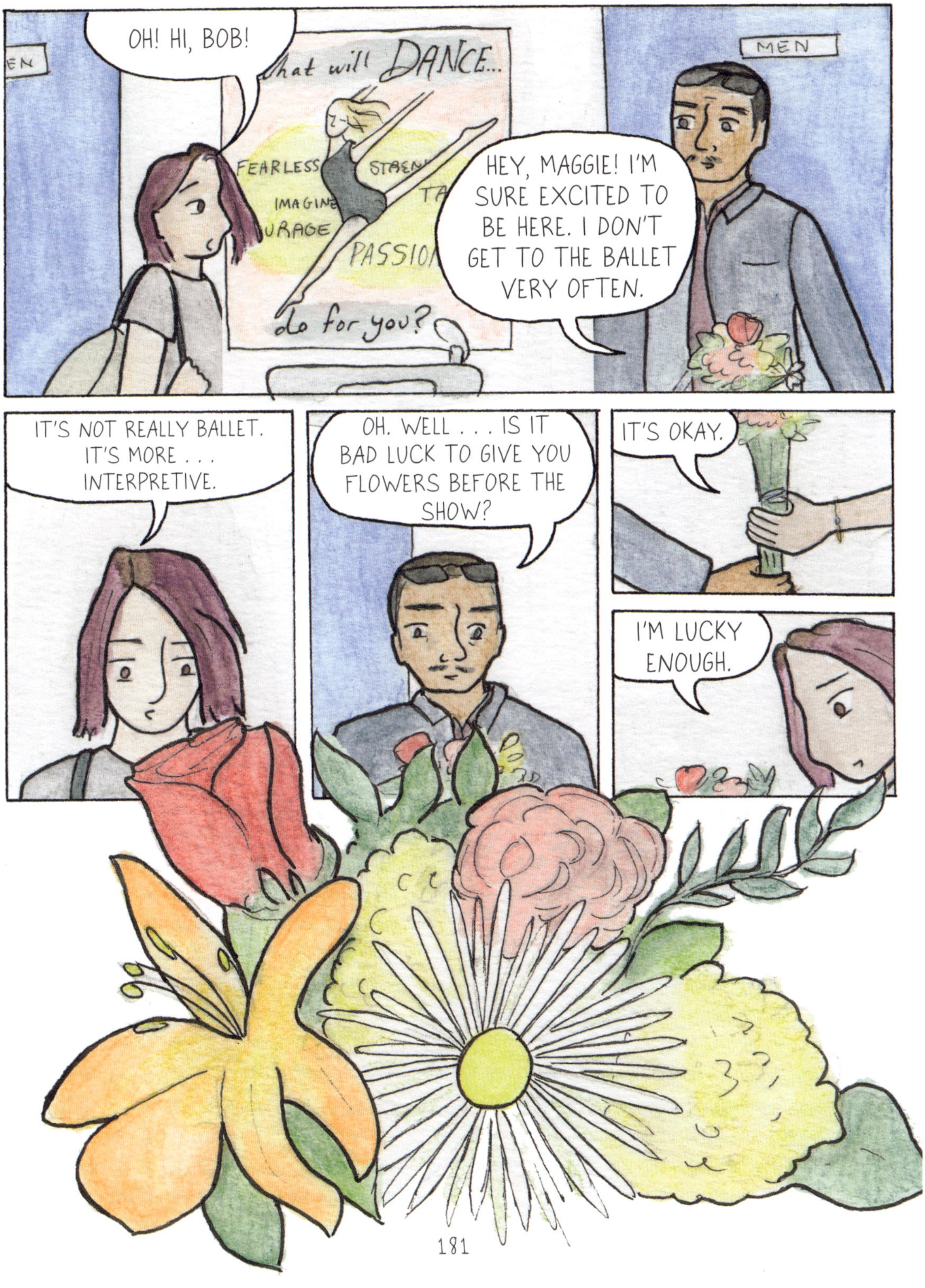
OH! HI, BOB!
MEN
What will DANCE...
FEARLESS
IMAGINE
PASSION
do for you?
HEY, MAGGIE! I'M SURE EXCITED TO BE HERE. I DON'T GET TO THE BALLET VERY OFTEN.
IT'S NOT REALLY BALLET. IT'S MORE . . . INTERPRETIVE.
OH. WELL . . . IS IT BAD LUCK TO GIVE YOU FLOWERS BEFORE THE SHOW?
IT'S OKAY.
I'M LUCKY ENOUGH.

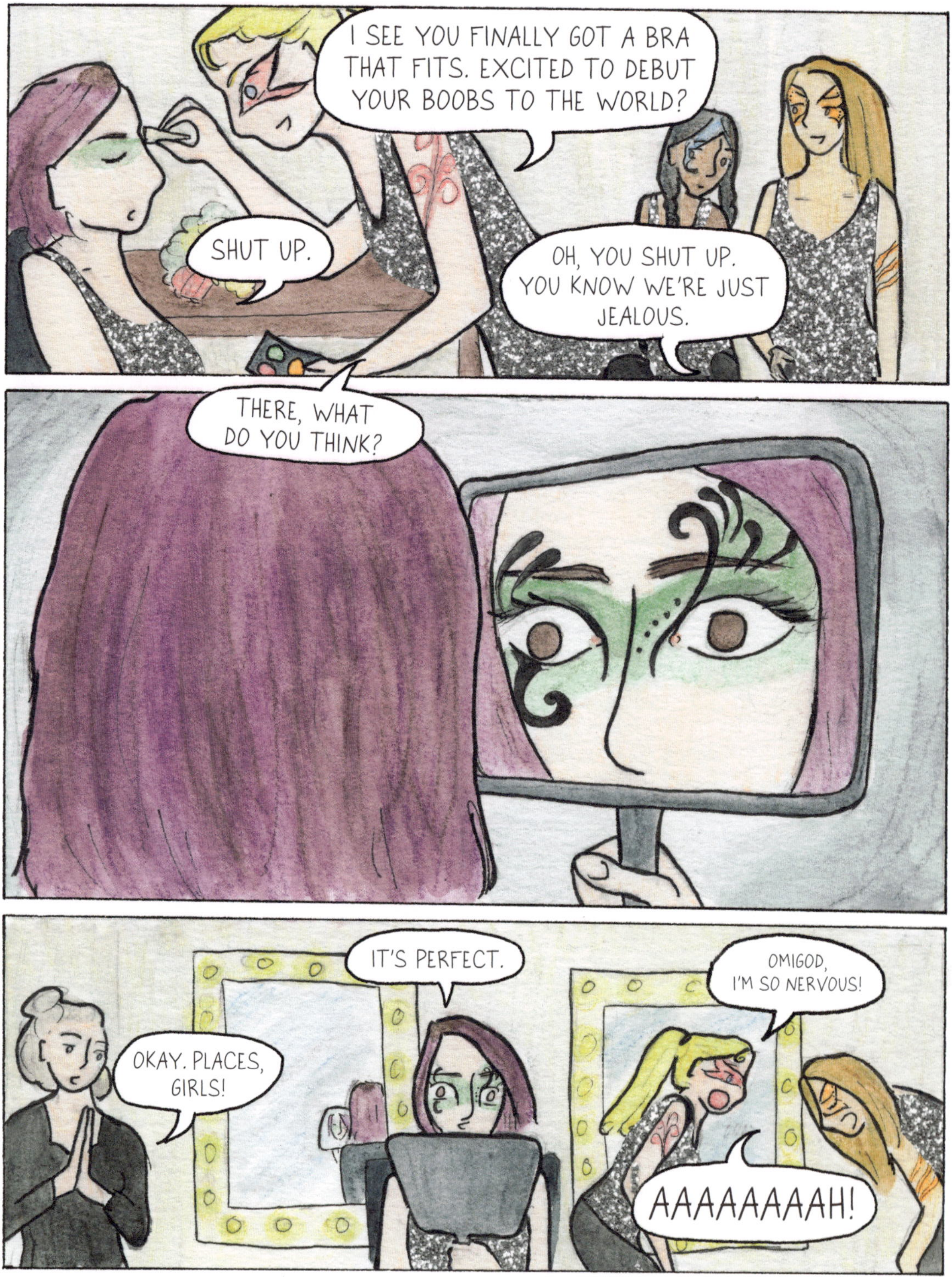
I SEE YOU FINALLY GOT A BRA THAT FITS. EXCITED TO DEBUT YOUR BOOBS TO THE WORLD?
SHUT UP.
OH, YOU SHUT UP. YOU KNOW WE'RE JUST JEALOUS.
THERE, WHAT DO YOU THINK?
IT'S PERFECT.
OKAY. PLACES, GIRLS!
OMIGOD, I'M SO NERVOUS!
AAAAAAAAH!

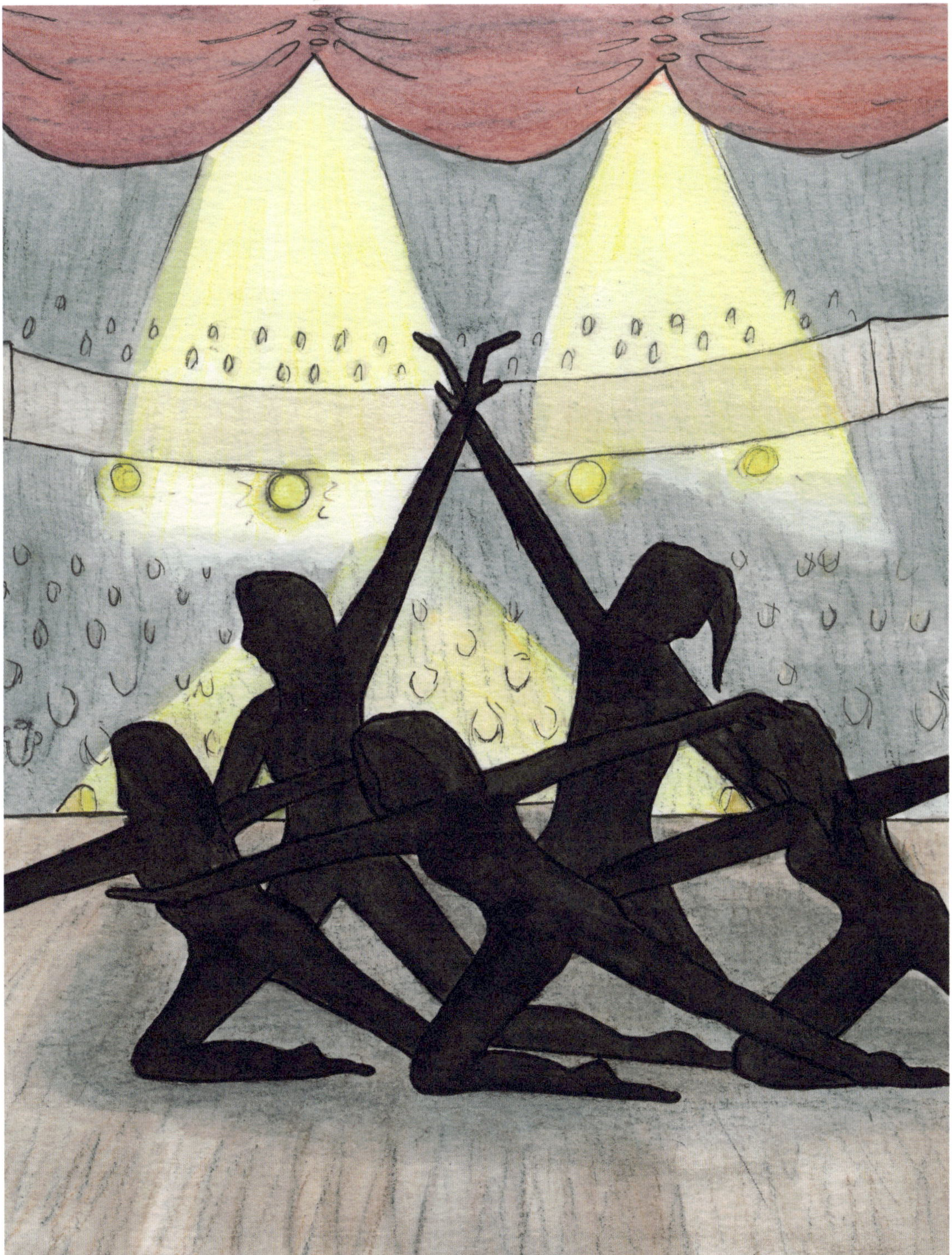

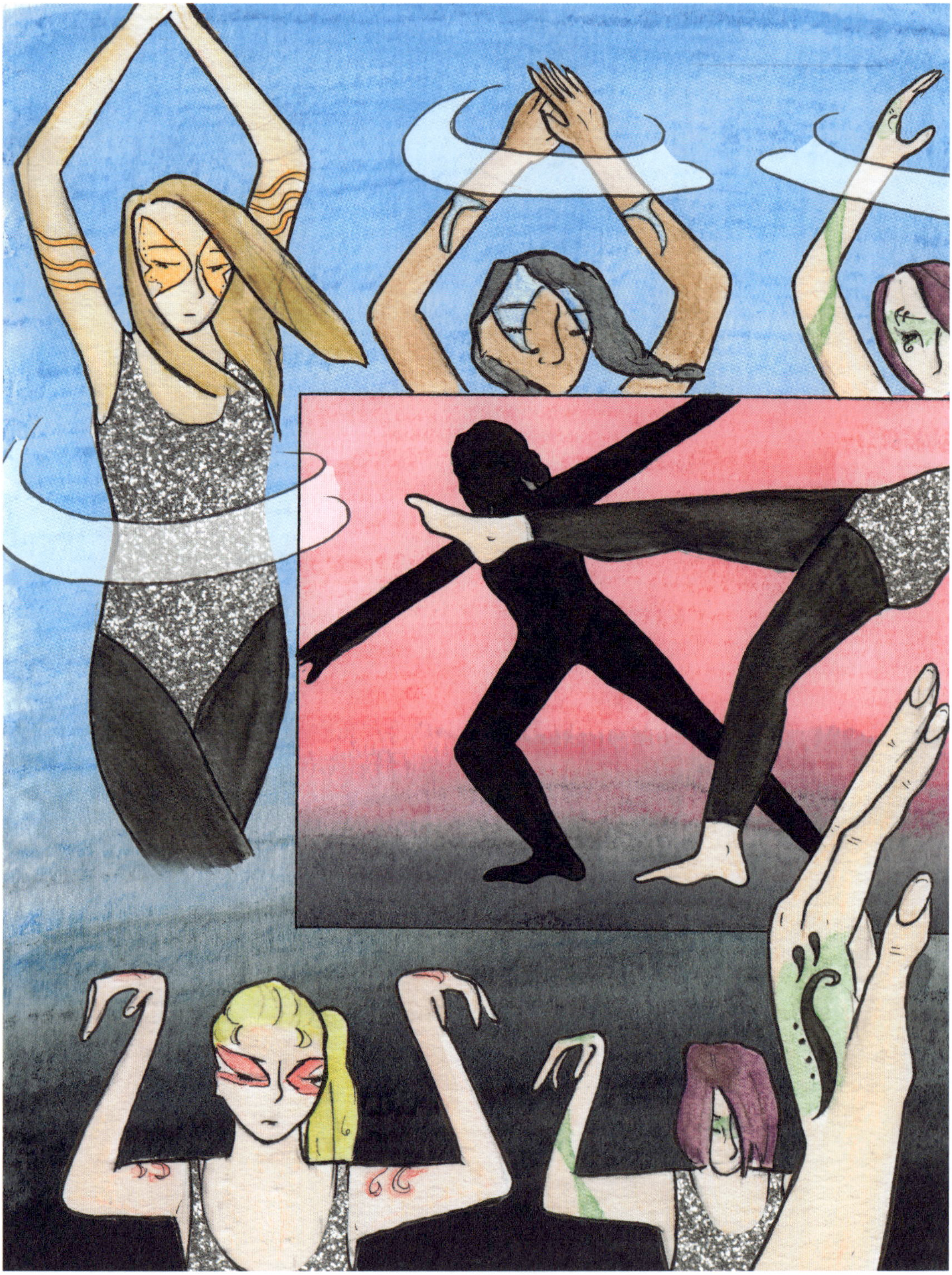

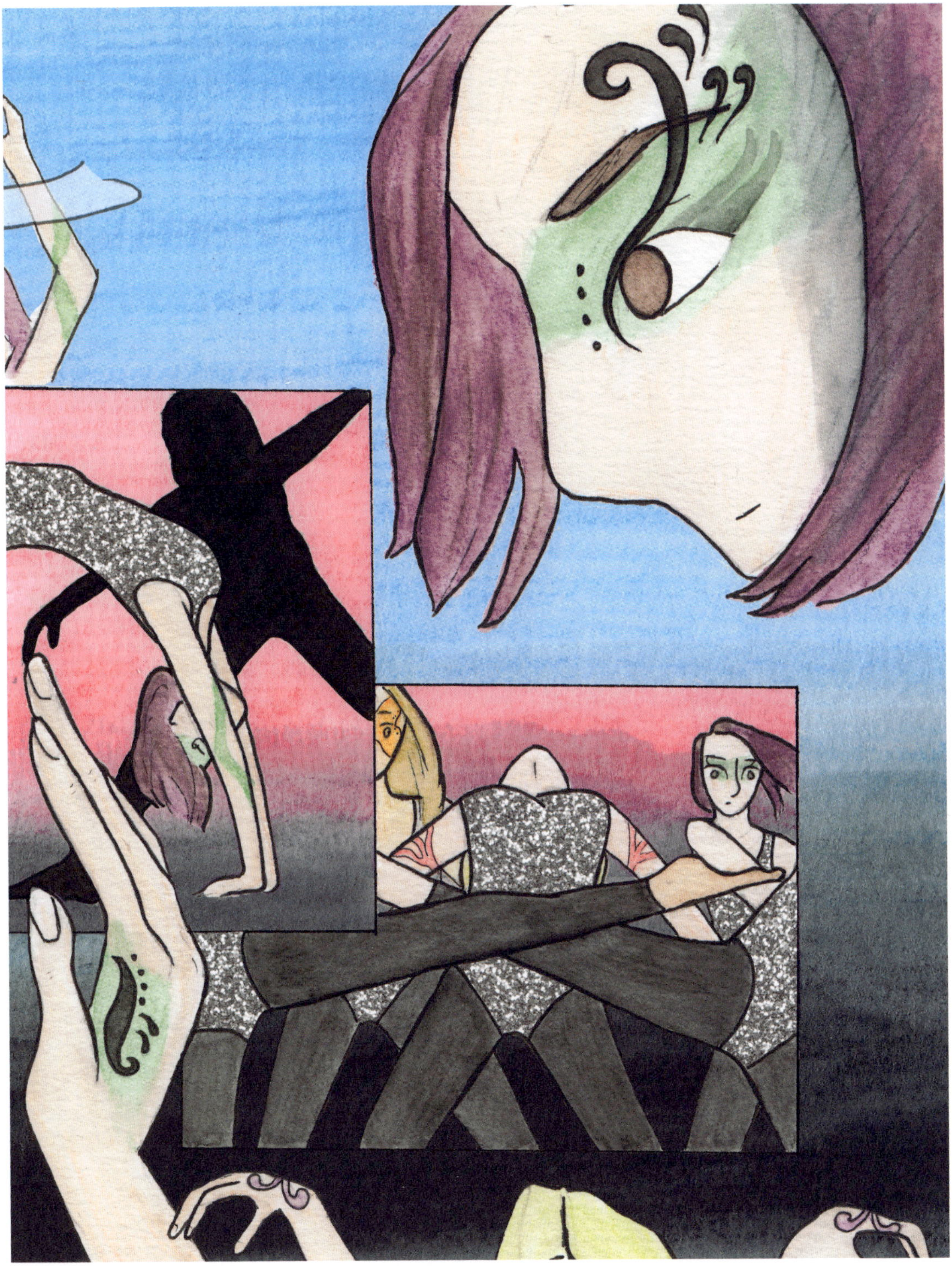

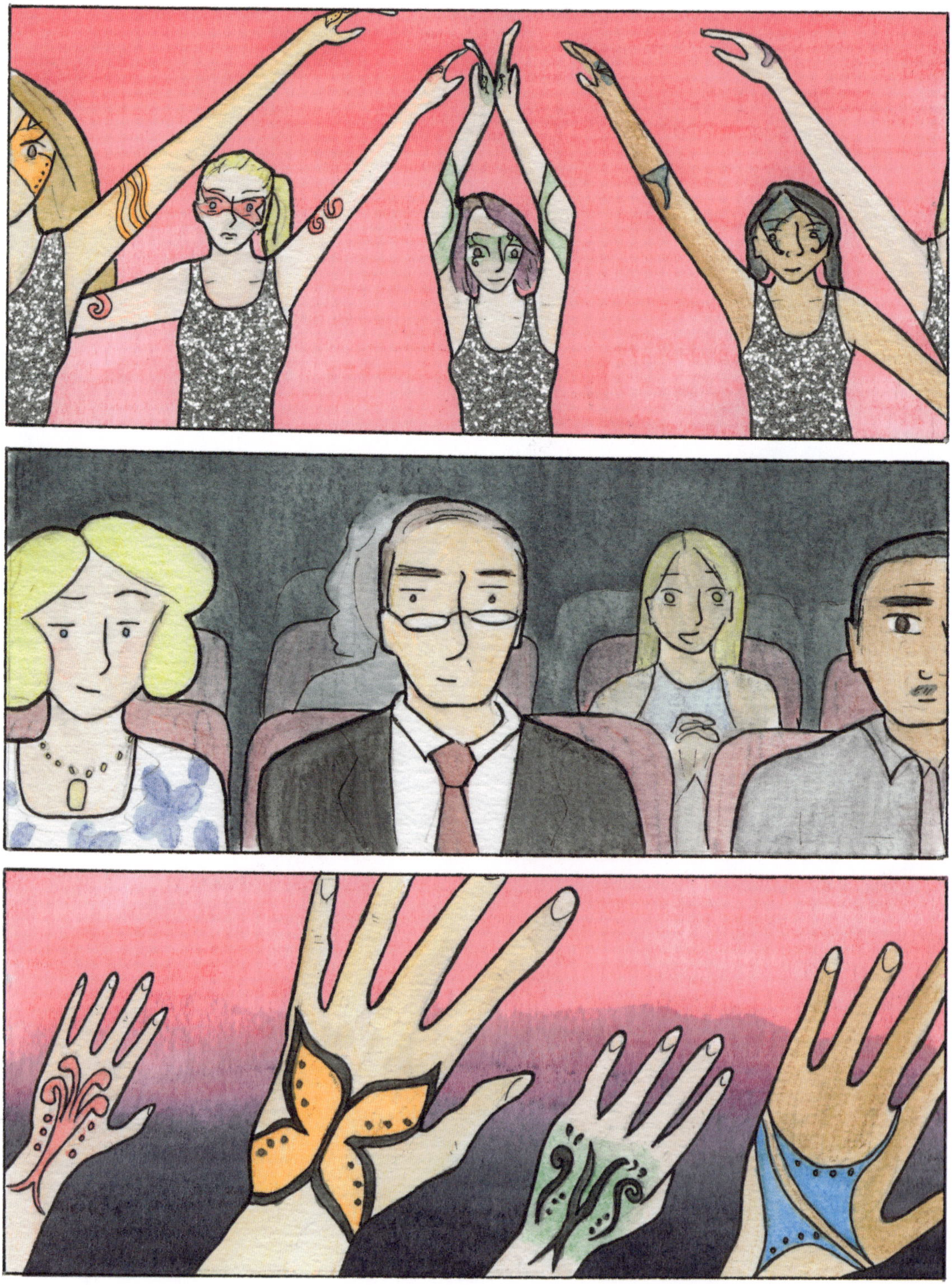

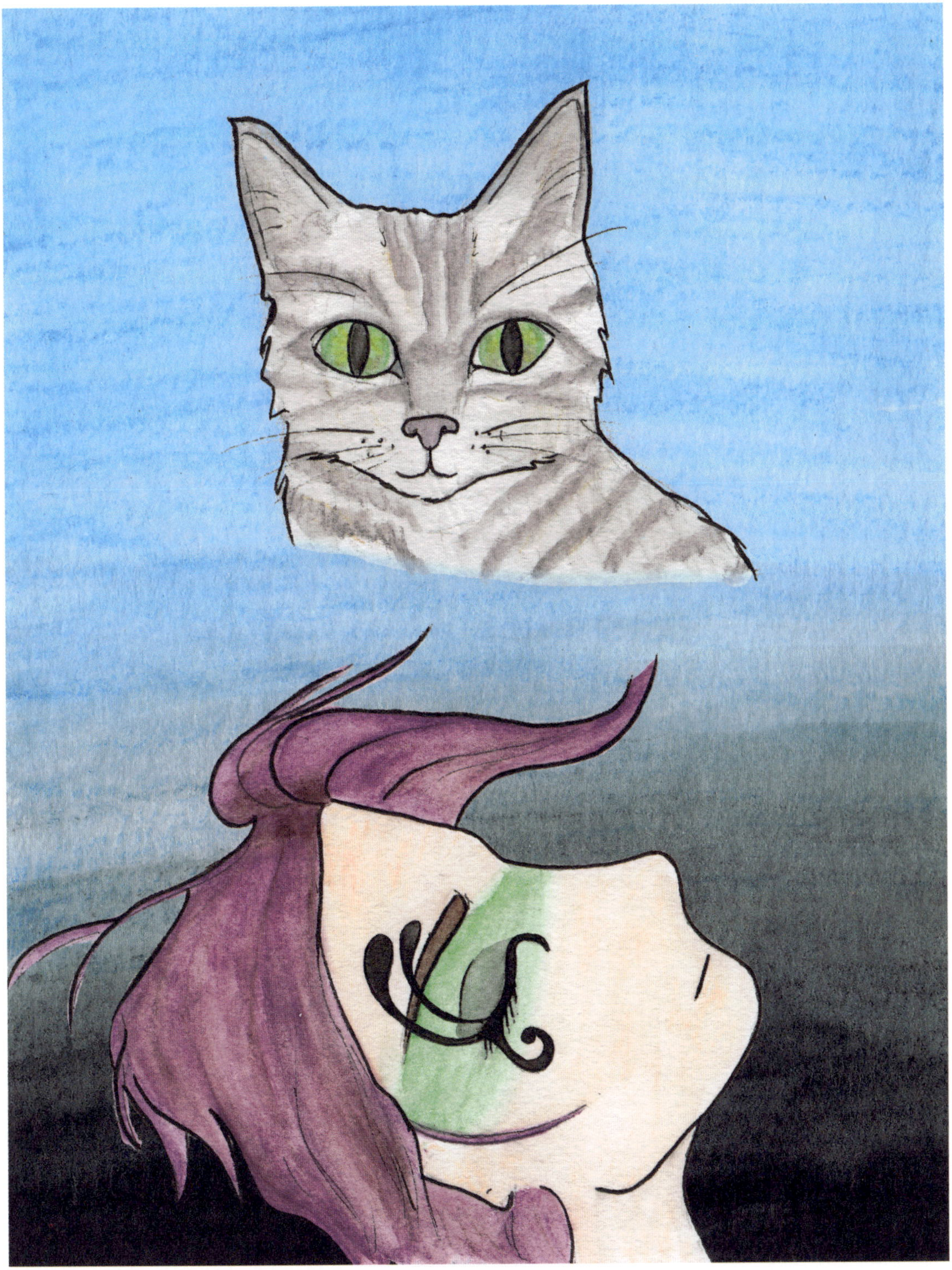

All that lives must die,

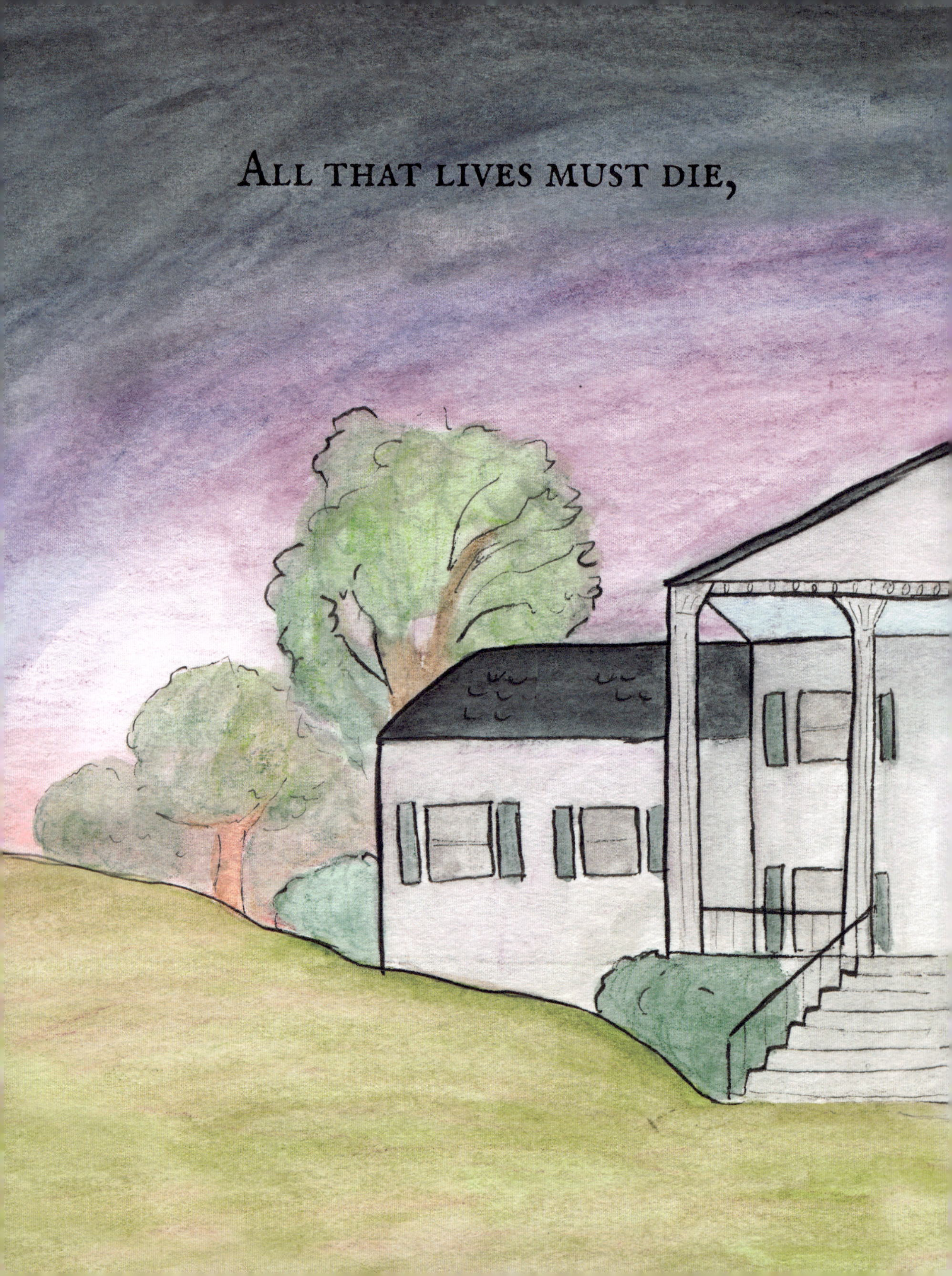

Passing through nature into eternity.

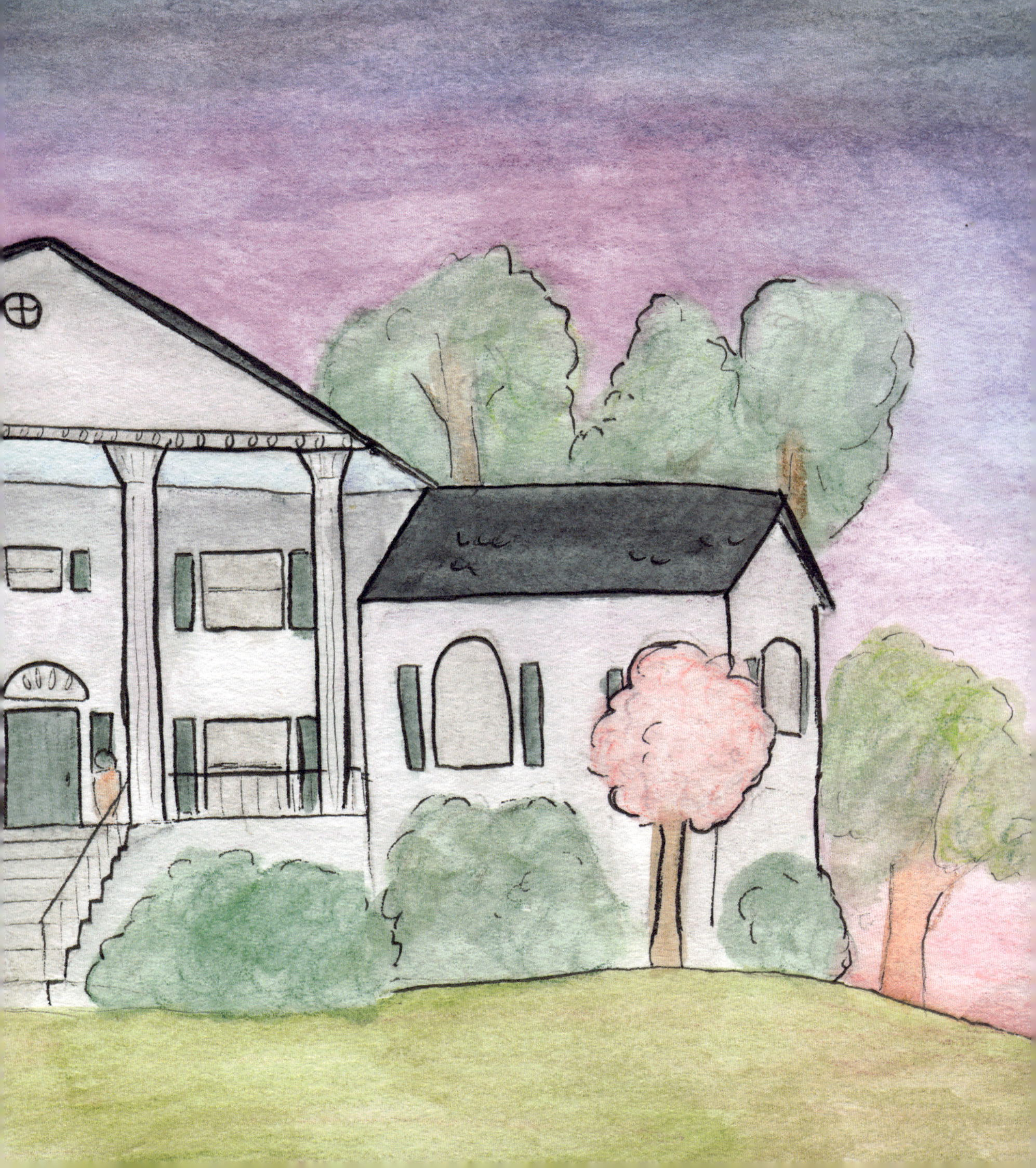

FEB 1964

# A NOTE FROM THE AUTHOR

This is a ghost story, but it's also a memoir. Some things in this book occurred just the way I told them. I did lose my cat inside my own house. I never found her, and the mystery of what really happened still haunts me. I did come out in high school — a school of extreme wealth and privilege — but no one took it seriously. My dad really is a federal judge, and I learned a lot about the world in his courtroom. Did I literally see a ghost? Maybe not. But this story is still true, because it's about how it feels to confront the past — your own or someone else's — which is just like seeing a ghost.

# ACKNOWLEDGMENTS

All my thanks to Katie Cunningham and Stephen Barr, who helped me turn a small, odd idea into something meaningful. To Lisa Rudden and Nico Carver for their tireless support, and to Nick King for the words "live as cat, die as cat." And to my mother for putting up with me.

First edition 2018

Library of Congress Catalog Card Number pending
ISBN 978-0-7636-9419-7

18 19 20 21 22 23 TLF 10 9 8 7 6 5 4 3 2 1

Printed in Dongguan, Guangdong, China

This book was typeset in Maggie Thrash.
The illustrations were done in watercolor pencil
and pen, and completed digitally.

Candlewick Press
99 Dover Street
Somerville, Massachusetts 02144

visit us at www.candlewick.com